TH
CIRCLE

BARBARA HATLABAN

ISBN 979-8-88644-105-5 (Paperback)
ISBN 979-8-88644-106-2 (Digital)

Covenant Books
11661 Hwy 707
Murrells Inlet, SC 29576
www.covenantbooks.com

This book is dedicated to Stephen Hatlaban III without whose bullying this author would never have written anything.

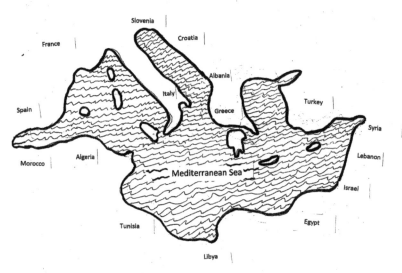

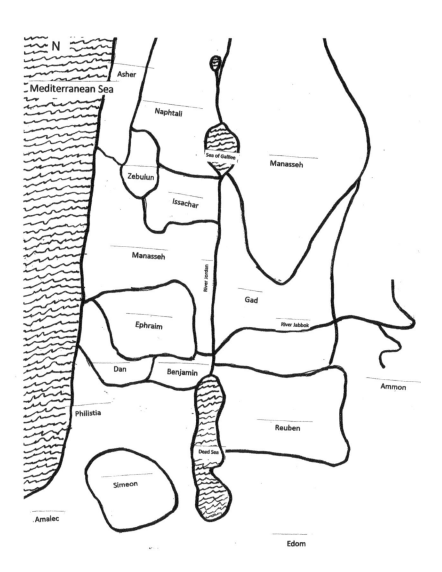

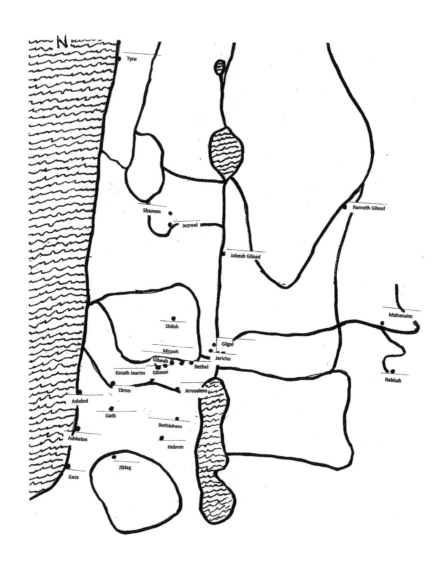

N

Tyre

Shunem

Jezreel

Ramoth Gilead

Jabesh Gilead

Mahanaim

Shiloh

Gilgal

Mizpah

Jericho

Gibeah

Kiriath Jearim   Bethel

Gibeon

Ekron   Jerusalem

Rabbah

Ashdod

Gath

Bethlehem

Ashkelon

Hebron

Ziklag

Gaza

CHAPTER 1

Year 418

Ouch! My foot hit a patch of wet leaves, and I went down hard on my back. Blue skies. White clouds. Right where they should be. I lay there for just a moment, staring at the sky, my head ringing. Every child under the age of twelve in the town of Gibeah must have been out in the field that afternoon, celebrating a perfect spring day. I got up, shook my head, and rubbed my scraped elbow. I quickly grabbed my stick as the tightly rolled ball of rags came my way. The ball was in the control of one of the larger boys. He was pretty fast, but I was faster. I darted out with my stick, inserted myself practically under his arm, and whacked the ball away from him. The ball was mine, and it changed direction with a swat of my stick.

The game was simple, surely a game that children play the world over. We had a field, we had two teams, and we had two goals. The plan was both to knock that ball through the other team's goal and to prevent the other team from maneuvering that same ball through our team's goal. There weren't a lot of rules otherwise, though it would be a foul to grab the ball with one's hands and run with it. We used our feet and our sticks to direct the ball. The ground under our feet was hard and uneven. I realized that when my head unexpectedly came in contact with it.

We played in a field that was meant for crops, but that wasn't planted yet. I saw my best friend, Sarah, out of the corner of my eye, and passed the ball to her. Right as I hit the ball, she tripped over a stone and went down. I sped up, recovered the ball and, while approaching our opponents' goal, took a wild swing and sent the errant ball flying into the woods. *No! Ouch!* I blasted after it and practically impaled myself on the dead and pointed limb of a tree. I heard a crack as the dead branch broke, and I heard my garment tear. I had a bleeding hole between my breast and my shoulder and saw my sleeve hanging by a thread. I pulled the sharp stick away, held it against the longer stick I was using on the ball, and made a mighty effort to hit the ball out of the woods. It landed at the edge of the field. I attempted to toss my torn sleeve back into place, and it stayed put for about a minute. All I had to do was not move.

I emerged from the woods and saw that the game was breaking up. It was suppertime. My damaged sleeve was hanging down in front of me, and my shoulder was bare. Sarah approached me and tried to put my sleeve back in place. She had a small piece of cloth in her hand and addressed my injury. We were surprised to see that our game had an audience. As always, my brother, Esh-Baal, was a witness to anything I did that could qualify as questionable. He made a typical snide remark.

"Showing off our assets, are we, Michal? You're indecent!"

With as much dignity as I could muster, I retorted, "Have you ever played a fast game, Esh-Baal? Or are you content with watching?"

It felt like Esh-Baal watched me a lot. Was I interesting?

He muttered something under his breath and slithered away in the direction of the house I shared with our mother and sister. Slithered—I mentally compared him to a snake. Sometimes Esh-Baal seemed devious and underhanded. He was going to give our mother warning of what she could expect when I walked in. Esh-Baal was tall, like our father, but he didn't have our father's bulk and muscle.

Sarah had a dirty face and dirty elbows, but her clothing was intact. She looked at me and couldn't quite suppress a grin. One of the other players had claimed the rag ball. Sarah had put down her playing stick, and so had I, and then I realized I was still holding the sharp stick that had caused my minor injury. We noticed a young couple standing on the edge of the field, apparently watching the game. We didn't know them. The wife held an infant. We walked past them as we headed home and heard the young man say to his wife, "In just a few years."

The wife smiled and agreed. Their child was destined to play in the fields, get dirty, and rip his clothing.

Sarah's house and mine weren't far apart. Gibeah was divided into neighborhoods, and the neighborhoods were made up of extended families. Sarah and I were half sisters, and we lived in the same neighborhood. We walked each other home and left each other to face our mothers alone. Mother met me at the door, and I heard the inevitable sigh. My sister, Merab, was home. She'd played the game with us for a while, but she fell, skinned her knee, and gave it up. I assumed Esh-Baal had been here, but I didn't see him now. I knew what was coming. Mother and I would take a trip to the stream. Mother had another tunic for me in her hands, and off we went. Rizpah and Sarah were at the stream when we got there, though Sarah was mainly washing her arms and her face.

Mother pointed me toward the stream after taking off the damaged tunic. She noticed my puncture wound and remarked that there was a salve to put on it after I'd washed. I was aware of my unbound hair flying in my face and everywhere else. I'd worn a covering over my hair when I left the house, but it was undoubtedly hanging from a tree. I didn't have it and I didn't remember losing it. My mother didn't demand that I try to wash my hair, which would have meant submerging myself in the chilly stream. She saw to it that I washed the upper part of my body and my face along with the wound. I put on the clean tunic and we went home. Mother tackled the task of putting my hair to rights. Mother, Merab, and I were sitting beside the hearth. I was shivering.

"Mother, what did Esh-Baal tell you?"

Merab gave a small, if possible, ladylike snort. "What does Esh-Baal ever say? I can't believe you care."

"Esh-Baal was questioning my mothering skills as usual," Mother replied. "He thinks you're running wild and you're not modest."

For the first time, I realized that as Esh-Baal criticized me, he was also criticizing our mother. He was implying that I needed more discipline and structure, and our mother wasn't providing it.

"Merab was there. Is she running wild too?"

"Well, she didn't come home with half-a-tunic. I put the same salve on her knee that I used on your cut. Merab didn't require a trip to the stream. You and Sarah, I do not begrudge either of you a childhood. But something will have to be done about this tunic, and you're going to do it."

Mother found a needle and some thread and gave them to me. "I'm not asking for a work of art, but I want this tunic made wearable."

The three of us looked up and were somewhat surprised to see my father at the door. My mother got up quickly and gestured for him to sit down near the hearth. "Would you like something to drink?" she asked.

My father smiled. He looked at me and said, "I see our hooligan has destroyed some more clothing."

My mother suggested that maybe I would be more careful in the future if I had to do the mending myself.

My father gave my mother a quick kiss and then stated his purpose. "I can't stay. But, tomorrow, we're *all*, and I mean *all* picking rock. It's almost time to plow."

My father caught the face that Merab made. "Yes, Merab, you too. And, yes, your hands will get dirty."

Picking rock was an annual job, and it was dirty. The village children, boys and girls, walked the fields looking for chunks of rock that had pushed their way up over the course of the winter. Nobody would pretend that picking rock was fun, but sometimes these tasks became social occasions. I knew Sarah would be there. So would Esh-Baal! Every winter, new rocks made their way to the surface. The objective was to remove anything large enough to damage a plow. The rocks would be set to the edge of the fields, and then my father would come around with his donkey cart. The stones were removed to two communal piles that lined the pathway going out of or into, depending on one's perspective, the village of Gibeah.

Our father didn't live with us. He had a private mudbrick house off to one side of the neighborhood. Our family structure was complicated in that my father kept a concubine, who happened to be Sarah's mother. My mother was the wife. Oftentimes, husbands and wives lived in the same dwelling, but these were families of one man and one woman.

My father left and I remembered the stick. I had brought the pointed stick home with me, and it was lying outside the door to my mother's house. I decided to make a present of it to Esh-Baal. Esh-Baal lived in a dwelling with other boys and unmarried men. It wasn't hard to get into the building, and when I went, nobody was inside. They were sitting in the backyard, drinking beer. It was cool outside, though shortly after sunset, it would become uncomfortably cool. I planned my secret visit for some time between supper and bedtime. I knew where Esh-Baal slept and slid the stick into his bed. I was resigned to not knowing the outcome. I mean, how badly Esh-Baal got poked. I had no doubt that he'd know who put a stick into his bed. But he certainly wouldn't be telling anyone, at least, not if he was seriously stabbed. He didn't like me, and I felt the same. Tattletale! Still, I knew he'd get me back if the opportunity arose. I resolved to be watchful.

CHAPTER 2

Year 418

The rock-picking went fine. The entire village had organized for the work, and though it was indeed a long day, we walked all the fields that supported our town. I wore the tunic I had mended. It didn't look very fashionable, but it held together. I wouldn't have wanted to wear one of my better garments to pick rock. The children put the rocks at the edges of the fields, and the men picked them up and loaded them on the donkey cart. There were two donkey carts. One was my father's, and the other belonged to one of the neighbors. They were situated on either side of the field that was being "picked." Once the fields were picked, we children were excused. The men completed the task of relocating the rocks to the two piles that lined the path. I was aware of Esh-Baal and he was aware of me, but there were people everywhere. If he and I were having a private feud, this wasn't the setting in which to continue it. He made a couple of half-hearted attempts to trip me, but I avoided him.

It was a sunny day in the first month. The people of the village were all back to doing the more mundane chores which, after the rock-picking, felt easy. Sarah and I were out and about together, as we often were. We gathered wood on most days that were dry. It was nice to set up a store of wood for sloppy days. We hadn't wandered far from the compound, though we were outside of it, walking along the edge of the woods. We'd walked along the path and between the two large piles of stones. We were picking up dead pieces of wood off the ground, trying to be mindful of snakes. Snakes weren't common, but they did exist. I have to admit that I wasn't really giving Sarah a lot of attention. I just expected her to be enjoying the spring weather like I was, in addition to providing a service to the community.

As it happened, she'd been preoccupied all day, though I hadn't noticed. Sarah gave me my first lesson on female status, not a concept to which I'd applied any attention up until then. What she said specifically was, "Our father loves my mother more than your mother."

I just looked at Sarah in surprise. I didn't know how to answer except in the form that children's answers often take. "Does not!"

Sarah continued with, "Look how many children my mother has!"

We were part of a farming culture. Sarah and I knew early on where babies came from. I knew that my mother had five children,] and that I was the youngest. My brothers were quite a bit older. Jonathan, Abinadab, and Malki-Shua were married, though Esh-Baal still lived in the young men's barracks. I must have been seven or eight years old at the time. I knew that Rizpah had many children, and I didn't even know how many. She was pregnant and near to her time.

We'd picked up as many branches as we could carry. We walked back into the village along the path and stacked our wood against the side of the hall. The hall was big enough for the residents of Gibeah to hold large gatherings, but it wasn't congenial. We children were told that this hall was a lot more comfortable than the hall that had preceded it, but it was still too dark and too poorly ventilated. Our village had a grove of trees, oaks and sycamores, conveniently located, and if the weather permitted at all, we preferred to gather there. My father used the hall for military meetings.

I realized that mother was almost always in bed at night with Merab and me. Rarely was it just Merab and me. I liked having our mother with us, and it didn't occur to me that her presence was due to the fact that our father wasn't inviting her to his bed. I was a child. I did what any child does when it's looking for reassurance. I went to my mother. Of course, I told her what Sarah had said, but the reassurance wasn't forthcoming. My mother did something I didn't expect and burst into tears. We had a discussion eventually, but not in that moment. In that moment, a servant appeared with a message for Mother. Rizpah was in labor.

Mother dried her eyes, pulled herself together, and said to me, "Michal, you're old enough. Merab, Michal, come along!"

We went to Rizpah's dwelling where my mother and another older woman delivered Rizpah of a son. Rizpah's labor was the first I ever saw. Childbirth was the purview of the women of the community, and it was important that young girls learn about it early. Sarah and her sisters were there, too, but only to observe. My mother and the midwife did the real work. Rizpah was in labor for maybe half a day. We learned that this length of labor was relatively easy, and it could have lasted much longer. We heard gossip about outcomes, not all of which were positive. In the case of Rizpah and what turned out to be her tenth baby, the outcome was excellent. Rizpah was exhausted but healthy, and her new son was also healthy.

Nobody really enjoys listening to a baby cry, but the noise was one of the things my mother and the midwife were looking for. The new baby announced his presence. He was tiny. It wasn't a big bellow. But it was enough. The birth had been very uncomplicated. My mother must have wondered all through the process about the statement Sarah had made to me and about what Rizpah was telling *her*. Mother was the wife.

For the first time in my short life, I wondered about wives and concubines. Why had my father not married Rizpah? Did Rizpah have any say in it? My father was allowed to take more than one wife, but he never did. Rizpah did have community status just for childbearing. She had given my father nine healthy children, three of whom were sons. I found out later that one of Rizpah's infants had died. This was a huge grief for a mother. My own mother had not had to bear it. Rizpah came through this immediate childbirth experience with no ill effects. The child was healthy, and that child was a son. There was rejoicing in the compound. When my father arrived to see his new offspring, he named the baby Mephibosheth.

I also thought about Sarah and me. We were best friends, weren't we? I thought we were, but what did she think? How different was it to be the child of the concubine as opposed to the child of the wife? Was my status different from her status?

I have always admired my mother for being forthright. It's easy to let a certain amount of time elapse and then forget the question. As a rule, my mother didn't do that. She may have been relieved that she had the opportunity to mull over the topic in her mind before trying to put it into words.

The three of us were alone in the house again in the evening. Mother began with, "Merab, did Michal tell you what Sarah said yesterday?"

Merab made some disparaging remark about not being very interested in anything Sarah had to say.

Mother told her. Merab looked puzzled and then angry. Mother said, "Sarah believes that one can measure love by measuring the number of resulting children. Have either of you considered love, what it feels like to the person who loves, and also how it looks from the outside?"

I piped up, "Is it love when a man beds a woman? I think that was what Sarah was trying to say."

Merab looked uncomfortable and said nothing.

"A man bedding a woman is one of the outward manifestations of love. *One* of them. It is easy to confuse love and lust. Women are more likely than men to do so. Lust is simply an animal instinct that abates when the physical urge has been satisfied. It is something sheep do. Do sheep love each other? Probably not. They perform the act of mating and then go their separate ways. They certainly produce plenty of lambs! If I had to define love, and it's not something I think about too often, I'd be more inclined to call it a commitment and a partnership. It is enduring through good times and bad. It is about affection and enjoying another person's company. It's much more than thirty minutes of pleasure.

"If your father invites Rizpah to his bed more often than he invites me, it could be all about her ability to conceive children. I'm not sure I'd call that love. I am confident that Abner loves Deborah. I am confident that Deborah believes that, but she has no children. It seems clear that I won't bear any more children. I have five beautiful children, and I praise Elohim!

"I do understand why a child asks such questions as he or she is learning to make sense of the world. However, it isn't productive, at least for adults, to look in on other people's relationships and draw conclusions. People on the outside will never have enough information. Does your father love Rizpah more than me? I don't believe that. Your father and I have been together a long time, and if we are past the stage of showing love in public, then so be it. It would make me uncomfortable anyway. Love is your father's protection of me and his daily providing. Love is my running of the household, maintenance of our dwelling, cooking meals, and perhaps caring for him when he's sick or wounded."

CHAPTER 3

Year 418

My father was a king. Do kings ordinarily pick rock? No, but in my father's case, it wasn't so much that such labor was beneath him. It was more about being home at the appropriate time, and my father usually wasn't. He had grown up a farmer and valued the land, but as king, he was more a soldier than anything else.

I was born a princess and so was Sarah. We sometimes called each other "Your Highness," but always with irony. We thought about our status while we were doing laundry, gathering firewood, and carrying water. If we were looking for privilege, it would have helped if our mothers had been queens. Our father had no palace, and our mothers had no real status beyond that of any other woman in the village. We daughters performed the tasks of the women of the world and didn't think too much about it.

I do recall once when my mother heard us using the phrase "Your Highness." We were children and were jesting with each other, but she didn't like it. She was absolutely determined to hang onto the life she'd had in our village before my father took on the public role of king. My father was not a king when he married my mother. I knew that on very rare occasions, my mother would be approached by someone else, usually a woman whose husband was standing in the background and usually somebody she didn't know, to deliver a suggestion to my father. She was not receptive. She didn't seek that sort of attention.

Interestingly enough, Rizpah did. I saw that same scenario play out between her and members of our community and saw her smile and move her hands as she did in any earnest conversation. I was never close enough to hear the words. She was approached more often than my mother was, and I concluded she was more gracious about it. It may also have been that the people who approached her were counting her children!

Was it helpful for people to seek access to my father through his women? I'm tempted to say no, though certainly, I wasn't privy to any of the talk that went on in my father's quarters. It didn't feel to me like my father valued suggestions that came through women. People who wanted access to my father didn't know that, though it was predictable. Our culture cared for women, but it didn't ask their opinions, pretty much ever. My mother and my father were both governed by the roles of males and females as defined by our society, and they preferred to stay within those parameters.

My mother said, "Be careful what you say and understand what could result. You don't and can't know who's listening. You and Sarah are playing, but it won't always be this way. You're both growing up and you both could be used as messengers to your father. Ask yourselves if you want that. Still, your brothers are more likely to be pestered in that way."

Very shortly after the rock-picking chore, and on the next sunny day, my father and the men of our village plowed the fields. We children felt a minor bit of apprehension. If one of us missed a large rock and one of our neighbors broke a plowshare, we would be held responsible. We hoped we'd done a good job and the plowing would proceed without incident. Many of the men plowed with donkeys. The plowing for the entire village was done first, and after that, the planting. Our community grew wheat and barley. There's always a feeling of relief when the fields get planted in a timely fashion. Once the planting was done, the men looked for rain. As king and a leader of men, my father was very likely to be involved in battles in the springtime. Occasionally, he'd be available to help with the plowing and the planting, but when he wasn't, the men of the village who weren't away from home with him would make sure his fields were planted.

I remember just a bit of controversy about the planting. There was a philosophy that some of the land needed to be left fallow. It helped the soil to recover, and then, when that field was planted the next year, the yield would be greater. However, it also meant that this particular field would have no yield at all in the current season. The ancient laws given to Moses suggested that any field should be given rest every seven years.[1] Our community observed this law, though not rigidly and not without dissent. The men left two fields fallow that spring.

The main focus of our village was crops and livestock. And in my short life, I found the routine to be tedious. Pick rock, carry water, gather wood—every day looked like the last. I made the mistake of complaining to my mother. In a fit of impatience, my mother said to me, "Boring is good! So much of what isn't boring is downright terrifying!" Mother was relieved when the so-called boring tasks of the day moved along placidly and uninterrupted.

When my mother used the phrase "downright terrifying," I wondered if she referred to my father's battles. We residents of Gibeah were quite distant from my father's battles. His battles, at least so far, hadn't been fought on our soil. When he went into battle, which was most years, was my mother downright terrified? It was obvious that when men went into battle, some were killed. The possibility must have weighed heavily on my mother's mind.

I watched Rizpah, too, especially after Sarah had made a comparison between the two women. Rizpah and my mother seemed to get along, but then my mother wasn't one to be governed by emotion. Rizpah was slightly younger and had an obvious spring in her step. I caught her skipping to the well once, albeit with an empty pitcher. She didn't skip back, carrying water. Rizpah had a wide smile and a lilting musical laugh. Sometimes when she spoke, I caught just a hint of something foreign. She had a slight accent, but only when she said certain words.

Rizpah was a good worker, but she was a dreamer. My mother got impatient with her at times. Rizpah was quite beautiful, even after ten pregnancies. She had milky skin, dark wavy hair, and she was curvy. She wasn't one to see for herself what needed to be done.

---

[1] Leviticus 25:2–5.

She did what she was asked to do as long as she got direction from my mother or my Aunt Hadassah.

Was my mother beautiful? She was certainly attractive but maybe not beautiful. She was tall and lean with smooth skin and dark wavy hair. She emanated energy. It was because of Mother and Aunt Hadassah that the routine tasks of day-to-day living were accomplished in our compound. The two of them worked, and they also delegated. My mother and Rizpah were entirely different types. Mother wasn't one to accept excuses. If a task needed to be done, and she'd designated a "doer," there wasn't any discussion as to whether or not the prospective "doer" felt up to it.

I heard my mother say more than once, "It's a job. It doesn't matter how you feel about it."

CHAPTER 4

Year 386

It was one of those evenings when Mother, Merab, and I were all in the house, and it wasn't quite time to sleep. It wasn't exactly cold, but one could expect the nights to be cool. We had a low fire glowing in the hearth. My mother wasn't always expressive, but occasionally, she would talk to us about her life. Mother started off by posing the question, "Do you know what I meant when I said boring was good?"

Merab responded, "Do you mean not having to run away from raiders?"

Mother said, "That's exactly what I mean. We all have to appreciate peace, satisfaction, and even daily tasks, just because they reflect the absence of something really frightening, like enemy tribes. The Twelve Tribes, including Gibeah, are surrounded by enemies. There are constant raids, either against the Twelve Tribes or initiated by them. Have you watched the boys with their wooden swords, practicing to become warriors? The favorite enemy is the Philistines who live along the coast of the Great Sea. There are many foreign peoples along the borders of the Twelve Tribes' territory, just waiting for the opportunity to reach out and take something. The Philistines are closest. Still, Gibeah, as your father's seat of government, has been peaceful since the Twelve Tribes got a king. It was not always so.

"The last raid that affected me specifically took place maybe two years before your father became king. The Twelve Tribes had a leader at the time named Samuel, but Samuel wasn't a warrior. He was more of a diplomat, politician, or priest. He did not fight battles. Jonathan was seven years old, Abinadab was six, and Malki-Shua was five. Esh-Baal hadn't been born, but Rizpah had three young daughters in addition to Abinadab.

"It was early morning after several dry days. Gibeah awakened to shouting, horses' hooves, and swirling dust. The men of the village knew exactly what was happening, and despite the element of surprise, they stood at least somewhat ready. Weapons were a big problem. Your father actually had a sword he'd captured in a previous raid, but most of the men wielded farm implements.[2] I didn't stay to watch. Rizpah, my Aunt Hadassah, and I rounded up the children and fled into the woods. Aunt Hadassah made sure she included my mother-in-law in the escape.

"Poor Mariamne! You know she's Aunt Hadassah's sister. Back then, she wasn't who she became later, but she was failing. And she wasn't very old. Aunt Hadassah loved her and tried to get her grandchildren to pay her some attention. It was hard. She wasn't interesting and she was having some difficulty making sentences out of words. Back then, she did talk, but she was hard to understand. We also suspected that she didn't understand what was being said to her. To say the least, she was confused and may well not have understood why a large group of us was hurrying through the woods. We all did what we could to guide her and make a path for her.

"We were quite a large group of mainly women and children. Rizpah was doing the best she could with a brand-new infant, and those of us around her were trying to be mindful of her as well as Mariamne. We fled to Gallim, which was a town close to Gibeah but with a significant patch of woods in between. We found shelter there, and we also fulfilled the duty of warning the residents that there were Philistines on the move.

"We spent three nights there in Gallim, being sheltered by generous residents. It was boring. Yes, being away from home and far from the daily tasks is boring! We tried to be mindful of the usual chores of the village and to help where we could. The boys spent one lovely afternoon playing the game with the rag ball and the sticks with the children of Gallim. We watched the game, perhaps because

---

[2] 1 Samuel 13:22.

we didn't have a lot to do while we waited for word of our loved ones. It was a tense time for the families of the men caught up in the task of defending our towns.

"I ended up spending more time with Mariamne than I otherwise would have. All of us did, and Aunt Hadassah was grateful. Mariamne was aware of us back then, and she knew my name was Ahinoam. She knew I was married to her son. I saw a hint of a smile at the corners of her mouth. Aunt Hadassah knew her better than anyone, and she insisted that her sister understood what we said to her. It's just that her responses—and in those days, she did respond—were garbled. I can honestly say we tried, but it wasn't a satisfying experience. We all appreciate it when our words are met with the other person's ideas.

"When our group entered Gallim with news of an attack, some of the men of Gallim immediately trekked through the woods to Gibeah with whatever weapons (or farm implements) they could lay their hands on. Everyone had basic knives, of course. We got our first news of the outcome when they returned. We were apprehensive and showed it. There were a lot of serious expressions and a lot of pacing back and forth. What was at stake was our husbands for certain and possibly our freedom. We were alive, and so were our children, but we hoped to keep our husbands and hoped our lives wouldn't change dramatically for the worse.

"The men of Gallim came back with good news. As they entered their town, we noted that they looked exhausted and that some were wounded. However, they had that look of triumph as well. The encroaching Philistines had been routed. There were burned buildings as always happens in a raid, but not a lot. The men of Gallim could state for a fact that your father had survived. My husband was distinctive. He was the tallest man for miles around and was easily identified.

"Some of the men of Gallim knew Uncle Hur, Hadassah's husband, personally. He, too, had survived. There were casualties, but not compared to the Philistine casualties. The men of Gibeah and the men of Gallim had won quite a victory and had taken some booty. One highly prized commodity was weapons. We saw some swords and a javelin that had been taken by the men of Gallim. We were assured that the men of Gibeah had also taken items of value. But the best assurance was that we could go home and that most of us still had homes. We spent one more night in Gallim and then headed back to Gibeah the next morning following the same path back through the woods.

"Our village healer, Deborah, had fled to Gallim with the women and children. She was married to my husband's cousin, Abner. The village of Gallim had its own healer, but when Deborah offered to assist with the wounded, she wasn't turned away. None of the men of Gallim had been killed. I have never taken a strong interest in healing, but I was very grateful that somebody did. I watched Deborah heat water for cleansing and infuse it with herbs. She and the healer from Gallim both strongly advocated hot water and clean bandages. You may have noticed we used hot water and clean rags when we assisted Rizpah with childbirth.

"I was so glad to see your father once we all got back to Gibeah. We had a joyous reunion that I shared with Rizpah. Hur and Hadassah had a joyous reunion. Your grandfather, Kish, survived, as did his brother, Ner, and Ner's son, Abner. Abner and Deborah had a joyous reunion. Ner was a widower. Kish and Mariamne—well, I wish Mariamne had been able to convey to Kish that she was glad to see him. Maybe she did. She didn't say anything but she presented Kish with a wide smile. Their house was intact, and Kish took his wife home. He wasn't one for public displays of affection. He took care of his wife's physical needs but had no idea how to relate to her, and neither did the rest of us.

"Clearly, our village had been the site of a battle. There were burnt buildings and partially burnt buildings, and there was evidence of blood. But the men had gotten rid of any corpses before the rest of us came home. We were grateful for that. Our men had wounds. Your father had a sword gash on his chest. All the men with their cuts and bruises looked like they'd survived a battle. There were a few broken bones. We begged for details, and the men probably gave us a short and simple account. To a man, they were very quick to give credit to their fellow townspeople. Hur was a raging lion. He killed a Philistine, took his sword, and killed four more. He had a slash on the side of his face. Your father and his father fought side by side and dispatched numerous Philistines. Ner and Abner, fighting as a team, did the same. The reinforcements from Gallim were valiant.

"After the dust settled and the surviving Philistines fled, there was the usual effort to strip the bodies. My Uncle Hur, though a ferocious fighter when his family was threatened, didn't think much of raiding in general. He did take a heavy gold ring off the thumb of a Philistine that he personally killed, and he kept the sword he'd taken early on. But he didn't strip any bodies. The rest of the men didn't leave anything of value on any dead Philistines. They dug a pit and covered the bodies quickly.

"We were fortunate that our men weren't severely wounded. Deborah had spread a wet rag over your father's chest and let the liquid soak the wound. Your father was seated. She got out a needle and thread, just like the one I used for mending. Your father cringed. He didn't make a sound, but I saw the grimace.

"Deborah asked me, 'Do you know what I'm doing?' as she stuck the needle into my husband's skin.

"'You cleaned the slash, and now you're stitching the edges of the skin together,' I answered.

"Your father interjected, 'Ouch! Get on with it!' He didn't like being treated like a teaching opportunity.

"Deborah added, 'There is more to wound-cleansing than water, though water is essential. This particular water was infused with rose petals and rose bark, though I added what I had of frankincense and myrrh to the mix. I didn't have much. Next time we see a trader from the far south, I will hope to buy more.' Deborah finished stitching. 'A wound like this could fester. We try hard not to let that happen, and the frankincense and myrrh seem to help. We grow roses here, and those help as well.'

"Deborah brandished the needle in the direction of Uncle Hur's face, and he flinched. 'I'm fine,' he said.

"Aunt Hadassah had to interject, 'My warrior husband! You have earned a very distinguishing scar.'

"You've both seen Uncle Hur's scar. He got it in that raid. Uncle Hur didn't say anything in response to his wife's comment, but he looked uncomfortable. He wasn't looking for recognition as a warrior, but there would be the inevitable scar and there would be no hiding it.

"Deborah offered him the soaked rag and he applied it to his face. She used the soaked rag on the rest of the wounded men, but she didn't give stitches to anyone but your father.

"We were thrilled to be home. There was a conversation among our village elders, specifically Hur, Ner, and Kish that wasn't confidential. The men were sitting outside Kish's house, and we were doing the housekeeping tasks in the background. The men were puzzled as to why the Philistines picked Gibeah. Gibeah didn't glitter in the sun. It was a very ordinary village made of very similar mud brick houses. If Gibeah had wealth, it wasn't obvious.

"Hur was grateful that this particular raid had been spectacularly unsuccessful, and he said, 'Praise Elohim!'

"Our village acknowledged Elohim as God, but none of us were very religious. Ner and Kish were more militant.

"Kish said, 'We cannot simply overlook this act of aggression. We need to retaliate. It's time to launch a raid on Timnah.'

"Ner agreed, 'We do.'

"But Hur said, 'The Philistines don't have anything I want. And Gibeah is in no position, on its own, to go raiding anywhere. We don't have the population for it. I'm not prepared to support a retaliatory raid, but the two of you can look around and see if the men of Gallim are interested in doing any such thing. I'm feeling blessed right now. And one more thing, if you do come up with some allies who are interested in launching a raid, it is imperative that you not take all the men of Gibeah or all the men of whichever town opts to join you. I cannot defend this town by myself, and it may indeed need defending.

"'And speaking of which, we all see very clearly that one sentry at night isn't enough. Malachi was the first to die. We as a village need to make sure his family isn't forgotten. Did the Philistines view Gibeah as an opportunity? They may not have expected a huge return, but they thought they could take something without a lot of effort. Our village showed more readiness than they expected, and for that, I am proud of us.'

"The conversation ended when Hur stood up to leave.

"He said, 'We were lucky. I'll be paying a visit to Hilkiah and Zebulon after supper. We need to discuss better security measures. I hope they'll agree to take up the matter with the city council. Maybe if we ask for four sentries, we'll get three.'

"Our village came together to repair damaged buildings. This took precedence over organizing a raid. Ner and Kish still wanted revenge against the nearest Philistine city. There was a delegation to Gallim, and it included Ner, Kish, Abner, and your father. I was adamantly opposed, and so were Deborah and Rizpah.

"I spoke for the women of Gibeah when I said, 'We were spared! Have some gratitude.' I also pointed out that your father's chest wound was still healing and he still moved stiffly because of it.

"The men of Gibeah, and maybe all of the Twelve Tribes, were reluctant to be influenced by their women. So they set off anyway in an attempt to create a band large enough to destroy a Philistine city, in this case, Timnah. They tried Gallim first, the city that had protected Gibeah's women and children, and found that the population was enjoying the peace. Yes, there was wealth to be gained by raiding, but there was also great risk. The men of Gallim pointed out that the Twelve Tribes had very few real weapons and that the Philistines would have the advantage on that basis alone. The men of Gibeah proceeded to Nob and got the same answer. After that, they abandoned the idea and returned home.

"We women breathed a collective sigh of relief. I was able to hear the four men when they sat outside our home in the evening and had a discussion.

"Your father agreed that the Twelve Tribes needed weapons. I heard him say, 'What we really need are blacksmiths. We take our scythes and plows to the Philistines for sharpening, and nobody questions it. We've concentrated heavily in recent years on farming, and there's nothing wrong with that until we have to defend ourselves. Looking to the future, we need to think about training some blacksmiths or capturing some. We could manufacture our own weapons. We need weapons, and our young men need training.'

"I know that after this raid, Gibeah did provide three sentries to watch through the night. I assume Uncle Hur spoke to the city council, but it's also possible that the city council might have come to this conclusion without him."

CHAPTER 5

Year 418

It was raining. Was it always raining? My father's perspective on rain was a lot different from mine. He wanted rain pretty much whenever there wasn't either planting or harvesting to do. I thought a little about my father's life as a soldier, a life I knew nothing about. How would a soldier regard rain? Surely it made everything more difficult and less comfortable.

When it wasn't raining, there were a lot more chores for the children. On this day, we children were hurrying toward the hall just as quickly as we could and being cautious about the slippery mud underfoot. There were partial stone paths, and we walked on those as soon as we came to them. There was a stone path to the door of the hall. For myself, Merab, Sarah, two of Sarah's sisters, and three boys from the young men's quarters, the hall wasn't that far away. It was part of our family compound. There were children from other parts of Gibeah also heading for the hall, and for them, the distance was greater. They got wetter than we did.

By the time we arrived, we were cold. We took off whatever outerwear we had and hung it up on pegs inside the door. It wasn't close enough to the fire to be efficiently dried, but there was an effort not to drip all over the floor. Hur was already there, and he'd laid a welcoming fire in the hearth. We gathered around it for a few minutes, trying to warm up.

The village children who were roughly my age were being taught to read. Hur was our teacher. As with any group of children, some were more enthusiastic than others. Merab was determined to learn to read. Our mother had a task for her that could be done on rainy days, specifically teaching her to weave. Merab was interested in that, too, and hoped she could do both. I give my mother credit for not standing in Merab's way or mine, though I don't claim to be quite as dedicated as Merab was.

Mother wasn't sure girls needed to know how to read. Mother couldn't read. Father approved in his somewhat distant way just because any sort of knowledge could be valuable. He was surprised that Hur would take the trouble to teach girls, though. Hur was convinced that any gender could learn to read, and why shouldn't girls participate? By the time all the students had arrived, we were a group of about twenty. Some children, like Merab, were inspired to learn to read. Other children were specifically sent to the hall by their parents. They were unmotivated and made minimal effort.

Hur owned several valuable, and somewhat fragile scrolls. My father owned two. These were the works that we children were learning to read. Hur also had a large piece of vellum on which the children practiced writing characters. Writing was a lot harder than reading! Hur was the most educated person in our community. Clearly he could read and write, but he also knew something about history and knew something about civics. I never found a subject that didn't interest him, though he was more well-versed on some subjects than others. Hur was patient and also enthusiastic. He taught us to read, but he also taught us to love learning.

Hur told us about Moses, a revered leader of the Twelve Tribes who'd lived about 400 years earlier. It was Moses who had led millions of the descendants of our patriarch, Israel, out of Egypt and slavery and into the region of the Jordan Valley. He knew something about Moses's family, specifically his older sister, Miriam, and his younger brother, Aaron. The journey took longer than it should have. It took forty years, and it was largely a matter of skirting the borders of the hostile nations between Egypt and the Jordan Valley. Hur tried to help us visualize millions of people, including children and livestock, on the move, which really can't be done quickly. Still, forty years was extreme. Before the end of it, tempers flared.

Hur described an unlikely conflict between Moses, his brother, and his sister. For whatever reason, well into the journey, Miriam and

Aaron decided to take issue with Moses' Cushite wife. Hur believed that the disunity made Elohim angry. There was a huge migration underway, and Miriam and Aaron were focusing on something trivial. When the three of them got together for a discussion, Miriam came away with leprosy.[3]

I had to pipe up. "Stop! Wait! If Miriam and Aaron were both criticizing Moses's foreign wife, why didn't they both get leprosy?"

Hur answered, "Surely you don't believe I know the mind of Elohim. Elohim doesn't owe any of us an explanation. Miriam got leprosy, and Aaron didn't. Happily, she experienced leprosy for only a week and was then readmitted to the community. I know one thing. Miriam is remembered in the annals and not for having leprosy. She was a noted poet and singer. Aaron made a place for himself as a high priest. This was a talented family. Moses found his calling in politics, Aaron in religion, and Miriam in leading in worship."

As the conquering armies of the Twelve Tribes occupied their new homeland, the land itself was divided into tribal areas and tribal governments. Our tribe was Benjamin, and our territory lay to the west of the River Jordan. We were young enough that we'd never traveled anywhere. We understood that we were members of the tribe of Benjamin, but we had no idea how our tribe fit into the much larger group of twelve. Hur had a papyrus map of the geography and the layout of the tribal lands. It was fascinating.

Hur was interested in local government, and he tried to pique our curiosity. Hur knew the leaders of Gibeah personally and made some effort to get to know the leaders of Benjamin. He was involved in local government, either cheering on the leadership from afar or trying to make the leaders think twice about what they were proposing. He hoped that we children would get involved in our community as we grew older. I wondered why Hur wasn't an acknowledged community leader but he wasn't. He was the man to whom the tribal elders could go if they needed a volunteer for a project.

The hall had a few high windows. There were sheepskins hanging in front of them, which kept out the worst of the rain. There were

---

[3] Numbers 12.

doors on either side for ventilation, but in the rain, it wasn't practical to open them. The doors were cracked, and some water came in. The hall didn't have hard-packed dirt floors that would have quickly turned to mud on wet days. We were grateful for the floor of lime. There were a few stools along the wall, and some of them even had sheepskin cushions. We learned that in earlier days, the hall had been even more primitive, but once my father began to host tribal elders and generals, he'd added the stools and some torches.

There was also a chair for my father that had armrests. It was positioned near the hearth and covered with a blanket. We were not allowed to sit on it, though we were guilty, when Hur wasn't looking, of taking off the cover and looking at it. Hur could have lit the torches, but he was cautious about it. They smoked. He lit two, roughly in the center of the hall and on either side of it.

On this day, the outdoors was dark and overcast. The indoors was dark. Our sources of light were two torches and the hearth. We children had a few school days with pleasant weather, but again, oftentimes, we had other tasks on nice days. Now and then, Hur would hold classes near the woods under a spreading tree. Children may not be able to concentrate well on a glorious day when they'd rather be playing games. But the hall had its own drawbacks, specifically that it was actively gloomy.

Hur sat on one of the stools. We children quickly occupied the stools along the wall, and the rest of us sat on the floor. The glowing hearth was warm on a chilly day. The burning wood crackled and threw our tiny sparks that died on the lime floor.

I truly liked Uncle Hur. I liked that he thought girls could and should be taught to read. The men of our community, specifically my father and grandfather, weren't so liberal. A man had a place in society and a woman had a place, and usually, the two didn't overlap. Women's tasks didn't include reading. Another man of our family who was less impressed by gender was Ner, my grandfather's brother, though he really didn't spend time with the children in the way that Hur did. We all knew Hur a lot better.

Hur was a gentle, easygoing man who tried hard to care for the people around him. Still, I vividly remember making him angry on this dreary indoor day. I like to think that being a child is an excuse. Maybe it is. Human beings learn as we go, and children have more to learn than adults. Happily, Hur didn't stay angry with me for long. What I did was to take the papyrus map too close to the hearth. There were sparks in the air, and the papyrus was highly flammable. I was cold, and I was also looking for light.

I felt a firm hand on my arm and heard Hur's voice. "Girl, what are you doing?" He yanked me away from the fire, none too gently. Hur didn't raise his voice to me, but there was something noticeable about him when he was angry. The scar on his face became prominent, and sometimes he fingered it. Maybe it throbbed in stressful situations.

"I'm sorry, I'm sorry," I said.

"Michal, you know that papyrus could catch fire. And if you dropped a flaming papyrus on the floor of the hall, the whole place could burn."

"I'm sorry," I said again.

The lesson of the day, in addition to a little bit of geography and some reading, was to be aware of my surroundings. It's a good lesson for us all.

So our group backed up from the hearth, which wasn't ideal just because the hall was so dim. Hur turned the lesson toward writing. We children sat on the floor with the piece of vellum in front of us. Hur provided an ink pot and a goose feather. We took turns trying to copy the characters off one of Hur's scrolls in such a way that others of our culture could interpret them. Hur was quite complementary to Merab. She seemed to have a knack for drawing characters accurately. My efforts weren't too bad, but they weren't quite as neat and as sharp as Merab's.

CHAPTER 6

Year 418

It was laundry day. Laundry day was nobody's favorite day, but if there was good news on this day, it was just that the weather was so cooperative. In fact, there were occasions when my mother took Merab and me to the stream when it wasn't the community's laundry day. We really hated that. Mother was determined that the clean clothing would dry quickly, and of course, the specified village laundry day wasn't always pleasant. In my mother's defense, she didn't bring us to the stream alone very often. It was usually for something specific; for instance, blood on one of my father's tunics. And when that happened, there were other things to wash as well.

On the village laundry day, the banks of the stream were speckled with women and girls. We got the social connection that everyone craved, and we also got an additional element of safety. Wet laundry was heavy and cold. And sometimes the stream was swollen and fast. There were occasions when laundry day was put off for a week. The stream could be treacherous. A woman who braved the stream alone took her life in her hands. If she slipped and lost her footing and was weighed down by her clothing, the result could be catastrophic. Drownings occurred, but happily not often. Usually, there were enough of us on the banks to look out for each other.

I looked around for Sarah, and she and I washed the clothing entrusted to us as we chatted. Merab was in a group of three other girls her age, and mother was holding a conversation with the midwife who'd assisted at the birth of Rizpah's baby. Sarah and I finished our part, grabbed an armful of heavy, wet clothing, and headed back toward our dwellings. The two of us had a very nice conversation and some laughter. I thought about what she'd said about our mothers and almost brought up the subject, but I was afraid I'd spoil the mood. I liked our relationship, and maybe it was better if we didn't compare mothers. Mother finished the task she'd assigned to herself and left the stream with Merab trailing behind her. There were two spreading trees not too distant from our house on which we hung the clothing to dry.

Mother and Merab went into the house and sat down at the loom. Mother was a good weaver. She mainly produced rugs, many of which were small and off-white or gray but a few of which were richly dyed. Mother wove wool. As mother's skills increased, her signature rugs became two-colored. The house we lived in was fitted with a blue and yellow rug in front of the hearth along with other smaller and plainer rugs scattered throughout. Merab was operating the loom, and mother was overseeing.

Sarah was occupied with a task given by her mother. I wandered around, not really knowing what to do with myself. I was glad the laundry was done, but now what? Days like this, without designated tasks for everyone, weren't that common. I decided to go visit my Aunt Hadassah. I liked Aunt Hadassah. She usually made time for the village children, including me. Aunt Hadassah was quite an accomplished cook, and sometimes she let me help her. She introduced me to any number of herbs that she used to season food, such as dill, caraway, cumin, turmeric, fennel, and thyme.

On this day, there was a pot bubbling on Aunt Hadassah's hearth, and the aroma was wonderful. But it wasn't suppertime. Aunt Hadassah was simmering a small piece of mutton in an herb broth to which she'd later add vegetables. Most meals consisted of fruits and vegetables. The meat would simmer for several hours.

As I arrived, Aunt Hadassah was preparing to leave. She said, "Hello, Michal! How was laundry day?"

I answered, "Fine," when there really wasn't much else to say about it. It happened, and it happened without incident.

"Would you like to come with me to look in on your grandmother?"

I couldn't muster any enthusiasm, but then I wasn't doing anything else either. I agreed to keep my aunt company. My Aunt Hadassah visited her sister most days. She would go sometime before the traditional evening meal at such time as my grandfather wasn't likely to be home. It wasn't so much a matter of trying to avoid my grandfather. It was more a matter of not wanting to intrude on the two of them and of not wanting to be in the way. I actually think my grandfather welcomed Aunt Hadassah's presence. His marriage can't have been ideal, and it took some of the pressure off of him.

Grandfather and Grandmother lived only a few minutes away. Aunt Hadassah started the conversation with, "Good afternoon, Mariamne! Have you eaten today?"

Wait, there was no conversation. There was Aunt Hadassah talking and, hopefully, my grandmother listening. My grandmother didn't respond. She never responded. Aunt Hadassah watched her eyes and swore she could see comprehension there. Aunt Hadassah went rummaging around the hearth area to see what food might be available. There were some root vegetables that were hard.

My grandmother had few or no teeth. Hadassah settled on the end of a loaf of bread and some milk. She smelled the milk first. It passed inspection, and Hadassah proceeded to cut the bread end into bite-sized pieces. She poured milk on the pieces and hand-fed my grandmother. I didn't realize before that day that my grandmother didn't lift food to her mouth and eat it. Aunt Hadassah handed me the spoon, and I fed my grandmother. It felt uncomfortable. It felt like I was intruding on her disability, which I was, but then, apparently, if nobody took the time to feed her, she would die. Did my grandfather feed her? My grandmother did finish the bread and milk.

I tried talking to my grandmother. "Do you like it, Grandmother?"

"Please talk to her," my aunt pleaded. "She does understand."

What does a person say to somebody who doesn't participate in a conversation? I talked about doing laundry. It was the most recent event in my life.

"Have you been outside today, Grandmother? It's a beautiful day. My mother, my sister, and I just got back from washing clothes at the stream. The washing was our main chore for the day, and now Mother and Merab are weaving at the loom. You should smell the pot that's cooking at Aunt Hadassah's house!"

Of course, there was no food cooking on my grandfather's hearth.

I asked, "Who cooks for my grandfather?"

Hadassah said, "I do. So he'll get some mutton and vegetables this evening. Your mother and Rizpah help too."

"Does my father visit his mother?"

Aunt Hadassah shook her head. "Almost never. Your father is plowing, planting, harvesting, and raising his own children, and that's only when he's home. If he told me he doesn't have time for his mother, I would believe it, but I still wish he'd try. He stays busy. I am convinced that my sister appreciates visits, but for the visitor, they're not very satisfying. Your father doesn't sit still well, and that's what it takes to visit Mariamne. A visitor has to relax and just be. Your father needs to do." Aunt Hadassah picked up my grandmother's thin hand. "She knows we're here and knows who I am. I love her."

Did I see a little flicker in my grandmother's eyes when her sister said that? I don't know if my aunt was watching. If she was, she would have known for certain.

Visiting my grandmother wasn't such an odious duty as I thought it would be, maybe just because Aunt Hadassah was who she was. Sometimes it's not easy for a child to have a conversation with an adult, but Aunt Hadassah was different. She was a great listener and thought before she spoke. The three of us were sipping tea, and Aunt Hadassah would help my grandmother lift the bowl and would also dab at her chin with a napkin. Aunt Hadassah made it a point to speak to her sister, but as we just enjoyed each other's company, she focused on me. We chatted about this and that until I got up the courage to ask, "Why are some women wives and some concubines?" I wouldn't have asked my mother that or Rizpah either.

Aunt Hadassah looked surprised. Then she answered, "Oh, you're thinking about Rizpah. I think your father should have married her. She bore him ten children, after all. Did you know that Rizpah was a Philistine captive?"

31

"No. Is it a secret?"

Hadassah replied, "Maybe it is now. People don't talk about it. Your father took Rizpah as a young girl, almost certainly a virgin. As you know, if our warriors take slaves, they take them on successful raids against our enemies. They don't take many, and they usually kill the adults. Sometimes we can train younger foreigners in our ways and they can adapt. Your father clearly was besotted by Rizpah's beauty. You can imagine how your mother felt. Still, it is a man's right to take multiple sexual partners, and your mother didn't have grounds to object. She made the best of it, and I envy her serenity.

"Rizpah adapted. She speaks Hebrew very well. If someone were to tell me she misses her old life and her family, I'd be surprised. She acts like she's forgotten her former life, and maybe the bearing of children is part of that. She behaves like she's one of us, and our community has accepted her. Wife or concubine, well, I have never discussed her status with your mother. It's entirely possible that your mother didn't want your father to marry her, and he conceded. The other idea might be an old law that prohibits members of the Twelve Tribes from intermarrying with the cultures around us.[4] Did your father think that if he took a foreign woman and didn't marry her he could keep the law? There are problems with both possibilities. First of all, your father isn't known for caring what women think. He cares for your mother and he cares for Rizpah, but he doesn't value their opinions. Secondly, he's also not known to be religious. So back to your question—the answer is I don't know."

I don't know how long we stayed. We stayed long enough for my grandfather to stroll in.

"Hello, Kish!" said Hadassah. "I just finished getting Mariamne to eat something."

Grandfather mumbled his thanks and then patted his wife's shoulder.

"Hello, Grandfather!" I said. "How was your day?"

I would never say that Grandfather communicated with as much difficulty as his wife, and yet he didn't seem at ease trying to

---

[4] Deuteronomy 7:2–4.

talk to me. Maybe he'd have done better with Hadassah if I weren't there. He made a comment about the weather and then said something about the newly planted fields. The men were keeping watch at least until the seed sprouted. Birds would eat it if they got the chance.

Hadassah stood up to leave and then said, "There will be mutton stew at our house this evening."

Kish grunted an acknowledgment. I walked my aunt back to her house, and neither of us spoke. I continued on to my house, thinking all the way about my grandmother and my aunt who were sisters. What happened? Why was my grandmother the way she was and my aunt entirely different? What happens when a person ages? Is it all about aging or are there other factors? My Aunt Hadassah moved easily, spoke easily, and carried out the same tasks she'd done since childhood. My grandmother was a shell of a person who sat in one place all day. She *could* walk if she had to, but somebody would have to guide her. Most of the time, she did nothing and went nowhere. She was my grandmother, and I was supposed to have some feelings for her. I felt guilty. There was something about her that was frightening. Maybe it was simply fear on my part, fear of what age could do to a person. I knew then and there that if I got to choose, I'd rather be like Aunt Hadassah when I got to be her age!

I got to see how well Merab had done with the piece of a rug she was weaving. She'd made progress, but for the moment, I wouldn't have known it was a rug. I saw woven blue wool, and the work looked good. It's just that at this beginning stage, it could have been anything.

CHAPTER 7

Year 418

It was another school day, but this time, we children and our teacher, Uncle Hur, weren't in the hall. We had a stand of lovely shade trees along the path that led into and out of our neighborhood. The hall wasn't congenial, but there were drawbacks to outdoor learning as well. First of all, the insects were annoying. And, secondly, a lot of us had trouble paying attention on a fine day.

Today, Uncle Hur was lecturing on history. The Twelve Tribes had a national hero, Moses, who was succeeded by another national hero, Joshua. Joshua was a general. It was he who led the Twelve Tribes to conquer the Jordan Valley and occupy it. Uncle Hur wanted to give us all some background on the Hivite city of Gibeon, which was just to the west of Gibeah. I was daydreaming about sticking my bare feet in the stream and was having trouble differentiating between Gibeah and Gibeon. Sometimes Uncle Hur droned on like buzzing bees.

"Let me add one thing about Moses before we move on to Joshua. Moses led the descendants of our ancestor, Israel, out of slavery in Egypt. All of you know that our culture numbers its years, and you know that our present year is 418. Do you know the significance of the number?"

There was silence until one of the older boys ventured a guess. "Was this the year when our people completed the journey to the Jordan Valley?"

Uncle Hur said, "Well done. Almost! The number 418 is the number of years since our ancestors left Egypt or, more specifically, since they crossed the Sea of Reeds. We count forty years from that date until the Twelve Tribes reached the Jordan Valley. Our ancestors went to war. The Jordan Valley was inhabited when they arrived, and the residents fought for their homes in the same manner any nation does.

"So the Twelve Tribes made a treaty with Gibeon, not realizing that it was a neighbor.[5] And it wasn't just Gibeon. There were three other Hivite cities in the same vicinity—Kephirah, Beeroth, and Kiriath Jearim. Elohim had not sanctioned any treaties with the inhabitants of the area, and Elohim wasn't consulted. Joshua found out quickly that he and the rest of the leaders had been duped. They were angry with the leaders of Gibeon, who deliberately tricked the invading army into thinking they were a distant people. They were also angry with themselves. They could have inquired of Elohim. Elohim is silent sometimes when He feels we don't value His opinion.

"The armies of the Twelve Tribes did proceed to Gibeon and demanded an accounting. It is written the leaders of Gibeon weren't apologetic. They were trying to save their towns and populations from destruction and felt justified in their deception. Joshua didn't feel he could break the treaty just because the leaders of Gibeon did something underhanded. There were oaths involved. But he wasn't prepared to just forget the whole thing either. He didn't exactly enslave the population, though the result was similar to that. We see slaves as individuals who are guided by overseers and whips. The Hivites remained in their cities. Joshua decreed that their responsibility to the treaty would be that they would provide wood and water to the communities of their conquerors. That would be the price of the treaty. The Hivites agreed, and this has been their role for four hundred years."

I heard a subtle change in Uncle Hur's voice which brought my consciousness back to the present moment. He clearly realized that we pupils weren't focusing. It was just too perfect a day.

"I can just feel the excitement surrounding my modest history lesson," Uncle Hur said with irony. "You ask if there is any possibility that history is relevant to your lives. In this case, yes. In this case, I am combining history with very current events in Gibeah."

---

[5] Joshua 9:15.

The group of children was now paying attention.

"We have a scholar in our midst—well, not in the midst of this group. We have a local scholar who will be assisting with an updated treaty between the Twelve Tribes and the Hivite cities. I find it rather amazing that any treaty has been in place for four hundred years and that even after that time, there is an interest in extending it. Do any of you know who our resident scholar is?"

Right then I knew. I knew that Hur had a former student of whom he was inordinately proud.

I muttered, "Esh-Baal."

"Speak up, Michal."

I said louder, "Esh-Baal."

Uncle Hur confirmed my guess. "Esh-Baal will participate with two other scholars to modernize the ancient treaty. He is the youngest person involved. It was quite an honor for him to be asked. Small-town residents can indeed get tribal recognition. As a very young man, Esh-Baal is beginning to make his mark as a scholar for the Twelve Tribes. Perhaps if this effort is successful, Esh-Baal will become prominent. He was my student, and in some disciplines, he has surpassed his teacher.

"Moving on, here is a blank scroll and a quill and ink. I want everyone in the group to transcribe two characters onto the vellum, and after that, you're dismissed. Use this lovely day as it should be used."

I wasn't interested in treaties and wasn't interested in Gibeon. Maybe I should have been. It wasn't at all far from Gibeah. I was interested in Esh-Baal. I felt like every time I looked up, there was Esh-Baal, watching me, looking for some behavior he could criticize. I watched him, too, and if I could excuse my own spying, I would have said it was in self-defense. Was any part of me proud that my brother was participating in a nationwide endeavor? I was simply too young at the time for politics. As I grew older, politics became more relevant to my life, but not then.

I never saw the group of men who were updating the treaty. They met in Gibeon. However, Esh-Baal brought home a piece of the treaty on which he was working, and he mentioned it to our mother and father. I wanted to see it. I wanted to see if I could read it. I thought about asking Esh-Baal if I could look at it and then decided that I wasn't going to take no for an answer. Therefore, I wouldn't ask.

I knew the opportune times to sneak into the young men's barracks, but I also knew that if I wanted to read something, there had to be some light. My brother would be taking his piece of vellum back to Gibeon in two days, so I couldn't wait too long. I got my opportunity when the barracks was empty and the young men were out in the fields, checking for weeds. I found the manuscript in the area Esh-Baal occupied and realized that I could read most of it. There were words I didn't know. But one thing I noticed, Esh-Baal used "accept" when he should have said "except." I giggled! So now what? Should I let him present the manuscript that way and never see the outcome? Of course not! I was going to point out the error and gloat. Very conveniently, Esh-Baal came in from the fields right then and demanded to know what I was doing in his quarters.

"I'm proofreading your manuscript, Esh-Baal. Look at this—you used the wrong word."

Esh-Baal responded, "Good, Michal! You can read. Now get out of my space."

I left. I viewed myself as the savior of Esh-Baal's reputation. Esh-Baal viewed me as a nuisance. Still, he got to correct the error before he went back to Gibeon. He might even have gone back over the rest of the manuscript. Esh-Baal, while annoying, was also single-minded and thorough.

My brother spent quite a bit of time in Gibeon. Nobody questioned it until my father returned from a trip to Mizpah. He didn't stop to greet my mother; he didn't stop to greet Rizpah; he went directly to the young men's quarters to see Esh-Baal. In our village, there isn't a real option for privacy. Oftentimes, if there's nobody else in view, we can fool ourselves into thinking our conversation is private, but if we think logically about it, we know it really isn't. We live close together. Our shelters aren't sound proofed. We hear most of what goes on around us and we accept the inevitability of unseen family members listening.

I heard my father begin with, "I ran into Isaac in Mizpah today. The treaty you were hired to write was done two weeks ago."

I didn't hear Esh-Baal's response other than any number of I'm sorries. I know he said something, and that was when my father lost his legendary temper. Shouting makes it a lot more difficult to follow the conversation if a person wasn't meant to be included. If I am an eavesdropper, so be it. But I have no doubt the entire compound heard the angry words. Like me, nobody else may have understood them. When my father left the young men's quarters, suddenly there was dead silence on the compound. I wonder if my father noticed. My father retreated to the small brick house in which he lived alone and didn't really make his presence known for the rest of the day.

We members of the family didn't see Esh-Baal for the rest of the day either. I remember a vegetable stew that was quite delicious. Mother was using up a goose, and though there wasn't a lot of meat in the stew, a little bit added a lot of flavor. I could identify thyme in it too. Esh-Baal didn't join us. Our father did, and we all felt his black mood. We tiptoed around him and left as early as we could. Merab and I took the bowls to the stream to wash them. I saw my mother leave our house and take a bowl to the young men's quarters for Esh-Baal. Merab and I speculated about what had set-off our father. She and everyone else heard the raised voices, but not the words.

My brothers all left their quarters after supper and around sunset. Jonathan, Abinadab, and Malki-Shua left their respective dwellings and converged upon the young men's barracks. I noticed because of how unlikely it was for them to go there. They encountered Esh-Baal and two other young men, sitting outside sipping beer as the day cooled off. Jonathan, Abinadab, and Malki-Shua were all of a type—rugged, determined soldiers. They excelled when they practiced with their faux weapons and were all now focused on learning to use the real weapons they'd captured. They were tall and muscular, and they shared similar interests.

Esh-Baal wasn't one of them. He was tall but thin and, even at his young age, inclined to stoop just a little. He was a person who pored over manuscripts and scrolls, and it was affecting his posture. The other three had more in common with each other. The three of them sat down against the back of the building on either side of Esh-Baal. I saw the two young men who'd been sitting with him discreetly leave, walking from the back of the barracks to the entryway.

I saw my three older brothers approach the dwelling where Esh-Baal lived, but I couldn't see the back of the building where people sat after supper. Esh-Baal must have been surprised to be the object of his brothers' attention.

Abinadab spoke first. "Hey, brother! What, by Elohim, did you do to our father?"

Malki-Shua chimed in, "Esh-Baal on Father's shit list—who'da thunk? When did you start breaking rules?"

Jonathan spoke up, "Okay, Esh-Baal, spill!"

Esh-Baal must have been uncomfortable. His three brothers ordinarily tended to ignore him.

Esh-Baal said, "Well, Isaac, Naphtali, and I finished rewriting the treaty a couple of weeks ago. We turned it over to the Hivites of Gibeon for approval, and they approved it. Father encountered Isaac in Mizpah, and Isaac told him."

Malki-Shua observed, "But you just got back from there two days ago."

"Nobody asked me why I was going to Gibeon and I never explained. Up until now, nobody cared!"

Esh-Baal's voice rose a few notes when he whined. It was grating.

"So," said Abinadab, "we care and we're asking. Whatever you were doing in Gibeon made Father furious, and I have a very good idea what it might have been. Gibeon has some exceptional whorehouses."

Malki-Shua interjected, "You would know! So would Jonathan."

Jonathan defended himself, "It was *one* time. That sort of entertainment isn't for me. I was hoping to keep Abinadab out of trouble, but that didn't work out."

Esh-Baal whined, "If you've all visited ladies of the evening in Gibeon, why is father raging at *me*?"

Abinadab replied, "You got caught. For the most part, father doesn't monitor our activities. He probably has his suspicions but he doesn't want to know. You are quite a bit younger. I don't know if it will make you feel any better, but father worries about your safety. There is danger in whoring. There are angry pimps and there are social diseases."

Esh-Baal said, "I wish you wouldn't say whoring. You don't know Delilah. She's young and gentle and a slave. She's trying to buy her freedom."

I wish I could have seen the expressions on their faces. What I heard was raucous laughter that continued on for several breaths.

Jonathan gasped an apology. "I'm sorry, Esh-Baal. We know you believe that. Esh-Baal, this is a very bad idea. You're not aware enough at your age of how the world works. You have a tender heart."

Malki-Shua said, "Delilah, is it? For Father, a double curse. A prostitute *and* a Hivite!"

Jonathan asked, "Did Father forbid you to go back to Gibeon?"

"Oh, yes!"

"Are you going to obey him? We will not be watching you, Esh-Baal, and neither will he, especially when he's not home."

The discussion ended without an answer from Esh-Baal. The young men stood up to go inside, but just before the group disbursed, Jonathan spoke.

"Wait, Esh-Baal! I have something for you. I took this javelin from the Philistines, and I already have a good one. Do you want to practice with it? I don't need it."

If Esh-Baal answered the question, I didn't hear it. But he did take the javelin into his living quarters. Esh-Baal came around to the front of the barracks as his brothers left for their homes. I hurried home at that point. I contemplated how Esh-Baal made money. He did earn something for the treaty he helped to update. He was also quite an accomplished scribe. He wrote for some of his neighbors and read for them too. Presumably, he received some sort of pay. I wondered how much it cost to visit a prostitute. I didn't ask our father. Was Esh-Baal really going to practice with a javelin? I tended to be aware of his whereabouts and expected to notice if he took the javelin out into the yard.

CHAPTER 8

Year 418

The children of Gibeah were getting another history lesson. It wasn't raining, but the skies were gray, and there was a brisk breeze. We met in the hall. As usual, there was a fire in the hearth and two lit torches. Hur began by saying, "I know it's dim in here, but today, we're doing something different. It won't be quite as important to have light. We have a guest lecturer, and his name is Ner. Some of you are undoubtedly tired of the dusty old history of Moses and Joshua, but Ner will talk about recent history and about people all of you know. I truly hope you will be genuinely interested, but if not, I ask you to be respectful of the time being given to you by somebody who could easily find something else to do."

None of us had ever viewed Ner as a scholar or a teacher. He was sitting on a stool next to Hur. He didn't seem entirely comfortable, but he did have a very good grasp on what he wanted to say. He started out with a stutter or two, but once he got going, the words flowed easily.

He began, "Hur has educated you well on the subjects of Moses and Joshua. Were they kings? No, they were not. Joshua may have been Moses' protege, but he wasn't his son. In those days, both Moses and Joshua were acknowledged leaders of the Twelve Tribes, but there was a huge amount of input by the elders of all the tribes. There was also the question of the succession. With a king, it's easy. His son succeeds him. With Moses, Joshua, and those who came after them, the transfer of power was never guaranteed. Civil war could have erupted more often than it did when the acknowledged leader died, but usually it was just the various tribes going back to their various geographic lands and ignoring the larger nation.

"Did Hur tell you about Moses' prophecy? It is written that long ago, even before Moses was succeeded by Joshua, he predicted that like the other cultures of the Jordan Valley, the Twelve Tribes, would eventually demand a king.[6] Approximately 300 years ago, a man stepped up and declared himself to be king. He came to power in a bloodbath, as some kings do, with the execution of his seventy brothers. His name was Abimelech, and he was the illegitimate son of a warrior and judge named Gideon, also known as Jerub-Baal. However, he was neither preceded by a king nor succeeded by a king, and his reign, if you will, was only three years. He created no dynasty. He was not anointed, and there was no tribal consensus. He reached out and took something and didn't hold it long. He was an individual who died a bad death. He was killed at a siege when a woman dropped a millstone on his head from above.

"By this time, you all know who Samuel is. Samuel didn't believe that Abimelech fulfilled the prophecy. I know Hur promised you a history of people you know who are still alive, but let me give you a short foundation of tribal government. Eli and Samuel may be ancient figures to all of you, but I knew them. To me, they're recent history. Eli and Samuel were the two nearest predecessors to King Saul. They were not kings. I was only a child when Eli died. I don't pretend I knew him, but I did see him once. The most memorable thing about him was how fat he was. Very similar to Moses and Joshua, Samuel was Eli's protege and not his son.

"I did actually know Samuel somewhat and did have opportunity to have conversations with him. Samuel was older than I, but not by a lot. He had the energy of a much younger man and did a lot of traveling. He would offer sacrifices to Elohim in the towns he visited and would host feasts. I heard from Samuel's lips something about his early life. His mother brought him to Shiloh and Eli when he was five years old. He was the first child of a woman who'd been childless for many years. As many women do, she felt shame for being

---

[6] Deuteronomy 17:14–17.

barren. She promised the child to Elohim if He would favor her with one, and Elohim did. She kept her promise. So Samuel became Eli's apprentice and learned the ways of the priesthood from early childhood. We've been talking about the difficulties of transferring power when a tribal leader dies. Both Eli and Samuel were righteous men with unrighteous sons. We can all be grateful that in these cases, the biological sons weren't given power.

"When Moses recorded his prophecy about a king, he listed certain requirements. The first condition was that Elohim would select the king. Samuel positively swore that Elohim had selected Saul and that the first condition had been met. The elders of the Twelve Tribes had been witnesses. Hur and I were both witnesses. There were other parts to Moses' speech that suggested that the king not have many wives and not amass great wealth. It is clear that some men, such as Abimelech, will take a prophecy and try to forcefully insert themselves into it. The effort didn't end well for him. Our King Saul did not seek power nor did he slaughter any relatives to get it.

"We are three brothers, Kish, Hur, and I. We are bound either by blood or by marriage and the three of us have some shared experiences that are more binding than anything else. At least to some extent, we can read each other's moods."

CHAPTER 9

Year 387

"My brother, Kish, was out of sorts on one otherwise lovely morning. You could always tell when he was out of sorts, though he didn't throw noisy tantrums. He paced back and forth outside his dwelling, scuffed up the dust with his sandals, and muttered to himself. On this day, the muttering was mainly two words.

"'Dorcas! Ebenezer! Dorcas! Ebenezer! Where in Sheol are you?'

"Kish's two donkeys had disappeared. Disappeared to where? How could livestock disappear in our small village? He approached his son.

"'Saul, I need you to go find two stray donkeys first thing. Dorcas and Ebenezer will make mischief among the neighbors if they are allowed to roam free too long. I can't imagine that they've gotten far.'

"Saul set out with a young servant, Asher, after breakfast. Where can a donkey hide? When Kish ordered the search, he expected his son home with the donkeys before nightfall. Saul and Asher must have been gone about a week and a half. The donkeys were only gone a day. As predicted, a neighbor found them in his shed, eating his hay. The compound knew that Kish was looking for donkeys, and the neighbor knew where to bring the miscreants.

"A week and a half is a long time to search for errant donkeys. Kish was about to organize some village men to look for Saul and Asher, but before he made that happen, Asher showed up. He brought news that was astonishing. Saul had taken a place among the prophets, coming down from the high place of Gibeah, and he was prophesying. Saul did not prophesy. This was entirely out of character. Saul had always been taller than anyone else in the village. It made him distinctive, but other than that, he wasn't one to call attention to himself. Hur coined a phrase that was repeated a number of times.

"'Is Saul also among the prophets?'[7]

"When Saul appeared in the compound, he was nothing short of ebullient. He was praising Elohim, dancing, and prophesying. The first person to greet him was Ahinoam and he told her that she would be the wife of a great king. Not only that, but he told her that her daughter would be the wife of a great king. Ahinoam at the time had only two sons. Ahinoam...Ahinoam wasn't one to tolerate nonsense. She looked...is there a combination of impatient and astonished?

"Ahinoam's thought processes were more agile than most, and she quickly came back with, 'I have sons. Will I be the mother of a great king?' Her question immediately broke the mood. Saul's face darkened and then went blank. If I hadn't been watching Saul at that moment, I would have missed the transformation. It was surprising. He had been full of joy and not afraid to express it, and he transformed back to the rather reticent individual who was familiar to us all. Ahinoam must have noticed, but she was probably relieved to see the version of her husband that she knew. I wonder what she thought about the prophecy or if she thought about it. Ahinoam is very practical.

"*What* great king? There were kings all around the region of the Twelve Tribes, but it isn't customary for the descendants of Israel to marry them. And none of them seemed to be obviously great. They ruled small territories on the outskirts of the Twelve Tribes' territory, and except for the Egyptians, they weren't known for establishing long-lasting dynasties. The other obvious problem for Ahinoam was that she was married, though of course, women become widows all the time.

"Practical, yes, Ahinoam handed Saul and Asher clean clothing. She made an eloquent gesture toward the creek. Saul had been prophesying, and we were amazed. We wanted to hear all about it.

---

[7] 1 Samuel 10:11, 12.

But the two of them were grimy. Ahinoam and Rizpah prepared a meal while Saul and Asher got cleaned up. Their timing was impeccable. They entered the creek in a minor drizzle and exited rather quickly in a thunderstorm.

"It wouldn't be true that the women prepared a feast. But they did prepare food for the entire compound, which was unusual. Normally, a woman takes charge of feeding a smaller group within the compound, perhaps just those in her dwelling, though it's customary for her to see to the needs of any of her own sons living in the young men's quarters. Preparing a meal in this case meant bread that had been baked the previous day, along with some olives and figs. Also, Saul had brought home two loaves of bread, acquired on his travels, that were still fresh.[8]

"All the girls helped to bring refreshments into the hall. This was the old hall. I know the improved hall can still be a dark and mysterious place, but the old wooden hall was dismal. Hur had a fire lit, which helped, but at the time, there were no torches. The doors were cracked open for ventilation, but as you might expect, the rain came in as well. The paths between compound buildings had become muddy and slippery. The present stone walks were added later. We all did our best to balance whatever items had been entrusted to us, and we got everything into the hall without mishap. Several of the girls carried pottery bowls in baskets. We needed a number of them since they were used for both food and drink. Saul and Abner brought large containers of beer.

"The men had seated themselves on the rugs they had brought into the hall, and the women passed around bowls with supper in them. Hur had brought a rug for Hadassah. Saul helped transport the beer but was rather distracted otherwise. Asher brought rugs for Saul, Ahinoam, and Rizpah. Saul and Asher took places near the hearth. They were both shivering. It always feels good to be clean, but the stream was chilly. The children settled themselves on the floor. Even the old hall had a floor of lime.

---

[8] 1 Samuel 10:4.

"We enjoyed being together and listening to the drumbeat of the rain. We all got along relatively well for living in close quarters. Saul's speech was shorter than expected. He and Asher had gone to a number of neighboring towns, looking in vain for the donkeys.

"Saul said, 'We went north, first to Geba and then to Michmash. We asked everyone along the way if they'd seen any donkeys out foraging for themselves, and nobody had. This was several days after we left Gibeah. We sat down and puzzled over what to do next. We understood that our family would soon start wondering what had happened to us. Asher had a splendid idea. We were close to the region of Zuph, which was just a bit further west. Asher pointed out that the holy man lived there, and perhaps since we'd come this far, we shouldn't give up without consulting him. I was reluctant. I knew about the Holy Man, but I'd never met him and wasn't sure how he'd feel about a total stranger asking for favors. I'd brought nothing with me. But Asher had. He was willing to give a gift of the quarter of a silver shekel he was carrying. So we went to Ramah in the area of Zuph to try to see the Holy Man. Do holy men do donkeys? I'll admit to being a little embarrassed about asking. But we went.

"'It was the strangest thing. We didn't get to talk to the holy man, Samuel, right away. First we observed a sacrifice presided over by Samuel. I've witnessed sacrifices before, but not recently. Gibeah has a high place and an altar, but I haven't been there in a while. Samuel performed a sacrifice, and immediately after that, there was a feast. Both Asher and I ate well. I ate especially well. There was a joint of meat that Samuel had set aside for me as if he were expecting me. It was right about then that he made mention of my father's donkeys, and I hadn't even gotten a chance to ask. He simply said the donkeys had been found. So Asher and I headed home after the feast.'

"Hur and I had met Samuel previously, but this was Saul's first encounter. We demanded details. Saul told only the barest outline of events. He repeated that Samuel said the donkeys had been found and the two of them went home. There wasn't anything to add. We tried a different approach and insisted that Saul explain his sudden ability to prophesy.

"Saul said, 'I can't explain it. It's a feeling of unbearable joy that must find release. I wanted to see my family, but I had to go first to the high place of Gibeah. I knew there were priests and prophets there, and I needed to join them. I took a place among them, and they didn't seem surprised to see me. There were sounds coming out of my mouth. Was it words? I don't remember any of them. What did I say? This sensation has never come upon me before, and for all I know, it won't come upon me again. They danced and I danced. Before we knew it, we'd come down from the high place and into the town. I wasn't aware of time or distance. I felt tired but exhilarated. My body and mouth were active, and my thoughts were completely at peace.'

"I wasn't tactful. I asked, 'Do you expect us to believe that? We are the ones who know you best, Saul. You don't sing, dance, or prophecy, or at least, not in public.'

"Saul said, 'This is the only explanation I can give you. I'm not saying it well, and you're not particularly accepting, but it's the best I can do. We, the men of Gibeah, have been invited to a meeting of all the tribes of Israel. It will be held in Mizpah. I intend to go, and I hope the men of our family will come along to support the effort. Samuel will send word as to when.'

"I remember thinking when Saul informed us all that Samuel had called a tribal meeting in Mizpah, did he have a successor in mind? It would be advantageous to everyone if there wasn't a huge gap between Samuel and the next national leader. Samuel wasn't getting any younger."

Hur said, "There is a lot to tell about the circumstances under which Saul became king of the Twelve Tribes. I had hoped to get into it a little further, but now the sun is setting, and it's time for supper. When we meet again, it's possible that Ner won't be available, but I can continue the story. I was there too.

"As for Saul's prophecy, I heard it with my own ears. Ahinoam is the wife of a great king, whether she prefers to acknowledge the fact or not. Merab and Michal, the daughters of Ahinoam, have you ever heard about the prophecy? I am confident Ahinoam thinks about it, but I've never heard her speak of it."

CHAPTER 10

Year 418

The following day, we were back to the usual routine. Our village had gotten the rain that had threatened, but the following morning was bright and hopeful. The ground was still soggy and covered with puddles. Sarah and I were sent out to gather branches and sticks to burn as we did on most days. Our compound was made up of houses quite close together, though there was an obvious gap between the neighborhood and the surrounding forest. We left the compound proper by means of a well-worn path. It was along this path that men of the family had been stacking up rocks from the fields for many years. Anyone leaving or coming into the compound by this route had to keep to a fairly narrow stretch of path. A driver could get a donkey cart through it if he was careful.

Sarah and I walked through, as we always did, trying to keep our feet dry. There was still a significant puddle straddling the path just as we left the compound.

We were children. There were limits to what we could carry, and we had to carry anything we picked up to the communal wood-pile that leaned up against the hall. The woodpile had a loose covering over it to keep out the worst of the weather. We were hoping the storm had knocked down some branches, which would be easy to gather and for which we wouldn't have to go far afield. We did find our respective armfuls not too far from the point to which we had to carry them. We gathered what we could and headed back along the path to the entrance to the compound.

We never saw it coming. Our arms were full, and we couldn't see the ground in front of us. Suddenly, both of us were face-down in the puddle. Our loads flew everywhere. My chin came down hard on one of the branches I'd been carrying and jarred my teeth. Happily, my tongue wasn't in between them! Later on, I discovered I'd earned a black eye from the experience. I looked at Sarah who was picking herself up.

I said, "Sarah, are you all right?" She looked disgusting—and disgusted. There was blood on her lip and on both of her hands.

Sarah said, "I think so. Ouch! I'm bleeding. Michal, I wish you could see yourself!"

Neither of us was injured. I found my feet and assumed my appearance was pretty much the same as Sarah's. We looked at each other and couldn't quite suppress the inevitable grins. Then we thought about our mothers, ruining the mood. I turned around, looked closely at the path, and found a narrow rope strung across it at ankle-level. I pulled up a short stake with a rope attached that came out of the ground quite easily, and I flung it away from the path. There was another short stake on the other side of the path. Esh-Baal! He must have observed us leaving and set up his little trap immediately behind us. If he was sitting in his usual spot in his quarters, he wouldn't have seen our humiliation. However, the entire compound would observe us as we made our way to our dwellings. We weren't going to get any dirtier. We picked up most of our loads and proceeded to the woodpile.

The reckoning came when we had to face our mothers. I didn't witness Sarah's conversation. I can tell you that my mother was appalled. She didn't let me into the house. She walked me down to the stream, and that's where we found Sarah and Rizpah. Sarah and I walked out into the stream, fully-clothed. It was cold! We got the worst of the mud off our clothing and also addressed our faces, arms, and legs. When my mother and I got back to our house, my mother brought a blanket outside and wrapped me up as she tried to pry me out of my wet, sticking clothing. It was an ordeal. All the while, I was wondering if my mishap was going to require another laundry day. In our childhood, none of us had much clothing. I had two changes of clothing that fit and partly because I got Merab's outgrown clothing. Merab's clothing came to me in pristine condition.

I told my mother about the rope stretched across the path. I didn't mention Esh-Baal, but I had no doubt he was the reason a rope came to be there. I shivered for a while in front of my mother's hearth after I got out of my wet clothing, and I assume Sarah did the same. My clothing was incredibly dirty, but this time, it wasn't torn.

The next time I saw Esh-Baal, it was outside his dwelling. He smirked at me.

"Nice black eye you've got there, Michal! Been fighting?"

"You're an ass, Esh-Baal! Of course I know who strung a rope across the path in front of a big puddle."

"Guess what, Michal? I know who put a sharp stick in my bed. It may interest you to know I found it before I got into bed. You're way out of line, Michal. The time is approaching when you'll be some unlucky man's wife, and if our mother won't instruct you, your husband most certainly will. Your accommodation skills need practice!"

"My accommodation skills? You think I'm supposed to accommodate you? Not likely!"

CHAPTER 11

Year 480

Michal struggled to rise from the sheepskin on which she'd been sitting. Her legs were stiff. Getting up was harder than it used to be. Thankfully, Abishag was at her side, as usual, and helped her up. She offered Michal a bowl of beer, and Michal sipped. The two women were older than their audience, though Michal was obviously the older of the two. In fact, Michal was the oldest resident of the women's quarters, of either of the women's quarters. There were two—one in the palace of the old king, Michal's and Abishag's late husband, and one in the palace of the present king, the son of the old king. Michal and Abishag remained in the old palace where they'd lived as their younger selves, but now the women's quarters was filling up with wives of the new king. Michal's and Abishag's husband had many wives, but the new king was putting him to shame. Solomon had hundreds of wives, and it was becoming a problem to house them. Space was at a premium.

Michal stretched her legs and back and said, "Ladies, I promised to tell you my story. Please indulge me a little longer if it appears that I'm telling other people's stories as well."

The ladies watched an elderly man make his way through the public area of the women's quarters and to the spot where Michal now stood. The man could well have been older than Michal, and though he walked slowly, his back was still straight. As he approached Michal and Abishag, he inclined his head in a small bow. Asher brought messages from other parts of the complex to Michal who was the senior healer of the palaces.

"Highness, the daughter of Pharaoh has requested your presence."

Michal took another sip and replied in a scratchy voice, "Greetings, Asher! I have begun telling my story to this appreciative group of women who seem interested. What does the daughter of Pharaoh want with me?"

"She didn't say."

"No, she wouldn't, would she? I have no objection to attending her, but it's always helpful to know what to bring with me. Abishag and I will bring a variety of herbs and hope we bring the right ones. My voice is giving out, but give me five more minutes."

Michal's voice was raspy but understandable. "Ladies, you may know that I am a worshipper of Elohim who has declared Himself alone to be God. I do not believe in a pantheon of gods. I promise I will not preach to you. You come from many cultures and believe a variety of things. My purpose, especially for those of you who are new to Jerusalem, is simply to acquaint you with some of our laws. I am about to visit the daughter of Pharaoh, Solomon's chief wife, and in the back of my mind, I wonder if anything I have to say to you about religious laws is even relevant under this king. But what you need to know is that such laws exist. Are they enforced? Probably not, but can you ever know that for certain?

"Right now, this gathering knows as much about Moses as I do. He was a national hero of 400 years ago, and on that basis, we all need to be careful what we believe about him. The information has been passed down through the generations, and there's a possibility it's been embellished. But we know this due to an artifact that I personally haven't seen—Moses gave our people Ten Commandments engraved on stone tablets, and these tablets are kept inside the ark of God. Have I ever seen the ark of God? At a distance. I caught a glimpse of it as it was being brought to Jerusalem, but it's not an artifact that's generally visible to the population. The ark of God is extremely sacred, and only priests get to see it. It is now housed in Solomon's grand new temple.

"As for the stone tablets of the law, the first three commandments tell how Elohim expects His people to treat Him. We are not to value anything more than Elohim. We are not to create idols out of wood or metal, and we are not to misuse the name.[9] We all swear. Many of you will swear on the name of your gods. Do not swear on the name of Elohim. One of my brothers did so once, and I heard it. He wasn't struck down by divine lightning, but I remember being surprised by it. The penalty in the days of my father and husband was death by stoning.[10] To me, the law is not theoretical. It has been enforced in my lifetime, though, to my knowledge, not under Solomon.

"Asher, one more moment. Zeta, are you here?"

A young woman came forward at Michal's request. There were many striking young women in Solomon's harem, but the majority had dark hair and dark eyes. Zeta was unique. She had extremely fair skin, orange hair, and blue eyes. And she had a gash between her shoulder blades.

"Zeta, I just want to look at your wound," Michal said. She and Abishag walked Zeta over to one of the windows where they had some light and took the bandage off her back. The wound was quite deep, and Michal had stitched it. The healers peeled back the bandage and applied their noses. Nothing. The bandage wasn't soaked with blood, and they replaced it. Abishag noticed Michal's hand moving up toward her jawline. Michal had a thin white scar that she sometimes fingered. It was an old wound. Abishag thought perhaps Michal had a special empathy for people with wounds just because she'd been wounded herself. Still, Abishag had never asked about it.

"It looks good," Abishag commented, "and it has no odor."

Michal added, "Zeta, you are healing nicely, Now stay out of knife fights!"

Michal was making light of how Zeta came by her wound, which wasn't exactly a knife fight. She was stabbed in the back.

Michal pondered the concept of the harem as an institution. There were too many different cultures represented in too small of a physical area, and truth be told, the harem put hundreds of women

---

[9] Exodus 20:3–7.
[10] Leviticus 24:13–16.

in the position of vying for one man. Women aren't by nature any more peaceful than men. Violence erupted out of sheer frustration. The ultimate status symbol in the harem was a pregnant belly. Zeta wasn't pregnant, but she'd been given a valuable ring by her husband, Solomon.

Gifts are dangerous things, mused Michal. One woman, getting special attention and letting it be known, put herself in harm's way. *On the other hand, if I were given a gold ring, I'd wear it too*. This particular assailant had seen the ring and made a huge attempt to take it. But she was neither strong nor skillful with a knife. Zeta was bleeding and on the floor but never lost consciousness. She closed her fist and hung on for dear life, screaming all the while. Two eunuchs ended up removing the attacker and sending for Michal. Removing the attacker to where? Michal hadn't asked. She didn't know every woman in the harem and she didn't know of any individual who was *this* mercenary. She wondered how many of the residents of the harem were overtly crazy.

Michal sighed audibly. As the number of women in the old palace grew, so did the tension. Michal wasn't aware of any members of the harem who'd been murdered, but she did know of one who'd disappeared without a trace. Maybe she ran away. Or maybe not.

Michal asked Abishag, "What do you think we should bring to the princess's palace?"

Abishag replied, "We need the essence of poppies as a painkiller for sure. Maybe something to cleanse cuts, such as rose petals or ground mandrake. Some clean rags, we're guessing."

Michal and Abishag stopped by Michal's sleeping cubicle before leaving the old palace. Michal kept bowls of dried herbs on a shelf near her bed, all appropriately labeled. Michal was putting her writing skills to good use. They scooped up a variety of samples and then left for the daughter of Pharaoh's palace, each carrying a basket.

Dusk was falling as they crossed the garden. Solomon had put in a formal garden that connected the four main buildings of the royal environs—the old palace, the new palace that Solomon had built for himself, the daughter of Pharaoh's palace, and the ornate temple to Elohim. The garden was a very popular gathering place, especially in the cool of the evening or the morning. Michal and Abishag dodged women on the stone pathways. Michal mused about stone pathways. They made a big difference on wet days. One's sandals could remain clean. She mused about the wall around the garden. Did it keep reluctant women in or the undesirables out? Was it for the protection of the women? Michal had heard the phrase "for your own protection" so often that she'd begun to question it. It sounded insincere.

What she did know about the wall was that it provided shade; in some cases, not necessarily desirable shade. She regretted her lost herb garden. Michal had always tended a garden, mostly containing plants that could be used in healing. She'd tended various herb gardens at various homes, and she'd had one in Jerusalem right where one section of the wall now stood. Oh, Solomon hadn't deliberately built over her garden. If there had to be a wall, the standing wall was in an appropriate place. Michal had to move her plants out of the larger garden-park just due to lack of sunlight. She still had a garden, and her garden still had its own fence, but it was now further away. Solomon's garden had a wall and huge shade trees. Michal recognized its magnificence and artistry when she was feeling open-minded.

Michal and Abishag passed close to the fish pond. Solomon had it constructed and then had lilies planted in it. The lilies were thriving. The pond had large rocks around the perimeter that acted like stools. It had been stocked with fish. There were ladies there, watching the fish and waiting for sunset. Michal reached out and touched a frankincense bush that was one of several lining the path. There were myrrh bushes too. Michal thought, *This isn't the climate for these, though so far, they're surviving.* She and Abishag valued frankincense and myrrh for their healing properties. The garden also boasted almond trees, fig trees, and olive trees in addition to the larger shade trees.

It was a short walk, and the two ladies walked in silence. They'd been to the daughter of Pharaoh's palace before, and neither of them looked forward to the experience. With night falling quickly, the place would be even darker. It had a sinister quality that was hard to describe logically, but both women got the same feel from the place.

The place was dark, even in the daytime, and a little bit creepy. They were waved through the entryway by the guard, who was undoubtedly Egyptian. Michal and Abishag had never encountered anyone in the princess's palace who wasn't. Immediately across from the door was a large, at least human-sized statue of the goddess, Bastet. Michal thought the statue of the woman with the cat's head looked almost evil in the torchlight. She felt her skin crawl. There were offerings there, the usual spices and perfumes, but their senses were assaulted by another smell. The perfume wasn't enough to hide the scent of spoilage. Abishag tried not to gag.

Michal spoke what they both knew. "Somebody offered milk to Bastet." They followed the torches on the wall past the statue and entered the next room. The princess's secretary met them and escorted them to her.

The princess spoke first, "Greetings, Michal! Abishag! Are you both well?"

Michal answered, "Greetings, Amneris! We are well and hope you are also."

Michal wasn't one to stand on ceremony, especially when the individual in question addressed her by her given name. Abishag was more reticent, but then, she wasn't the daughter of King Saul. She returned the greeting with, "Good evening, Your Highness."

Amneris invited them to sit. She had a chair next to her hearth, and in front of it was a small table. There were three candles on the table and two stools positioned beside it. The room was very warm. Michal wondered about the land of Egypt, and though she'd never been there, she'd heard that it was hot and dry. Was the princess perpetually cold? There was an almost overpowering odor of incense. Michal and Abishag sat down on the stools and waited for the princess to speak.

Amneris said, "I invited the priestesses of Elohim because I need a love potion. And because I'd like the two of you to look in on my daughter."

Michal and Abishag exchanged glances. Michal spoke first. "A love potion? You mean with chanting and crystals? Abishag and I are not priestesses. We are merely worshippers of Elohim. And we very much fear that your request would be perceived by the lawgivers of the Twelve Tribes as witchcraft."

Abishag added, "The practice of witchcraft is forbidden to us.[11] And so we really have no good knowledge of it. Michal and I have never tried to make a love potion."

Michal asked, "Surely you have Egyptian servants who could provide what you need?"

Amneris said, "I invited the two of you because my servants aren't providing anything that works. I need my husband not to ignore me. And I thought you were priestesses. No matter. Shall we take tea?"

A servant brought ornate bowls to the table and poured tea. Michal and Abishag sipped. Amneris stroked the rim of the bowl with her fingertip. Michal glanced at Amneris who was a dark beauty. It was hard to know whether there was hair under her elaborate wig. Michal knew that some Egyptians shaved their heads. She watched the interaction of the princess's rings with the candlelight. Her gems flashed color in a way that was almost mesmerizing.

Michal changed the subject. "You mentioned your daughter. Is she ill?"

Amneris answered, "She has or had a fever."

Abishag asked, "Is she thrashing about? Does she utter words or sounds that are meaningless?"

Amneris seemed deep in thought. Michal took another sip and thought about how warm the room was. She realized she was slumping on her stool and made a conscious effort to straighten up her back and neck. She stood up, somewhat unsteadily. But then again, standing up in and of itself was becoming strenuous. She noticed that Abishag wasn't alert either, and she shook her shoulder. Abishag seemed groggy. Michal broke the silence and asked, "Amneris, just how worried are you? Should we see your daughter now?"

"Yes, come with me." The daughter of Pharaoh stood up languidly and glided into the next room. Her white clothing was loose

---

[11] Exodus 22:18.

and flowing. The fabric was thin and moved with the princess, outlining her slender form.

Michal and Abishag followed Amneris into a room that was much cooler and didn't have the overwhelming odor of incense. Abishag was shuffling and leaning heavily on Michal. They couldn't help but notice a stone figure with a woman's body and the head of a lion. It wasn't as large as the statue of Bastet, but it was large enough, standing like a sentinel in a corner of the room. The statue was surrounded by bowls of red liquid. The room was dim. Michal wondered if the liquid was blood, though there was no blood scent.

"The priestess of Sekhmet has already ministered to Khepri, and possibly her efforts were enough," said Amneris. "My daughter is very important to me, and I value the help of all gods."

Amneris's Hebrew was very good, though she had a noticeable accent. Her voice was soft and soothing. The child was sleeping on a bed at the side of the room, and seemed tranquil enough. Michal gently touched Khepri's cheek and concluded, "If she had a fever, it has broken. Perhaps by morning, she'll be hungry. If Abishag and I were to do anything for her at this time, it would simply be to apply cool damp cloths to her forehead and chest. Still, there is no need to wake her up. Sleep is a great healer."

When the princess's secretary showed the two ladies out of the palace, it was dark. Both ladies felt enormous relief in the cool evening air. The rooms of the palace were stifling. Michal and Abishag were surprised to find Asher waiting for them just outside the door. He had another manservant with him. Abishag was obviously unsteady. As they walked back to their quarters in the old palace, Abishag leaned on Asher. She didn't speak. Michal wasn't feeling well, but she did wonder aloud why Asher had met them.

Asher said, "I have contacts among all the servants in all the palaces. I am not fond of the atmosphere in Solomon's new palace, but the princess's palace is a place of wickedness. It's a dangerous place for those who don't belong there. I honestly wasn't sure what I was going to do if the two of you hadn't come out shortly. Next time, I need to consider that. Did she say why she called you?"

"She thought we could make her a love potion. She also said her daughter was sick."

"Was she?"

"I don't know. All I could tell was that she was sleeping. Still, there was a statue of Sekhmet in the room, and there were offerings there. The princess may have believed she was sick."

"What offerings?"

"It looked like bowls of blood."

Asher sighed. "No, it wouldn't have been blood. It would have been red beer. Was there any odor of fermentation?"

"Now that I think about it, yes. That must have been what it was, but at the time, I couldn't identify it. There were many odors in that palace."

"What do you know about Sekhmet?"

"Nothing. I assume she's an Egyptian goddess of healing. Just at the entrance to the palace, there was a huge statue of Bastet, the woman with the cat's head. Then in Khepri's room was the woman with the head of a lioness. The Egyptians make very unlikely statues!"

"There is an old story about Sekhmet, one in which she was sent to destroy humans. The other gods changed their minds and tried to stop her. She was feasting on human blood and wouldn't stop. So they took beer, turned it red, and she drank it. A lot of it. She became drunk and stopped killing. You observe that the Egyptians make unlikely statues. Yes, indeed! It's also unlikely that they look to a very destructive being for healing. Perhaps the lion part is the destroyer and the woman part is the healer. A dilemma!"

The four of them arrived at the old palace, and Asher asked if Michal and Abishag wanted something to eat. "Suppertime is over, but I can find something for the two of you."

Michal asked, "Abishag?"

Abishag shook her head.

"I am most definitely not hungry. We both need our beds."

*****

Michal was awakened rather late the next morning by Asher. He said, "Abishag cannot attend you this morning. She has a pounding headache. Can I help you up?"

As Michal struggled to sit, she realized she had a pounding headache too. "Asher, help me outside—quickly!"

The two of them made it out the door, and Michal threw up. There was almost nothing in her stomach, but she heaved anyway. She asked, "Is Abishag ill?"

"Yes. Did either of you eat or drink anything in the princess's palace?"

"We had tea. We didn't eat anything. Asher, does Amneris hate us? I wasn't aware of any conflict between us. We are wives of a dead king. We cannot be a threat to her. I have viewed the princess as annoying, but I hadn't thought her to be dangerous."

"Desperate people, men or women, can be dangerous. The servants over there do believe that for a while, the princess was afraid for her daughter's life. By the time you and Abishag arrived, the worst was over. I do not begin to understand the mind of a princess, but it certainly appears she tried to drug you both. To what end? If she wanted to kill either or both of you, I don't know a good reason. Did you make her angry by, in her opinion, refusing to make her a love potion? Maybe. I can only advise caution if you are summoned to that palace again. I seriously doubt the princess hates either of you, but I also firmly believe that she doesn't consider either of you at all. You're both expendable and unworthy of notice. Let's get you back to bed."

CHAPTER 12

Year 388

My Uncle Hur was giving another history lesson. He was still leading up to that point where the Twelve Tribes chose a king, but he wanted to include background.

"Between the time when King Saul, who wasn't king at the time, went to Ramah and the time he went to Mizpah, a year passed. Saul was never good at waiting. Samuel made it clear to Saul that he needed to be part of the tribal meeting at Mizpah, but he was less specific as to the 'when' of it. Saul was tense, so tense that we all noticed. He did a lot of pacing and didn't sleep well.

"In the meantime, Saul decided the family should celebrate Passover, which wasn't something any of us had observed up until then. Passover was traditionally celebrated in the spring, and Saul wasn't willing to let the season pass without acknowledging it. Samuel had made a big impression on Saul, and Saul wanted to show solidarity by celebrating one of the ancient festivals. Samuel believed that if he could persuade the Tribes to observe mutual holidays, it would promote unity. He traveled from his home in Ramah with some regularity, especially to Mizpah and Gilgal, where he offered sacrifices and presided over celebrations. It was at these gatherings that people from the further-away tribes would come to Samuel with their complaints. Samuel was reputed to be a good listener as well as a wise man. Very often, both aggrieved parties would leave satisfied.

"Passover was traditionally a seven-day event. Saul wasn't willing to abandon the fields for seven days, so he focused on the Passover dinner to the best of his knowledge. He and I talked about it. Like I said, we'd all heard of it, but up until then, only in a theoretical way.

I helped do some research and determine what the meal would have looked like. The Passover dinner included roast lamb, which was very much welcomed by the whole community. We didn't eat much meat. There were items of interest that Saul tried to explain to Ahinoam and to Rizpah, such as unleavened bread. Unleavened bread? Really? Why? But Saul was insistent, and Ahinoam and Rizpah ended up creating a number of large crackers for the feast.

"Saul butchered a lamb. Several young boys were enlisted to turn the lamb on a spit over an outdoor firepit specifically designed for the purpose. Saul also wanted to include bitter herbs. Ahinoam had horseradish in her garden, and she harvested one of them. She diced the root into tiny pieces. When the lamb was done cooking, Saul made a point to remove meat without breaking any bones. We were given portions in the usual bowls along with a condiment of horseradish and some cabbage from Ahinoam's garden. We each took some of the cracker, which Rizpah had broken into manageable pieces.

"We took our bowls into the hall for a communal meal. The doors were propped open this time, and at least until sundown, we enjoyed some light. Ahinoam provided two candlesticks. Saul said the meal should be eaten standing up, but in the end, we were at a loss as to how to accomplish that. Asher had spread rugs and hides along the walls of the hall. Saul said the first blessing to Elohim while we all stood, but in order to eat with a minimum of mess, we ended up sitting on the rugs while we ate. Again, this was the old wooden hall. There weren't any stools or torches in it. The food was delicious! I liked the cracker. I'm not sure it was superior to bread made in the usual fashion, but it had an interest all its own. Saul asked several blessings throughout the meal.

"After the meal, there was a lot of uneaten horseradish left in bowls. The family wanted to please Saul. They did taste it. Ahinoam asked Saul what was the point of the horseradish, and he didn't know. He knew that our ancestors had eaten it. I tasted some with my lamb. The flavor was strong and was certainly an acquired taste. I was one of the people who left some in my bowl. Saul brought Passover back to the town of Gibeah, and once he became king, it was celebrated regularly by the tribe of Benjamin. I assume it is celebrated to some degree by the rest of the tribes. All of you have been introduced to it earlier than I was.

"Samuel was trying to do more with the Twelve Tribes of Israel than bring back Passover. He was trying to bring back Elohim. We believed that Moses and Elohim had a unique relationship. We believed in one god who could not be artistically represented, at least during those times when we thought about god at all. In the time of Moses, there were laws specifically written down regarding the creation of images and also regarding the "oneness" of Elohim.[12] Samuel tried to impress upon us that we needed divine forgiveness for our daily shortcomings and that blood would facilitate that forgiveness.[13] I knew so little about worship. Still, the notion of atonement through sacrifice or blood is universal. The cultures surrounding the Twelve Tribes all practice it.

"We in Gibeah weren't particularly religious. The observance of Passover made an impression on me, and I started to think about Elohim more often. We can witness sacrifices if we wish. Gibeah has a high place with an altar and a priest. There are sacrifices offered there, but a person has to specifically go there to see one. I began to make it a point to go there occasionally, and when I did, I brought a male lamb. Elohim accepts animal sacrifices of various beasts, but the male lamb is the most common.

"One item of interest—Elohim doesn't require human sacrifice.[14] The nations surrounding the Twelve Tribes actually put their children on fiery hot altars and give them up to their gods. I absolutely cannot conceive of such an act. A child is a family's best asset and a jewel in a mother's crown. Is that the point? A child is the most valuable thing that could be offered to appease potentially angry gods? Samuel, priest of the Twelve Tribes, offered animal sacrifices only.

"Was Samuel a sacrifice? The Twelve Tribes don't practice human sacrifice, but I do wonder if that's how his mother felt about

---

[12] Exodus 20: 3,4.
[13] Leviticus 17:11.
[14] Leviticus 20:2.

it? At the time she turned her son over to the high priest for instruction, he was her only child. She would go on to have more children, but she didn't know that. The sacrifice of Samuel didn't require his death. It required his life.

"So we celebrated Passover. The festival dates back to that time when the descendants of Israel were preparing to leave Egypt forever. Pharaoh wasn't receptive to losing a huge number of useful slaves, and he needed persuading. Moses did various demonstrations in the name of Elohim which finally culminated in the deaths of firstborn sons of the Egyptians. Elohim's messenger 'passed over' the houses of the enslaved Twelve Tribes without taking any lives. The members of the Twelve Tribes set themselves apart from the Egyptians that night by painting lamb's blood on their door frames. Blood, albeit not human blood, remains a symbol of atonement.

"In my musings about Moses or maybe, more specifically, what we know about Moses, I see a parallel with Saul in that both were reluctant leaders. They did not seek power. Neither Moses nor Saul were assertive people, though both eventually learned to command. Moses was flanked by his older sister, Miriam, and by his brother, Aaron, all of whom became acknowledged leaders. Saul drew support from Samuel."

CHAPTER 13

Year 388

The children sometimes got frustrated with Hur for cutting a story short due to something trivial like suppertime. Still, we were beginning to realize that he couldn't simply go on talking indefinitely. If he talked for a long time, his voice got raspy. And if we thought supper was trivial, our mothers didn't.

The next time the children and Hur were available for lessons, we expected to hear about the meeting at Mizpah. We had a pleasant day and met outside under the big sycamore tree. Hur began, "I was one of the elders of Gibeah at that time, and it was my privilege to accompany the group to Mizpah. The group from Gibeah included Saul, Abner, Ner, Hur, and Kish. Hilkiah and Zebulon went, though some of the city's political leaders did stay behind just to oversee daily life."

The children were distracted by a young man who approached the group. There were excited cries of, "Jonathan! Jonathan!" My much-older brother had entered our circle and seated himself down next to Hur. Jonathan was a legend. He was a local hero. He was quite tall, though not as tall as our father. He was very fit and still handsome, though his tanned and windblown face was showing signs of middle age.

Hur said, "Thank you for welcoming Crown Prince Jonathan. He has agreed to share his impressions of his father's return from Mizpah."

Jonathan began, "I will admit I have some reservations about attempting to teach anyone anything. Hur is a natural teacher, and my limited skills will probably fall short. All I intend to do is talk about the return of the delegation that went to Mizpah. Hopefully, Hur will talk about the meeting itself because I wasn't there.

"I have been in this school situation before, but at the time, I was much younger, as were the other children of the group who are now all close to my age. The circle is round! Hur was my teacher long ago, and we met in the old hall. Even back then, Hur wanted to add different voices to the education of the children. One memorable visiting teacher was Samuel. I loved Samuel because he had such a deep knowledge of the history of the Twelve Tribes. I like history, though clearly, there would have been young people who didn't understand the relevance. To my knowledge, the young people in the hall were courteous, regardless. Samuel was a figure to be respected even when the subject at hand was history.

"At the time we learned that our father was now a king, I was nine years old. Abinadab was eight, and Malki-Shua was seven. More often than not, Abinadab and I tried to tell Malki-Shua he was too young and send him home, but…well, looking at it from my present standpoint, one year younger than Abinadab and two years younger than me wasn't all that young. We rarely, maybe never, succeeded in getting rid of him, so oftentimes, the three of us did what we did together.

"We heard it before we saw it. There was an unmistakable sound of approaching horses, and our community had no horses. There was also the sound of a number of marchers and of weapons jangling. There was a hint of something in the background rolling, like a cart or wagon. The pathways between towns are much better suited to people walking or riding a mule. It's possible to pull a wagon along them, but there are constant ruts. The roads back then weren't any better than they are now. They're very hard on any wheels and any beasts doing the pulling. What we heard were distinct thuds followed by curses.

"We weren't the only ones listening. The neighborhood heard what we heard, and the sounds were threatening. Raiders! The men of our family were gone, though there were men left in town. The men began to collect whatever weapons could be found, and if not weapons, then anything sharp. The women and children prepared to evacuate.

"We three—myself, Abinadab, and Malki-Shua—were children at the time. But I thought we could get closer. None of us were adult-sized, and all of us could walk silently. It would have been better not to abandon the town, which is always a huge undertaking and entails a certain amount of risk. It wasn't easy, but we persuaded our mothers to allow us to spy. The women were all trying to get supplies together, and they were distracted. The three of us followed the sound, and we were somewhat surprised that there didn't seem to be any effort at stealth. When we got close enough, we could make out voices and conversations in normal tones. It was the voices that caught our attention. The two soldiers in the lead on horses didn't look like anyone we knew. But we knew the voices—Father and Uncle Abner! We ran back to the village and shouted loudly, 'Wait, it's Father!'

"The women paused their preparations and stood by, but like us, they didn't recognize anyone in the lead as the procession entered Gibeah. There were a *lot* of men, some of whom were clearly soldiers. This wasn't just the small number of representatives who'd made the original journey. And when my father appeared at the head of the procession, he looked different. My father could be recognized just from his size, and we did recognize him, sort of. He and Uncle Abner were both sitting on horses. I'd never seen my father on a horse, and happily, he got a very large horse. Both of them were wearing helmets. I'd never seen my father in a helmet. He was holding a javelin. Our village elders followed Father and Uncle Abner, and the soldiers brought up the rear.

"For a few moments, Mother, Rizpah, and Aunt Hadassah were in shock. It was easier to recognize Uncle Hur, who wasn't mounted and wasn't wearing a helmet. Once they got close enough, the women recognized the village elders too. When my mother found her tongue, she mumbled a greeting and then immediately asked, 'Who will house these soldiers?'

"My father dismounted and said, 'They have tents.' I watched Father get off the horse and noticed just a slight hitch in his posture. I'm certain it hurt!

"Mother asked, 'Where can tents be pitched in our village?'

"Father thought about it for a moment. 'In the fallow fields! That's the ideal place. We have unplanted fields this year, and soldiers could pitch tents there.'

"Aunt Hadassah brought up the next practical concern. 'How will this number of men be fed?'

"'One of the soldiers is an army cook. We will repair the outdoor hearth and oven for his use. And the cart is full of grain and vegetables. Our village received many gifts at Mizpah.'

"Father directed the soldiers to the area on which they could pitch tents. Uncle Hur, Uncle Ner, and Grandfather didn't say a word. Father didn't have to make an effort to gather the family together. We were all there. Uncle Abner opened his mouth with the most unlikely of pronouncements. 'Long live the king!'

"Father finally removed his helmet, and underneath was a thin gold circlet. 'Samuel put this here,' my father pointed to his head. 'I never told you everything about my first meeting with Samuel. There were no witnesses, not even Asher, and it didn't feel real. Samuel anointed me. What did that mean? I thought only priests were anointed. It was an odd sensation. Asher was on the road home at the time, and I caught up with him immediately after Samuel poured oil on my head. If it didn't feel real to me, how could I expect any of you to believe it? The Twelve Tribes don't have kings. I never asked Asher if he noticed my oily hair. Asher notices pretty much everything, so I suppose he did, but he didn't comment.'

"Uncle Abner picked up the narrative. 'After the elders of the Twelve Tribes arrived in Mizpah, Samuel gave a little speech. He wasn't confident that the Twelve Tribes should have a king just because the surrounding nations did. He felt a king was an affront to the leadership of Elohim, but he also understood that this was what the Twelve Tribes wanted. Samuel wanted Elohim to pick the individual and to make His wishes known to all of the Tribes. He set up a public demonstration. Elohim had favored the tribe of Benjamin, and Samuel set out to prove it. He spoke out the names of heads of the clans, one by one, and ended up with the clan of Matri. He went on to name Uncle Kish and after that to name Saul.

"'The family expected Saul to come forward when he heard his name, but he was nowhere to be found. Uncle Kish was looking frantically. One of the servants eventually found my very tall cousin not exactly hiding with the baggage but not exactly being part of the crowd either. Uncle Kish, were you embarrassed?'

"Grandfather looked like he was still embarrassed. He didn't say anything.

"Uncle Abner continued, 'This was when we all heard the first chants of 'Long live the king!' Samuel appeared with the circlet he meant to use as a crown. It's not a heavy crown, and perhaps Saul will want something more substantial, but it has the appropriate symbolism—a circle to surround a head or head of state. Samuel must have planned ahead. Some of the leaders of the Twelve Tribes also planned ahead and brought gifts. Saul and I were given horses and helmets. Saul has a heavy javelin.

"'As with anything else, the consensus wasn't unanimous, but there was the support of the majority. The tribes support Samuel, and because of him, Saul also. A few leaders rather pointedly turned their backs and gave nothing. But as you can see, soldiers coming from all of the Tribes are prepared to support the designated king. A leader with an army behind him wields great power.'

"Father continued, 'Our people have had a very haphazard method of transferring power for all these years. Maybe a royal family will make a difference there. Anyway, 400 years passed, and it was actually Samuel to whom the elders went regarding this inefficient transfer of power. I assume these elders were members of the governments of all of the tribes. The tribe of Benjamin was represented, and I met some of the tribal leaders. Samuel told me what had led up to the gathering at Mizpah. He wasn't happy about it, but after consulting Elohim, he realized that a change in leadership was inevitable. Samuel and I are partners. The two of us are fulfilling an ancient prophecy.'

"Mother made a comment about Samuel's sons. 'As far as I can tell, Samuel was preparing his sons for leadership. This idea of a king of the Twelve Tribes still seems foreign to me, but then Samuel's sons are the most corrupt individuals in the country. They are quite focused on personal gain, whatever that takes. I'm very glad our nation won't be led by them, but I also ask in the end, what difference does it make? There will never be a guarantee, whether judge or king, that the leader's offspring will be either good leaders or interested in governing on the peoples' behalf. How do you know about this prophecy? How does Samuel know?'

"Father said, 'There are some chronicles written down, but Samuel's information comes directly from his mentor, Eli. Eli led the Twelve Tribes before Samuel and had similar issues with his sons. Think for a moment about our sons, Ahinoam. I will be grooming Jonathan and Malki-Shua to be king, starting right now. They may be children, but it's already clear that they're ethical individuals. Our boys aren't the sort to take advantage of their position at the expense of anyone else.'

"Abinadab, Malki-Shua, and I were standing right there, listening to every word. We never heard the name Abinadab. He didn't say anything, but I have every confidence that he noticed. I love Rizpah. She's my second mother. If I were to tell this group that Abinadab had the wrong mother, I believe you would all know what I meant. I have no intention of disrespecting Rizpah, but how is it fair to limit a man's options based on his parentage? Abinadab is fearless and could undoubtedly get men to follow him. He has an acknowledged place at my right hand, but he will never be king. My father didn't marry his mother. It's just the way things are.

"We all stood respectfully while Father and Uncle Abner were talking, but we three boys were staring at the horses. One of the soldiers took the two horses after the group started to break up, and another soldier took charge of the mules that had been pulling the cart. We boys followed the soldier with the horses. Please understand, I have my own horse now, and the creatures aren't so exotic. But at the time, we were all fascinated. Horses are beautiful animals, though these particular horses weren't built for speed. They were both tall and heavy and could probably have plowed a furrow very quickly. Father and Uncle Abner never used these animals for farmwork. They were war horses, and as Father and Uncle Abner started fighting battles, the horses' season of rest was the same as Father's and Uncle Abner's.

"The soldier first took off the saddles. He kept the bridles on long enough to rub down the animals, and we three boys were allowed to help. All of us had some experience with caring for animals, but not horses. We led the soldier to a fenced paddock where he took the bridles off and turned the horses loose. Then we showed him where Father stored the donkey cart he used at rock-picking time. There was room in that shed for the saddles and bridles.

"The children got to have a look at the wagon that had come from Mizpah and its contents. There was a lot of food in it, which wasn't too exciting. There were a few other items of interest—some gold bars, some silver bars, and some quality weapons. My father wanted a heavier crown, and he had to travel to Gilgal for a gold-smith. He took some of the gold on the wagon and he took the circlet that Samuel had given him. He had a crown made for himself. It was rather simple, but it did contain more gold and there was a polished piece of lapis lazuli at the very front.

"I admire Father's crown. It is a royal symbol without being ostentatious. When Father holds meetings in the hall, and my broth-ers and I are in attendance, he wears it. He looks very distinguished.

"Gibeah changed overnight. Father changed overnight, and so did Uncle Abner. Mother resisted. Mother, of course, was never a queen, and she was never required to play that role, but she wasn't so sure she wanted to be married to a king either. The biggest thing that changed for her was that her husband was now absent a lot. She, Rizpah, and Aunt Hadassah all continued to do the tasks they'd always done. Rizpah was the most romantic of the three, and she was more intrigued by the new atmosphere of the village. Gibeah had become a seat of government. It didn't change the lives of the women. Rizpah may have wanted it to, though Mother didn't.

CHAPTER 14

Year 388

"Gibeah became a military outpost, Father became a king, and Uncle Abner became a general. My father put his newly-acquired soldiers to use more quickly than he or we might have expected. He also took his new title seriously. Can a man transition easily from a farmer to a king? There was an opportunity, and my father took it. Jabesh Gilead seemed destined to be persecuted once per generation. It was located within the tribe of Gad, but too close to the Ammonite border. The elders of Jabesh Gilead sent out an urgent message for assistance to the Tribes of Israel.

"Benjamin was near Gad and in a position to help, though the River Jordan separated the two tribes. Father was full of a positive spirit at times that completely transfigured him. I know Uncle Hur knew about my father's team of oxen, but the rest of you probably didn't. Oxen are expensive, but they are worth their price. They do so much more work than donkeys in a shorter period of time. My father had oxen, and young as I was, I realized how much he valued them.

"Father did something unexpected when he received the message from Jabesh Gilead. He killed his oxen, cut them into pieces, and used messengers to deliver chunks of rotting flesh throughout the Tribes of Israel. Now these were the same Tribes of Israel to whom the leaders of Jabesh Gilead had already appealed, begging for reinforcements. If the other tribes felt justified in ignoring the plight of the citizens of Jabesh Gilead, they thought better of ignoring Father. Rotting flesh must have some power.

"Father's first taste of war, as opposed to random raids, was a big success. He mustered 330,000 men at Bezak, from all the tribes of Israel, made them into three divisions, and utterly slaughtered the Ammonites. He was an absolute hero to the citizens of Jabesh Gilead. The Ammonites had surrounded the city, and when representatives of Jabesh Gilead came out to sue for peace, the Ammonites made a condition that they would poke out the right eyes of all the citizenry. Paying tribute was one thing, but…my father became a leader of men and a warrior of renown.

"The battle against the Ammonites allowed my father to achieve one of his goals—his army captured two blacksmiths. My father didn't know a lot about what a blacksmith required, but he was willing to learn. He kept one blacksmith in Gibeah and positioned the other in Gilgal. Both were grateful for their lives after the total destruction of their nation's army. Both knew their trade and were able to articulate the needs of a smithy. Two blacksmiths wasn't enough. We needed them to train others and allow the Twelve Tribes to spread iron-working skills across the land.

"The Philistines were undoubtedly watching from afar with great interest. A neighboring nation had mustered an army of 330,000? Surely they didn't know the exact number, but they saw the obliteration of the Ammonites. There was a new threat much too close to them that they hadn't acknowledged before. They may also have wondered how their neighbors, the Twelve Tribes, no longer needed their assistance with the sharpening of farm implements.

"After my father's initiation as the leader of armies, he was given yet another confirmation as king from the Tribes of Israel. Uncle Hur will remember this. Again, he was there. The elders and my father all went to Gilgal this time, and Samuel presided over a second anointing. My father's new crown was ready and Samuel crowned him. Then my father came home. Gibeah was home, and my father never saw any reason to live anywhere else.

"Father pondered how to use the gifts of gold and silver he'd been given. His village was Gibeah, and he wasn't inclined to move his government to a larger, more prominent city. He initiated a minor building project, mainly focused on the young men's barracks and on the hall. He made improvements to the young men's barracks, and he also built another large barracks in the same vicinity. He needed to house the soldiers that had become his personal retainers in a more permanent dwelling. It was the idle soldiers who actually took on these building projects. Soldiers can't be away fighting wars during all seasons, so winter became the time for building.

"Father never built a palace for himself and he never had a throne room. This was when he razed the hall and rebuilt it. He started a campaign to make a huge number of mud bricks, which he wanted to use instead of the former wooden frame. The new structure was larger and had windows. The thatched roof and the lime floor were the same, but my father added torches and furnishings. There were new rugs and stools that remained permanently in the new hall. There was one carved chair. Other kings wouldn't have named it a throne, but it was quite a step up from a stool.

"The last improvements added by my father were several stone paths. He and the soldiers used the rocks that had been piled up on both sides of the pathway, though they had to be selective. The stones weren't dressed and some would have been inappropriate. But chiseled or not, some stones were easily able to be worked into an earthen path. The task was labor-intensive. My father had no intention of making stone paths to every house. His modest effort included his own dwelling, the soldiers' barracks, and the hall. Stones don't stay in place very well if they're only grounded in earth. The new path needed constant maintenance, which it didn't get. But early on, when it was new, the stone paths added elegance to Gibeah."

CHAPTER 15

Year...

My father came to power around the year 388, and he reigned over the tribes of Israel for forty-two years.[15] I was born right about in the middle of his reign, so anything that happened during the early years is oral family history. Oral history can be unreliable, but in this case, there weren't that many intervening years. If I wasn't there to see my father's actions, at least the people from whom the information came had been witnesses.

My father had a troubled life. It's got to be easier to be a farmer than a king, though of course, power is addictive. My father evolved from a farmer into a king almost overnight, and his cousin, Abner, was equally transformed. Abner became the general of my father's forces. My brother, Jonathan, also rose to be a warrior of note, though he never was given a title. My father may have thought that "king's son" was enough. Abner, Jonathan, Abinadab, and Malki-Shua were valiant men, though Abner was significantly older.

My mother had more children during this time. So did Rizpah. My youngest brother, Esh-Baal, was born in the year 400, Merab was born in 408, and I was born in 410. Esh-Baal was never a warrior. He was very smart, even as a child and, later on, excelled at diplomacy in those unusual circumstances in which a diplomat was required. There was very little diplomacy, though my brother did some limited negotiating.

In my father's early days as king, he was very zealous for the laws that Elohim had given to our people through Moses. As a king, my

---
[15] 1 Samuel 13:1.

father now had power to right some of the wrongs of our culture. My father made a concerted effort to stamp out witches.[16] It may not be possible to stamp out witches, but he certainly sent them into hiding! My father also attempted to enforce the laws of Elohim regarding sexuality. My father believed that Elohim didn't intend intercourse to be a casual activity, done for two people's pleasure. It was a serious act of commitment. The laws of Moses specifically condemn adultery. There was a tendency on the parts of some individuals to treat intercourse as recreation. Intercourse has always been a private thing, though in those odd cases in which the perpetrators were caught, my father had no qualms about having them, usually both participants, stoned.[17] It was also during his early years as king that my father was most joyous and most likely to prophesy. I never saw any of this. I only heard about it.

My father started out in a close friendship with Samuel. Samuel was not a military man. My father was humble enough in the beginning to realize that he could learn from Samuel. Samuel had a unique relationship with Elohim, and my father was interested. He didn't have much background in religion, but he deeply respected Samuel. He had no background in governing. Samuel was well-versed in both. The town of Ramah, where Samuel lived, was part of the territory of Benjamin and not far away from Gibeah. The young men of Gibeah had devoted about a week to repairing an old dwelling that hadn't completely disappeared with the residents' quest for bricks. Father fixed it up so as to provide housing for Samuel whenever Samuel was in town.

Samuel, at his age, couldn't be expected to make do with a tent! In those early days, Samuel visited Gibeah often and did his best to offer my father guidance. Samuel was an experienced leader of men, but he knew his role was almost over. My father was preparing to lead the nation and he wanted to be mentored.

My father had given up the life of his youth and was trying desperately to define the role of king. Truth be told, he was enjoy-

_____

[16] 1 Samuel 28:9.
[17] Deuteronomy 22:22–24.

ing the title. As my father won victories and gained confidence in his position, he relied a little less on Samuel and Samuel's advice. Elohim spoke directly to Samuel, and Samuel spoke to my father. For a while, my father aligned himself with Samuel and Elohim.

But something happened. Slowly, as his powerful position started to feel more natural, my father felt less need for the advice of an old man. And as Samuel began to feel more like a nuisance and less like a mentor, my father found himself edging away from Elohim.

My brother, Jonathan, grew up and easily became Father's favorite. The two of them shared interests and skills, specifically those of very successful soldiers. Jonathan attacked a Philistine outpost at Geba, which was just north of Gibeah. I don't know whether Jonathan had my father's blessing for that endeavor or not. It was an act of aggression and caused the Philistines to mobilize. Jonathan defended his action by saying that the Philistines were a coastal people and had no business manning an outpost as far inland as Geba. He might have been right, but he forced our father's hand. The Philistines responded and caused our father to respond. Father and his army camped at Gilgal, and the Philistines mustered at Micmash.

My father was waiting for Samuel to come to perform the offices of a priest. My father didn't offer sacrifices. Samuel did, and Samuel had agreed to come to Gilgal within seven days. He didn't. My father's troops were deserting in droves. To Samuel, time was always fluid. My father was desperate and, in the end, offered the sacrifices himself. Of course, Samuel appeared right about then and was not impressed. My father apologized. He admitted he had not sought guidance from Elohim. For the first time, Samuel suggested to my father that his line would not become a dynasty. Interestingly enough, whether my father had angered Elohim or not, his army won the battle. The Philistines became confused and turned on each other, and then the troops who had deserted my father's army reappeared and gave chase. It was a rout. My father's troops took the usual spoils including weapons.

The family learned of these events from my father. He used to come home and talk about battles, though it helped a lot if his efforts resulted in victories. He was enthusiastic and open in the early days of his reign. On that particular occasion, he was still able to be reprimanded and still able to feel regret. I specifically remember hearing him talk about past battles and past armies. This battle became a very painful lesson to him on the fickleness of human beings. He began his new career with a huge following and a huge victory over the Ammonites, and this battle at a Philistine outpost, and not a very large one, was a revelation. The deserters returned to help end the battle and share in the spoils. Victories are wonderful things, but this event turned my father cynical.

Another time, my father routed the Amalekites. Samuel had been very specific that Elohim wanted the Amalekites utterly destroyed, down to their women, their children, their livestock, and their possessions. My father won a famous victory at Amalek. He wasn't quite willing to destroy everything. He kept the best of the livestock, the best of the spoils, and he kept the king alive. Samuel, in the name of Elohim, ended up pursuing my father who had left the ruined city and proceeded to Carmel.

I am not aware that my father ever did anything like this again, but he erected a monument at Carmel to his victory.[18] I didn't see it. I'm told it was a stone tower with inscriptions on it. My father called it a record of the battle with the Amalekites. It was, but others suggested that my father built a monument to himself. Abner said that the designation for Elohim appeared once on the tower, and my father's name appeared multiple times. Abner didn't like it. The Twelve Tribes weren't monument-builders like the Egyptians.

Long ago, in the time of Joshua, three tribes got together and built a massive altar that was not associated with the worship of Elohim at Shiloh and was not sanctioned by the other tribes. It was never intended to be used for sacrifice, though it was shaped like an altar.[19] The other tribes almost went to war over it. It was perceived as an act of rebellion. Happily, the three tribes that erected it were allowed to explain, and the explanation was accepted. It was intended

---

[18] 1 Samuel 15:12.
[19] Joshua 22:10–30.

as a sign of solidarity for the coming generations, not a sign of separation. So if the building of monuments wasn't unprecedented, it was rare and somewhat risky.

In the case of my father's monument, at least nobody suggested a civil war. There was some underlying disapproval and there was some approval too. Many soldiers were proud of the part they'd played in the victory and had no problem with a commemorative monument.

After my father erected his monument, he left Carmel and went on to Gilgal, which is where Samuel confronted him. It was clear that my father had left Amalek with a huge herd of cattle and sheep. Samuel heard them, as did everyone else in the vicinity. To this day, I don't know how Samuel knew the Amalekite king was still alive, but he knew. He was so angry when he arrived that he killed the Amalekite king right in front of my father.

It was here that my father and Samuel parted company. My father went home to Gibeah, and Samuel went to his home in Ramah. Samuel, who was quite old now, ended any participation in affairs of state. My father never saw him again.

At Gilgal, Samuel had told my father a second time that Elohim had rejected him and his house from being king due to disobedience.[20] My father was angry. He had built a nation, built an army, united a group of tribes that could be quite independent, and had won great victories. Per Samuel, Elohim wanted a king who would obey him. My father made some remark about obeying Samuel, which is how it felt to him.

My father changed after Samuel left. He may have complained bitterly about Samuel and his demands, but somehow, his joy was gone. My father had been blessed with a positive spirit, allowing him to prophesy, but unfortunately, there are also other spirits. My father was crazy, at least at times. He would sink into himself, a little like his mother, or he would have screaming matches with the people he loved. Would he have been happier to have lived out his life as a farmer?

---

[20] 1 Samuel 15:23.

One of my father's dubious victories was over the Hivite city of Gibeon. Gibeon was a very close neighbor to Gibeah, but its people weren't descendants of Israel. My father knew there was a treaty in place between the tribes of Israel and the Gibeonites, dating back to the time of Joshua.[21] His own son was part of the group of the scribes enlisted to update the old treaty, so he can't have claimed ignorance. Abner recounted the story to the family, and while he remained loyal to my father all his life, he did try to talk him out of this particular course of action. My father was slowly becoming less rational and less willing to listen to advice. His wishes prevailed, and his armies sacked the city and put most of the inhabitants to the sword. They burned the town as successful raiders do. We were appalled that our father would desecrate a 400-year-old treaty, and my father never felt led to justify his actions.

I knew that my brother, Esh-Baal, went to Gibeon with some regularity, and that Gibeon had a well-known high place and several well-known brothels. In my father's eyes, did Gibeon corrupt his son? I never heard a plausible explanation, though if this was a reason, then my father indulged in a personal vendetta. If Esh-Baal was the reason, then there's a certain irony in his having been part of the delegation that rewrote the treaty.

It made me sad. My father was a king. He could have addressed his son. My father's zeal for morality had waned quite a bit by the time he and Abner leveled Gibeon. As my father's reign continued and as he grew less and less likely to listen to anyone, it became clear that he had no qualms about using his position for personal vendettas. As for Gibeon, there were the usual few survivors who lived to rebuild the city. My father never had to answer for that mistaken enterprise. He was dead. But his successor did.

---

[21] Joshua 9:15.

CHAPTER 16

Year 420

My mother had commented earlier that she wasn't very interested in the art of healing. However, she became highly skilled as a midwife, which isn't so different from being a healer. I wanted to cultivate both skills. By the time I started following Deborah around, she was approaching middle age. She had no children. I was young enough that it didn't occur to me that her situation might have been unsatisfying for her. I only knew that she had a lot of time for me, and that was good. Deborah and Hur were my first mentors and I am thankful for both of them.

Deborah first noticed me watching her when Gibeah's warriors would return from raids with wounds. She would treat the wounds, and if I was standing there, she would explain what she was doing. Our community was responsible for teaching young people and especially any young people who expressed an interest. Interest was encouraged. I was grateful to be learning to read and was fascinated by childbirth. Deborah wasn't a midwife. She was involved in another dimension of caring for our fellow humans. She began to invite me to assist her in her search for healing plants.

Mother's garden was an important part of my childhood. Oh, never let it be said that Merab and I enjoyed weeding it, which was one of our childhood duties. We did enjoy the produce of it as did others in the neighborhood. Rizpah and her daughters helped as well and ate of the fruits of their labor. My mother grew peas and cabbage for food and cumin, dill, horseradish, and mustard for seasoning. She had a small stand of fig trees and one olive tree that she tried to nourish and protect, and she made sure the rest of us participated.

Deborah introduced me to poppies. We happened upon a clump of poppies, and she knew exactly what they were. She was excited. I say a "clump" of poppies when I probably mean a hundred. And Deborah knew how to extract from poppies the substance that was for humans a phenomenal painkiller. It wasn't without its risks, but the rewards were great. I watched Deborah slit a pod, for lack of a better word, with the small knife she carried. As she did, a milky substance oozed out. I was mystified. She advised me that we were going to make slits in every pod, allow the milky substance to dry, and collect it the following day. Deborah could be very energetic, and to "milk," if you will, one hundred or so plants with multiple pods per plant was ambitious.

If I thought that was time-consuming, I hadn't yet seen the effort to collect the sap. We did come back the following day with permission from my mother, and the task took most of the day. We carried baskets and bowls. We harvested every plant and returned home with quite a good supply of the dried milky substance. I was exhausted, and I assume Deborah was too.

Deborah explained that we'd store the sap in its dry form, which was portable and which would keep well. She'd show me specifically what to do with it when the need arose, and like many healing herbs (like henbane), it would be dissolved in water in order to administer it.

Deborah always made the disclaimer, "Medicine is poison if you use too much!" Before she discovered the stand of poppies, she had relied on a plant called henbane to ease pain. If Deborah was afraid of poisoning her patients, henbane was a good reason. I knew the plant. It was actually quite pretty. One dried the leaves and simmered the result in water, creating a sort of tea. But as I learned over the years, henbane is terribly unpredictable. Poppy syrup has its risks but fewer than henbane. Deborah commented that henbane could kill animals (and people), but she assured me that animals avoided it.

Deborah taught me what she could, and I was grateful. I still had a lot of unanswered questions, and later in life, I realized that expecting one person to have all the answers wasn't fair. Ideally, there would be various individuals with whom to compare information. Deborah didn't know everything and never pretended she did. She knew how to harvest the poppy sap, dissolve it in water, and try to persuade her patients to drink it. It wasn't pleasant. Sometimes for children, she added honey. But in terms of dosage, it was strictly trial and error. I absorbed whatever Deborah could teach me about finding the appropriate plants at all and about which parts of the plants to use. Deborah, when called to a sick bed, proceeded with caution. She tried small amounts first, which was understandable, but which also took a long time. She had a healthy respect for herbal remedies.

On the days when Mother didn't have tasks for me, and Deborah invited me to accompany her, there were two possibilities for the day. Sometimes we went on a quest for medicinal herbs, though we were also on the lookout for anything we could use to season food. The other possibility was to visit people who were feeling poorly and who'd requested a visit.

We habitually carried baskets. We only brought bowls when we were dealing with poppies, but bowls are heavy. We would look for things like alfalfa, nettles, roses, dill, garlic, caraway, chamomile, and almonds, plants that are easily transported in baskets. We saw mushrooms, but Deborah was hesitant. She wasn't well-versed in mushrooms, and too many of them were deadly poison. Many people enjoyed mushrooms, and presumably, these were the people who knew *which* mushrooms. I was curious. But I'd have to learn about mushrooms from someone else.

Deborah and I looked for common plants and usually found them, but Deborah was constantly looking for the unexpected— like the poppies. One day, the unexpected took the form of a low plant with wide leaves and purple flowers. I thought it was pretty, but without guidance, I would have walked right past it. Deborah immediately saw value. She stopped for a moment and considered how it might be harvested. She got down on her knees and took out the knife she carried.

I expected her to cut off the flowers or maybe the whole top of the plant. She used the knife to dig the dirt around the plant, and it became clear that the root was the goal. When she'd loosened the plant, she tugged the whole root out of the ground. I was astonished. The root was reminiscent of a human body—hairy arms, legs, torso.

Deborah told me the plant was called mandrake, and it was rare. She said we would cut the root into thin sections, dry them, and grind them up so as to be dissolved in water. She was elated, but with caution. Mandrake had fertility implications, but like henbane, it was volatile. Because it was rare, she hadn't had a lot of experience with it. She knew about it from her former mentor.

I have admitted to being grateful for Deborah's willingness to teach me, but I'm going to add a spiteful comment. In a sense, I *did* earn the education. Harvesting healing plants was only part of the effort. After the harvest, there is the task of rendering the plants or seeds into a form that can be dissolved in water or oil. Sometimes, as in the case with almonds, it's a matter of making them into oil. Some of the preparation is incredibly labor-intensive. And if it's not, it's tedious. A lot of this preparation fell to me, and clearly, I understand why. Deborah was the teacher; I was the student, the apprentice. I agreed that the novice always gets the grunt work, but still, my labor had value.

Seeds are ground to powder to the best of the grinder's ability with a mortar and pestle. I ground a lot of seeds. It hurt my hands. We used the olive press to extract oil from the almonds. Hallelujah! I can't imagine grinding almonds in a mortar and pestle. I'm told it can be done, but Deborah and I didn't have to do it that way. We were allowed use of the olive press during the periods when it wasn't needed for olives.

I worked hard on that mandrake root, but in all fairness, so did Deborah. We sliced the root as thin as we could, and after the pieces were dry, we ground them in the mortar and pestle. Dried herbs can be stored for a long time and they're easily dissolved. As for the leafy herbs, it was just a matter of drying them. So they needed to be laid out or hung from the ceiling, though clearly, that preparation wasn't such hard work. Once they were dried, then they were finely ground, usually by me.

After that, reading and writing became imperative. If I needed a reason to value reading and writing. It was the labeling of ground-up herbs that all looked alike. Both Deborah and I made sure the finished products were labeled, and certainly, I continue to do that to this day.

Another thing I learned during this time, just as a general rule, was to wash my hands. Our people are fastidious about washing, but Deborah understood better than most the danger of walking around, doing the day's tasks, with residue of herbs on one's hands. She pointed out that it was easy to lift one's hands up to one's mouth or eyes in an absentminded way, and it would be better if there were no grains of henbane or mandrake on them. I've carried over this practice of handwashing to my midwifery tasks and I demand that my assistants do likewise. We can argue that it might not be necessary, but I would argue back that it can't hurt and it's not that big an imposition.

Sometimes I would accompany Deborah to visit unwell members of the community. I remember Deborah's ointment for a colicky baby. She used crushed dill mixed with olive oil and massaged the baby's stomach and back. She also used crushed dill seeds, seeds that I had crushed in the mortar with the pestle, and steeped them in hot water. We waited for the water to cool. Deborah and the mother got the baby to drink some. The baby seemed to settle, though Deborah and I never knew for how long.

In peacetime, when we weren't addressing wounded soldiers, the majority of Deborah's calls to action involved children. We visited a home in which a child had been burned. Deborah had made a wash out of a large number of rose petals steeped in water. She applied that to the child's arm first and, afterward, got out the almond oil. I had watched her make an ointment out of a tiny bit of the dried mandrake and almond oil. Deborah applied it to the burn and wrapped up the arm in a clean rag. The child had been crying when we arrived but had quieted. It appeared that the ointment had worked for pain-relief at least. Deborah left a small amount of plain almond oil with the mother and said she could apply that in a day or so. As burns go, this one was less serious.

Deborah was summoned for a child with a broken arm. When we visited the family, she made sure she'd taken some poppy juice with her. Ideally, the child would drift off to sleep before she touched him, but if not, at least he'd be relaxed. She administered the poppy juice, let the child drift off, and then lightly touched the break. She felt the good arm for comparison, and in this case, the break wasn't complicated. The bone was in place. So she advised the family that the child had to keep his arm immobilized for several weeks. She found a thin, straight stick, and bound it across the break. This was after she'd wrapped the arm very lightly in a thin rag to protect the skin from the stick.

Deborah was very sincere in her desire to help. She was absolutely determined to do no harm, and to that end, she was very conservative in her dosages. She knew that some of her efforts had been less than successful. Sometimes it's less about the healer's skills and more about the severity of the illness in question, but it's a distinction that can be lost on a grieving family. She was aware that small doses lengthened the process, but she was adamant.

"Yes, I know small doses take a long time to act, but there's no help for it. You're impatient, Michal. You're well on your way to becoming an effective healer, but impatience is your enemy."

I countered, "He's in pain!"

"Yes, he is, and I regret that. We're all in pain. Pain is a part of life and can't be avoided. What can be avoided, at least temporarily, is death. I will *not* be a party to anyone's death through sheer impatience. Believe in your remedies and allow them time to work."

My mother taught me better. My mother believed that there were certain ways a child needed to address his or her elders. I couldn't help myself, or maybe I didn't try hard enough. "Everyone is *not* in pain! What does that mean? A broken arm hurts."

If Deborah was able to be patient while her herbal remedies worked, she was also patient with me. "Michal, you have compassion which is absolutely critical if you would be a healer. But your compassion in a stressful moment will never excuse sloppiness. Be thorough. Most pain is a temporary condition. If in your haste to help a victim of a broken bone you don't set the bone properly, that person is permanently disabled. Sometimes you will have to put your compassion aside for the long-term benefit.

"Insofar as my oblique statement that everyone is in pain, don't think that pain is just one thing. You see a child who is responding to pain, and you feel compassion. Do you feel the same compassion for your father arriving home wounded and not obviously displaying any reaction? Your father knows that everyone is in pain, and he knows there's no point in whining. His pain is no worse than that of his soldiers. The child hasn't been in the world long enough to know that his pain isn't the worst of all pains.

"Many people have pain that's not visible. Whether you recognize another person's pain or not is irrelevant. It's still real to the person who feels it. Have you ever met a man who couldn't feel anything? I have met very few, thankfully, men who broke their backs or necks. I can't help them. I'm not a miracle-worker. They feel nothing, including pain, and maybe they'd give everything to feel again. Such men don't live long with those injuries, and to my mind, it's a blessing."

"So when you speak of pain, you're talking about men and wounds?"

"Not necessarily. And perhaps I use the word *pain* in its broadest definition. How about disappointment? Disappointment is a sort of pain, and unless the bearer goes around weeping, it's invisible. Disappointment is universal, except for those people young enough not to have experienced it. Life is never what we expect or hope. And the end result is that invisible pain. Some people are much better equipped to leave the past and look ahead. Some people feel the pain every day, but if they're wise, they mostly keep it to themselves. Turning inward is destructive, and in addition, the rest of the community can't be expected to want to socialize with gloomy people."

Deborah didn't yell at me as I deserved. She gave me an honest explanation and a lot to think about instead.

When my mother didn't have specific tasks for me and when I wasn't playing in the yard with other children, I might simply drop in on Deborah. I remember an instance in which I approached her house and heard sobbing. She was alone and she was sipping something. I saw a bowl with a label on it on the table, but I couldn't read the label from where I stood. Deborah wasn't expecting me. She was crying like her heart was breaking. Should I have gone in to make sure she was okay? A good friend probably would have done so. I was a friend of sorts, but I wasn't an equal. I was a child and a student. I made the easy decision and backed away before she knew I was there.

Is this one of my many regrets? I don't know. There is a huge dilemma in whether to try to offer comfort or whether to allow a person to grieve in private. I'm much more than a child now, but I don't have an answer. I specifically remember thinking about Deborah's secret pain.

I was concerned enough about Deborah that I didn't sleep well that night. I got up very early, before mother was up and assigning tasks for the day, and walked to Deborah's and Abner's house. I had resolved this time to at least ask if there was something I could do. I was trying to avoid Mother, but it was still pretty early to be calling on other households. I arrived at Deborah's house to find Deborah and Abner both awake. Deborah was crying loudly and almost screaming about insects crawling on her. I assume that at least some of their neighbors didn't sleep through it. Abner was holding her tightly and trying to assure her that nothing was crawling on her.

I made a split-second decision and walked in on them. Deborah didn't notice. Abner was surprised. I asked Abner if I could administer a little poppy juice tea to Deborah. He didn't have any idea what to do and conceded that it might help. I looked through the bowls for the appropriate label. At this point, I noticed that the bowl from the day before, still on the table, was mandrake. I put it away. Between the two of us, we got Deborah to sip most of a bowl of diluted poppy juice. It had the desired effect. Sometimes during periods of stress, the object is just to relax the patient enough for them to sleep. It isn't a cure. Time and sleep are cures.

If Abner had noticed the bowl of mandrake on the table, he didn't say anything, and even if he noticed, he may not have known anything about it. I assumed that it was mandrake tea that Deborah had been drinking when I'd last seen her. A fertility treatment? Maybe. If I'm right about that, I got to see some of the side effects of mandrake firsthand. I vividly remember making sure to wash my hands after I left.

I was attempting to isolate the healing plants that I knew about and see if I could place them at the edge of my mother's garden. It's so much easier to know where the plants are, especially if you need something specific, than just go out into the woods and hope to find them. I had added onion and garlic successfully. All of those plants are used in cooking and all are effective in relieving some ailments.

I asked Deborah if I should take poppies and introduce them to Mother's garden, but she was reluctant. She hadn't heard whether poppies grew successfully in a garden or not, and she was quite elated to have found some. In the end, she let me take one. Deborah was wise. It died. She and I both made note of the spot where we could find wild poppies.

Some of my childhood memories are a bit hazy. I remember better what I did than what I thought. But I know for a young person raised in an atmosphere of peace, it was easy to assume the adults in my life were competent and secure. Perhaps that's a credit to those same adults. But when Deborah very unexpectedly admitted, "I'm afraid of being labeled a witch," I was shocked. Witchcraft was forbidden by Elohim, and not only that, my father had launched a campaign against the practice. He had witches stoned.

Of course I said something stupid like, "I know you're not a witch!"

Deborah laughed. "Thank you, Michal. It would be nice if society accepted what you think, but in general, it doesn't. There is a certain danger in attempting to provide healing to a patient who is very ill. Some illnesses are beyond my capabilities or anyone's capabilities. Herbal medicine isn't well-understood by most of the population. Oh, if they're ill, they'll happily try anything, but the danger for the healer lies in failure. Success isn't a problem. Herbal remedies are a mystery to people who aren't familiar. I could say ignorant, which is a rude way to phrase it, but people fear what they don't understand. Do my dried-up, ground herbs look like living plants? Not anymore. To some, our efforts look like magic. You and I know what hard work goes into dried herbs!

"I thank you for your vote of confidence, but there is danger in professing the art of healing. There is danger when the patient dies, and some patients die. Some families can't accept it. They need some-body to blame. It might be even more dangerous to be a midwife, like your mother. Childbirth is hazardous. But she is protected. She is the wife of a king. I am protected. I am the wife of a general. I have seen male healers. I do believe they're less vulnerable than female healers, though I could be wrong. Females, whether healers or not, need protection from males.

"I'm grateful to have that, but I still resent the superstitions of our culture. I am rambling about the human condition which isn't likely to change for my convenience. Thanks for listening to my musings about things I can't change, and neither can you. I hope you'll continue on your course as a healer. You have talent. There are risks and there are rewards. It would help to marry a powerful man!"

CHAPTER 17

Year 420

When the task in question was childbirth, it was my mother who gave me guidance. I assisted her, to our mutual relief, with what turned out to be a happy event. I couldn't help but think about Deborah's cautions the whole time.

One of our neighbors gave birth to a girl. I was becoming well-versed in the ways of the midwife, and I was now allowed to do more than observe. This was another one of those hoped-for outcomes—both mother and child were in good health. I asked the baby's mother, as she was putting her new daughter to her breast, what the baby's name was. She answered, "Bathsheba."

As my mother and I were leaving, we encountered some family members who were waiting outside the door. One, of course, was the baby's father, Eliam. He was shifting his weight from one foot to the other, completely unable to stand still. He addressed us with, "Can we go in? Can we go in?"

My mother smiled at his excitement and answered, "Absolutely. You have a perfect daughter. All is well."

Eliam's father and mother were there, standing watch with him. When my mother said the baby was a girl, Eliam's father just grunted. My mother gave him a smile, which he ignored.

As the two of us left, my mother asked me, "Do you know who that was?" I didn't. "That's Ahitophel, one of the major politicians for the Twelve Tribes. They say he is very wise."

I'd heard the name Ahitophel, though I didn't know in what context. It turned out that Ahitophel and his wife lived in Giloh, which was a good bit south of Gibeah. He and his wife were here for their grandchild's birth. The information didn't really mean anything to me at the time, but it was one of those tidbits that a person remembers the next time the name comes up.

It wasn't long after Bathsheba's birth. The day began in a very ordinary way. At first, the weather was good, and the residents of our community were all out doing the usual daily routine. The daily routine took the form of many outdoor tasks, men in the fields and women carrying water and gathering firewood. For whatever reason, my father was home. He'd led his men on a successful raid against the Philistines, and all of them were resting from that exertion. Resting could be done in a group with bowls of beer just outside one of the dwellings. Resting inevitably included healing for some. Resting also included walks around the fields of ripening grain, more often than not, just to look.

A servant found my mother right where my mother could usually be found. My mother had made the daily bread dough and was letting it rise. She stopped what she was doing and gave the servant, obviously in distress, her full attention. "Rachel, take a breath. Calm down and tell me slowly."

"Please hurry, please hurry, the lady Mariamne has hanged herself!"

My mother's mouth fell open. I had just come back from dumping an armload of firewood on the pile at the hall, and I witnessed her shock. I didn't hear the words, but I followed her. Mother dropped her basket and hurried across the compound to find Aunt Hadassah. Aunt Hadassah was home, sorting vegetables for her pot, when my mother interrupted her with, "Aunt Hadassah, come now!"

The two women ran to my grandmother's dwelling with my mother leading the way. Actually, Aunt Hadassah didn't really run, but she could still set a swift walking pace. The servant had cut my grandmother down, but she was clearly dead. Aunt Hadassah gasped. I cringed. I saw my grandmother, her tiny, withered, crumpled body and her distorted face. I looked away as quickly as I could. Mother asked Rachel to go find my father and grandfather. She went looking for them in the fields.

Of course, my father and his father returned to the compound as quickly as they could. They were dumbfounded. Should they have been? Should any of us have been? My grandmother sat in one spot, very silently waiting for death, ignored by her family. I do not intend my words to be a criticism of my grandfather. It's very risky to try to analyze another couple's marriage from the outside. None of us understood how my grandmother came to be the way she was, and none of us, except Aunt Hadassah, tried very hard to be kind to her.

Maybe the biggest surprise lay in my grandmother's timing. She was very old by this time, probably over seventy years. People of that age die of natural causes all the time, and perhaps my grandmother wouldn't have had long to wait. There is a stigma attached to taking one's own life. Some view suicide as a form of murder. There must have been something in my grandmother's life that she couldn't bear anymore, not even for another half day. But of course, by this time, she couldn't verbalize anything, even if she'd been willing to confide in somebody. Suicide is very hard on a family, but again, my grandmother may not have felt a lot of loyalty to the family that had rejected her. Poor Aunt Hadassah! She had tried so hard.

Aunt Hadassah located a shroud. The men took my grandmother's body outside and put her onto it, and the women prepared the body for burial. Ideally, the body would have been left outdoors until burial, but it started to rain. The men moved the body and shroud to a corner of Kish's dwelling, and the women finished the preparations indoors.

Hur was arguing loudly with Kish, standing in between buildings in the pouring rain, as both of them got soaked. The whole compound probably heard them.

Hur said, "It must be told—"

And Kish countered, "Not by me!"

Ner was there, also ignoring the rain, and I made out his low voice but not his words.

*****

The next day dawned bright but cool. We buried my grandmother in the tomb of Grandfather's and Uncle Ner's father, next to Uncle Ner's wife. Merab and I went to speak to Aunt Hadassah. Is it odd to try to console the deceased's sister instead of her husband? By the end of the burial ritual, Grandfather was falling down drunk. Aunt Hadassah had reached an accommodation. She knew that her sister had been desperately unhappy. None of us were quite sure how Elohim regarded suicide. We all believed that death was a beginning, not an end. Aunt Hadassah was unwilling to contemplate a cruel, rigid god and comforted herself by believing that her sister was at peace. None of us had to judge such actions, and for that, we were grateful.

Don't let it be said that we had no compassion for our grandfather. We did visit him, albeit not while he was drunk. After that unpleasant day, we tried to be more mindful of our grandfather and what his needs might be. Our mother, too, tried to help care for Kish. He wasn't one to cook his own meals or tidy up after himself.

The day we buried my grandmother was a day given over to contemplation and conversation. We allowed the daily tasks to slide and made an extra effort to support one another. Aunt Hadassah was actively grieving. I'm not so sure about Grandfather, but he wandered around like he was lost. Being drunk didn't help! The entire family came together to prop each other up, especially Aunt Hadassah and Grandfather. It was a day of rest.

Sarah and I talked together several times about what "must be told." Was what "must be told" the reason our grandmother had given up on life? We were very curious and wondered if Uncle Hur really did intend to tell some family history that Grandfather didn't want told.

CHAPTER 18

Year 358

Yes, he did, but the telling wasn't immediate. It was summertime, and Uncle Hur was waiting for another lull between Father's battles. He wanted Father, Uncle Abner, and the other men of the community who participated in war to be there. Grandfather was adamantly opposed, and in the end, Uncle Hur simply suggested that he not attend. The moment arrived, and my father was interested to hear what Uncle Hur had to say, whether his father approved or not. Uncle Ner, as one of the three elders of our community, seemed not to have a strong opinion, though he exhibited no enthusiasm. All of us vividly remembered the suicide of our grandmother. Or maybe more to the point, we remembered our grandmother in life, a shell of a person.

This time, the meeting was at the edge of a grove of trees. The day was brilliant, and the shade was welcome. We heard a bird or two singing vehemently, and we heard the persistent and rhythmic throbbing of the brook. There wasn't much noise of the human variety. We were all curious. We were all quiet in anticipation. As predicted, my grandfather absented himself. It turned out to be another day of drinking for him who, in the past, hadn't been accustomed to making a spectacle of himself. Some of us sat on rugs under the trees. Most of the children just sat on the ground.

Uncle Hur began to speak. "History is fluid and open to interpretation. If you would learn history, learn it from somebody who actually saw it. But beware, if there are battles involved, the victors tell the story in whatever way suits them. The vanquished, of course, are dead. Time smooths the rough edges, and perhaps that's a blessing. Ner has told me that he has no interest in speaking on the subject that I'd like to tell, but I am asking him now to be a witness. Either my words are true or he will provide a different interpretation." Ner nodded.

Hur continued, "Memory is tricky, and again, this might be a mercy. Some memories are easier to live with than others. It has been said and said and said and said[22] that Israel had no king and that everyone did what was right in his own eyes. But understand this: the law was given by Moses four hundred years ago. We lacked enforcement, not law. And we *did* lack it, no question.

"Gibeah was a lawless place in my youth. The residents knew it. They did not go out alone, especially after dark, nor did they allow their children to do so. I remember a young woman who was grievously assaulted and hit in the head. She never spoke again. She was able to manage the tasks of a very young child after that, but not without supervision. She died young, and perhaps it was for the best.

"There was the body of a boy found naked and bloody in a shallow grave. These events happened close together. The boy's father went to complain to the city elders, though I didn't know then exactly who. I was a youth and didn't know the city elders and took no interest in community affairs. The father was never seen again. It was the eleventh month. Our stream was very high and fast-flowing. If his path had taken him by the stream, we never found any trace of him.

"All of you are aware of the immutable laws of hospitality. If a traveler enters your house, you are responsible for him. The wickedness of Gibeah and of the tribe of Benjamin in general became widely known when a member of the tribe of Levi passed through Gibeah. He was heading into the territory of Ephraim, and he arrived in Gibeah at sunset. He had a woman and a servant with him. Our city lived up to expectations in that one of our residents took the three of them into his home for the night.

"What happened after that was unconscionable. In the darkness, some of the city fathers of Gibeah (I found out who they were well after the fact) surrounded this resident's house and demanded that

---

[22] Judges 17:6, 18:1, 19:1, 21:25.

the Levite be turned over to them. They intended to rape him and said so. The homeowner eventually talked the mob out of that particular action, but instead, the resident had to turn over the woman to them. They abused her all night, and in the morning, she died on the doorstep. She was the Levite's concubine and was precious to him. So why did he turn her over to the mob? Why does anyone do anything? The Levite lived. His concubine died. Was there a real choice? It didn't matter. Gibeah was responsible.

"The Levite put the body of his concubine on a donkey in the morning and continued on his way. He got to his home. He cut the woman's body into twelve pieces and shipped them to the other tribes, asking for justice against the tribe of Benjamin. Cutting up a body is a very strange thing to do, and some might call it sacrilegious. But what was stranger still was that this unconventional course of action piqued the national interest. The tribes came together, mobilized, and camped against Benjamin. They actually mustered in the town of Mizpah, which is part of the territory of Benjamin.

"The tribe of Benjamin received one of these body parts, a desiccated foot. I didn't see it, so you can accuse me of telling events that I didn't see. My father did see it, and he was appalled. Decaying body parts really aren't part of the usual dinner conversation, but my parents discussed it in the hearing of the children and rather indignantly. The message accompanying the foot, in the case of the tribe of Benjamin, wasn't one of mustering soldiers for a united front against an enemy. We learned to most of our great surprise that we were the enemy. The other tribes were coming together to demand justice of Benjamin. Benjamin was expected to find the murderers of the dismembered woman and turn them over to a national tribunal. The vast majority of us had no idea what was going on. If we knew anything about a Levite, a servant, and a concubine, it was from months ago. We had never been aware that our fellow tribesmen thought it an act of war or that this atrocity was worse than other atrocities. The murder of a guest is truly heinous, and this action brought the tribe of Benjamin to the attention of the larger nation.

"The army of the eleven tribes gathered in Mizpah and announced its demands from there. If Gibeah's tribal elders would turn over the offenders for trial, they could avert a war. The tribal elders, who turned out to be the offenders, refused. The armies of the rest of the tribes started a battle and were at first repulsed. The Benjaminites were cocky and self-satisfied. A second battle ensued, and the Benjaminites fought back effectively again.

"I fought in these battles. If there was ever a time when I saw value in war, it was then, though let me be clear. It's a lot easier to see value in a war your side is winning! It was also true that we Benjaminites were defending our homes from invaders. We were under attack. We were becoming convinced that Elohim was on our side. A forlorn hope and entirely without merit. Elohim doesn't condone rape, murder, corruption, and whatever else was happening in Gibeah.

"We did know in general that Gibeah wasn't a safe place at night. That was our clue. If you read the chronicles, you will see that Elohim punishes wicked nations again and again and again, and He uses armies to do it. As you might expect, the armies of eleven tribes of Israel were too much for one tribe and the one tribe that has always been the smallest anyway. The entire territory of Benjamin was eventually overrun, our cities were burned, and our families were annihilated.

"Six hundred of us, including Ner and Kish, retreated to the Rock of Rimmon, where we were pinned down. All of you young men seeking glory in battle, you haven't seen glory until you've killed your brother!"

Hur burst into violent sobbing. Asher approached with a bowl of beer. Hur took some sips and struggled to regain his composure. Then he continued, "Mahlon was fifteen. He was lying in the dirt and the blood with a javelin through his middle. It pierced his backbone, and he couldn't move his legs. We were being pursued. He was barely conscious, but he wanted me to leave him. I did, but I slit his throat first." Hur sipped his beer. He didn't make a sound, but his body was vibrating with emotion. "We spent four months on the Rock of Rimmon. The River Jordan was to one side of us, and the armies of the tribes of Israel were to the other. It was a miserable time.

"We were the last 600 men of the tribe of Benjamin. We were in survival mode. We had some tents, not enough. We had no food unless somebody managed to kill a bird or maybe a deer. The river was there, wide and deep. And fast. It was difficult to get water from the river. The banks were steep and slippery. If a man lost his footing, he was dead. Some did. We gathered rainwater to the best of our ability and barely hung on to life.

"Morale was terrible. If we survived, what was left? The towns of Benjamin had been destroyed, as had our families. I remember Kish was ill. He had a fever and was babbling. We did what we could. There was a tent we found for him, and we made sure he got water. To this day, I'm surprised he lived. There was almost no shelter from the sun and rain.

"I have tried to piece together what might have been the thinking of the attacking tribes of Israel. I mean, why four months? The Rock of Rimmon wasn't a fortress by any stretch of the imagination, but the armies of the eleven tribes only ventured onto it in small incursions. Small raids by small groups. We who were living on the Rock could expect to starve at some point, but in terms of military action, it felt a little like a stalemate. The power wasn't in the hands of 600 men. The power to overwhelm lay with our attackers, and they didn't use it.

"After four months, the armies of Israel repented of the idea of decimating one of the Twelve Tribes. A delegation came to us with an offer of peace, and we all left that desolate rock. We were flabbergasted. Why *now*? Had we Benjaminites been taught the appropriate lesson? It is written an eye for an eye and a tooth for a tooth, a life for a life.[23] Really? The vengeance against the tribe of Benjamin was almost complete, much more like the concept of the blood feud, which in theory could continue for generations. Moses's law replaced it or officially replaced it. All of you have probably heard of isolated instances of blood feuds.

"I have considered the situation at leisure and from afar, and it does occur to me that if indeed the city of Gibeah had been willing to turn over the perpetrators of the original crime to the armies of

---

[23] Exodus 21:23–25.

Israel, maybe the result would have looked more like the life for the life. Maybe we had our chance. But we can never know, and what we got was the extreme blood feud. Mizpah wasn't razed, and it didn't have to be rebuilt. I do not understand its place within the borders of the territory of Benjamin. Surely it can't have been without sin. But the attack against Benjamin was launched from Mizpah, and it must have been spared on that basis.

"If I am allowed to add one observation, based on my years in the world, know this: your actions and decisions affect other people, and you may never even know who or in what way. If you see evil, it is not okay to ignore it and go about your business."[24]

Hur paused for a moment and sipped his beer. Asher brought him a second bowl. We wondered if he was finished talking, but as it happened, he wasn't.

Hur continued, "So we were 600 men, give or take, with no families and no homes. The tribes of Israel, always good for swearing oaths, had sworn before Elohim that they would not give their daughters in marriage to the disgraced remnant of the tribe of Benjamin. So what to do, what to do. The armies of Israel decided, after their blood lust had been appeased, not to annihilate an entire tribe. Elohim had decreed long ago that his people, the Twelve Tribes, should not mix with the neighboring peoples who didn't acknowledge him.[25] We survivors went back to the lands of our heritage and began to rebuild. It was a place to start. We had to do something.

"That period of my life was downright depressing. I had Kish and Ner, and we had a few neighbors whom we'd known before the battle. We three were there for each other, and with great effort, I can find it within myself to thank Elohim that I wasn't alone. But none of us felt much hope during that period, and some of us did indeed kill ourselves. The usual platitudes exist—this, too, shall pass, and things will look better in the morning. In my personal experience, things did get better. In Mariamne's, I'm not so sure. I can look at her and understand what desolation feels like. Elohim bless her!

---

[24] Deuteronomy 21:21, 22:21–24.
[25] Deuteronomy 7:1–4.

"I have asked myself at what point this oath before Elohim was agreed upon by eleven tribes. Clearly, the initial effort was to destroy the tribe of Benjamin. No need for an oath against a nonexistent tribe! So did the tribes swear this misbegotten oath after they decided to allow the survivors of the Rock of Rimmon to live? They must have, but it makes no sense to me. I don't expect to arrive at an answer to that question in this life.

"In the meantime, the armies of the Twelve Tribes—wait, it was eleven tribes—had a plan for the continuation of the tribe of Benjamin. The women of Benjamin were dead. I still grieve over the waste. I still grieve after all these years for my mother. The victorious tribes first had to ascertain whether any cities had refused the Levite's original call to arms, and they were in luck. Jabesh Gilead had. Yes, Jabesh Gilead had the gall to say no to a war against a fellow tribe. To the rest of the tribes, it was a traitorous act.

"The eleven tribes of Israel went up against Jabesh Gilead, slaughtered its inhabitants right down to the livestock, burned the city, and saved 400 virgins. The city was obliterated. The armies of Israel handed off 400 virgins to the 600 survivors of the Rock of Rimmon for wives. They also helped the rest of the Benjaminites to secure wives. This time, the women were kidnapped without killing the families. A small improvement! As long as the women were taken by force, their families were not guilty of breaking an oath that was sworn by other members of other tribes without their permission.

"We, the lowliest of the low, rebuilt, took the wives that were offered, and brought children into the world. All of you are living in the new town of Gibeah. The surrounding towns of the region of Benjamin are new as well. The men of Gibeah who are my age are mostly men who experienced the Rock of Rimmon and who refuse to talk about it. It was a painful time. We will join our fathers in due time, and the event will be forgotten. It will be replaced by the next excess. There is never a shortage of excesses.

"A lot of you consider me to be unconventional, especially in my view of women. I won't disappoint. I am about to sit down and allow my wife to continue the narrative. Before I do, Ner, do you have anything to add?" Ner shook his head.

CHAPTER 19

Year 358

Aunt Hadassah stood up. "I realize that some of you would rather not listen to a woman speak in public. This gathering can be loosely defined as family and maybe not exactly as 'public.' But we have a dilemma. My husband has just suggested that if you would learn history, learn it from somebody who lived it. I, too, have a story. Would some of you be more comfortable if Hur told it for me? He could. I have told it to him, and he knows my story. But he wasn't there, and I have a voice. Those of you who object to hearing my story from my voice are more than welcome to leave. I will take no offense." Nobody moved.

Hadassah went on, "I am from Jabesh Gilead. Jabesh Gilead is in the tribe of Gad and to the east of the River Jordan. I left Jabesh Gilead about fifty years ago, but I still consider myself to be a native. It was a lovely place to live before the armies of the Twelve Tribes decided to obliterate it. Villages tend to be rebuilt. Settlements are settlements because they have access to water. Jabesh Gilead has access to both the Brook Cherith and the Jordan River, though the Brook is slightly closer. Saul, I don't think I ever thanked you for rescuing those whom I once called my people. Jabesh Gilead lies too close to the powerful Ammonites, and it lies on arable and desirable soil.

"Hur began his story by relating some of the sins of his city, even though at the time he was only peripherally aware of them. Mariamne's and my early story was the same as that of the young women among us in Gibeah. We did the things women everywhere do—carry water, seek out firewood, and do laundry.

"Everything changed one early morning when the city was asleep. Our first indication that something was amiss was the noise of shouting, of livestock, of horses' hoofs and the swirling dust and the smoke that was making us cough. It was completely unexpected, and we had no idea what it was. The dust was fierce.

"As we began to be able to see, we saw foot soldiers and mounted warriors killing our neighbors and burning their houses. Clearly, we needed to run, and we tried. My father grabbed a scythe and ran at an infantryman, but you can guess how that turned out. A scythe isn't much of a weapon. My mother grabbed my hand and my three-year-old brother. My sister, Mariamne, was directly on our heels. We raced toward the surrounding trees but never made it. I watched my mother and my brother put to the sword and awaited my turn.

"Instead, the mounted warrior pulled me up in front of him on his horse, drew me away from the fighting, and dumped me on the ground near some other girls. Mariamne and I watched our town burn. Well, it was more a matter of hearing and smelling than seeing. I could have watched the slaughter of more of my neighbors, but I sat with my face in my hands and refused to look up. I remember Mariamne had one arm around me with her face in my shoulder. We couldn't look. We couldn't move.

"The noise abated. The smell of smoke filled my nostrils and my consciousness. Sometimes odors are very memorable, and I still remember that day whenever I smell smoke. There were other odors. Blood has an odor when there is a lot of it, and burning flesh has an unmistakable odor."

It was Aunt Hadassah's turn to falter. She didn't break down but looked very close to it. Asher responded with another bowl of beer. Aunt Hadassah sipped for a moment and then went on. "Some of you have fought battles. You know whereof I speak. For those of you who haven't, understand this: the actual battlefield experience is utterly indescribable. Therefore, I will stop trying.

"After our city was destroyed and I found the courage to look up, our little group had grown to 400 girls. These were friends of Mariamne and me, or at least some were. We were surrounded by soldiers, and at the time, we didn't know *what* soldiers. We assumed

Ammonites. If we had been told that we had been taken prisoner by the armies of Israel, we would have been shocked. Well, more shocked. We were already pretty shocked.

"We all expected to be raped and murdered, but instead we started a long march to Gibeah and other towns of the tribe of Benjamin. These towns were in various stages of being rebuilt. We found out that we were destined to be the mothers of the new tribe of Benjamin. We crossed the River Jordan at Gilgal, and some of us left the group there. Some of us stayed in the more northern cities of the territory, and the last few of us made it down into Gibeah.

"Here we were parceled out to whichever man spoke for us. It was an uncertain, horrible time following a grueling journey. We had watched everything dear to us destroyed, right down to our pets, and we'd left with the clothing on our backs. We were exhausted, ragged, and filthy. Our childhood was effectively over, and we needed to become wives and in short order. It turned out that we were to be wives and not slaves, which was a relief of sorts.

"Mariamne and I somehow stayed together all the way to Gibeah. Hur spoke for me. Kish spoke for Mariamne. Mariamne's and my stories overlapped, pretty much from the beginning. We were raised in the same household, we endured the destruction of our town and family, and we made a new beginning together in Gibeah. We made a new beginning, but I'm going to take a moment to share what the beginning looked like on the day we arrived.

"As we were coming into Gibeah, right on the outskirts, one of the soldiers escorting us produced a large bowl of water. We were told to share it to wash our faces. After that, we were taken to the village square. All of you are familiar with the village square. Raiders can't burn it! It's made of stone. We were taken to the block where slaves are auctioned off and told to stand there. The experience was chilling. We had all been contemplating slavery the whole journey from Jabesh Gilead to Gibeah. There was no exchange of money at this time, which is interesting in a way because traditionally, a wife comes with a bride price. Still, to expect men who'd spent the last four months on the Rock of Rimmon to have money or anything else of value would have been hopeless. The beginning of my marriage wasn't traditional.

"Hur took me to the house he was repairing for us. It wasn't finished, but it was close and would shelter us. I was making a new beginning, and believe it or not, the first entry I made into our not-quite-rebuilt house became one of my favorite memories. Hur, please don't be embarrassed. When I entered the house, right in the middle of the floor, was a large tub almost full of water and with a few rose petals scattered over the surface. There were small pieces of soap along the edge. I was surprised. The water wasn't hot, but it wasn't frigid either. Hur had drawn it from the stream two days earlier.

"We were both feeling rather shy at this point. Hur handed me clean clothing, turned his back, and left. I was utterly thrilled to get out of the rags that were covering me. The tub wasn't really deep, but it was wide enough to accommodate my body. The whole experience was wonderful. It was awkward, but I managed to wash my hair. A tub of water isn't a large gesture, but it improved my outlook enormously. I was going to be cared-for. I was going to be loved. My future looked bright. The clean clothing fit reasonably well and felt good. Hur's and my first act as partners was to get the tub out of the middle of our dwelling.

"Hur and I celebrated our marriage that night. For those of you who are unfamiliar with a wedding night, I'll refer you to your mothers. We got to know each other in a very intimate way. Hur, don't blush! That's not why I bring up the subject. I wanted to say that in the night, I woke up screaming. That can't be an auspicious start to a marriage. Then I felt strong arms around me and I felt a heart beating against mine. After a few moments, I felt safe and drifted back to sleep. The next night, it was Hur's turn to wake up screaming. I put my little arms around him, and if I didn't exactly make him feel safe, at least he knew he wasn't alone. There's value in not being alone. He, too, went back to sleep in a little while. The houses in the new town of Gibeah aren't soundproofed, and they're quite close together. Anytime we woke up in the night, we were made aware that our neighbors were having nightmares too. It took a number of months before the new town of Gibeah was mostly quiet at night.

"Mariamne had a child, Saul, who was the object of much rejoicing. Elohim bless you, Saul! It is so difficult for a woman to be childless! My sister had a son. We were blessed. I also brought a child, a daughter, into the world at about the same time. I was doubly blessed. My husband and I had been through terrible times, both of us. And somehow we managed to support each other and move forward. When Hur spoke for me, I got the gift of a lifetime. A loving marriage.

"Kish could not get past the violent events of his youth. He couldn't face Mariamne. Mariamne represented a period of Kish's life that he was trying to forget. Of course, Mariamne felt abandoned and rejected. She tried to find a space without pain. I do not want any of you to leave this gathering and go tell Kish that I blame him. I most certainly do not. Kish did the best he could. There is great fault to be found, but not with Kish. And not with Hur and not with Ner and not with me. I think about Jabesh Gilead and what the town did. It did not show solidarity with the rest of the tribes, apparently a crime punishable by death. I am tired of death. I grieve for my sister, but maybe more specifically, I grieve for the child she once was. She wasn't always a shriveled-up old woman. May she find peace."

CHAPTER 20

Year 480

Michal paused and repositioned her legs. She was sitting on her usual sheepskin with her back against a wall of the public room in the women's quarters. "Ladies, I do appreciate your attention. But my voice is giving way and I'm tired. Should I assume that you're tired? I won't. Some of you have more energy than is practical in these circumstances. Before we adjourn for the night, I would like to continue to teach you just a bit about our history and our laws. Across the centuries, the laws have been enforced with varying degrees of severity.

"It will not surprise any of you to learn that sexuality, at least for women, has been and can be quite restricted. As we have all noticed, a man may take unlimited wives and concubines. A woman may not. Do many men collect women? I have to hope not. Elohim sanctioned the union of a man and a woman, but this harem is a purely human construct. If the man, specifically Solomon, is gratified by such a situation, I am surprised. Perhaps a man could have two or three wives and be satisfied, but hundreds of wives is extreme and incredibly unsatisfying for the wives except for the chosen few! I've come to the conclusion that harems like ours are rare just because very few men have the wealth to collect women. The kings of the world believe it's a privilege to be married to them. And in the case of this huge harem, *married* is a rather flexible term. Traditionally, marriage implies a public ceremony and a consummation. To those of you who've never met your 'husband,' is the word even valid? We have food, we have shelter, we have slaves, we have fine clothing. The kings of the world believe we ought to be grateful.

"Our present king is tolerant in many ways. However, if any of you are caught with a lover, I'm not sure that tolerance will apply. To my knowledge, it hasn't happened (yet). Adultery is traditionally punishable by death.[26] I have never watched an execution, but they did indeed occur under my father's watch. In fact, they were public, and some people watched them. Some of you are bored and frustrated. These feelings are understandable, but again, be very, very careful. There are laws against doing with a woman as you might do with a man. The practice is detestable to Elohim, and even if it weren't, you'd still be guilty of adultery.[27]

"Since we're talking about sexuality, let me speak from a strictly practical perspective to those of you who are virgins. Some of you, whether you've met your husband or not, aren't virgins no matter what your fathers told Solomon's representative. Do you who are not virgins share horror stories about sex with those who are? I am an anomaly in this place, a woman who has had more than one lover, and it's not a secret. It puts me in a position where I could compare lovers, despite the fact that it's not very nice to do that. I do not want to add to anyone's fear of sex.

"Did I say that a woman can't have more than one husband at a time? I am about to refute my own words. The woman was me! I don't know of any other woman in this position, but I was. I'll get to the circumstances in just a bit. Both lovers in my life made an honest effort to please me. David was young, enthusiastic, and energetic. The two of us explored sex together and concluded that it was good. If Paltiel lacked some of David's energy, he made up for it in experience. I was blessed and I am grateful. If/When you are called to Solomon's bed, and if you feel apprehensive, now would be the time to hone your acting skills. Men's and women's bodies were created to be joined together. The first time, whether it's sex or anything else, is the hardest. I've met Solomon a time or two, though clearly, I haven't slept with him. He's not cruel. Go willingly as a student who desires to be taught, and put on your brightest smile. Solomon will be kind.

---

[26] Leviticus 20:10.
[27] Leviticus 20:13.

Keep an open mind and try to relax. Some of you will die virgins and childless. That would be worse.

"I am not here to judge any of you. I am not here to judge Solomon. I'm not even here to judge our culture which is less than perfect. We will all be judged by history, and I, for one, am not looking forward to it. I have regrets. There are many beautiful bodies being wasted in this place, and if I could change it, I would. Our quarters are surrounded by soldiers, some of whom are young and handsome. It will be for each of you individually to decide whether the risk is worth the reward. I will not be watching any of you, and I would prefer not to know."

The ladies were distracted by Asher walking at his usual languid pace across the room. Abishag was about to help Michal up, and when Asher got to her, he took her other arm. "Wait! Ouch! Getting up is harder than it used to be!"

Michal stood up unsteadily but quickly found her balance.

Asher said, "Highness, please come to attend Bathsheba. She is poorly."

Since the group of wives didn't seem to be in any haste to disperse, Michal addressed them again.

"Like Abishag and myself, Bathsheba is one of the few remaining wives of the old king. She is bedridden and she is in pain. She will die soon. We cannot really help her, except insofar as to ease her pain with the poppy mixture. Sleep can be a blessing. We will minister to Bathsheba first, and then we'll look in on Maacah, who has also survived long after her husband. To my knowledge, Maacah isn't in pain. But she has lost her mind. She thinks she's a child and needs assistance with almost everything. She has a daughter, Tamar, living in the women's quarters, and her daughter provides the majority of her care. Abishag, are you ready?"

Michal added, just as they were leaving, "Do all of you know that Bathsheba is Solomon's mother?"

CHAPTER 21

Year 423

I met David when he came to Gibeah to attend my father. My poor father! His days of joy and prophesying were long over. David was recommended to my father for his musical ability. My father made arrangements with his father to allow him to stay in Gibeah. When my father slipped into his almost unresponsive state, which was happening more and more often, David played the harp for him.

As a person who tries hard to practice the art of healing, I was astonished. I had contemplated my father and what could be done for him, but I'd never considered music. I do not play any musical instruments. In the case of David and my father, the harp was magical. My father responded and almost got back to his younger self. This was a sort of healing with which I'd had no experience, and I watched in awe.

David came from Bethlehem. He was the youngest of his father's sons. He had seven brothers. The servant who recommended David to my father called him a warrior and a brave man.[28] But when his father sent him to my father, he'd been keeping his father's sheep. I puzzled over how a shepherd made a name for himself as a warrior and a brave man. Apparently, David was needed regularly to tend his father's sheep, and in the beginning, David divided his time between Bethlehem and Gibeah.[29] He was an armor-bearer for my father when he was in Gibeah. David was very young. If he had seen battle, I would have been surprised. David spent his summers at his

---

[28] 1 Samuel 16:18.
[29] 1 Samuel 17:15.

father's house, which was when my father would be most likely to be on the battlefield.

It was midsummer and had been a while since David had visited Gibeah. As always, he cared for his father's sheep when he was in Bethlehem, where his family lived. He unexpectedly appeared on the battlefield one day when my father was harassing the Philistines. Three of his brothers were serving in my father's army, and David's father had sent David to check on them. I wasn't there, but I think I can accurately describe what happened just because so many people were witnesses. And the accounts were similar enough that I absolutely believe the event happened.

The armies of Israel and the armies of the Philistines were having one of their many shouting matches. The Philistines camped on a hill in the vicinity of Socoh, and my father's forces camped on a hill overlooking the Valley of Elah. The valley lay between the two armies. The battle-hardened soldiers spent forty days hurling insults at each other from a safe distance. One particular Philistine named Goliath, who was absolutely enormous, came forward every day, demanding that the armies of Israel produce a champion to fight him. His voice was huge, like the rest of him, and nobody in my father's army volunteered.

For whatever reason, my father didn't recognize David, and neither did Abner. He was just a young shepherd who approached my father's troops on their side of the Valley of Elah. He hoped to contact his brothers and bring back word to their father. The first thing David heard was the mighty challenge of the giant Philistine. David had a huge respect for Elohim and felt that the Philistines were insulting the Lord directly. He volunteered to be the Twelve Tribes' champion.

There was the usual discussion as to how to approach the confrontation. My father wanted to deck David out in armor, but in the end, he didn't insist. There wasn't any armor that fit David, and he was just too awkward in it. A soldier needs time to practice wearing armor and wielding weapons. David headed into the valley wearing his usual shepherd's attire.

The soldiers from both armies watched from their positions on their respective mountains while David and Goliath made the trek into the valley. David had a staff and a sling. He moved lightly and gracefully. His opponent in full armor moved ponderously, always with his shield-bearer slightly in front of him. Both armies were caught up in the suspense of the moment. It took a certain amount of time for the two combatants just to come to a place to face each other.

David's accuracy with the sling was legendary, not that Goliath would have known nor cared. Goliath made it quite clear that staves and slings barely qualified as weapons. Goliath's expertise with the javelin was also well-known. Like everything else about Goliath, his javelin was enormous. But David turned out to be faster. David slung a stone, only one, and hit the Philistine in the head. Two armies looked on in amazement. They didn't see the stone fly, but they did see Goliath fall. The Philistine's champion lay stunned on the ground, and two armies watched a shepherd cut his head off with his own sword. In the meantime, the unfortunate armor-bearer faded into the forest.

The encamped Philistines abandoned the effort and ran, as the armies of Israel pursued them as far as Gath. Gath was the giant's hometown. Many Philistines died on the way. My father's armies looted the camp and obtained much booty. As always, there was a real effort to acquire weapons. My father was elated and apprehensive. He had Abner ask David about his parentage, and David told him, though David must have been puzzled. Had he changed so much? My father had sent messengers the previous year to his father requesting his services, so at one time, he'd known who David's family was.

In my lifetime, I have known of more giant men than just Goliath. Goliath had a brother named Lahmi who was just as large. He was killed by one of David's Mighty Men, and I will get to the Mighty Men in due course. David's nephew, a son of his brother, killed another enormous Philistine, also in Gath. These men had a mutual ancestor named Rapha.[30] The chronicles suggest that when Caleb, a contemporary of Joshua, was awarded the city of Hebron for his family, he drove out a colony of giants, who then settled in Gath. In another battle, another of David's Mighty Men killed a giant Egyptian.[31] I have never seen any of these very large men, some seven feet tall. But I have heard enough soldiers' tales to know that such men weren't isolated cases.

Oh, I did see Og's bed with my own eyes. Og was not one of the giant men with whom David's troops fought. Og was the enormous king of Bashan back in the time of Joshua, when the tribes of Israel were conquering territory in the Jordan Valley. Og's iron bed was thirteen feet long and six feet wide. Og, of course, is long dead, but his bed was stored in Rabbah for centuries. It was part of the spoils that David took from Rabbah later in his life and brought to Jerusalem.

After David killed Goliath, my father extended his invitation, to use the term loosely, for David to become part of his court. *Court—* another term to be used loosely! It was more a matter of living in Gibeah and being available to my father. My father was constantly looking to build up his army,[32] and he perceived David as an asset, at least initially. When David arrived, he brought his three nephews, Joab, Abishai, and Asahel. The four of them were seldom seen apart. They all moved into the young men's quarters of our compound. These were the sons of David's sister, Zeruiah, and due to their ages, the four of them were more like cousins. Zeruiah must have been twenty-five years older than David. When David came to Gibeah, he brought three shepherds with him. All the young men were untried in battle, though per David, all could use a sling with accuracy.

David was called upon regularly to play an instrument for my father. David played several instruments and he also sang. His voice had changed from his earlier days in our compound, but if anything, it was deeper and more powerful. When my father got into one of

---

[30] 1 Chronicles 20:4–8.
[31] 1 Chronicles 11:23.
[32] 1 Samuel 14:52.

his moods, the music made a huge difference, and the whole family was relieved. When my father was burdened by his demons, we were all affected by it. And when David played and sang, we all heard it. Oftentimes, we'd drop what we were doing, maybe just briefly, and listen. My brother, Jonathan, found a fast friend in David. The two of them had much in common, though Jonathan was somewhat older.

As for me, I fell in love with David, the new David that my father and Abner hadn't recognized. He *was* slightly changed, and it was all about maturing. He was a little taller and a little broader, and his hair was a little longer. David was just a bit above average height, which made him shorter than Jonathan. His best feature was his vivid blue eyes. He had dark, wavy hair, and when the sun shone on it from just the right angle, it took on an auburn tint. David was very handsome, and I wasn't the only one who thought so.

I have often wondered how quickly after my father invited David to Gibeah he regretted it. Should my father have given David a heartfelt "thank you" and sent him back to Bethlehem? David was young, extremely charismatic, and extremely successful. Was he ambitious? Probably that too! Some would say that Elohim favored him, and he did acknowledge Elohim more than the average person.

David wasn't just a musician. He quickly became a warrior and then an effective leader of men. I would see David and his nephews practicing with their newly acquired weapons in one of the more open spaces of the compound. They would spar but with caution. It was good practice, but weapons, of course, were designed to cause injury. The four of them were careful, and the worst I saw after their mock battles were some bruises and cuts. Occasionally, Jonathan, Abinadab, Malki-Shua, or all three would join in the practice. I remembered the javelin Jonathan had given to Esh-Baal, but I never saw Esh-Baal try to use it.

My father began to rely on David and his nephews to lead men into battle. David was a natural soldier and earned himself some renown. My father was torn between rejoicing in David's victories and being jealous of him. There was a chant that went up from the people who lined the walkways as the victorious soldiers returned home. They shouted, "Saul has slain his thousands, and David his tens of thousands." My father heard this more than once, and he was vain enough by this time to be very reluctant to share the glory. My father hadn't always been vain. Being a king changed him. If David earned glory, so did his nephews. The four of them were often spoken of as a cohesive group, though David always stood out just a bit. Well, in my eyes, he did!

CHAPTER 22

Year 424

If my father had reason to be suspicious of David, why did he want him for a son-in-law? Maybe it was all about keeping David where he could see him, but still, in the end, even the marriage option didn't accomplish that. While David was becoming an adult in the fields of Bethlehem, Merab and I were becoming adults in Gibeah. My father thought to marry David to Merab. David hemmed and hawed, insisting that he was nobody to be a king's son-in-law. To this day, I wonder why. Merab was a lovely and accomplished young woman.

My father gave it up and married Merab to a worthy husband named Adriel. The marriage ceremony wasn't a huge event. My father collected the traditional bride price for Merab. Merab had a new garment, I remember. And when it comes to memories, her marriage day is my favorite memory of her. She looked young, demure, graceful, and extremely attractive. The ceremony, if you will, was the lifting of a veil, the touching of hands, and a journey to Adriel's town. There were two mules and a cart. My sister arrived in Meholah in style! As the two of them departed, I saw Merab's hand very subtly creep over to Adriel's hand, and I felt a pang of jealousy. Adriel was older than she, as was the usual custom, but happily not a lot older. He was handsome enough in a rough way. It was clear Adriel was a working man and nobody's decoration.

My sister was happy. She got pregnant almost at once and had her first son. If Merab had married David, would anything have been different? I wanted to marry David, and I was glad when my sister didn't. My sister suffered greatly at David's hand, and I'll get to that later. I was becoming adept at midwifery, and I wish I could have assisted my sister in childbirth. But she and Adriel lived in Meholah, which really wasn't close by. I never found out about Merab's labor until it was over.

My father was still of a mind to have David as a son-in-law, and that left me. Correction: that left me *if* there was a necessity to use a daughter of the wife as opposed to a daughter of the concubine. I haven't really reconciled wives and concubines in my mind, but there did seem to be an advantage to being the wife or a child of the wife. I had made that transition from child to woman, and my father used women to advantage. Nobody really disputed the fact, including me. I just reserved the right not to like it.

My father broached the subject of marriage again to David, though this time, the bride was me and not Merab. I wasn't included in the negotiations. I have to assume that David was either ready to become a king's son-in-law or he preferred me to Merab. A bride price is usually money or land. My father made a very unlikely proposition to David, and I did see some logic in it in that David had neither money nor land. His father was wealthy, but he was the youngest son. My father wanted a hundred Philistine foreskins for the privilege of marrying me. That's when it started. That's when it became clear that my father wanted David dead.

I regret that my father wasted time and energy in the belief that David was a threat to him. And believe me, he wasted a *lot* of time and energy, almost devoting the last years of his life to the elimination of David. Did my father have so many valiant warriors that they were disposable? There is something incredibly flattering about having a man go into battle for you. But it's also the same principle that I've spent my life rebelling against. Women as prizes or women as symbols. David, of course, was up to the task, and he defied my father by not getting himself killed. He proceeded to do battle with the handiest Philistines and brought back two hundred foreskins. David had a following, his nephews and any number of others.

So I became David's first wife. We had the typical betrothal period after my father accepted the bride price. My father wasn't entirely gracious about it. Despite the fact that David had just devastated a Philistine battalion (or because of it?), we enjoyed several months of peace. I never asked David why he accepted me as a wife and not my sister. It's entirely possible I didn't want to know. I was focused on being allowed to marry the man I loved, and I didn't analyze too deeply. But in my latter years, I wonder. I would never have considered myself prettier than Merab. She and I were very different, personality wise. David and I had happy times, at least at first, before my father's bizarre behavior came between us. I'd gotten my heart's desire. So many women never do.

David applied himself to designing our first house. My new husband was creative in very many ways. The house he and his nephews built for us was quite different from others in the compound in which we lived. It was of mud brick, which was the available building material. But the outside was whitewashed, and it glistened in the sun. More notably, it had two stories. It was the tallest house in Gibeah. I wondered where David's ideas came from. How different was Bethlehem from Gibeah? Our house was unique. We had the usual floor of lime downstairs with the usual hearth.

I had never taken the time to note what went into the building of a house, but when the house was destined for me, I took an interest. The mud bricks themselves were works of art and took some time to create. The basic recipe was mud, water, and straw. The mixture needed time to blend, which was about a week. Then the mixture was shaped in molds into uniform bricks, and that took another week just to make sure the product was dry enough to hold its shape. After the bricks were removed from the molds, they still needed additional time to dry. So all this occurred before any walls went up. David was meticulous. He hadn't ever built a house before and he relied heavily on workmen who had. His bricks were sturdy and his walls were straight. Our house was eye-catching, mostly due to the whitewash, and it was also well-built.

My mother wove a magnificent rug as a wedding/housewarming present, and it sat in front of the hearth. She used shades of cream and green, and it was quite large. It might have been my mother's masterpiece. The only thing upstairs was our sleeping quarters. The upstairs ceiling was rather low, but it was adequate for its purpose.

There were windows front and back that allowed a wonderful summer breeze, along with a nice view of the town. I'll concede that they also allowed a draft in the winters, but then I had bedcovers and had David. Who could ask for more?

Ner and Abner also gave us a wedding present, even if weddings in general weren't huge events. And I still don't know what they were thinking. They gifted us with a statue, or maybe an idol, and it was heavy. I thought it was ugly, though I didn't say so to Ner and Abner. David thought it had artistic merit. Somehow, David and his three nephews wrestled it up the ladder and into the sleeping loft. They stood it up in a corner. I never liked it, but eventually, I came to ignore it.

It started with the bride price. I didn't foresee that things between my father and my husband were never going to get better. My father had a notion that if he needed a spy in David's house, this would be me. But even before he gave me to David as a wife, he knew I loved David. So for him to expect me to be loyal to himself if I had to choose between them wasn't very practical. My father personally tried to kill David and more than once by hurling a javelin at him.[33] These attempts took place while David was playing his harp, so it became clear that the music was no longer enough to chase off my father's demons.

My father set me up to choose between himself and my husband, and I made my choice. It was Jonathan who heard it. He told me of my father's latest plot to kill David and when. I helped David escape one night through the bedroom window. The ground wasn't that far down, and we used a rope tied at one end to the statue. It was heavy enough to bear David's weight. Yes, the statue came in handy! With some effort, I afterward maneuvered it into our bed and piled up the bed clothes on it as if somebody were sleeping there. I told the usual attendants that my husband was sick. When my father finally blasted his way into the room and found David gone, he was furious. It's always difficult to be screamed at, and my father had taken to doing quite a bit of screaming.

---

[33] 1 Samuel 18:10, 11.

"You disloyal bitch! You clearly came to be because your mother was an adulterous woman!"

"Father, please stop trying to kill my husband. He has done you no wrong. He has won victories in your name! And your accusations against my mother are truly unreasonable."

"Girl, you are in no position to tell me how to treat one of my subjects. You do not understand David's ambitions. In fact, you don't understand much!"

"Father, David threatened my life. I was afraid not to help him."

"You helped him two days ago. Don't try to tell me you've been afraid of his absent person for two days. You disgust me!"

My father was losing his mind. David was the enemy. I cried a lot over my disaster of a marriage. How does a young wife cope with the constant absence of her beloved husband? It's so difficult when the two people you love most don't get along, and in the case of my father and David, "not getting along" was an understatement.

Young person that I was, I assigned blame. I blamed my father. At the time, my father held all the power, and at the time, he didn't feel led to compromise. David left Gibeah and returned to Gibeah with dizzying regularity. He went to Bethlehem and got at least some protection from his family. That option didn't work long-term, but David used it for a while. When my father began pursuing David with an army, David stopped putting his family in a position of defying the king.

David and I shared the fierce passion of youth when we could. Those nights with David were the best nights of my life. It was splendid to be David's only wife. But unlike my sister, I failed to conceive. There was the anguish of youth mixed in with the passion. Youth has certain expectations. Youth believes that certain things are true of women and/or marriage in general and doesn't concede that there are exceptions. It's *difficult* to be the exception. I thought I would be like my sister and conceive immediately, but it wasn't to be. It took a long time for me to come to terms with that reality.

I thought about Deborah and thought about mandrake. I assume she still had some dried mandrake. It's not like a healer has lots of opportunity to use it or needs very much of it for a dose.

Mandrake was widely believed to have fertility properties, but even in my youth, I was a skeptic. How can one measure, when a woman becomes pregnant, whether the mandrake was effective or whether she got pregnant in the usual way? I didn't know, and I'd seen the aftereffects of what I presumed to be mandrake. Deborah was fine by this time, but she also didn't remember the incident. I decided I could wait a little longer.

Long ago, when our love was new, I benefitted from my husband's musical ability. David played the harp, the psaltery, and the flute, though his favorite was the harp. He had a glorious singing voice. I sang with him in the privacy of our quarters sometimes. My voice wasn't like his voice, but it was good enough to complement his song. He wrote small compositions for me and sang them to me. It was very romantic. I am nostalgic. I'd almost forgotten about that.

In those early days, David and I did some whispering in the privacy of our loft bedroom. Privacy—we knew that whispering was mandatory if we wanted to keep our conversation between ourselves. David told me something astonishing. My father was making a name for himself as a powerful king. This was before David had met him or any of the rest of us. David was keeping his father's sheep and not paying a lot of attention to the larger issues of the Twelve Tribes. He did know that a leader had emerged who was putting the Philistines to flight.

"Samuel came to visit my father. I wasn't there when he arrived, so I only know how my family viewed the whole incident. The city elders of Bethlehem were quite apprehensive. Samuel was a legend. And even if he weren't, it was well-known that Samuel had quarreled with your father. Bethlehem was a peaceful town, and none of us were looking for tribal drama. Somebody actually asked if Samuel had come in peace. After I met Samuel and established something of a relationship with him, I realized how ironic the question was. In peace? Samuel didn't lead armies of destruction. I have to believe that Bethlehem was afraid Samuel's visit might attract the wrath of your father, but Samuel himself wasn't a violent person. Samuel only inflicted violence on the rams and lambs he sacrificed!"

I whispered back, "I never met Samuel. I hear that he used to visit Gibeah, but I hadn't been born then. When I came along, he and Father had parted ways. Father mentioned him now and then but never said anything nice about him. Still, the two of them must have gotten along at one time."

David replied, "I met Samuel when he came to Bethlehem to include my family in a sacrifice to Elohim, or so he said. Looking back on it, Bethlehem was quite far from Samuel's usual wanderings, so if my family was afraid the visit would be noticed, it was with good reason. There was a sacrifice, and my family participated, but that wasn't really why Samuel had come. I missed it, being in the fields with the sheep. My father and the town wanted a plausible explanation for your father if his spies were watching Samuel. We didn't want any trouble."

"Do you like him?"

"I do. Your father thinks what your father thinks, but I see no malice in him nor great ambition. He and your father aren't on the same course, though your father feels threatened by him. Samuel is very wise, and if circumstances allow, I'll take the opportunity to let him teach me.

"Anyway, after the sacrifice, my father was asked to produce his sons for Samuel's inspection. My seven brothers were presented, and Samuel simply told my father that the Lord hadn't chosen any of them. Chosen any of them for what? Father never asked the right questions! Father sent my brother, Shammah, out to the fields to look for me, and I remember he wasn't very happy about it. He was designated to watch the sheep until I returned, and at that stage of his life, he felt that shepherding was beneath him. However, he did it, and I went to the house to meet Samuel.

"In the presence of my father and brothers, Samuel anointed me with oil from a horn. Samuel said that Elohim had rejected your father from being king and that I was to replace him. I know oil isn't magic, but the anointing made me feel different. There was a tremendous peace and a tremendous power, if you can understand that. I'm not saying it well. It's hard to describe. The entire town was afraid of Samuel, and nobody was willing to question anything he did. We all just hoped he'd leave quickly, and he did. He headed for his home in Ramah, and I went back to the fields. At the time, I was grateful for the solitude. I needed to think. I brought my harp to the fields and played for the sheep.

"And guess what? The next thing I knew, somebody had recommended me to your father to play music for him. So I came and I saw that my music helped your father's spirit. For a while. Now I'm asking whether somehow your father found out that Samuel had anointed me. My father and my brothers were witnesses, and if anyone else was there, I don't know about it. But the household is large and there are many slaves in it. Others probably knew. Your father is treating me more as an adversary than a son-in-law. I know Samuel anointed your father."

"Samuel anointed my father twice, though I was never a witness."

David's revelation gave me pause. *Did* my father know of Samuel's relationship with David's family? It might explain a lot. My father was determined that Jonathan should succeed him as king. Suddenly I was afraid. I choked up and tried hard to be quiet about it.

"What does this mean, David? Will you kill my father to become king?"

I have to believe David had thought about it because he took a long time forming his answer. He finally said, "Michal, please don't forget that he's trying to kill me and there are witnesses to the fact. If I am to become king, and sometimes that notion seems very distant, Elohim will have a plan allowing me to keep my hands clean. To answer your question, no, if I can possibly avoid it, I will not kill your father and Jonathan's father. If the two of us are face-to-face with weapons drawn, I probably won't let him kill me. But if I am the anointed of Elohim, so is your father. There will be another way."

CHAPTER 23

Year 424

I met Zeruiah when she came to Gibeah for her brother's marriage to me. She stayed about a month, living in an empty dwelling that her slaves fixed up for her and meeting the people who were now part of David's life. I found her fascinating.

Zeruiah was the first independent woman I'd ever met. She was a force to be reckoned with. She wasn't exactly tall, but she was taller than me. She had a habit of standing very straight, which made her appear taller, as did her thinness. She and David shared the remarkable blue eyes. When Zeruiah spoke to me, her deep blue gaze went right through me. She was willing to spend time with me, possibly because I met her gaze. She was intimidating, and I've come to believe it was intentional. I tried hard not to let her know I thought so. She wasn't tolerant of people who seemed weak.

There were two reasons I sought out Zeruiah. First, she was David's sister, and I was looking for anything about him that anyone could tell me. On that score, I was disappointed. Zeruiah was long away from her father's house by the time David came along. Zeruiah's father, Jesse, had many children with multiple wives. Zeruiah wasn't the oldest, but she may have been second or third. She laughed when I tried to question her about David. She told me that I knew him better than she did.

She had made the effort to come to Gibeah to try to get to know him a bit. She hadn't been totally successful. She found him unoccupied a couple of times, and he was willing to talk but never for very long. Her brother was busy, and he was probably less interested in a relationship than she was, despite the fact that she was his best friends' mother.

Clearly, Zeruiah also came to Gibeah to see her sons, and though they were glad to see her, they, too, were busy. Along with David, they were serving my father, and they were also practicing diligently with whatever weapons could be found. They were more willing to specifically make time for her than David was. I enjoyed the company of Zeruiah's sons, and I made a comment to her about Joab, who was the closest of the three to my age. I felt like Joab was one of those rare males who was willing to treat me as a person as opposed to a woman. Why should being recognized as a woman bother me? It doesn't bother most women.

Which brings me to the other reason I wanted to meet Zeruiah. I wanted to know how she functioned in the world without a husband and whether or not she liked it. Please understand at this time, I was a brand-new wife, and everywhere were stars and rainbows. My future was full of promise, and I was sure that being married to David was all I could ask for.

Zeruiah said, "My sons are honorable men, and Joab has just taken a wife. I am pleased that I got to be a witness. He seems to love Damaris very much. I am a widow and have been in the world much longer than you. I'm glad you and Joab get along, but be careful. There are always people watching, and some of these will either actively wish you ill or simply use your behavior to entertain themselves. I do know whereof I speak. It doesn't matter if you didn't do anything wrong. It can matter if you're perceived to have done something wrong, and it can matter a lot."

"I hope this doesn't mean I shouldn't speak to Joab or to Abishai and Asahel, for that matter?"

Zeruiah looked at me and then said, "I see a little bit of myself in you, and I doubt there's any stopping either of us. It's just a caution. It's just advice, maybe useful, maybe not. You have the power to cause trouble for yourself, and you also have the power not to. I doubt I'm saying anything you haven't thought about."

Zeruiah told me a bit about her own marriage. Ezekiel was significantly older than she, and she was his second wife. Girl children and boy children learn separate daily tasks, and these separate tasks are fairly universal. Girls are expected to marry, bear children, and defer to their husbands.

Ezekiel was rather rigid. He knew without a doubt what a wife's daily tasks were and how they should look at the end of the day. His mother was still alive at the time, and she supported her son wholeheartedly. Zeruiah had two young boys, Joab and Abishai, and was pregnant with Asahel. She faced a barrage of criticism on a daily basis. Her husband didn't physically abuse her, but nothing was ever enough or good enough. It was exhausting. Zeruiah pointed out that her husband's wealth, at the time he died, made a huge difference in her options. Poor women didn't have options!

Zeruiah was lucky she bore sons. If she hadn't, her day-to-day life would probably have been even worse. Due to the duration of her marriage, she had no children other than the three sons.

Ezekiel died suddenly. Zeruiah knew she was supposed to grieve. She tried, but she didn't miss Ezekiel. She created a new day-to-day routine for herself during that loosely defined period when a widow is expected to mourn. Ezekiel and Zeruiah had been living in Hebron, but with his death, she moved her family back to her hometown of Bethlehem. She was heavily pregnant. She made the journey anyway, in part to escape her mother-in-law. Asahel was born. The birth was ordinary. She and the child were healthy. She had a lot of support from friends in Bethlehem, and her parents were still alive. She had a few slaves who were invaluable in the effort to raise three boys.

Zeruiah wasn't surprised when her father approached her about another husband. She was still of child-bearing age and was a vigorous person. She was reasonably attractive. That was obvious even in her fifties, which was when I met her.

She was not amenable to marrying again. She did her father the courtesy of meeting several eligible men who may well have been attracted by a wealthy widow. Zeruiah had no illusions. She knew what she wanted, and it was freedom. She cultivated a nasty tongue, which wasn't a tool she used on me. Actually, by the time we met, she had become a lot less prickly.

Zeruiah may have been a little lonely in Gibeah, and I did visit her with some regularity. I hope she viewed me as a friend. She shared some confidences about that period in her life, which was almost as stressful as anticipating Ezekiel's needs (which seemed to be what he expected).

Some people are smarter than others. Zeruiah told me of one would-be-husband who expounded at length on what he was looking for in a wife. Is this really the best way to woo an independent widow with money? She countered by telling him what she wanted in a husband and, at the end of the discussion, called him an old woman. There may not have been a greater insult. Zeruiah remembered that conversation with humor.

She also confided to me her deep dark secret and a memory that was much more painful for her. She started talking and she couldn't stop. Some men expect women, maybe all women, to obey them. Zeruiah encountered one of her father's possible choices one late afternoon to her great regret.

"I was alone in the house, though Asahel was there. He was maybe a year old at the time. Joab and Abishai were both outside playing with other children as they do on warm summer days and evenings. My father wanted me to meet a man from Mizpah named Nahum. Nahum stopped by in the early evening. I wanted to honor my father, but I truly wasn't in the mood. I had a tendency not to be terribly polite, though I'm working on that."

Zeruiah paused and sipped her tea. "I remember thinking it was time to nurse Asahel, and I suggested to Nahum that we meet the next day. Instead, he sat down very close to me and put his hand on my shoulder. I had never met this man before. I found his behavior suspect. I stood up and moved away from him. I firmly and not-too-courteously demanded that he leave.

"Asahel wasn't immediately within reach. He was dozing on a rug in the corner. Nahum was shocked that a woman would presume to give him orders. On the first day we met, he slapped me. I have no doubt he was shocked when I slapped him back. He punched me in the face, then in the stomach, and then in the eye. With one colossal jerk, he tore my garment almost off. I was about to be shown what a woman's place was, and if I was lucky, I'd survive it.

"As you have guessed, the concept of fighting back wasn't foreign to me. Oh, when I was married, it would have been. I was the most submissive wife in town. But I wasn't that person anymore, and there was no turning back.

"He punched me again in the ear, and he grabbed for my arms. My head was ringing, and I was dizzy, but I was absolutely terrified. Did I scream? I doubt it. I don't remember. I remember Nahum's big hand on my throat.

"Do you know that when your emotions become strong enough your physical ability gets stronger as well? There was a pottery bowl I could reach, and I grabbed it and broke it. I flung all my weight in the direction of Nahum, holding out the broken pottery and aiming at his throat. I am not a brawler. This was my first and only brawl. But I was very, very lucky. I did reach Nahum's neck with the jagged edge of the bowl and did back him into one of the pillars of the house. His neck was immobilized against the pillar, and I pushed with all my strength. When the blood gushed out, I was covered in it. So was he. At the time, I didn't notice. All I noticed was when his grip on me weakened. I sank to the floor in a corner and couldn't move. I could hear Asahel in a remote way, but it was so distant. He was crying, and I couldn't help him.

"I don't know how long I cowered in a corner. If my feet were to move, my brain would have had to direct them, and it didn't. I don't know how long Asahel was crying. Obviously, at some point, Joab and Abishai came home. Abishai tripped over the body in the doorway and landed near me. I knew who it was, but I still couldn't move. Joab stepped around Nahum and tried to communicate with me in my corner. He tugged on my garment, and most of it came away in his hand. Joab and Abishai were scared. There was a *lot* of blood, and though some of it was mine, most of it wasn't.

"Finally, Abishai left and went to my mother's house. My mother came back with a slave and was speechless. There was a dead man in the doorway, and her daughter was covered in blood. The slave picked up Asahel, and my mother sent her to bring my father. She came to examine me and to see if I was alive. My hand was clutching a jagged and bloody piece of broken pottery, and she pried it loose. It dropped to the floor. She got me to my feet and led me back to her dwelling, Joab and Abishai following behind. My mother stripped off what was left of my garment and laid me on a bed. She sponged me off as gently as possible. It became clear that my face was the most injured part of me. My face blossomed into a rainbow of colors, and it certainly hurt. So did my abdomen. But I escaped without broken bones or missing teeth. I wasn't injured, which was a blessing.

"Michal, I fought for my life or at least I believe that. I also wondered whether Asahel was in danger from an extremely angry man. He wouldn't have been in a position to be a witness. He wasn't talking yet. But this was not my finest moment. Killing a fellow human changed me. I do not recommend it, and it hasn't happened to me again. I have never been alone with a stranger since that event."

Jesse wasn't aware that Nahum had violent tendencies and he was shocked. He and some male slaves removed the body. It didn't matter to Zeruiah. She never lived in that dwelling again. There wasn't an arrest or a trial. The evidence was compelling. There was nothing secret about the altercation. The whole community knew very quickly. I called the killing a dark secret, but it was never a secret to those living in Bethlehem. It was just one of those things in a person's life that they're not proud of. A regret—time eventually smoothed the raw edges of the memory.

Jesse knew it would be absolutely futile to look for another husband for his daughter in Bethlehem. Zeruiah's sons grew into men without a stepfather in their lives. Clearly, there was no shortage of male influence in Bethlehem. Zeruiah made a life for herself, being involved in her sons' lives and becoming involved in the community. Her new goals didn't require a husband.

Zeruiah's name is in the annals of history where very few feminine names exist at all. But I smile to myself just a little—the context is Zeruiah as Mother. Her name is associated with her offspring, Our culture truly values childbearing. I have to wonder when my mind is otherwise idle, *why* Joab, Abishai, and Asahel aren't known as the sons of Ezekiel. They're the sons of Zeruiah.

CHAPTER 24

Year 425

My father was very angry when I helped David escape from our house in the dead of night. David would leave Gibeah for a while, and then he'd return. This became a pattern. He'd sneak into town and go looking for Jonathan to see how my father was feeling. I saw them talking once in the dim morning light just before dawn. What was I doing out of bed at that time? I've never been a sound sleeper. I wake up at all different hours of the night, and sometimes, especially if it's hot, I take a walk. I'd rather be able to sleep well, but there is something to be said for the early morning before others are up. It's a special time of day, and if I can't sleep, at least I can appreciate the solitude and the silence. In this particular instance of David returning, he came to our house, so I didn't have the burden of pretending not to have seen him.

I missed my husband. But there were times when I wondered why he came back to Gibeah at all. It was fairly well-understood by this time that my father's mind was slipping. He was absolutely capricious. David never knew whether he'd be received as a son or as an enemy. Maybe I flatter myself to think I was a reason for David to make the somewhat risky effort.

Unfortunately for my father, David had a second ally right within his family—my brother, Jonathan. David and Jonathan developed a strong friendship pretty much from the moment they met. My poor father! His children were disloyal. Jonathan became aware that my father was plotting again to kill David, and this time, he didn't involve me. He warned David directly, and again, David left Gibeah. My father's face turned purple when he realized that David had gotten away and called Jonathan all manner of names, some of which were very unflattering to our mutual mother.

His rage reached epic proportions. He made the huge effort with Abner and some of his soldiers to knock down my house. Should I give him credit for making sure I wasn't in it? Probably not. Abner made sure nobody was inside, and he even gave me ten minutes warning. I grabbed my mother's rug and ran.

How does one knock down a well-built house? There's an art to it. First my father burned the parts that would burn, specifically the thatched roof. The flaming thatch fell onto the wooden floor below it and caused that to catch fire. After that, a relatively small battering ram was all that was needed to flatten my whitewashed brick walls.

The next time I saw my house, it was a pile of whitewashed, if sooty, bricks surrounding my and David's mostly burnt possessions. The heavy statue had fallen through the floor. The largest part of it was covered in debris. I would venture to guess that an item like that would survive a fire, but I never attempted to salvage it. I did walk through the wreckage and I did pick out a few less-damaged items. I took away some of the bowls and picked up two of David's musical instruments. They were damaged, but to my eye, not too badly.

I walked past my former address in the days following and was saddened by the sight. Predictably, the bricks began to disappear. Bricks are resilient and reusable, and there's a certain amount of tedious labor required to make them. The community was always building something. After a while, the remains were almost gone, though a passerby could still tell there had been a dwelling in that spot. The statue disappeared. If somebody saw value in it, they were welcome to it. I still wonder if either Ner or Abner rescued it?

After Jonathan warned David away, the dynamic changed. David was no longer leaving Gibeah for a few days or a week and then returning. He stopped taking refuge in Bethlehem. He now had a large following. When David left, his nephews went with him, as did about 600 other shiftless men. Shiftless is an unflattering assessment. And for some of David's hangers-on, it wasn't true. But some of these men followed David for lack of any better options. They had no skills, and in some cases, their families had rejected them.

If David had an army, so did my father, and the feud took on a much grander scale. Interestingly enough, David tried hard to keep his promise to me not to kill my father. David and his men spent their time eluding my father, who was doing the chasing. I didn't see David again for a number of years. My father kept coming home to Gibeah during the winters, but he and David persisted with their disagreement over several battle seasons.

So what happened to me in the meantime, a wife without a husband and a woman without a dwelling? My mother had become ill. My father spent way too much time pursuing David, but he also had countless enemies all around the territories of the Twelve Tribes and fought countless battles with them as well. With my father and my husband gone, I spent many nights in my mother's house being available to her. To that end, I'd moved some of my belongings to her house, and when my father destroyed my dwelling, most of my clothing wasn't in it. My mother suffered in the manner that Bathsheba suffers.

I got what many people don't get—I got the chance to say good-bye to my mother. I had to watch my mother's condition worsen, but still, without that intimate period of time, we never would have had the conversation. My mother was the least emotional person I've ever known. I found out in her time of weakness that she did indeed feel emotions and feel them deeply. It started out like this.

"Daughter, you have no children and there are no signs that you are pregnant. Has your husband rejected you?"

Since my mother and I had never shared our innermost thoughts, I was caught off guard. "No, Mommy. He loves me. I hope there will be a baby soon."

I thought about suggesting that David and I were apart too much for me to conceive, but it sounded like an excuse. And my mother was well aware of the fact.

My mother said, "I hope so too. Some women are childless, and it's just one more burden to bear. Abner and Deborah have no children. Deborah occupies herself, but if she thinks about it, it causes her pain."

Deborah and I ministered to my mother to the best of our limited abilities. Deborah prepared the poppy juice and it did ease mother. I had brought poppy juice and wanted to give some to Mother, but she said, "Wait. I appreciate the sleep it brings, but let me speak for a moment." She gasped and tried to ease her body into a more comfortable position. "The prophecy—"

I honestly thought my mother had taken no notice of the prophecy. She never commented on it after my father had declared that she would be the wife of a great king. I thought she was much too practical for such ideas. I had to spoil the moment by saying something stupid.

"Mommy, sip the poppy syrup first. We'll talk of my father's prophecy when you're feeling better."

I would like to think my mother taught me a lesson. Maybe my mother would be gratified to learn that she'd taught me anything. Since that conversation, I have never again pretended to a dying person that they weren't dying. It took some physical effort for my mother to express anger, but she did.

"Michal, I will never feel better. Please don't insult me. If I am to talk to you, it has to be now. I am the wife of a great king. My husband is a great king. At the time he was declared a king and he became a king, it didn't feel possible. I saw his life change completely, and I saw his personality change too. Is he happy? No. He is tormented.

"Did you know there was more to your father's prophecy? In that very odd moment, when your father did something, I wouldn't have believed if I hadn't seen it. He prophesied that my daughter would be the wife of a great king. I had no daughter at the time. I had sons, and I would have welcomed some favorable prophecy regarding them, though again, the whole event didn't seem real anyway. I blurted out some comment about being the mother of a great king, and that was the end of any prophesying by your father. Once that prophetic spirit left him, he didn't remember anything he'd said. I completely disregarded the daughter prophecy when Merab and you came along, just because I had no intention of raising a couple of princesses, whatever that means. I wanted strong young women who would someday become good wives, good mothers, and assets to their communities. I was afraid that 'princess' implied indulgence and self-centeredness."

Mother's face contorted into a grimace, and she paused. I offered her a bowl of beer, and she sipped.

I asked, "So do you think the prophecy pertains to me or to Merab? Is it believable at all?"

"If I were to look at Adriel and at David, I would say David was the more likely of the two to become a king. I also see just how much David threatens your father. I wonder what my husband knows that I don't know? As for me, what does it mean to be the wife of a great king? Nothing. And I'm grateful. Since I married your father, I got the life I wanted. I got the house, I got the five children, I got my garden, I got the role I wanted in the community. My life became more difficult when your father became bizarre. I believe that becoming a king made him crazy. Was it important for him to become a king? Samuel thought so.

"For me, the prophecy was true and I take no pleasure in it. Will you be the wife of a great king? When your father came down from the high place of Gibeah and prophesied, his prophecy was true. If his prophecy was true, it is my opinion that it was meant for you and not Merab. Will it make you happy? Will it make David happy? I very much doubt it.

"My daughter, my daughter. I am sorry you have no children yet, but I am enormously grateful that you are willing to care for me during my illness. I'm going to say something now that you've never heard from my lips, and I don't say it just because I am grateful to you. Before I die, I need to make sure you know I love you."

I blinked and I blinked again. I hated to think that my mother, in her final days, might be following my father down that road of insanity.

She had to have known what I was thinking. "Michal, just because I never said it didn't mean that I loved you and Merab any less. I wanted sons. A woman's husband always wants sons. A farmer wants field hands. A king wants heirs and soldiers. I know you and Esh-Baal have a strained relationship, but if you can, for my sake, try to be kind to him. Your father has never actually said it, but I believe

Esh-Baal is a disappointment to him. Esh-Baal knows it and pretends he doesn't care. It's got to hurt.

"I'm glad I had sons, but I'm glad I had daughters too. A woman wants daughters for her own. I loved you and Merab. You were so different, but I was very proud of both of you. I wish I could see Merab again, and I wish I could see my grandchildren."

"Mother, should I send for them?"

"No, no, it's too late. It would be a terrible journey for all of them. I might let you do it if I thought I'd live long enough for them to get here, but it's too late. I hope you see Merab again, and if you do, give her my message and my blessing."

"Thank you, Michal, for caring for my garden. You are being schooled in the art of healing, and from what Deborah says, you're catching on quickly. You have a skill of your own, something not given to you by a man. Elohim bless you, Michal! I will take some of that poppy juice now."

Mother slipped away peacefully one late afternoon. I'm glad she died in peace, but the dying took a long time. She stayed in the house where her children were born and ran the compound as she always had. My father didn't have a harem, and my mother didn't attempt the role of the chief wife. She wouldn't have liked it! After my mother died, I simply remained in her house. I made certain that her garden was maintained. It was invaluable for daily food, and I was still trying to cultivate plants that had healing qualities.

I once asked a visiting trader about cultivating poppies, and he asked if I had tried planting them in the fall. I said, "Of course not. Who does that?" He swore by it, and I did try it with one poppy. I dug up the bulb in the fall, cut off the stalk as per instructions, and transferred the bulb in the eighth month to the garden. The poppy did come up in the spring, to my surprise, and it flourished. I proceeded to move more poppies to my mother's garden, though I hope I was respectful of the nature of poppies. The stand of wild poppies still exists and thrives. I never tried to take every plant.

CHAPTER 25

Year 426

David and his men traveled swiftly from here to there, always with my father in pursuit. The rumors of atrocities carried from town to town. My Uncle Hur's word, *excesses*, popped into my mind. My father was so intent on killing David that he committed sacrilege against a community of priests. This community was important because it was here, at Nob, where the tabernacle stood.

The tabernacle was an extremely elegant tent that symbolized the worship of Elohim for the Twelve Tribes. Originally, the tabernacle was built to be portable. It was constructed in the Sinai Desert after the Twelve Tribes had successfully put Egypt and slavery behind them. It was carried by the priestly tribe all the way from there into the Jordan Valley. During the period when the Twelve Tribes were conquering the Jordan Valley, while Joshua's headquarters was in Gilgal, it was there. But Joshua had it moved to Shiloh, where it remained for over 300 years. It was in Shiloh when Samuel was a boy, serving the high priest who ministered there.

My father had the tabernacle moved to Nob. The high priest of the tabernacle admitted to helping David, and my father ordered eighty-five men to be killed. My father had some difficulty finding a man to carry out an order to kill priests, but of course, there is always one. Excesses—the priests of Elohim were treated like an enemy people, massacred with their wives, children, and livestock. My father's guards refused to do it, to their credit, but there was an Edomite in my father's entourage who was a witness to the interaction between David and the high priest. Doeg and his men did the killing.

After Nob was leveled, my father had the tabernacle moved again, this time to the high place of Gibeon. This was after my father had almost leveled Gibeon. Gibeon's high place had escaped my father's wrath, and the rest of the city was in the process of being rebuilt. One of the priests of Nob escaped and made his way to David's forces. David got a firsthand report of my father's latest act of insanity.

It was during one of those unusual and very welcome periods of peace when my father and his forces were at rest when I had my first and only conversation with Jonathan. It's not that Jonathan and I disliked each other. It's just that our paths didn't cross, and we had nothing in common. Except that now we did—David. I was married to David, and Jonathan was his best friend. Jonathan came to see me at our mother's house. I asked if he was hungry, and he said no. We went to sit outside at the back of the house. I brought two bowls of beer.

Jonathan had just participated in one of my father's eternal pursuits of David. Father discouraged Jonathan from coming along because he didn't trust him. Jonathan was only there on this occasion because Malki-Shua was ill. One night, Jonathan sneaked away from Father's encampment. He was determined to see David, and he did, though he found himself captured by David's men when he got too close.

Jonathan described the scene. "I really was rather fearful. I needed to see David but knew I was taking a risk. David surrounds himself with some very questionable human beings, and I was aware that I could have been killed before whatever guard even thought to ask who I was. I found myself with an arrow pointed directly at my face, and behind it was a bowman I didn't know. Elohim protected me. The guard did ask what my business was, and I told him. I have no idea whether he believed I was the son of Saul, but he wasn't taking any chances and brought me to Joab. Joab seemed to be David's second-in-command. Joab took me to David.

"I'm here to bring you news of David, and he really is doing okay, though at first I didn't think so. He had no joy. He was exhausted from living on the run. It rankled that Father was trying to kill him for reasons that weren't obvious. I have to believe he sometimes got impatient with some of his followers. Some of them enjoy violence, and a lot of them are rather ignorant. They all view David as a hero or a savior, and while he's aware of that, he also perceives some of them to be unpredictable if he makes a decision that they don't like. I wouldn't guarantee that he views himself as a hero or a savior!"

I had to ask, "How did he look?"

"I could see the tiredness in his eyes, and it was there in his movements too. He hadn't changed a lot physically. He seemed healthy, if not enthusiastic. We talked all night. I did my best to give encouragement. We talked together of Elohim and of David's and my future.

"I don't see myself as a king, ever. He and I talked about that. Our father wants to establish a dynasty in the worst possible way, but it isn't to be. I told David I'd support any claims he made to the throne. Throne! Our father has a big wooden chair with armrests, but maybe someday, the Twelve Tribes will have a throne.

"Did you know that Samuel anointed David to succeed our father? David's entire family was there to observe, but they were afraid. They enjoyed the peace of their town and preferred that the news not get back to our father. Of course, the news *did* get back to him, but it was a secret for a while."

I answered, "Yes, I did know. David told me in whispers one night. I didn't know what to make of it. I tried to get David to promise not to kill our father, and I don't think he wants to. But he did point out that our father is hunting him. Jonathan, there is every possibility that this conversation will get back to our father. Does he know you visited David?'"

Jonathan said, "I told him, but I told him after I got back. I decided to face his wrath sooner instead of later as I was absolutely confident that my little nighttime adventure wouldn't be secret for long. I really expected a diatribe including rather nasty slurs about Mother, which he uses with some regularity. Father is still obviously seeking David's life, but somehow he doesn't seem as single-minded as he used to be. He wasn't pleased and said so, but not with the usual screaming and swearing. Sometimes I wonder if he's becoming resigned to a lesser role for his family, and sometimes I wonder if he's just old.

"I got back to camp in the early morning hours and went to my tent. I get a little disgusted with our guards sometimes. It wasn't nearly difficult enough to get into camp and to my tent unobserved. I know where the guards are stationed, but still, if I had been in my tent and if the intruder was an enemy, I would probably have been killed.

"I'm interested to learn that David told you he wouldn't kill Father. On two occasions that I know of, David got close enough to our father to kill him, and he came away with proof. One time, he cut off a bit of our father's garment, and another time, he stole our father's javelin. After both of those incidents, the two of them talked, and Father felt bad and left off the pursuit. Father told me that during one of his odd periods of repentance, he'd gotten David to swear that when he came to power, he wouldn't attempt to wipe out the family of Saul. I know our father believes in the prophecies of Samuel, and yet he tries to thwart them. Is our father doing battle against Elohim? I wonder. Our father has victories over the nations that surround the Twelve Tribes, but he and his army haven't been successful against a shepherd-turned-soldier with a ragtag following.

"I have nothing against the sons of Zeruiah, but I must add Joab was *not* impressed when David refused to kill our father. He thought that David's troubles would be over if Father was dead. Everyone was very weary of this unstable lifestyle. I know David can't come back to Gibeah, and for this, Sister, I am sorry. I wish David's band could find rest somewhere unknown to Father. I know and Father knows that David could have killed him. David refers to our father as 'the Lord's anointed.'"

"Did he ask about me?"

"Not exactly. At the risk of sounding very insulting, your name didn't come up. It wasn't that kind of conversation. But on that subject, you need to know that David has taken two more wives, Ahinoam and Abigail. He took Ahinoam first, and I know nothing about her except that she's from Jezreel. He took Abigail when she became a widow, and her story is a bit more interesting. Her husband, who was wealthy, lazy, and drunken, insulted David's men and refused to send gifts. When she found out, she was petrified and tried to make amends. I don't know a lot other than that, but her husband died, and David married her. I didn't meet either one of them."

"Jonathan, you have no idea how much I appreciate whatever news you have for me. Please don't hesitate to tell me anything, even if you end up telling me that I have competition as a wife. It was inevitable."

Jonathan took his leave. I knew that David couldn't come home, perhaps until Father died. And if he did return to Gibeah with two wives, what would that mean to me? Gibeah—when my father died, what was in Gibeah for David? Surely he'd be more inclined to return to Bethlehem. Life was changing at a rapid pace. I contemplated David and Jonathan's secret conversation, and I contemplated my royal brother pledging support to an outlaw in the desert. How incredibly ironic!

My father was troubled by an evil spirit, and now he didn't have his favorite musician to play for him. He was more arbitrary than ever. There are times when I contemplate Abner. Did my father even understand how fortunate he was to have Abner's loyalty? It can't have been easy for Abner, though hopefully, he became adept at gauging my father's moods, and maybe hiding his own opinions.

I found out that David and his men and their families had been welcomed by Achish, the Philistine king of Gath. If Jonathan hoped for a refuge for David away from our father, this was it, but to my mind, it wasn't ideal. Father may have been David's enemy, but so were the Philistines, at least traditionally.

David and Achish had a complicated relationship. David had met Achish on a previous occasion when he was being chased by my father, but it was initially a short stay in Gath. David and his men first went there after David left Nob. Achish's officers hadn't forgotten the chants of the women of the Twelve Tribes after David's victories over the Philistines, and they complained when David was given sanctuary in Gath. David concluded that Gath wasn't a safe haven, and he feigned madness. Achish didn't try to detain him. David and his men left hastily. It was Gath's champion that David had very pub-licly killed. The circle is round!

David returned to Achish a second time, and this time, the Philistines didn't feel threatened. Or maybe it was all about keeping the refugees out of Gath. David didn't pretend he was crazy either. Achish ceded the city of Ziklag to David and his men, which kept them out of the way of Achish's Philistine soldiers. I mourned a bit for the man I married. Two other women were with him, and I wasn't. And Achish—what was he thinking? He must have thought that the warrior who had taken 200 Philistine foreskins for a bride price could be tamed somehow. He took a big risk, though David never turned on him directly.

CHAPTER 26

Year 427

I was in Gibeah, living in my mother's dwelling. I had replaced Mother's hearth rug with the grand one she'd made for me, and every time I looked at it, I thought of her. I missed her. I missed my husband. I tried to keep busy and still assisted Deborah. If I allowed myself to dwell on it, I was rather unhappy. I was married to an absent man who hadn't given me a child. I was beholden to my father for protection.

Protection was no small thing. Our territory was surrounded by enemies who simply waited for an opening to launch a raid. It wasn't particularly comfortable being dependent on my father. He was positively erratic by this time, and I was grateful that my mother didn't have to deal with him. I wanted some sort of change in my life, but I didn't know where to begin. I got some satisfaction from tending my mother's garden.

My father had spent many years being a farmer and respecting the land. Now these past years, he'd been more of a soldier than anything else, but fertile land was still a prize to be desired. I'd never heard the name Paltiel. But he apparently owned a prime piece of land that abutted my father's holdings and that came with both a large pond and a producing vineyard.

Paltiel lived in Jezreel. It was not convenient for him to own land in Gibeah, and he made my father a proposal. He would take me as his wife and cede the adjacent property to my father as a bride price. What was Paltiel thinking? I have never been a great beauty. My looks and demeanor were very like my mother's. I was young, of course, and youth is more valuable than any young person knows. I wasn't a virgin and wasn't a widow.

My father was intrigued at the whole proposition. He knew I had a husband. He'd accepted a very unusual bride price for me. Nobody knew better than my father that my husband wasn't dead. My father and I had a very public and very spirited discussion as I was returning from the market one afternoon. I was carrying a basket with a loaf of bread and some fruits and vegetables.

My father confronted me and said, "Michal, I have a new husband for you."

I didn't even attempt to hide my astonishment. "Father, I have a husband. In fact, I have a husband whom I love. I truly wish you would allow him to come home."

We were not alone. It was a busy market day, and various members of the community were observing our conversation.

My father continued, "There is a man I was acquainted with a long time ago who has taken an interest in you. I am not prepared to turn down the bride price he offered for you. And by this time next year, you'll be a widow!"

I was getting angry and raised my voice. "Then we'll wait until this time next year! I will not let you make an adulteress of me!"

It would be an understatement to suggest that my father wasn't interested in my opinion. Both of us were getting angry. We shouted at each other in public and drew spectators. My father closed the gap between us, and he backhanded me. He knocked me down. I don't know who was more surprised, my father or me. He'd never done that to me before nor to my mother either. Neither my husband nor my mother had ever hit me hard enough to knock me down. I may be fortunate that my father didn't break my neck. He was a big man with big muscles, and he was used to knocking soldiers around.

My eyes grew very wide. I looked up at my father, and he looked down at me. Was he going to apologize? No. The words he actually spoke sounded more like, "I do not argue with women." He turned away, and Abner helped me up with his usual smirk. I'm pretty confident Abner thought it was high time.

The whole town watched while I retrieved the contents of my flung basket. My father, with Abner standing by, actually threatened to tie my hands behind my back and tie me to a mule. I could face my new husband, if I can call him that, either bound to a mule or with an attitude of willingness. And an attitude of obedience, I might add. I had pride, more then than now. If I had appeared in physical fetters, would Paltiel have beat a hasty retreat back to Jezreel? I did as I was told, reluctantly. And if Paltiel noticed a big bruise on my cheek, he didn't comment on it.

This was my farewell to Gibeah, to my family, and to my mother's garden. Like my sister, I got to travel in style when I left Gibeah. Paltiel was a wealthy man. He was significantly older than I was. We had the cart pulled by two mules. I was able to bring some of my belongings. My father accepted the proffered bride price. I found out what it was. Did he ever find the time to enjoy his fruitful new piece of property? Believe it or not, I hope so, but I wonder. He simply wasn't home much.

Paltiel took me to Jezreel in the north. This was the first time I had ever traveled anywhere, and while I was getting to know Paltiel, I was also fascinated by the scenery. There was a road of sorts, though it was thoroughly rutted. My possessions did remain on the cart for the entire journey, but Paltiel and I did not. It was so uncomfortable! We saw some glistening mountain peaks, but from a distance. We crossed the River Kishon. I'm sure the Kishon is a real river at some times of the year, but happily for us, when we crossed, it was more of a stream. The mules weren't intimidated. Jezreel itself was incredibly beautiful. The farms there prospered, and it was also part of a well-known trade route.

I liked Jezreel. The town was set up in neighborhoods, similar to Gibeah, though I found that out as I explored. I found out who was related to whom. I liked Paltiel, though I didn't love him. Paltiel loved me passionately. Be that as it may, I still didn't conceive. Paltiel took me to his house, which wasn't new like the one I shared with David, but it was of similar construction—mud brick with a second floor sleeping level. Paltiel had rugs too. There was quite an elegant one in front of the hearth, royal blue with a black border. It was lovely, but it didn't have quite the quality of my mother's rugs. Or was I just prejudiced?

With my move to Jezreel, I got to visit my sister, Merab, a few times and met my nephews and my niece. It was such fun to play with Merab's children. I made sure to convey greetings to her from our mother. Merab wanted me to describe our mother's last months, and I tried. The memories brought tears to her eyes.

"She actually said she was proud of me? Mother simply didn't take the time to say things like that. I just wish I could have known when she was alive. I tried to be a good daughter. I tried to win her approval, and maybe I got it, but I never knew it."

"Merab, I had no idea you felt that way. You *were* the good daughter. How could Mother not have approved of you? I was the one who was always in trouble."

"Michal, I was the conventional daughter. I'm not sure how good I was. But one thing that might interest you, many times, after Mother was done giving you a piece of her mind, and you were walking away, I caught a little smile on her lips. I actually think she delighted in your spirit and also believe she tried hard not to crush it. You and I were different, but she didn't love you any less."

I met Paltiel's children and grandchildren. Paltiel had been a widower for many years. He had a son and a daughter and five grandchildren. Paltiel's children seemed a little bit apprehensive that he'd married the king's daughter. I'm not sure how they thought I might act, but hopefully, I acted like any other adult female. I did my best to care for Paltiel as a wife, and they noticed. Paltiel and I saw his children with some regularity, and eventually, they seemed to accept me. I hope they were comfortable in my home. Yes, my home—the home in which they grew up.

It was finally my turn to leave the only town I'd ever known and the members of my family who still lived there. Sarah had married shortly after I did, and she traveled to her husband's town. It has always been customary for young wives to leave their childhood homes and travel to where their husbands lived. Up until then, that hadn't been my reality. My husband, while he was serving the king, lived in Gibeah.

It's important to have friends, and the making of friends, especially later in life, is a challenge. I didn't know anyone at all in Jezreel, and I barely knew the man to whom I was married. Married. Was I married? My father and Paltiel said I was. My first friend in Jezreel was Paltiel's daughter-in-law. She had children, and I didn't, which makes a difference. But the two of us had any number of conversations about herbs, sitting over cups of tea or taking long walks. I never felt like I knew enough to teach. But we'd talk about what worked and what didn't, and I ended up learning from Susannah. She also learned from me.

Susannah had a very nice typical mud brick house that was larger than most. Her husband, Paltiel's son, worked in partnership with his father, and both of them earned a nice living, mainly conducting trade. When Paltiel was away, so was Ezra. Susannah and I kept each other company. We were sitting outside of her house in the cool of the evening, sipping tea. I had grown up on beer, and tea was a bit of a revelation. But it was one of the trade goods bought and sold by Paltiel and Ezra, and Susannah had acquired a taste for it. I was in the process of acquiring one. I always associated hot drinks with healing or medicine, but tea just felt good going down. It had an interesting flavor. Susannah's children were out and about, doing what children do on mild summer evenings, playing with other village children.

Susannah broached the question, "Michal, do you want children?"

I looked at her. I wasn't expecting a conversation quite this personal. I'd had the conversation with my mother, and it was when I was quite a new wife. Susannah looked back at me with dark, concerned eyes. There was no malice in them. This was a raw topic. I felt the tears start to flow.

"I want a baby more than anything else in the world," I said between sobs.

Susannah got up, moved her stool closer, and put her arm around me.

"I believe that most women want children, but I wanted to make sure before we started to talk about options."

"Do you mean mandrake? It's not easy to find, and also, it's dangerous. There are side effects."

"I've heard of mandrake, but I've never worked with it. I've never even found any, not that I'd necessarily recognize it. I've got some stinging nettle we could try. That's supposed to help, and there are no side effects."

"When Deborah was training me, that's one of the plants we'd look for. I remember that both of us wrapped the stalks in rags before pulling them up. We tried not to touch the plants themselves. We dried the leaves, and I don't recall doing anything else with them."

"I'm going to make us both some nettle tea. Let me warn you, the taste isn't quite like what we're drinking now. I'll have some with you."

"So you've drunk nettle tea before, and you have children?"

"Does it work? I don't know, but yes, I have drunk it and for fertility reasons. All I can say is, it doesn't hurt! We'll sip a little tea together, and then I'll give you some nettles to take home. You'll have to do your own pulverizing, though."

After drinking Paltiel's imported tea, the nettle tea was rather noxious. Susannah made a face. I asked her if she wanted more children, and she replied that she was ready for another baby.

"I would like a larger family, but I am also concentrating on being grateful. I have two beautiful children now."

Susannah's two beautiful children made their way back home in the hopes of getting supper. I picked up my dried nettle stalks, around which Susannah had wrapped a rag. When I got home, I took the leaves and ground them with a mortar and pestle, and I sipped one more bowl. Ugh! I was going to try this preparation in earnest when Paltiel came home.

It was Susannah who gave me lessons on mushrooms. Our first lesson occurred one pleasant day when Susannah's children thought she was taking them for a walk. Her children were full of energy, and they ran on ahead. Susannah and I followed the path more slowly, and we took a few detours into the woods. We women had a tendency to carry baskets pretty much everywhere. Baskets are absolutely essential. The children were happy to be outside and weren't paying a lot of attention to us. Susannah showed me one type of mushroom that was easy to identify and that was safe to eat. She also showed me a couple of species that weren't. I knew Paltiel ate mushrooms. I learned which mushrooms were safe to eat and learned how my husband liked them cooked.

I have never been a talented cook. I cooked of necessity and made meals that were edible, if unimaginative. Susannah was an excellent cook and took the time to teach me a few tricks. I learned about mushrooms from her, and she also taught me to make her personal variety of lamb stew. Paltiel was impressed! Paltiel was a very tolerant husband. He was the most uncritical person I knew.

I choked down a bowl of the nettle tea every evening until Paltiel returned from his business trip. When he came home, I told him about Susannah and her nettle remedy. Paltiel's immediate response was, "Then we'll have to do something about that!"

Paltiel, while a bit advanced in age, was vigorous. He was a fairly big man, at least if I'm not comparing him to my father. He grabbed my shoulders, and his mouth came down on my mouth. I felt myself being lifted up and carried into the sleeping room.

I gasped. "I see you missed me!"

Paltiel was an excellent lover. I just knew with the cups of nettle tea and Paltiel's best efforts, I would conceive. I was disappointed when my courses began right on schedule. There were nettles left, and I resolved to try again.

I was in Jezreel for a number of years, keeping Paltiel's house and being his wife. I consulted anyone who used plants to their best advantage and tried to continue my education. I kept a garden. Susannah taught me that many of those same herbs that had healing properties could also be used to season food. I had a row of poppies and had one henbane plant along with a number of miscellaneous food plants. I made one effort to transplant stinging nettles and was spectacularly unsuccessful. They were dead within a week. It wasn't a problem to find wild nettles. They were abundant along the river banks.

I had some concerns about the more volatile plants in my garden, and I asked Paltiel for a fence. He had the servants set up a stout fence around my plants with a gate that faced our house.

Paltiel was kindly disposed toward me. My life with David seemed very distant. I eventually asked Paltiel how it came about that he gave up a vineyard for a woman who wasn't technically free.

"Did you want to become the king's son-in-law? And if so, did you get any benefit from it?"

Paltiel said, "As a businessman, I am always looking for contacts and alliances. It felt like a good thing to be the son-in-law of the king. It's hard to know whether I have benefitted. There are a few people out there who know my wife is King Saul's daughter, and maybe these men are more inclined to meet with me and listen to me. Probably more men don't know, and it's not the sort of thing I'm likely to bring up in conversation. As a general rule, my associates don't care who I'm married to!

I asked Paltiel if he'd ever been a soldier. He was living both in Gibeah and in Jezreel when my father came to power.

"Your father launched a huge and successful mission against the Ammonites just after he was declared king. I wasn't part of that army, though I would have been young enough to be. I had two homes, and I was in Jezreel at the time. Once when I was there, the Philistines were camped at Shunem. We in Jezreel felt threatened, and the young men started training in earnest. I was part of that group, but we never went to war. The Philistines turned their attention elsewhere. I cannot claim to have endured the hardships that soldiers endure. I don't think I'd have made a good soldier, and even though soldiers come away with loot sometimes, I don't regret my non-participation. I don't care about glory or fame, and there are safer ways to earn wealth."

I thought for a moment about my brother, Esh-Baal, who also was no soldier. Would he and Paltiel have had interests in common? I'm not aware that Esh-Baal ever engaged in trade, though he might have been good at it. I remembered my mother's wish that I be kind to Esh-Baal. I never got the chance, and maybe it was just as well. I'm not sure I could have been. Esh-Baal could be petty, and so could I! Paltiel could not.

Paltiel surprised me by admitting that when he'd lived in Gibeah all those years ago, he'd noticed me.

"My wife and I used to watch the children bat the rag ball back and forth between goals. You were unmistakable. You were an aggressive player. All the boys' eyes were on you. I remember you had a friend, and you and she would keep possession of that rag ball for long periods, handing it off to each other. It had to be annoying to the boys who wanted to be superior. You were different from most girls, more independent and less predictable. My wife and I would bring Ezra to watch, and though he was just a baby, he seemed fascinated. You should know Ezra played some very successful games with the rag ball in his youth!"

"I remember! I remember a couple with a baby whom I didn't know. It never occurred to me to try to make your acquaintance. You and your wife watched us, and so did others."

I needed to know how Paltiel felt about me being married. "What kind of a marriage is this, Paltiel? Are we really married? Or am I still married to David?"

"Do you or did you love David?"

"Paltiel, what a question! I did. Yes, I absolutely loved David when the two of us were together. But, right now, that feels like another life. I don't know how to answer you."

"Michal, you know I love you. You have given me the treasure of your youth. You seem comfortable with us here in Jezreel. Last time I was in Gibeah, and before that it had been a while, I started to realize how long I'd been alone. And how long you'd been alone. Did David abandon you? It seemed that way. I decided that if I wanted to speak, I should do so or forever wonder what could have been.

"I negotiated for you with your father and took him at his word. There will be a winner and a loser in this ongoing struggle between Saul and David, and I have placed my wager on King Saul. I am very grateful that you are with me, but your father has been much slower at resolving this conflict than I expected him to be. I am rather impatiently awaiting word of David's death. And when it comes, we will have a proper celebration."

I said nothing. There was nothing to say. I am perceived by some as being outspoken, and rightly so, but in that moment, I was silent.

CHAPTER 27

Year 480

Michal paused. It was getting dark, and it was close to suppertime. She stood up with some effort. Abishag was close by, as always, and helped steady her.

"Let's adjourn to supper, ladies, and meet again tomorrow. I am going to add my usual admonition about the culture in which you now find yourselves. Not all of you had happy childhoods. However, our laws declare that you will at least pretend to honor your father and mother, and they also specify punishments for disobedience. Some parents are more deserving of honor than others. If you must criticize your parents harshly, please do so in private.[34]

"Some of you are undoubtedly wondering why I, the person who screamed at my father in public, have the right to give lectures on respecting parents. I have thought about it over the years. I have drawn conclusions about the laws of Elohim in general and not so much as they pertain to specific incidents and individuals. If I can generalize broadly, the laws of Elohim are intended to define our relationships with Him and to define our relationships with each other. I did respect my father and mother for most of my life. I did my very best to care for my mother when she needed me most. I did not respect my father in that particular disagreement, and I embarrassed us both. I wholeheartedly believed he was wrong.

"My father and I were not the only individuals involved. There was also my absent husband whose voice was not heard. My husband paid the agreed-upon bride price to my father, and then my father

---

[34] Leviticus 20:9.

drove him off. Now my father felt he was entitled to a second bride price for the same daughter. I regret that I made a fool of myself in front of the whole town. And I don't. I think if I had done my father's bidding without protest, I would *really* have regretted it. I made sure the town was aware that I had resisted my father's scheme to the best of my ability. I left town shortly after the altercation. I don't know if I would have garnered any sympathy from the witnesses. But I might have.

"For those of you who would break the law, consider this—you may be confident that you won't get caught, and maybe you won't. But if you are, it would be better if the results of your deception were not obviously for your own benefit or your own gratification. The law is not for me. The law is not for you. The law is for us and to protect us from each other.

"Ladies, I will return to this room tomorrow to continue my story. But I am asking for your indulgence. You've undoubtedly realized by now that my story isn't just *my* story. It involves other people with whom my life was and is linked and, in some cases, who were far away. You will realize that I wasn't there when my father died and that I wasn't tracking the movements of my husband, David. I learned of their circumstances after the fact, and for the most part, I heard the stories from more than one set of lips. For the sake of continuity, I will relate how events transpired and in their chronological order.

"My Uncle Hur had my Uncle Ner as his witness to correct his memories if need be. I have no one, and I can only hope I am conveying my story as honestly as possible. I am trying."

Michal and Abishag headed in the direction of the dining area. Their audience got up slowly and stiffly, and some of the women shook out the rugs or hides on which they'd been sitting. Everyone was ready for supper.

Michal paused as she noticed Asher heading toward her. Abishag tried not to cringe. She whispered, "Supper will be delayed. Asher has a task for us."

"Highness," he greeted me. "Good evening, Abishag. There is need of a midwife at the other palace."

"Do you know who is in labor?"

"Her name is Ahsia, and she's a Moabite princess. I am not an expert on labor, but her women would like you to come quickly."

Abishag sighed. Michal tried not to.

"All right, we are on our way."

The two ladies stopped by Michal's sleeping cubicle to gather a variety of herbs and also whatever clean rags could be found. They both washed their hands in a basin near Michal's bed. Then they stepped out into the evening air and proceeded into the garden. The sun was setting. It was probably a lovely sunset, but the majesty of it was obscured by the trees. Michal and Abishag hurried across the garden on their way to the palace that housed the majority of Solomon's harem.

Abishag commented, "This palace makes me very uncomfortable. The atmosphere is different from the old, familiar palace in which we live. I feel like there are evil forces here."

Michal answered, "Yes, I agree. It's an eerie place. But it's probably no worse than Pharaoh's daughter's palace. The women whom Solomon has married have brought their gods with them, and these gods war with Elohim. We hope Ahsia is blessed with a very ordinary labor and we can be out of there shortly. Oh, while we're here, we must look in on Naamah. She's pregnant and near her time."

Michal and Abishag entered the new or newer palace and felt the atmosphere change. There was incense in the air that made it oppressive. There were no empty rooms. There were women everywhere. One woman they noticed sitting motionless very close to the entryway seemed to be meditating in front of a small statue that sat on a high shelf. There was an incense dispenser in front of her with a thin stream of smoke. Michal and Abishag stepped around her.

As they moved through the palace, they saw niches carved into the stone walls, all of which housed stone or wooden figures. Occasionally, they saw a woman there as well, bowed in worship. They did not see images on the grand scale that adorned the palace of Pharaoh's daughter. Also, this palace was cooler, which helped.

Abishag whispered, "Do you recognize these images?"

Michal said, "No, but probably Baal, Chemosh, Molech, maybe Ashtoreth—I can't tell one from another. I know it's none of our business how Solomon lives, but our city was much different under David."

They came to the birthing room where they'd both been before. They heard groans from a woman obviously in labor but who was surrounded by six women. The women stood up when Michal and Abishag entered and allowed them to approach Ahsia, who at that moment let out a scream and a curse. Michal and Abishag got down on their knees.

Michal said excitedly, "The baby is crowning! Ahsia, you're almost done. Push!"

"I can't! Ahhhhhhhhhhhhhhhhh! Curse Chemosh! *Ahhhhhhhhhhhhhh!*"

The baby's head appeared, and Abishag supported it as the rest of the baby slid out of the mother. "*Ahhhhhhhhh!*"

Abishag picked up the baby. Michal noted that the afterbirth had followed the baby out of the mother as was desirable. She applied some clean wet rags to the mother. Ahsia relaxed, exhausted.

Michal said, "Ahsia, you have a perfect son. He's beautiful!" One of Ahsia's ladies produced a cloth in which to swaddle the baby. The baby started crying. "Do you have a wet nurse?"

Another woman came forward and bared a large, full breast. The nipple was big. The baby's mouth was tiny. Still, the baby seemed to know what to do. He opened his mouth very wide and latched on.

"Ahsia, we know you're not feeling very well right now, but everything looks fine. You will heal quickly, and you have a lovely son. Very soon, you will be able to enjoy him."

One of Ahsia's ladies asked if Michal and Abishag would take refreshment. They'd missed supper and were hungry, but they declined. Neither wanted to spend any more time than necessary in the new palace.

"Can somebody direct us to Naamah? I'd just like to make sure she's feeling well. Our next visit to this palace will probably be for her."

One of Ahsia's ladies led the way to a chamber that housed several ladies. This chamber was more opulent than the birthing room. There were stools and tables and shelves, and there were statues on the shelves. There was a window, but it wasn't obvious after sunset. There were two torches on either side of the door and numerous candles on tables. Some of Naamah's ornaments glittered gold or silver in the candlelight. Michal and Abishag inspected a very pregnant Ammonite princess sitting on a stool that had a sheepskin over it. Naamah was uncomfortable and not as gracious as she might have been. She insisted she was fine, which was always good to hear. She and her ladies were having supper.

Michal and Abishag took their leave. They walked back through the corridor and out the front door, into the garden. Both took deep breaths of the unscented night air. They were silent on their way back to their own quarters.

CHAPTER 28

Year 430

I never saw my father again. He died on the battlefield, fighting Philistines. In fact, he died at Mt. Gilboa which isn't all that far from Jezreel. It's to the south and east. I heard a rumor that my father consulted a witch before he died. If he did, it was another one of those erratic bits of behavior that went against everything my father had once stood for. If my father really did this, he was desperate.

When the word came to us of my father's passing, it wasn't the news that Paltiel wanted. He retreated to his chambers for a few days. My position, and his, was tenuous, and he didn't know what to do. Paltiel eventually returned to his daily routine as if nothing had happened. He and I had been living together as husband and wife, and the community accepted us as such. If there was something we should have *done*, neither one of us knew what.

The details of my father's death spread slowly across the territories of the Twelve Tribes. We never knew what was true or what was false except for the number of people who repeated the news in the same way. There were two versions of how my father came to die. The shorter report was that he was badly wounded and fell on his own sword to avoid being killed by a Philistine. It didn't surprise me, and I didn't dwell on it. Battles are dangerous.

The other version seemed a bit more far-fetched. An Amalekite showed up to speak to David. He claimed that he delivered a death blow to my wounded father. The enemy in question was the Philistines, not the Amalekites. So whose army was this Amalekite part of? He could have been a slave, of course. There are always slaves in battle.

My father had been commissioned to wipe out the Amalekites and hadn't done a good job of it. The Amalekites had raided Ziklag and kidnapped the women and children who lived there with David and his men, though they hadn't actually killed anyone. They burned the village like typical raiders. The women expected to live out their lives as slaves. They were nearly overcome by fear. The forced march was hard on all of the prisoners. The women were advised to keep up or die. David's two wives weren't trying to protect children on this journey, but some of the women were. Ahinoam and Abigail did their best to help. The raiders and their prisoners ended up in a sort of valley that had a deep ravine to one side and was difficult to find.

I tried to find out where David's forces had been that allowed the Amalekites to come and destroy Ziklag. Did David feel that while he was in Philistine territory, he wasn't vulnerable to other enemies? It's true that my father didn't bother him there. David and his army had been negotiating with the Philistine ruler, Achish, while the Amalekites took advantage of their absence.

I also found out exactly what David and Achish had been negotiating, and I was shocked. There is irony here. David was proposing to add himself and his men to Achish's army, which was heading for Mt. Gilboa to do battle with my father. Achish thought adding David and his men to his army was a fine idea. Achish's Philistine commanders strongly disagreed. It was utter folly to use a band made up of the Twelve Tribes to do battle against the Twelve Tribes. The Philistines wouldn't budge. Achish finally ended up sending David home with David protesting all the way. Would David really have supported the Philistines over the Twelve Tribes? Over my father? I don't know and I can't know. I comfort myself by believing he really wouldn't have and my evidence was David's unwillingness to kill my father. But I don't know.

It was Achish's army that killed my father and brothers. David did not participate. He was sent back to Ziklag in a timely fashion that allowed him the chance of following the raiders. If David had followed Achish's army to Mt. Gilboa, the families and property would have been lost forever. And David may not have survived.

When David and his men returned to the devastation of Ziklag, David's men were ready to stone him. They were very, very angry that Ziklag had been left unprotected. It makes me remember my uncle Hur's admonition that somebody has to stay behind to protect the home territory. David clearly hadn't done that. They began a pursuit and happened upon a slave of the Amalekites who'd fallen ill and who'd been left behind. The slave wasn't feeling very loyal, and he gave direction to the best of his ability. David and his men found the raiders, surprised them, and won a great victory. They took back all the women and children. They took back their own items of value along with lots of other items of value, including weapons.

David avoided a mutiny that day. David was a man who inspired loyalty as a general rule, but if his men hadn't recovered their wives and children, it's not clear what would have happened. Would history have been changed? As for the Amalekites, they lost the battle, but 400 of them escaped on camels with the clothing on their backs. Another failed attempt to annihilate the Amalekites!

David was confronted soon after all this happened by an obviously unrelated Amalekite who claimed to have participated in my father's death. He brought items to David in Ziklag that lent credence to his story. He brought my father's crown and gold arm band. So he was definitely there and close enough either to my father or my father's body to take them from him. Why do leaders wear expensive jewelry into battle? My father did it. I witnessed it. And David did it too. Solomon doesn't, but then Solomon doesn't fight battles. I can tell that soldiers of other cultures wear valuable items into battle just by looking at the plunder brought back by a successful army. So the concept is fairly widespread. Does a crown rally the army around the acknowledged leader and provide a focus? If it does, it would also present a target to the enemy. I remember my father's crown, which was fairly heavy and was made of precious metals. But comparatively speaking, it was a rather plain circlet with one jewel.

All that aside, how does a stranger on a battlefield, surrounded by either soldiers of the Twelve Tribes or soldiers of the Philistines, get items of value off the battlefield and all the way to Ziklag? David said the man had a mule with two saddlebags full of flour. He buried my father's property in the flour and was successful in explaining himself to any soldiers who stopped him on the way. He was wearing old, ragged clothing in an effort not to be noticed. Still, the mule alone would have had some value if a small group of men who had weapons decided they wanted it. The whole journey must have required at least some luck.

David took ownership of the crown and the arm band but wasn't convinced that this Amalekite had helped my father to die. It was something about the way he told the story and how he obviously expected to be rewarded for eliminating the old king and clearing a path for new leadership. The Amalekite must have been quite shocked when David and his advisers immediately tore their clothing and started mourning loudly for my father.

David had a different perception of my father than one would expect, even during those times when my father was trying to kill him. Jonathan told me he referred to my father as "the Lord's anointed." He executed the Amalekite. He wasn't feeling charitable toward Amalekites at the time. My aunt made a small effort to describe a battlefield, but she really couldn't, and I've never seen one. Hallelujah! I know my father's preference, if he had to die, would have been to die in battle. My brothers—Jonathan, Malki-Shua, and Abinadab—also died on that day, though I heard no more rumors of suicide. Please understand these events happened long ago. I tell the story in the nonchalant way that people can do when the intervening years have softened the naked emotion. I did grieve at the time. Paltiel and I both grieved.

David was a politician. When he took a huge amount of plunder from the Amalekite raiders, he spread it around liberally. His men got their property back, along with a certain percentage of the gain, but David made sure the cities in the area, possibly cities that had been raided at one time or another, got portions of the spoils. One of the cities to benefit in this instance was Hebron. And it was to Hebron that David moved his entourage after abandoning Ziklag. David believed that once my father was dead, he could move out of Philistine territory.

Abner survived the defeat on Mt. Gilboa. Is it likely for a general to survive when his sovereign doesn't? I wasn't there, and the people I knew who were there were dead. I wasn't readily understanding how Abner could have lived, and since there wasn't anyone left who could tell me what had happened, I forced myself not to think about it. Even if I had become privy to some hidden truth, it wouldn't have changed anything.

My father's son, Esh-Baal, also survived, which was less surprising. He hadn't participated in the battle. As time went on, he would have found himself in a very precarious position. His family, from whom he derived protection, was dead, and in addition to that, he had survived a deposed royal family. Abner's position was similar in that he'd been attached to this same royal family in a very prominent way.

Abner did something completely unexpected and joined forces with Esh-Baal. The more I think about it, the more unlikely it seems. Abner and Esh-Baal can't have had anything in common. But my brother had something Abner needed, which was my father's name. And Abner had something my brother needed, which was military expertise and a loyal following. The two of them, along with soldiers loyal to my father, set out for Mahanaim in the east. Esh-Baal was crowned king there. The tribes of Israel weren't as united as one might have hoped, despite my father's and Samuel's best efforts. There was always a rivalry or maybe even an animosity between the northern tribes and the southern tribes. With Abner's help, my brother became king of a region that included Jezreel, Asher, Gilead, Ephraim, and Benjamin.

Of the two of them, Abner had the stronger personality. Did my brother want to be king? I think back on my father, taken away from the perfectly comfortable lifestyle of a farmer and thrust into a life of leadership, battles, and intrigue. Since my father made it plain how much he wanted to keep his status and pass it on to Jonathan, I guess he must have liked it, though he was a much stronger man than Esh-Baal. We citizens of Jezreel had some vague knowledge that the balance of power had shifted and that we had a new king. It didn't affect our daily lives. The seat of government at Mahanaim was on the other side of the River Jordan.

Samuel and my father had unified the Twelve Tribes to such a degree that they didn't war against each other. My father's death and the rise of Esh-Baal, Abner, David, and Joab changed that. For a while, Esh-Baal and Abner stayed on their side of the River Jordan. They had some understanding of David's place in the hierarchy, and they bided their time, consolidating their power. Joab had been acting as David's second-in-command for any number of years. Abner and Joab were very competitive individuals who eventually involved the armies of the Twelve Tribes in their petty rivalries. They participated in regular skirmishes.

There was an incident at Gibeon.[35] Gibeon was a good distance from Mahanaim, and it was not clear what Abner and his army were doing there unless it was a test to see what Joab would do about it. Joab wasn't long in bringing his army and confronting Abner. Gibeon had a large pool from which the residents got their drinking water. Both armies sat down and rested there, albeit on opposite sides of the pool. Abner got up to speak to Joab, and the two of them decided on some entertainment. Each army would provide its best representatives to fight hand-to-hand in front of the audience. The chosen young men got up and faced off, but the contest was never hand-to-hand. All of them, Abner's men and Joab's men, produced daggers and stabbed each other.

The rest of both armies proceeded to do battle, and Joab's army won. Abner and his men retreated toward Mahanaim. Joab's brother was specifically pursuing Abner and wouldn't stop. Abner tried to warn Asahel off, but Asahel wouldn't be warned. Abner turned around and killed him. Rumor had it that Abner was defending himself, but that wouldn't have mattered to Joab and Abishai. They were prepared to pursue the fleeing army all night, but Abner called out from a safe distance, "How long before you order your men to stop pursuing their brothers?"

---

[35] 2 Samuel 2:12–23.

Joab's brother was dead. Abner killed him, and there were witnesses to corroborate the fact. Still, the notion of the entire Twelve Tribes as brothers resonated with Joab who then blew the trumpet to call off his army. He had known Abner and Esh-Baal in Gibeah, long ago in peacetime. Were they brothers? Joab's army stood aside while Abner's army made its way across the River Jordan and back to Mahanaim.

CHAPTER 29

Year 430

Something memorable did happen while I lived in Jezreel, but it's not one of those events that I prefer to remember. Should I tell it at all? My Uncle Hur and Aunt Hadassah told stories that affected them profoundly but that their contemporaries refused to discuss. If I truly want to tell my story in any responsible way, this is part of it.

My husband was away. This was nothing new. Paltiel was a successful trader, and he traveled regularly. I went to the home of a couple in Jezreel to assist with the birth of a first child. Oftentimes, there would be another midwife to help, but this time, she couldn't come. I did the best I could by myself.

The birth was not normal. In theory, the child is born, and after the child, the mother passes the afterbirth. There is a great danger when the afterbirth is out of place, and it blocks the passage for the child. Jael was in labor for a day and a night. I believe that the child had probably died, and then Jael died. It was awful. I knew this condition was possible, but I had no training in what to do about it. I had never actually seen it. Jael's husband was beside himself. I delivered my sincere condolences and then left him alone with his extended family.

The following night, I was arrested. For those of you who remember Deborah's caution to me all those years ago, you know why. The mother was lost, the child was lost, and I found out later a cow and a calf of this same family also died that day. The cow, which was pregnant, had gotten loose and had pushed down part of the fence around my garden. She'd eaten the henbane. She delivered a stillborn calf and then died. I don't know to this day whether the townspeople associated the animal deaths with my garden. My garden, after all, had been fenced, and they couldn't have known what was in it. The dead calf was dropped not too far from the broken fence.

The grieving father and his family whipped up the community into a fury. They dragged me from my house and threw me, almost literally, into a little stone structure with a dirt floor and a locked door. I remember trying to speak and feeling somebody's filthy hand clap over my mouth. The crowd was chanting loudly and was not willing to listen to the words of a witch. I could hear the commotion through the walls but couldn't make out any words. I could also feel a cold rain seeping in. The floor was turning to mud.

I don't know how long I was there. Probably less than a week. I was locked in a dark place with no way to gauge the passing of time. If I ever learned anything about worship, it was then. I made my best efforts to pray. There was nothing else I could do there. I did get food, but not at regular intervals and not from anyone who would speak to me.

I was imprisoned long enough to just see if I might be able to tunnel under the wall. Yes, admittedly an act of desperation, dirt floor or no! There was no light. I didn't know whether it was day or night, and I didn't know how well the little hovel was guarded. The uppermost soil was malleable, and I did get an arm under the wall. The lower soil was extremely hard-packed, and my upper body strength wasn't enough to deal with it without tools. I only managed to get my hand outside the prison, and when I did, I felt a sharp blow from the handle of a knife. *Ouch!* But it wasn't the blade of a knife. Clearly, there was a guard, and clearly, my most subtle digging efforts created some amount of sound. I withdrew my arm quickly and didn't try again. Even if I could dig a tunnel large enough for my body, where would I have gone? I doubt there would have been a hiding place for a notorious person such as myself.

I have considered why I was held for days in this place. I expected to be tried as a witch, and I thought perhaps there was an effort to produce some witnesses and a judge. There must have been discussion about how to proceed, but I wasn't in a position to hear any of it.

165

When the door opened, it was drizzling. I was filthy, though that was the least of my worries. The crowd outside was still angry and still looked more like a mob than a group of citizens planning a trial. I heard maybe one or two voices speaking for me, but I have no doubt they were afraid. I had assisted in a lot of successful childbirths. But a mob thrives on fear and anger, and it believes what it believes. Facts are irrelevant.

The residents of Jezreel had dug a shallow pit away from the houses of the town. I walked in the drizzle in between two large men with some of the more intrepid townspeople following behind. I heard loud voices. I heard the words *witch* and *Beelzebub*. If the crowd was speaking in sentences, I didn't catch any complete thoughts. The men beside me were silent. They took either of my arms and dropped me into the pit. The crowd would then toss rocks down on me until I died and have a built-in place for my grave.

My husband did not suddenly and unexpectedly appear to save me, but my brother did. Esh-Baal, Abner, and a contingent of soldiers arrived to pull me out of the pit. I never thought my brother would be my defender, but in that moment, I was exceedingly glad to see him. The people of the town weren't necessarily aware that I was their new king's sister, though some of them undoubtedly knew. The presence of the soldiers caused the mob to hastily disperse.

My brother didn't address the crowd in any way. He sat on his horse, a large horse with some royal-looking trappings with an unsheathed sword across his lap. I'd never seen my brother look so commanding! Abner helped me up on a horse, and I went to visit Mahanaim for a while. It wasn't an easy journey in the rain. I was coughing and sniffling.

I remember the rain, I remember the horse, I remember crossing the River Jordan. Happily, the river wasn't high at this time, and the crossing was easy insofar as river crossings go. I do not remember dismounting. I was feverish. I remember waking up naked on the floor of a room. There was a thin rug under me. One of my brother's female slaves was ministering to me. I felt the warm water on my skin, and it was heavenly. She was cleaning me up with a wet rag, and it was quite a task. When she saw that I was awake, she motioned me to a large tub. The water had been warmed, and there were rose petals in it.

The slave woman never spoke but communicated with gestures. I didn't know at the time, but she had her tongue cut out. I tried without success to ask her name. She got me into the tub and then went to work on my hair. She washed it first and then made a valiant effort to untangle it. In the end, she did cut some of it. While I sat in the tub, she handed me a bowl of steaming tea. I had enough experience with herbs to know that there was crushed thyme in it. I can't claim to have liked the taste so much, but the hot liquid felt good on my raw throat. There was clean clothing for me. Once the anonymous slave felt I was free of vermin and comfortable, she helped me dress and showed me to a bed. I was asleep in seconds.

I was incredibly grateful for my brother's hospitality. I wasn't exactly bed-ridden, but I was weak. The opportunity to rest was just so welcome. When you can't find the strength to accomplish much, your thoughts can take over. I've spent my life mulling over relationships between people, and now I wondered about women and about slaves. We in the harems of kings really don't have a true grasp on the day-to-day realities of less-privileged women. I was a man's one wife twice, first a young David and then Paltiel. It's *entirely* different from being one of multiple wives. A woman can be beaten by her husband or father. Women are given in marriage every day to men they don't know and didn't choose. Women are taken from their families and moved to a husband's town. Women are not allowed to come and go as they wish. Do women and slaves have common ground? Do husbands ever cut their wives' tongues out? I hope not! Not that I know of.

Esh-Baal and I had a conversation about the tongueless slave.

"Esh-Baal, what happened to her?"

"I don't really know, and neither does my steward. It is awkward to own a slave who can't communicate, which is perhaps why she was sold. She didn't cost much. She does take direction well. My steward didn't ask a lot of questions, and obviously, she can't answer for herself. I need you to know, Michal, that this sort of thing doesn't happen in my household."

The household called the slave Yasmin, though nobody knew what her birth name was. I have pondered the reason for cutting out a slave's tongue, but the only thing I can think of is if she was responsible for serving at military meetings, and the company needed assurance of her silence. Am I overthinking? Maybe it was no more than revenge for some unfortunate remark. Slave owners can be cruel and impetuous. So can husbands!

Asher is a slave and a eunuch. He has been with my father's family all his life. We take battle captives and, instead of killing them, force them to serve us. Many captured boys are killed. A few are kept alive, but if they are, they are usually deprived of their ability to father children. Have any of you ever considered slaves? Or are they just pieces of furniture that you expect to be there when you want one? I listened to my aunt's story, and it made an impression on me. My sister-wives, Abigail and Ahinoam, had a similar experience. We are all one battle away from becoming enslaved!

I have had adventures. So has Asher. When my father and brothers died, he was a slave without a master. He was in Gibeah. I was in Jezreel. Asher didn't try to get to Jezreel. He attached himself to David in Hebron, or more specifically, to my brother's son, Mephibosheth. Mephibosheth is a common name. I had a half-brother named Mephibosheth, but this Mephibosheth was Jonathan's son.

When I eventually got to Hebron and found out Asher was there, I requested him for my household. Mephibosheth agreed. Asher is a very capable individual who runs my household. I am continually amazed that he is as strong as he is. He is older than I, though I'm not sure how much. I made a comment once that if my memories and my story are inaccurate, there is nobody left to protest. It's not true. There is one, though if Asher ever decided to voice an opinion, it would surprise me greatly.

I'd never visited my brother's capitol. It was a pleasant town. My brother had overseen some improvements. He gladly took some time to show me around and was quite proud of his town. I was staying in a room in his house. Esh-Ball hadn't erected a palace such as David made for himself and us. It was a large mud brick dwelling with multiple levels and with windows. Windows are such a luxury. The walls were thick enough to protect from some of the summer heat and the winter cold. If my brother's main model was my father's hall, this was a huge step up.

There were pleasant wooded areas, and there were flowers. There was even a small fish pond with shade trees around it. At the time, I'd never seen one before, and I spent some quiet hours there, just watching the fish. Once I regained some of my stamina, I went for regular walks. Esh-Baal had done very well for himself. He and his wife had a comfortable life.

Never before had I gotten to have conversations with my brother as two adults. I had to know,

"Esh-Baal, how in the world did you and Abner show up in Jezreel before I was killed? Jezreel isn't exactly nearby."

"I was actually surprised to learn that you were in Jezreel. Oh, I knew that Father had sold you, if I may, to another husband, and I knew what he got for you. You're a valuable woman, Michal! Your conversation with Father on the day he told you his intentions was the talk of the town. The old despot! You and I had our differences growing up, but I will admit to being proud of you that day. I doubt I ever once stood up to Father. Anyway, I did know that you'd left Gibeah, but I never inquired as to where.

"There was a messenger who started early one morning, and if I understand it correctly, he started out before you were even arrested. He saw the townspeople organizing into a mob against you and left immediately. As it was, we were barely in time. If you don't mind my asking, exactly what was the disturbance all about?"

"For your information, your sister is a witch. I am a midwife, Esh-Baal, and I have never refused to assist at a birth. Childbirth is risky. Many things can go wrong for the mother, for the child, for both. I did my very best. It was a long and complicated birth, and they both died.

"Have you ever seen a mob, Esh-Baal? There is no reasoning with a mob and there is no rule-of-law with a mob. We say we value witnesses and we say we value trials, but mobs don't. A mob is like an organism with no intellect but a lot of emotion. It would be nice if you don't have to deal with these situations regularly, but let me make sure I thank you for dealing with mine.

"I truly want to know if this witch still has friends in Jezreel. Are you going to tell me who?"

"Michal, you have a good understanding of what mobs do. So you must know that people who aren't part of the mob fear it. In answer to your question, yes, you do indeed have friends in Jezreel, but I'm not prepared to mention names. This sort of violence tends to burn itself out rather rapidly. Of course, in the meantime, very often, the object of the mob's wrath gets killed. You didn't. You'll go back to Jezreel and find that nothing has changed for the townspeople. Most of them will probably be embarrassed and not bring up your arrest. Things have clearly changed for you. It may be that some of your true friends will identify themselves to you."

Esh-Baal and I talked about various things. He'd read a lot and knew a lot. Esh-Baal's wife was a gracious lady, maybe not overly assertive, but then neither was Esh-Baal. The two of us got along well. Esh-Baal had neither multiple wives nor any concubines. We talked about Abner. Esh-Baal valued him but wasn't sure of his loyalty.

Insofar as our father's last battle was concerned, Esh-Baal had only Abner's explanation. It was plausible, but it wasn't provable. It was also commonly used. Abner was hit on the head and knocked unconscious. He was perceived to be dead. He regained consciousness as dusk was falling. He realized his situation and slowly and carefully made his way away from the battlefield. Esh-Baal took on the role of ruler with Abner's support. Their public relationship seemed stable, but behind closed doors, they had lots of arguments.

"I don't trust him. That's an awful thing to say. When he and I embarked on this course, it seemed the best option open to me or maybe to either of us. Does Abner want to be king? I don't know. If he does, he's subtle about it. Right now he's serving a king in the same capacity as he did under our father. Does he view me as an acceptable replacement for our father? If you asked me for specifics, I couldn't give you any. But it's this little remark and that little remark that makes me think he doesn't have a lot of respect for me.

"The soldiers, my army, if you will, are loyal to Abner. If he decided to assassinate me, I doubt they'd object. And speaking of which, he and I had words about that debacle in Gibeon. I still have no idea what he thought he was going to accomplish, but I'm frustrated with the waste of lives. And whether or not he had any choice but to kill Joab's brother, this dispute isn't over."

"Esh-Baal, were you ever anointed?"

"No. There aren't any priests in Mahanaim who would have been qualified to do it. I was crowned with a very simple gold circlet. We heard what our father's first crown was supposed to have looked like, and mine was similar. Abner crowned me. Most of the population of Mahanaim turned out, and nobody objected. My next building project will be a high place with an altar, and perhaps some priests might be persuaded to come here to live."

I stayed with Esh-Baal until Paltiel came home, and then I was escorted back to Jezreel. Once the pain and the anger of the bereaved family died down, Jezreel was peaceful again. Jezreel was usually peaceful, but the incident really left a bad taste in my mouth. Why are people so easily led? How can attitudes change overnight? I had friends in Jezreel or I thought I did. Esh-Baal assured me I still had some. My mother was never one to be ruled by emotion. She was right, but I discovered that a lot of people are perfectly happy to be swept along in the emotion of the moment.

Paltiel was appalled. He knew that his business would take him out of Jezreel again, though not necessarily any time soon. He wondered if he needed to make arrangements for me to stay in Mahanaim during his absence. Paltiel was robust but was heading into his latter years. He and anyone else his age knew that childbirth can go radically wrong in all sorts of circumstances. If the obvious solution is to blame the midwife, then there won't be any midwives. As it was, Jezreel had lost one midwife—me.

When I got back to Jezreel, my garden fence was fixed. The slaves fixed it before Paltiel got home. My garden hadn't been maintained in my absence. The henbane plant was dead, and I never tried to replace it. Other plants were dead too. Some need more water, some need less. The whole patch was weedy. I salvaged part of it and replaced other parts. I enjoy gardening. It's my opportunity to create order from disorder, and I get satisfaction from it. There is satisfaction in harvesting the fruits of my labor and eating them.

Susannah welcomed me back. In fact, since Paltiel and Ezra were both home, she organized a small party. It included Paltiel's daughter, her husband, miscellaneous children, and a slender young man I didn't know. Susannah said, "Michal, I want you to meet Hosea."

I learned that Hosea was an older friend of Susannah's son and that he was a professional messenger. He carried messages between towns and he owned a fast horse. "Hosea, you got word to my brother!"

Susannah said, "Michal, I know you intended to sleep when you got home from overseeing a childbirth that didn't go well. When you stopped here first just to talk to somebody, I saw how distraught you were. You didn't stay long and you talked about a sleeping potion. I'll assume you took one. Did you sleep through the commotion?

"I would have liked to have slept a little later into the morning, but the village was up and making a lot of noise. Early mornings, for those of us who habitually rise early, are usually fresh and quiet. That morning was different. There was tension in the air. Ezra was out of town, and I was nervous. Then I walked into the children's sleeping quarters and saw Micah up, standing still and just listening."

Micah chimed in, "The only words I could make out were *Michal* and *witch*. Everything else was noise, and there were a lot of voices. When Mother walked in, we both listened for a minute. We got very worried very quickly."

Susannah continued, "I asked Micah to go wake Hosea. Hosea agreed to carry a message and to leave immediately. I knew who your brother was. Happily, Hosea's horse hadn't had an assignment in several days, and he was well-rested. Thank you, Hosea, for a very speedy journey to Mahanaim! You didn't start a minute too soon. She's not a witch, I promise!"

I added my own thanks. I hoped I didn't look like a witch. I was wearing a blue linen sheath and a matching head covering. Suitably conservative, I hoped. Paltiel seemed to approve.

Hosea was a shy young man, but when he spoke, he said something completely unexpected. Hosea asked, "Are you really King Saul's daughter?"

"Yes, I am. I haven't seen my father in many years, and now he is dead. It all seems very long ago. I am King Esh-Baal's sister as well."

Hosea seemed to be impressed by my lineage, but I really didn't know what else to say about it. My father was a famous man, and I was his child, but I'd never lived like a princess. How do princesses live anyway? I was a businessman's wife and did the daily tasks of any other wife.

Susannah spoke up again, "Listen everyone! I have an announcement. Are you listening, Ezra? I'm pregnant!"

All of us voiced our congratulations simultaneously. Our small gathering made a lot of noise, about which the neighbors questioned Susannah and Ezra later. Paltiel was elated. Another grandchild! I loved Susannah like a sister and had nothing but well wishes for her. I had announced my retirement as a midwife rather loudly, so I made sure she knew that if she wanted me, I would be available to her. Our little party broke up soon afterwards. I couldn't help myself. Paltiel and I went back to our dwelling, and when he ventured outside to speak to one of our neighbors, I broke down and cried.

CHAPTER 30

Year 430

David and his men (and all their wives) were in Ziklag when the news came to them of my father's death. They were in the process of rebuilding their city, but with the death of my father, they decided to leave Philistine territory altogether. Ziklag was rebuilt, of course, and people still live there. Some of David's men had grown comfortable there and didn't follow him.

He and the men who went with him relocated to Hebron with their families. The men of Hebron welcomed David and anointed him king. David was declared king of the house of Judah. My father was also anointed twice. It was at this ceremony in Hebron that the elders of the city put my father's crown on David's head. David wore it that one time but, after that, had his own crown made. Solomon also designed his own crown. My father's crown and David's crown are probably moldering for all eternity in some hidden treasure room. David's crown was more elaborate than my father's, and the crown Solomon wears on state occasions is truly splendid.

Hebron was in Judah to the south, and David became king of that region upon my father's death. David and Esh-Baal had become kings at roughly the same time. They both rose after my father's death, but neither of them truly replaced my father. They contributed to the disunification of the Twelve Tribes. I am not a politician, but I did ponder whether one of them should have given way to the other for the greater good. They both guarded their pieces of the kingdom zealously.

We in Jezreel didn't care who was king of what. Our lives went on placidly, the seasons came and went. Susannah's belly grew. She retained her usual good cheer for the most part. She had an easy pregnancy. Paltiel and Ezra were making an effort to stay close to home until the baby came.

Our tranquility was shattered when we woke one morning to find about twenty soldiers on our doorstep. Twenty soldiers aren't silent. Paltiel and I did hear them as they were coming close to our dwelling. We all understood the danger of soldiers on the doorstep, but this particular group was small and wasn't actively burning anything. Abner was leading them. Paltiel stepped outside to ask what they wanted.

Abner replied, "We've come for David's wife."

Paltiel said, "Michal is my wife now. Her father accepted a bride price for her."

Abner said, "You know he had no right to do that. Saul accepted a bride price from David, too, and David was there first. He wants her back."

Paltiel asked, "What do you know about David? And when did David's business become your business? David is many miles away from Mahanaim."

I heard everything. What in the world was going on with Abner? How had his life become so inextricably linked to mine? I hadn't forgotten being forcibly yanked from my home in Gibeah and sent to Jezreel with a stranger. I hadn't forgotten being rescued from a pit in Jezreel, either.

Abner was supposed to be supporting my brother in Mahanaim, and here he was, ostensibly escorting me to Hebron in David's service. What happened? If he had some knowledge that David wanted me back, he was clearly negotiating with David, probably at my brother's expense. David wanted me back? Really? How incredibly unexpected! Abner had a reputation for ruthlessness. He also had a contingent of soldiers.

I stepped outside. I had to at least try. I announced loudly, "I'm not going."

Abner laughed. The soldiers found a horse for me, and I repeated, "I'm not going!" Abner dismounted along with two of his armed men.

"Michal, no one is asking for your opinion. There are various ways this task can be accomplished. You have heard discussion before of tying you to a horse, and that would be one way. It would be very uncomfortable, though, not that it matters to me. I am heading for Hebron, and so are you. Do you, Paltiel, wish to argue with my soldiers?"

Needless to say, the presence of horses and soldiers in our peaceful neighborhood caused those living near us to come out of their houses to see what was happening. This scene was so familiar. I had lived it before.

I said, "Wait. I need to get something."

Abner advised me, "Don't worry about your belongings. There will be ample possessions for you at the end of the journey."

I ran back into the house and retrieved my mother's bowl. The neighbors watched as Abner hefted me up on a tall horse. My horse was placed more or less in the middle of the company, and we all headed south.

Paltiel was devastated. He was sobbing. He tried to follow the caravan, and his son and some of his friends joined him. Abner rather forcefully sent them all home. They wouldn't have kept pace with us anyway. I wasn't sobbing, but I was shocked. It may be true that Paltiel was not the husband of my dreams, but he was kind to me, and I was happy. I loved his family. I had spent some labor over a garden that was producing, and I wondered if anyone would take care of it. Susannah might value it. She'd at least be able to identify everything in it! Before we got too far away, I asked Abner for the opportunity to speak to my brother. Mahanaim was way out of our way and across a river.

Abner asked, "Why do you want to speak to him? Do you think I am making this journey without your brother's approval? David asked Esh-Baal for your return, and Esh-Baal sent me."[36]

I was silent. I had loved David the way Paltiel loved me, but it was a *long* time ago. I didn't know what kind of a reception I'd get. I'd spent the last several years as another man's wife, though I was

---

[36] 2 Samuel 3:15–16.

bringing no children with me. I knew I would be going into an environment that included multiple wives, and I was quite apprehensive about that. Years ago, there were two wives. Were there more than that now?

Abner and I had a long ride-and-walk together. I have ridden horses now and then, but it's never been my favorite form of transportation. Riding made me hurt in places that I'd rather not talk about. Abner and I rode together, walked together, and talked together over many miles. So I can repeat Abner's impressions of what had gone before. If Esh-Baal had different impressions, and he probably did, I wouldn't know. Abner told me he was taking me to Hebron with Esh-Baal's blessing, though I would have liked to ask Esh-Baal.

Abner told me a little about my father's last battle on Mt. Gilboa. He said, "Our army was doomed from the moment Achish and his troops arrived. They must have outnumbered us, two-to-one. Achish himself was a formidable fighter. Did you know Achish killed Jonathan? Jonathan was a formidable fighter, too, but he took a wound to his sword arm early on, and he was rendered less effective by it.

"I know your father outlived Jonathan, but I didn't see his final hours. At some point, I lost my helmet, and after that, I took a hard blow to the head. I didn't have any other personal knowledge of the battle until I woke up surrounded by the dead. By the dead sons of the Twelve Tribes, actually.

"I was lucky the sun was setting. I laid still for another hour until I had the cover of darkness. Everything was silent. I knew the danger in staying where I was. The dead would be stripped, but probably not until morning. My sword was still in my hand, and for that, I was grateful. It was the only thing I took from the battlefield. Once it was dark, I slowly crawled away. I rested for a day in a cave. I made my way back to Gibeah. That's where I met up again with Deborah and Esh-Baal."

"How long did it take you to get to Gibeah? Did you walk the whole way from Mt. Gilboa? I know your head was wounded, but what about the rest of you?"

"It's true I didn't feel well, and it was also true that I didn't feel it would be wise to be seen. It must have taken me a month, going rather slowly and furtively. All the while Saul was king, Gibeah led a charmed life. When I finally reached it, it was the same orderly town it's always been. I was relieved. The traumatic experience was mine, but Gibeah was unaffected, and the people who were there when I left were still there.

"Esh-Baal and I hatched a plan. I look back and wonder how members of the defeated army came to be a king and a general of another region. Ironic! It's true that your father's army suffered a huge defeat, but we found out that there were survivors. The survivors, knowing that your father and I came from Gibeah, made their way there in the hopes of finding a rallying point. Between Esh-Baal and myself, we were able to convince these men to follow Saul's son. At that point, Esh-Baal and I had very few choices. We took a big chance and succeeded."

I asked Abner about Deborah and found out that she'd died. The trek from the region of Gibeah to Mahanaim was a long one. Mahanaim was way to the north and east and required crossing the River Jordan. They crossed at Gilgal. Crossing a river is never easy. Deborah got soaked and then couldn't get warm. The weather was bad. It rained day after day, and it was a cold rain. Eventually, it snowed. Deborah took ill along that journey and didn't recover. She was buried along the way. I wanted to ask Abner if he and Deborah had ever had any children, but that's always a tricky question, especially if the answer is no. I held my sometimes spontaneous tongue.

Up until Abner and I had a chance to chat, I didn't realize that the trip to Hebron was more complicated than simply returning an errant wife to David. Abner and my brother had quarreled. Oh, they always had their disagreements, but this particular quarrel wasn't likely to be mended. It culminated with Abner switching sides and offering his services to David in an effort to reunite the Twelve Tribes. This effort would oust my brother. If Abner was switching sides, so was I. I was only a woman, and no one required me to have any code of ethics. I was torn. Like Paltiel, my brother had been kind to me. I contemplated the concept of the Lord's anointed and knew that Esh-Baal hadn't been anointed. David had. Was David the new Lord's anointed?

So what provoked an irrevocable disagreement? A woman, of course! It wasn't widely known, but Rizpah had followed her lover's son to Mahanaim. She had taken her minor children with her, and she'd made a niche for herself. Why hadn't I met her when I'd spent some time in Mahanaim? I would have loved to have seen her.

Rizpah had actively avoided me. It wasn't that she disliked me, but she wasn't anxious to explain herself. She was the concubine of a former king. Was she important? She didn't know and wasn't taking any chances. When Esh-Baal and Abner left town, she followed.

Abner said, "At first I didn't realize Rizpah was part of our company. She wasn't trying to stand out, but it was hard not to. We had very few women among us, and Rizpah had children. Deborah tried to help her, and that was when I became aware that she'd joined us. Once I knew she was with us, I, too, lent a hand when necessary. It was a hard journey, and as I said, it killed Deborah. Rizpah was resilient. She protected her children and they survived. I never heard a word of complaint from her. Sometimes along the journey, I realized that I loved her. She wasn't young, and she'd borne many children, but to me, she was beautiful."

The relationship was a secret for a while, but when Esh-Baal found out, he was livid. He and Abner had a shouting match that reverberated across Mahanaim. Even back when I visited, my brother wondered if Abner wanted to be king. There is some overt symbolism in claiming the previous leader's woman or women, and it wasn't anything that Esh-Baal could just be expected to ignore. Abner knew full well why my brother was incensed. Esh-Baal took offense, and when he did, Abner took offense.

I am still trying to figure out if Abner had enough of being the power behind the throne and if he sought out an excuse to leave. Abner was a natural leader. Esh-Baal was not. He had a much more subtle nature. I don't know whether or not Esh-Baal, and his followers thought Abner would be back. Perhaps Esh-Baal believed he was happily rid of a threat to his authority. Abner had taken only twenty soldiers, so most of Esh-Baal's army remained in Mahanaim. And if Abner didn't go back? What about Rizpah? I knew my brother wouldn't take out his frustrations on a woman, and Rizpah would be safe either way.

Rizpah remained in Mahanaim with her children. I was pleased for her that she'd found another love, though I wondered what she thought of her love's new direction. He was heading for the court of a rival king. What would that mean to her future? Until Rizpah had taken a powerful man as a lover, nobody else took notice of her. But to Esh-Baal, she was the former king's woman and a symbol of his power. He hadn't been sure of Abner for a long time, and this relationship seemed like overt rebellion. But what about Rizpah as a person? She was still alive. She still had needs and wants. She hadn't asked to be symbolic of anything. Abner was prepared to care for her.

I have no idea what was going through David's mind about the whole situation, but what kind of reception could Abner hope to get from him? Abner had been highly instrumental in setting up a king as a rival to David, not to mention the fact that he'd been head of the armies of my father, chasing David hither and yon. Esh-Baal's forces and David's forces had been fighting each other since my father's death.

I pondered my place in this whole relocation effort and concluded that it wasn't about me at all. Abner may have thought he was controlling the game, but I wonder. Was the goal nothing more profound than removing Esh-Baal's best defense from his perimeter? David could be subtle too. David played the ends against the middle and let others do his killing for him.

On his way to Hebron, Abner did what he could in the towns we passed to undermine Esh-Baal to the residents. I overheard some of it, and it made me feel bad, though I never spoke out. I assume that Abner believed the things he was saying, and it's entirely possible that his words were by-and-large true. I have contemplated truth and what it is. I have considered half-truths. It occurs to me that half-truths might be worse than lies. Abner was repeating the negative things he knew about my brother and leaving out everything else. His words painted a rather bleak picture of an inept ruler.

The journey to Hebron ended at long last, and I was deposited at a large house where David's wives lived. I had my priorities, and the first was a bath. The other wives observed my arrival, which was understood, and of course I wasn't able to disguise my extremely disheveled state. All I could do was fix it as quickly as possible. I got a tub of not freezing water and a change of clothing. Two slaves took charge of my hair. A bath can make a huge difference in a person's outlook, and it gave me some fortitude. I was ready to meet the family.

David had a total of six wives, plus me and six sons. As always, I enjoyed playing with the children. Amnon was the oldest. He seemed like a serious child. He was quiet and shy, and looked for approval. Kileab was the second-oldest. He was loving and friendly but didn't seem to be in the best of health. He seemed fragile. Absalom was the third-oldest son, and he was full of personality. He was outgoing and mischievous. He was always testing the boundaries and always seeking forgiveness. He was a very handsome child with a beaming smile and thick curly hair. He never had difficulty getting pardon. The other children were younger and didn't have such well-defined personalities, but they seemed willing to be cuddled. I happily did the cuddling.

I thought about my future on the journey to Hebron and knew that being part of a group of wives would be very different from my experiences so far. David called me to his bed the first night I was back. He had changed greatly. I had changed greatly. We tried to make conversation, which had come easily to us in our younger days.

David asked, "How was your journey?"

I answered, "It was fine. It was long, but the weather was decent. Your servants were good enough to draw a lovely bath for me and find me a change of clothing. I'm very glad not to be facing more traveling tomorrow. David, I have to know, why am I here? You must know that I haven't been faithful to you."

"Michal, Michal! You are the wife of my coming-of-age and are valuable to me. I have friends in Gibeah. I know under what circumstances you were sent to Jezreel. I know there was nobody to protect you or speak for you. I also know that you were unwilling to return to me."

"I didn't feel I could face you. Maybe more to the point, I was completely unprepared to take my place among your many wives. At the time, I didn't know how many. I knew early on about Ahinoam and Abigail."

"Michal, you will always be my wife, and I'm glad to have you here. I almost said glad to have you back, but you're not back. You've never lived in Hebron before. The clothing my servants found for you is becoming, but it's time to get it off."

David's mouth found mine, and I gasped. His kiss was warm and familiar. My new clothing slid right off. I cannot pretend I didn't get pleasure from David's body. His older body was broader and very muscular. It was similar but was different. I did quite a bit of gasping that night. Both of us drifted off to sleep, satisfied, though when I woke up, he was gone.

Passion is good. I like passion. But I was hoping to regain the earlier emotional intimacy, and I was disappointed. It's hard not to just feel like a piece of property. David had gotten his own back. I wanted to hear him say, "I love you," but he didn't. He valued me. Is that enough? Was I a piece of silver or gold? I didn't get any particular attention after that, though it was probably true that I warmed David's bed as often as any of the other wives.

David was now marrying princesses or one, at least—Maacah, the daughter of the king of Geshur. This is the Maacah who still lives with us in the women's quarters. Ironically, David told me that when he was living in Ziklag, Achish, king of Gath, would question him every so often about which peoples he was raiding. David would always say he was raiding the Negev of Judah or the Negev of the Kennites when, in fact, at some of those times, he was raiding Geshur. David's raids were brutal. It's easy in peacetime to be critical, but in times of war, the goal was total destruction. David had a tenuous alliance with Achish, and he couldn't afford for word to get back to Achish that David wasn't conducting raids where he said he was. There was peace between David and Geshur after Maacah came to the women's quarters.

Her son, Absalom, was beautiful, outgoing, and reckless. Maacah also gave David a daughter, Tamar, who was and is equally beautiful. I was privileged to assist with Tamar's birth. Some of David's wives were more accepting of me than others. Maacah and Haggith were openly antagonistic early on. They despised my childless state and made constant remarks to that effect. It's not easy living with a group of women when everyone else is a mother. One starts to believe that the fault is one's own. It was doubly awkward because both David and Paltiel had children.

I am conscious of using the word *fault*, and I'm remembering my aunt's story. She used the word too. What is *fault*? And do people on the outside of the perceived "fault" have the right or the intelligence to judge? During these days, right after I'd been forcibly uprooted (again), I felt the pain of not quite fitting in. I never experienced a pregnancy, but children seemed to like me. I gained some level of acceptance just for assisting with childbirth and then later helping to care for the children.

Life in Hebron was quite different for me. It was my first experience as a member of a harem. Living in a women's quarters took some getting used to. I lived in one for most of my sojourn in Hebron and all of my sojourn in Jerusalem. I didn't know it at the time, but Hebron was an orientation of sorts. Our building wasn't guarded, and the wives came and went as we wished. Everything was less formal and less regimented than the lives we came to live in Jerusalem.

CHAPTER 31

Year 430

At the time I arrived in Hebron, David's wives were Ahinoam, Abigail, Maacah, Haggith, Abital, and Eglah. We were a small group. All of the women, with the exceptions of Maacah and Haggith, were daughters of the tribes of Israel. As you might expect, Maacah and Haggith, two foreigners thrown together, formed a loose alliance on that basis. There wasn't a royal palace in Hebron. David was a very new king and spent more time fighting battles than developing a capital. David had a dwelling, pretty much like the dwellings of his men, and we wives occupied a large building of our own.

Until I arrived, Ahinoam was the First Wife, which came with its own prestige. She knew about me and must have faced my arrival with a certain amount of consternation. However, she was the mother of David's oldest son, Amnon, which offered her some security and had its own prestige.

On the journey to Hebron, I was pondering exactly how to make my entrance, if you will, into this group that I hadn't chosen. I was very much aware that I was the first woman David had married, and I wanted to be recognized. I was also hoping to be liked. Diplomacy! It didn't hurt that David called me immediately to his bed.

The following morning, upon my return to the women's quarters, Ahinoam had vacated her preferred sleeping space in my favor. I didn't ask her to. She did. I felt I was entitled to First Wife status and First Wife privileges, though I was hoping to achieve all of that without making enemies. Ahinoam had an inbuilt sense of justice, for lack of a better term. Essentially, if she wasn't actually the

First Wife, she wasn't interested in pretending. And she was a very gracious, very accommodating lady. The daughters of the tribes are raised to accommodate, though, more specifically, to accommodate their husbands. At the time David married Ahinoam and Abigail, both of them knew that David already had a wife.

Ahinoam was from Jezreel, and she and I had many discussions about the place. Clearly, when she married David, she hadn't expected to be one of many wives, though also clearly, men in general were known to take more than one wife. She greatly respected her husband and loved her son. But there were things about Jezreel and her childhood that she missed.

Abigail's status had dropped from Second Wife down to Third Wife with my arrival. Abigail was another gracious lady, but she was a lot less submissive. She was a widow who had been married to a wealthy drunk. Early on, she'd taken a decisive role in the running of her husband's estate. She was from Carmel. I asked her once if she'd seen my father's monument. She looked at me blankly and asked,

"What monument? Oh, wait a minute. There is a road or, maybe more accurately, a hard-packed path that lies between Carmel and Gilgal. Last time I went that way, I noticed a pile of dressed stones along the path. I asked several people, and nobody knew how dressed stones came to lie in a heap there. Was there a monument there once? The stones hadn't put themselves there. The stones, even when I lived in Carmel, were being pillaged for building materials, and it wouldn't surprise me if they're all gone by now."

I answered, "I heard that my father built a monument at Carmel long ago to celebrate one of his victories. I didn't see it, but I heard about it from Abner, among others. Our people aren't known for building monuments, and Abner wasn't impressed."

My father's tribute to himself was very short-lived! Abigail was the mother of David's second-oldest son. I have to believe that life in the women's quarters was difficult for Abigail. She wasn't used to sitting idle. She may have been raised to accommodate, along with the rest of us, but she'd learned that she was competent. She never complained, but life in the harem was far from exhilarating. Still, she had her son who was her joy. She had no children with her former husband.

When Abigail married David, her life changed greatly. Oh, David was incredibly handsome, and Abigail's late husband was not. But when she married David, she left her luxurious life in Carmel and went with David to Ziklag. She met Ahinoam, and the two of them had an adventure together, which forged a bond between them. David, Ahinoam, and Abigail shared quarters in Ziklag.

Both Ahinoam and Abigail agreed that life in Ziklag wasn't ideal. The city itself was dilapidated, and the men who might have improved its buildings were rarely home. There was also the question of *which* men. David's ragtag followers were anywhere from 400 to 600 in number. David's nephews were among them, but many men gravitated to David who didn't have a lot to offer and who were less-than-ethical individuals. Some had been cheated out of what was theirs and left with nothing. Others were the cheaters who had been found out and were running for their lives. Some were disgraced soldiers.

Ahinoam and Abigail were both thrilled to leave Ziklag, its shabbiness, and its questionable culture behind them. Obviously, now there was also the task of rebuilding it, which was left to those who stayed. Abital and Eglah were very young and hadn't really experienced life outside of their father's house or their husband's house. They were both mothers early on, and they both seemed content. They weren't vying for status within the harem, and they seemed to accept their situation without question. Their attention was fully on their children. Even back then, I was the oldest person in the women's quarters!

Comparatively speaking, seven wives is a small number. But it's still enough for conflicts to arise. Is it common to dislike another person at first sight? I can honestly say that I didn't dislike Maacah at first sight, but she thoroughly disliked me. I didn't do anything to her unless she objected to my being First Wife. It didn't take me long to return her dislike. All of David's wives were beautiful, with the possible exception of me. Maacah actually looked a little like David. She had that thick, wavy, dark hair that glowed red in certain lights, and she had incongruous blue eyes. Her son, Absalom, and her daughter, Tamar, both had blue eyes. Her skin was a little darker than David's.

Haggith was an entirely different type. Haggith had pale skin and pale, light brown, very straight hair. She had almond-shaped green eyes. She was an exotic beauty. Maacah was a conventional beauty. I had an impression that Haggith, the mother of David's fourth son, Adonijah, wasn't terribly smart. If she were removed from Maacah's influence, she and I might even have gotten along. I didn't dislike her because she wasn't substantial enough to dislike. But she allowed Maacah to do her thinking for her.

Maacah and I were the only king's daughters of the group. I've admitted that I wasn't born into a royal line. Maacah was, and she delighted in it. She could name her forebears going back ten generations. She viewed me as an impostor as I sometimes viewed myself. But my father *was* indeed a king. He directed armies, personally fought battles, and he governed. He just wasn't born to the role nor did he establish a dynasty.

Maacah, with Haggith's approval, set out to make my life miserable. The other four wives refused to get involved. I would have welcomed any support that came my way, but at least at first, none did. In the beginning, the abuse was verbal. I was the "Barren Bitch" and the dried-up old woman. I desperately wanted to get pregnant and prove them wrong, but that didn't happen.

I am certain Maacah put some noxious substance in my food one day. She was standing much closer to me than she usually did in the dining area. She moved away when I noticed. But I ended up with diarrhea for a couple of days. I spent quality time in the privy during those days, and it gave me time to think.

Abigail had done something odd. Graceful, courteous Abigail bumped into me hard enough to send the bowl flying out of my hand. It shattered all over the floor, and a slave arrived immediately to clean up the mess. Abigail apologized profusely and several times. She never said another word about it. I wondered greatly about the substance that I didn't taste and, in the end, that I didn't even eat much of. The food itself was heavily spiced. I was utterly convinced that Maacah contaminated my food, but how much did she know about herbs? What would have happened if I'd have finished the serving?

The mind takes over when a person dwells on something. I was thinking too much about how evil Maacah was, and I started plotting. When Maacah came to Hebron, she brought various items as her dowry. Her pride and joy was a heavy, ornate, metal shelf that stood right near her sleeping area. She displayed her smaller possessions on it, and it allowed her bed behind it to feel slightly more private.

One quiet afternoon, when Maacah and Haggith were walking outside, I walked into the kitchen. Surprisingly, the kitchen was empty. I found a jar of grease, and I had a malicious idea. I spread the grease on the floor in the vicinity of Maacah's sleeping area. Grease is shiny, but unless one is looking for it, it blends with the tones of the floor. Let's just say I was successful. When Maacah returned, she was walking fast as she usually did. She hit that grease spot just right and went flying into her metal shelf. I wasn't watching. I restrained myself and joined the rest of the women after we all heard her scream. I arrived just in time to see a small household god fall off the top shelf and hit Maacah in the head.

The shelf itself was heavy and stable. It just wobbled a bit. Maacah didn't break any bones, but she sported a magnificent black eye for a while among other bruises. She glared daggers at me, and I glared right back at her. Neither of us said a word.

There was a grassy area outside our communal dwelling with a few shade trees. One of the slaves had planted flowers and made it quite attractive. It was a small garden, but it still qualified as a garden. We all walked there, just to get out and for exercise.

I went out one warm one evening, trying to get away from the closeness of the house and the other wives. When I walked outside, they were all still in the dwelling. I was alone, at least briefly, and I was enjoying it. I was very startled when I was hit in the back with a rock. I turned around immediately and, of course, didn't see anyone. I did see another rock go whizzing by my head.

That same night, when I came back into the house, I started to get ready for bed. I was about to say the house was quiet, but it wasn't really. The wives weren't noisy or boisterous, but the small children could be. There were six small boys in the house at the time and two small girls. There were slaves and nursemaids.

I spoke some sort of greeting to Abigail and Ahinoam, nothing in particular, probably just goodnight. And I went to my bed and for some reason actually looked at it before climbing in. I noticed a very slight movement under my blanket, and I whipped the blanket off the bed. I saw a sleepy snake. I forgot my mother's early training regarding public displays of emotion, and I screamed! The feud, if I can call it that, had escalated. Oh, the snake didn't bite me. If I'd gotten into bed without looking, it probably would have. A male slave arrived and knocked it onto the floor with a stick, dispatched it, and got rid of the carcass.

I've admitted to dwelling on negative thoughts from time to time, but we in the women's quarters got a big distraction from our paltry disagreements. Kileab, Abigail's son, became ill. If I want to sound snotty—and under the circumstance, that's not something I should want—Kileab was ill a lot. The usual scenario was that Abigail would spend a night or two at Kileab's bedside, hold his hand, and cover his forehead with cool, wet cloths. Abigail sought my advice this time when Kileab seemed sicker than usual.

There are some who perceive me as a healer. I can administer herbal remedies, and I know a little about plants. But what I do is alleviate symptoms. I do not cure ailments. There is a difference. I can maybe patch up a wound if the soldier-in-question comes to me early on. Wounds that become septic are beyond my capabilities. I have never cut off a soldier's limb nor assisted, though field surgeons do that. There is no guarantee that the soldier will survive such a shock, and many don't. But you'll see the occasional one-armed or one-legged soldier. A putrid wound is a death sentence. I assist with childbirth, minor accidents, and digestive ailments.

I will be the first to admit that illness is a big mystery. They say that fevers come from the air. I only wonder, if that's true, why we don't all have fevers? Did Kileab breathe some specific air to which the rest of us weren't exposed? Are some bodies heartier than others?

When Abigail came to me, Kileab was very ill. He was very hot and seemed to be delusional. He was flailing and seeing things the rest of us didn't see. He would make sounds, but the sounds weren't necessarily words. By the way, there were five of us around Kileab's bed. Maacah and Haggith were absent, but the rest of us did what we could to support Abigail. We put cool wet cloths on Kileab's forehead and his upper body. Abigail lifted up his head, and we tried to get him to drink some water.

I started mixing poppy juice. I knew that my actions were being scrutinized, and despite the fact that I should have been focused on Kileab, I had some concerns for myself. I had enemies in the harem and wanted my actions to be public and as well-understood as possible. I was also terribly afraid there was nothing I could do for Kileab.

I mixed the poppy syrup in front of all the ladies, and I mixed it with somewhat more water than usual. After all, this was a child. In front of the group, I put the syrup to my own lips and tasted it. I asked if Abigail or anyone else wanted to taste the mixture, and nobody did. I explained that poppy juice was not a cure for anything. It would help an ill person sleep. Sleep can be a cure in that it can help the body to heal itself. I tried hard to make it clear that I wasn't a witch and that the poppy juice was just an herbal concoction.

With Abigail's permission, I got Kileab to drink a bit of the poppy juice. In just a few minutes, he seemed to settle. He stopped babbling. I got up, left the group, and asked a slave to get word to the child's father, David. Then we all sat around Kileab's bed and conversed in low tones, but mostly, we watched.

David came, and with him was Joab. David sat down next to Abigail. Joab watched on the periphery. Kileab's breathing slowed. It became labored. And it stopped. Abigail let out a loud wail. We all wailed. David helped her up and took her back to his quarters. It is *so hard to* watch a child die! Two slaves came to remove Kileab's body and to prepare it for burial. We all grieved for Kileab and for Abigail.

After David left with Abigail, I made a point to speak to Joab privately. Did I think Joab could do something about my situation to which I had contributed? Probably not, but I wanted somebody on the outside to know that somebody on the inside was trying to kill me. Joab asked me who, and I relayed my suspicions. For those of you who are accustomed to the rule of law, understand suspicions count for a lot, especially if they're the suspicions of anyone in power. My experience in Jezreel taught me well about suspicions! Our culture didn't necessarily require proof-positives, which were difficult to obtain. I should have been apprehensive about naming a possibly innocent person, but I really disliked Maacah. It wasn't just about dislike. There wasn't anyone else in my circle who had the negative attitude, the access, and the nerve. I described my experiences to Joab, and he didn't offer an opinion. That wasn't unusual. Joab didn't ever say much.

Abigail was absent for about a week. We didn't know when to expect her back, but one late afternoon, when I'd come in from walking in the garden, I heard voices. I could identify Maacah's voice easily, but the other voice was softer and lower. Maacah said very clearly in her accented Hebrew, "You must denounce her. She killed your child!"

The other voice simply replied, "Kileab was ill long before Michal arrived."

"Why did you let that witch near your son?"

Abigail said, "I was the one who asked for her help. My son died, but that doesn't make Michal a witch."

Maacah went on, "You know she's been tried as a witch once, don't you?"

Abigail said, "To hear her tell it, 'tried' is an overstatement. Accused, yes." I heard soft sobbing and soft footsteps heading out of the room.

When I entered, Maacah was alone. "Witch," she hissed at me.

I had to ask. "Where were you and Haggith when Kileab was dying? How did you conclude that there was witchcraft involved? You weren't there!"

Maacah fastened one of her best hateful glances on me and left. I did find out where Maacah and Haggith had been that day but not from either of them. Asher heard it from one of their slaves, and he told me. They went to the high place of a goddess of Geshur. They left offerings of fruit and grain. At the time, I was a little shocked.

Everyone knew that the nations around us worshipped differently than we did, but it was a dangerous thing to do within the borders of the Twelve Tribes. Those days seem distant now.

Some of you may know that Solomon has actually built high places for the gods of Ammon and Moab.[37] I do not approve, of course, and I am grateful that the altars of Chemosh and Molech are at least outside of Jerusalem. I don't know what they look like. I do know that they didn't require the massive building project that Elohim's temple did, so perhaps they are essentially outdoor shrines with altars.

All of you have experienced great religious tolerance in this land that has adopted you, but understand Solomon's father was not so tolerant. In those days, being a foreigner wouldn't have absolved a person of responsibility. Foreigners living within our tribal boundaries were expected to conform. We of the Twelve Tribes worship one god, Elohim, and in times past, there have been severe penalties for those who didn't. It was in Maacah's and Haggith's best interests to be discreet.

So what did I do with the knowledge? Would you be surprised if I said nothing? I have been the one who has been tattled on both by my brother in our youth and by any wives who thought my conversations with Joab were illicit. I talked to Joab a lot more than some people thought was appropriate, but he was a childhood friend.

In my own experience with the bearing of tales, it hasn't felt to me like the bearer got any particular rewards for it. There were even times when the authority figure who was tattled to would have preferred not to know. Part of me would have reveled in getting Maacah into trouble. But part of me was also certain David wouldn't thank me. What would he have done about it? Put her to death? She was the mother of two of his children. Her father was still alive and still king of Geshur. It would have been awkward.

A couple of days later, I was called to David's quarters. It was dusk. It was light enough to find my way easily to a place I'd been before. I was crossing the garden when I heard hurried footsteps

---

[37] 1 Kings 11:7.

behind me. A young man was walking quickly, and when he saw that I was aware of him, he started running toward me. He got a little closer, and I saw the knife. I did the obvious thing and ran, but I wasn't much of an athlete. Nor was I dressed for running. The sandals I'd selected were appropriate for a liaison with a king, but not for covering ground quickly. It didn't take the young man long to get close enough to grab me from behind. I couldn't see the knife but felt it. I flung myself to the side as best I could, but my assailant was very strong. The knife was headed for my throat, and it managed to gash my face at the jawline.

What do people think when they're about to die? I'm told that people envision their regrets, and I think that's possible. I felt cheated. I hadn't lived long enough to have children. I felt a vague dissatisfaction with my life. I felt blood running down my face, but I didn't feel pain.

Suddenly, I didn't feel pressure from the assassin's body. I found myself standing alone in the garden, screaming, while the erstwhile assassin lay on the ground with an arrow protruding from his back. Joab and another soldier whom I didn't know were walking toward me. I was bleeding all over the new garment I'd put on for a rendezvous with my husband. Joab managed to tear off a bit of the bottom of his tunic and handed it to me. Even under the circumstances, I had to consider whether or not it was clean! I was quite near David's quarters by this time, and Joab asked, "Michal, what are you doing here?" I told him David had summoned me, and he responded, "No, he didn't. But we will head to David's quarters now."

I was taken into David's quarters where I met with a field surgeon. Let me state for the record, being the patient is a frightening and unique experience. The needle was as large as the horn of an ox! Well, not quite. The surgeon put the needle briefly into a flame before addressing my face with it. He also poured spirits on the wound, which stung badly. The surgeon sighed and advised me that I'd have a scar. I do. Depending on my mood, I either let my hair disguise it or pull my hair back away from it. You've all seen my scar.

I heard Joab and David talking softly in the background. Joab advised, "She can't live there anymore, or at least not if Maacah lives there."

David agreed and pulled me out of the women's quarters in Hebron. The two men also discussed the failed assassin. Joab didn't know him. His dress was that of Geshur, and Joab thought he might have been one of Maacah's retainers. He made a remark to David about the would-be assassin's ineptitude, and David retorted, "Then how did he get close enough to cut her?"

I thought about the age of the young man. He probably hadn't seen battle. But then how much expertise does it take to kill an unarmed woman? I'd be very dead without intervention.

I hadn't really been paying attention to the conversation because I was in pain and because of the surgeon's enormous needle. But I did look up at David's raised voice, and I did notice Joab's embarrassment. Joab muttered that his first arrow had missed. He murmured an apology to David, and seconds later, a louder one to me. My face was being stitched, and I didn't respond.

I never went back to the women's quarters in Hebron. David moved me to a small personal house in the vicinity of his. After the field surgeon finished, Joab escorted me there. I remember watching Joab's broad back as he left. When a person saves your life, it's an intimate experience.

Until we all left Hebron, I lived there alone with two slaves, which actually suited me fine. I missed Abigail and Ahinoam somewhat. The other four wives weren't friends of mine. I like children, but I didn't miss the chaos they create. With no children in the building, my new space was tranquil.

As became abundantly clear later on, this sort of solution was typical of David. Where his family was concerned and when problems arose, he wasn't good at facing them directly. He had no desire for my death and did accept the notion that it was his responsibility to protect me. So he did, but all without ever addressing Maacah.

CHAPTER 32

Year 430

Abner left Esh-Baal and offered his services to David. I can give a firsthand account of the desertion because I was there. I accompanied Abner to Hebron and knew about the feast that David prepared for him and his soldiers on their arrival.

Interestingly enough, Joab wasn't there. Joab had led a number of David's men on a raid, and they'd returned victorious. They brought back a lot of booty. Joab expected a big welcome and celebration, but he and his men were barely acknowledged. They arrived as the slaves were cleaning up the banquet David had just given. Abner left the banquet with the promise that he could bring all Twelve Tribes together under David's rule.

"You did *what*?" Joab's voice boomed out across the neighborhood.

"Quiet, soldier! You are not in command here." David's voice was loud, but not as loud as Joab's.

"Maybe I should be, *Your Highness*. If Abner had had the opportunity to take your life, you would be dead. He comes to you now from the northern tribes who have behaved like enemies and from your archrival, and you think you can trust him?"

"I have to try. I don't know how powerful Esh-Baal really is without Abner. If there were a way to unite the Twelve Tribes as they were under King Saul without bloodshed, I have to try. Abner says he can deliver the northern tribes to be united with the southern tribes."

"David, David, David, please listen to me. If Abner had any desire to unite the tribes, he would have worked toward it upon the death of King Saul. He doesn't. He and Esh-Baal caused the division in the first place. Something is going on with him, possibly between him and Esh-Baal, and he's using you. Can you ever trust anyone who betrays his lord and goes over to the enemy? He's a spy!"

"Can any individual really be required to pick a side and remain there for the rest of his life? Things happen, and good soldiers can be offended enough or appalled enough to leave. Joab, I have to try. If something happened, I don't know what. I have let Abner come in peace and let him depart in peace, and unless his actions contradict what he told me, you and I will leave it at that. I understand that he killed your brother, and I'm sorry."

I thought about Abner and Esh-Baal. They were so different. Maybe their partnership could never have been better than temporary.

The desertion of Abner brought about the death of my brother or at least I looked at it that way. I learned later on that the annals were recording my brother's name as Ishbosheth or man of shame. It made me sad. Esh-Baal was an honorable man for the most part, just not much of a soldier. But he was killed in his bed and was beheaded by his murderers, and maybe that's where the "shame" entered in. He died a bad death. The two men who decapitated my brother brought his head to Hebron and to David. I have thought about rotting flesh before and the impression it makes at the end of a journey. I personally find rotting flesh disgusting, but soldiers seem to take it in stride.

I grieved in private. I grieved for Esh-Baal. Then my mother's kind words about him returned to haunt me, and pretty soon, I was grieving for her. I did not go to supper that night. I had a little house to myself, and that night, I was blessed to have privacy.

People who committed murder of a member of my father's family expected to get thanks from David. David was unconventional. It was never a good idea to admit to killing any of Saul's family. The nations around us would certainly approve of the annihilation of the displaced royal family, but not David. David had made a promise to my father and he took it seriously. He put the murderers to death. He didn't cut their heads off, but he cut off their hands and their feet and made a public display of their bodies.

As a soldier, Joab must have been familiar with the concept of taking orders. He specifically defied his king. Unbeknownst to

David, Joab sent messengers after Abner, and Abner came back to meet with Joab. Joab killed him. David was appalled and promptly denied any responsibility.

Thinking back on it, David differentiated between killing in battle and killing outside of battle. In David's eyes, my brother was murdered. In David's eyes, Abner was murdered. In David's eyes, Asahel was killed in battle. David did not have Abner buried in Ner's tomb in Gibeah. He was buried in Hebron, and Esh-Baal's head was buried in his tomb.

David did indeed covet the kingdom over which my father ruled. He believed or at least hoped Abner could help win the hearts of the northern tribes. Esh-Baal and Abner were both gone now, and David had to try another approach. As it happened, the elders of the northern tribes, bereft of a leader, came to Hebron. They remembered the earlier days of my father when David was a very successful military commander. The elders of the southern tribes, together with the representatives of the northern tribes, anointed David a third time.[38] He was declared king of the Twelve Tribes, and his dearest hope was fulfilled—there was no bloodshed.

One advantage that David had that I wished my father would have had was people who would tell him no. Then again, toward the end of my father's life, it wouldn't have done any good. He listened to nobody, including his sons. But David had a group of thirty-seven men called the Mighty Men. Early on, Joab was named commander of the army, which was a separate title His two brothers were Mighty Men. Joab was one to stand up to David, and so were others.

I remember meeting a young man, also part of this elite force as he was preparing to depart for Gibeah. I saw Joab and Abishai standing with him, and I walked up to say hello.

"Good morning to everyone! What a splendid day!"

Joab said, "Good morning, Michal! Have you met Uriah? Uriah, Michal is David's most senior wife."

---

[38] 2 Samuel 5:3.

"Good morning, Uriah! How do all of you intend to spend this lovely day? I have no real plans for myself, though it would be a good day to stroll through the market."

Uriah answered, "I am just about to go find a cart and some mules. I am making a journey to Gibeah to claim my bride. Her father accepted a bride price some months ago. Abishai, where did you say I might borrow a cart?"

Abishai said, "Just go to David's stables. You will find any number of mules and carts there, and as one of David's Mighty Men, you're allowed to borrow them. The master of horses will help you find something suitable for a bride."

I asked, "Do you have a house for your lady?"

Uriah answered, "Yes. I have what I hope will be a beautiful house. In fact, that house is what's delayed my trip to Gibeah. I know all of you have lived there. Do any of you know Eliam's family?"

Joab said, "We know of them. Eliam is a Mighty Man, too, but I don't know him well. Maybe with his daughter married, he will move to Hebron."

Uriah headed off in the direction of the stables. I had to ask, "Joab, who are this man's people? I realize he has unlimited access to David, but he's not a son of the Twelve Tribes. He must be very trustworthy."

Abishai said, "Excuse me. I'm going to go help him." Abishai followed after Uriah.

Joab said, "Uriah is a Hittite. The Hittite empire is long gone, but even today, Hittites have a fierce reputation. Uriah's family has been in Hebron for several generations and is well-respected. David never shrinks from adding Hittites to his army."

"Did I meet Eliam long ago when a child of his was born? I think I did. I have a vague memory of my mother pointing out a politician who was part of that family."

Joab said, "That would be Ahitophel. He's the bride's grandfather. He's still active in community affairs, and he, too, has access to David. David values his advice."

"What of the old laws prohibiting the giving of a daughter in marriage to anyone not of the Twelve Tribes?"

"Uriah spent some time working around that ancient command. In the end, the priests, Abiathar and Zadok, agreed that Uriah's family had adapted well over the years to the Twelve Tribes' culture. They had never tried to follow Hittite culture or gods while living among us, and an exception could be made. Uriah is so excited. From what he says, his bride is very beautiful and will surely make him happy."

"Happy?" I asked a little bitterly. "I must not have made David very happy or I wouldn't be competing now with six women for his affection. Joab, are you happy with one wife?"

"Yes, very happy. It's quite a burden to put on another person, the task of making someone else happy, but yes. If I had to live without Damaris, I would lose a lot of joy. I thank Elohim for her! And Michal, you know that you were caught up in your father's plotting and that you weren't available to David. It's not all his fault, though at the risk of sounding judgmental, seven wives is a lot."

I turned to leave and decided I'd take a walk through the marketplace, even if I didn't really need anything. As I left, I saw Joab head off in the direction of the stables. I also saw Haggith. Haggith was standing by herself and didn't seem to be doing anything other than watching me, unless she was watching Joab. I felt a stab of impatience. Was somebody *always* watching me?

At the very end of my childhood, right as I was becoming a woman, David, Joab, Abishai, and Asahel moved to Gibeah. I was friends with all of them in those days and was glad to see Joab again. Joab and I shared many conversations, especially as David was becoming king and was less and less accessible. I viewed him as a friend, though it wasn't necessarily understood that men and women could be friends. I liked Abishai, too, but Joab was different.

When I saw him again, one thing I tried to get Joab to talk about was his brother's death. Joab didn't express himself to me. He and Abishai must have grieved in their own way. But they were soldiers. They saw a lot of death. Joab said, "I have avenged my brother's death, and there is nothing left to say."

I honored Joab's wishes by not saying anything more about the death of Asahel. I now knew that in Joab's mind, the death of Abner was linked to it. I didn't ever know Asahel that well, but my history with Abner went back to my childhood. Did I hate Abner? No! It puts a person in a terrible position when the family splits. In my case, the division was between my father and my husband. I wasn't really a player. I was thrown into my husband's camp, at least until I wasn't. I had fond memories of Abner in my childhood when David didn't exist and when Abner was married to a person who was dear to me.

Battle after battle takes a toll on a person, especially a person who is impacted by the results. I had deep suspicions of the general who survived a battle that his sovereign didn't. And, of course, after that, he became a personal adversary to me. No, I didn't hate Abner. I thought for a moment about Deborah and allowed one lone tear to roll down my cheek.

It was probably a week before I saw Joab again. I didn't see him every day. I greeted him, as usual.

Joab said, "I'm not supposed to be talking to you."

I was surprised even if I shouldn't have been. The words, "Why not?" slipped out of my mouth, though I knew immediately why not.

"Your husband thinks I'm too familiar."

"My husband has his informants, doesn't he? Joab, I value your conversation and whatever news you manage to bring. But if we want to chat and if we're forced to find a secret place, that's going to look even worse if we're found out. How can it be a problem to stand in the middle of the village square with people walking by?"

Joab answered, "I can handle David. But for the near future, I'll be limited to short conversations. Other things will claim David's attention before too long." Joab was as good as his word, and he walked away.

CHAPTER 33

Year 480

Michal paused. Her throat was dry again, and her legs were cramping. She tossed her head because her neck hurt, and her head covering went flying across the room. A discreet feminine laugh went up from the gathering. Michal's hand went to her scar and afterward to her silver hair. For the most part, Michal's thick hair was pulled away from her face in one long braid, which Abishag had plaited. Abishag offered a bowl of beer, and Michal sipped. Abishag sipped too. One of the slaves retrieved the head covering, and Michal put it back on. Michal thought back. When the palace was new, this public room had been a sterile place. Now it was home.

Michal surveyed the public hall of the women's quarters. It always surprised her that anyone was interested in her story. But the hall was full of women, maybe even more than had initially decided to listen to her. Then she smiled to herself and wondered how her concept of her own importance had become so exaggerated. These women are here because there's nothing else to do in this place! Still, there is satisfaction in being listened to for whatever reason.

For just a moment, she looked across the room and contemplated the various feminine garments. Many women wore linen, some of it dyed and some of it natural. Michal contemplated her own rather plain linen garment. There was quality there but no flamboyance. There were definite spots of color among the gathered women. The women from south of Egypt wore cotton in vibrant colors. Michal thought she saw a bit of silk here or there, but silk was dear and rare. The women wearing silk had almost certainly brought it with them from wherever. Women in the palace or rather palaces came from absolutely everywhere. There was the usual wool, though some weaves were finer than others.

A few women wore head coverings, and while it was modest to cover one's hair, it wasn't necessary in the women's quarters. The women's quarters were relaxed and informal, though if one had plans to leave later on, a scarf would be recommended. Some women wore sandals; some were barefoot. The weather was mild and the floors of the palace were smooth.

"I wonder whether some of you are curious as to why I make an effort to care for Maacah. Do any of you know Maacah? I certainly perceived her as a threat when both of us were young, but she is no threat now. And I can't, looking at her, bear a grudge. If she was deserving of retribution, she got it, and not by my hand. My hands are clean, at least in this instance. There is also Tamar to consider. Tamar is a beautiful and tragic figure, and Maacah is her mother. Far and away, she provides Maacah's real care. I just look in on them now and then.

"Many years ago, Moses recorded what he perceived to be the voice of Elohim, saying, 'Vengeance is mine, I will repay.'[39] I will tell you that I believe this to be a true saying, though I'm guilty of not necessarily following it when I should. The problem with the vengeance of Elohim is that it doesn't occur when we humans want it to and that more often than not, we're not allowed to watch. If you believe the saying, you take it on faith. A person's actions or choices will affect their future. In the case of Maacah, I do get to watch, and surprisingly, I get no pleasure from it. I wouldn't wish Maacah's fate on my worst enemy, which actually, Maacah was."

The ladies were becoming accustomed to Asher's interruptions. As he walked across the floor to speak of Michal, there were quiet conversations. The ladies were there to hear Michal's story, but when Asher came, they knew there would be a break. Abishag took Michal's hand as she struggled to rise. Asher arrived and took the other hand. Michal got to her feet and hung on to Abishag and Asher until her legs showed promise of supporting her.

---

[39] Deuteronomy 32:35.

Michal asked, "Naamah?"

Asher replied, "Yes. Once you leave this palace, you'll hear her screams. She's very sure she's the only one who's ever had a baby."

Abishag couldn't help herself. "Spoken like a person who's never given birth!"

Asher gave a little smile and said nothing. This palace housed any number of people who'd never given birth.

"Asher, we are almost on our way, but before this gathering breaks up, I just want to add the usual admonition. Our culture and our laws will seem odd to some of you. There are penalties for adultery, and none of you will be surprised by that. But we have a day of the week that is intended to be different from the days that are devoted to work, and this idea may be less well-understood. We do not work on the Sabbath day, which is the seventh day of the week. It is a day of rest and reflection. It is also a formal day of worship at Solomon's magnificent new temple. Many of us welcome the rest. We have a king who has demonstrated that he's not interested in imposing his own religious traditions on others. It may be that this particular king will be less interested in the penalty for misusing the Sabbath.[40] But in days past, there has been a severe punishment for not observing appropriately. Just let it be known, and if whatever you want to do on that day looks like work, be discreet.

"Abishag and I will assist the princess of Ammon with her first baby. Some labors are longer than others. We will expect to be here again the day after tomorrow."

They left by the front door, as usual, and traversed the garden. Michal mused, "I seem to come out here only when I'm hurrying off to some other destination. Both of us need to make it a point to come out here just to enjoy the place, when we have the leisure."

Abishag agreed but with qualifications. "I would love to sit along the pool one day and just watch the fish. But on pleasant days, everyone has the same idea. I can't always find the energy to fight the crowds."

The new or newer palace loomed ahead, and both ladies started walking more slowly. As promised, they could hear Naamah scream-

---

[40] Exodus 31:14, 15.

ing in another language. Sometimes the name Molech would be comprehensible, followed by what was probably an expletive. The ladies entered the palace without enthusiasm and were assaulted immediately by the cloying incense. There would be no incense in the birthing room, and they hurried that way.

Naamah's ladies moved aside for the two midwives. Michal and Abishag knelt down beside Naamah who promptly let out another shriek.

Michal said, "Naamah, you have to push."

"*Aaaagggggghhhhhhhh!* Leave me alone!"

Michal stood up, though not without difficulty. "As far as I can tell, Naamah will have an uncomplicated delivery, but she needs to do some more pushing. Push!"

"No! I can't. Water!"

One of Naamah's ladies went to get water, but Michal advised, "Just a little bit. Moisten her tongue. Can you get her up? She needs to walk around the room. The baby isn't ready yet."

Several hours later, the baby was finally ready. Naamah let out one last shriek as the baby's head became visible. The rest of the baby followed as is the case of an easier-than-some delivery.

"Look, look, a son! Naamah, you have a perfect boy child. Ahsia had a son, too, maybe a month ago. They can grow up together."

Naamah was in no mood to discuss other women's babies. "Who's Ahsia?"

As always, Michal made sure the afterbirth was delivered and then attended to the very tender spot through which the baby had made his entrance. One of Naamah's women swaddled the child. The child, feeling the unaccustomed air on his face, started to cry.

"Yes, the much anticipated baby's cry," exclaimed Abishag. "We have a set of healthy lungs."

The wet nurse stepped forward and bared a breast. The baby nuzzled for a minute and then caught on. Michal ignored the baby and turned her attention to Naamah. Naamah was understandably exhausted, but her post-birth body seemed very normal otherwise. There was no excessive bleeding and no unpleasant odor. Michal made sure she was clean and packed some clean rags between her legs.

Michal and Abishag prepared to leave Naamah with her ladies. The door was darkened by a very unexpected sight. Solomon! The baby's father had come to the birthing room. It wasn't customary for him to enter it, and he stood just outside. "Your Highness!" said Abishag and Michal in chorus.

Michal continued, "You have a beautiful son. Another beautiful son, I might add. He seems perfectly healthy, and his mother will regain her strength quickly. Should I ask the wet nurse to step outside?"

"Let me see my son. Then I'll go away and leave you ladies to do what ladies do. By the way, Michal and Abishag, thank you for coming."

The wet nurse held up the baby for Solomon's inspection. The baby was more interested in the breast than his father. He gave that small newborn wail, and the wet nurse reattached him.

"Your Highness, do you have a name for him?" asked Abishag shyly.

"Yes, he will be called Rehoboam," answered Solomon.

Michal wanted to know, "What did you name Ahsia's son?"

"Who's Ahsia?"

"There was another boy child born here about a month ago to a Moabite princess. Did no one tell you?"

Solomon looked confused.

Michal went on, "I do hope the child has a name by now."

As he was leaving, Solomon promised to look into it. Michal and Abishag set out for the old palace. They walked across a darkened garden and tried to make sure they picked up their feet. It was easy to trip over the stones in the path. As they were entering the palace they called home, Michal voiced what they were both thinking. "I'm glad Solomon was present for the birth of this son, but did Ahsia get any recognition at all?"

Abishag said, "Can he give proper recognition to all his children? How many wives is too many?"

Michal and Abishag were very tired but very satisfied that the birth had gone well. By now, it was late at night and supper was long over. Both of them were looking forward to sleep.

CHAPTER 34

Year 440

There were various things David wanted that other kings of the region had, specifically a palace and a temple to our God. Before he could proceed with either of those buildings, he had to consider a capital city. The elders of Hebron would have been more than happy for their town to be David's capital. The elders had welcomed David warmly and presided over royal anointings on two separate occasions. David just felt that Hebron was too closely aligned with the tribe of Judah. Jezreel, the town where I had lived for several years, was mentioned, but again, it was inside the borders of the tribe of Issachar and was well to the north. David wanted to bring the Twelve Tribes together, and he wanted a neutral capital.

He wanted a more centrally located city, nestled between the south and the north. There was a fortress called Jebus at the very southern border of the territory of Benjamin, and David resolved to conquer it. The location was good, but it wasn't much of a city. It thought itself impregnable. David and his army surrounded it, only to be taunted by its residents from the tops of the walls. In the end, David sent a contingent through the water system under the city, and these soldiers opened up the gates.

It was said that David offered the command of all his armies to the person who led the way into the water system and into Jebus and that this person was Joab. I once asked Joab about it, and he evaded the question. It seems like a flimsy reason for *that* kind of promotion, but then the person who led the others was clearly brave and/or reckless. David was surrounded by brave men.

The battle for Jebus was a lot shorter than its inhabitants might have expected. It was less destructive. David's men didn't burn the city nor did they butcher the inhabitants. David had his new capital, and he renamed it. Jebus became Jerusalem. David began improving it immediately. He enlarged it with some assistance from the king of Tyre. The king of Tyre sent cedar logs and skilled laborers. David built up the city itself and also created a royal palace.

I won't bore you with the details of our move from Hebron to Jerusalem as David named his new capital. It was arduous, it was chaotic, it was like any other move of a large number of people. We were blessed. The weather was good. It may be worth noting that I, with the help of several slaves, made the huge effort to move my garden. Of course, we couldn't move all of it. I pulled up samples of every plant I had and carefully packed them in baskets of earth.

I wasn't sure what to do about the poppies. Our move was in summer, not fall. I pulled up the poppy bulbs and cut off the stalks, resolving to set them aside until fall and hope for the best. I would plan to look for wild poppies in the environs of our new location, and in the meantime, I was transporting all of the dried plants, including dried poppy nectar that I had prepared. Each woman or her slaves was involved in packing and transporting her personal possessions, such as clothing, bowls, and rugs.

Once we got to Jerusalem, I knew my plants had to take priority. I looked for a patch of ground that offered good sunlight, and I set some slaves to tilling it. I am happy to state that most of my plants survived the journey, and I'm also happy to state that when I got around to planting the poppy bulbs, I found out in the spring that they'd survived too. I did some of the planting myself, but I had help from a trusted and talented slave. I had the usual fence put up after we finished planting. And, of course, the whole effort was done again when Solomon laid out his formal walled garden.

The king's household remained in Hebron while David was occupied with his first building project, which was what we now call the old palace. David was a very creative person who had seen a palace or two, specifically in Gath. He took some Philistine ideas and combined them with his own, ending up with a large multistoried mud brick building complete with windows and balconies. It is great fun to move into quarters that are new and in which nobody else has lived. It was up to the residents to make the place feel like home, which we did by each adding our personal touches.

When I left Hebron, I left behind my private house. The women's quarters in Jerusalem, when they were new, were the best quarters I'd ever lived in. I returned to the women's quarters with the move. I was First Wife, and the fact was not disputed. I rated a small, private nook for myself. I was wary of Maacah, but the two of us were never thrown together in the way we had been in Hebron. If I avoided her, she also avoided me, and our paths tended not to cross.

There were a few private spaces for the most senior wives. Many young wives simply spread out rugs and fabrics on the floor and slept in a mass. I was very grateful for a semi-private space because it was the only place I had to store herbs. My bed took up most of my small nook. It was separated from the main room by a low wall, and I enlisted a carpenter to erect a narrow set of shelves on that wall. It may not have been ideal to store dangerous herbs in such an insecure way, but it was the place where I had the most control. The vast majority of women took no interest in herbs and weren't curious enough to try to find out what I had.

Insofar as dried herbs are concerned, if a wife wanted to poison another wife, first she'd have to know which herbs were poisonous. Some definitely are if the prospective poisoner uses enough. But also, the wife-in-question would have to know how to read Hebrew. Some did, but it was a limited number.

I found a spot for my mother's bowl on top of the low wall. Was I worried that another wife would steal it? I knew it could happen. I had very little of value, though some of my clothing was well-made. Theft wasn't a big problem in the women's quarters. None of us wanted for anything, and we also knew that if we stole something, we'd have to hide it. That would defeat the purpose. We occasionally saw some violence.

David settled his wives from Hebron into their new quarters, and then he started taking many more wives. I did lose count. He took a lot of wives, and at some point, it didn't seem important to note how many. David had many children. I assisted at the births of some of them. It is no secret that when a man has numerous wives, he doesn't distribute his time equally among them. I still didn't conceive.

After David finished his beautiful palace, he was of a mind to create a temple to Elohim. He was dissuaded by the Holy Man who took the place of Samuel after Samuel died. Nathan pointed out that David was a man of many battles. Speaking for Elohim, Nathan advised that our present king, Solomon, would build a temple for worship. Solomon never fought war after war in the manner of his father and in the manner of my father. Can I point out that Solomon didn't have to? My father and David established a strong military foundation for a united Twelve Tribes that at least during Solomon's reign was not disputed by the neighboring kingdoms. Peace and safety are incredible blessings!

David may have been disappointed that he was not to be the one to build a magnificent temple to Elohim. But he distracted himself by designing the temple that now stands and also by amassing building materials. Solomon took on the actual construction. David went so far as to preplan how the temple would be staffed. He had a particular interest in music, and he designated singers. He also designated gatekeepers and treasurers. The Twelve Tribes had amassed beautiful and valuable items dedicated to Elohim and awaiting a permanent resting place, which is now the temple. David certainly dedicated much of the plunder from successful raids, but there were also treasures dedicated by Samuel, by my father, by Abner, and by Joab.

David redirected his spiritual energy toward the most holy object in the country. This was the ark of God that dated back to the time of Moses. It had originally been housed in the tabernacle at Shiloh but had various adventures of its own. During the time of the tribal leadership before Samuel, the army actually took the ark into battle against the Philistines and lost it. This was a huge tragedy. There was much wailing and grief among the population at large along with various officers' comprehensive efforts to deflect the blame from themselves.

The ark should not have left the tabernacle. When it was captured, the two priests who had accompanied it were killed. The

Philistines thought they'd captured the Tribes' magic, but it didn't work out for them. Eventually, after various mishaps involving Philistine gods, they sent the ark back, and it got to the lands of the Twelve Tribes, though never back to the tabernacle. It landed in Kiriath Jearim.

Right about the time the ark returned to the territory of the Twelve Tribes, Samuel was elevated to the position he held when my father met him. The ark resided in Kiriath Jearim for twenty years in the house of a man named Abinadab. David, with his new capital, wanted to bring the ark of God to his city, and to this end, he constructed a special tent for it, somewhat reminiscent of the tabernacle.

There were two attempts to bring the ark to Jerusalem. David assigned 30,000 soldiers and accompanied them himself to the house of Abinadab. Unfortunately, no one knew how the ark was intended to be treated. There were a few people who remembered what happened when the ark arrived in Kiriath Jearim, fresh from Philistine lands. The Philistines loaded the ark into an ox cart. After the ark was unloaded, some individuals of the Twelve Tribes were impertinent enough to look inside it. All of them died.

As far as David knew, it had worked out okay to transport the ark on an ox cart, and that's what he did. The procession got as far as the threshing floor of Nacon. One of the oxen stumbled, and one of Abinadab's sons reached out his hand to steady the ark. Uzzah died on the spot. David was both frightened and heartbroken, and he left off the effort for three months. David found the nearest house where the ark could be sheltered, which happened to be the home of Obed-Edom of Gath.

Obed-Edom had some reservations about sheltering such a powerful object. It was before his time, but he knew that the ark had wreaked havoc on his people, the Philistines. He ordered that his household not touch the ark, and he hid it away in a room that had nothing else in it.

David had not given up the idea of having the ark of God in his new city, but in the meantime, he tried to find an advisor who knew anything at all about the ark. David had a number of advisors, some of whom hailed from cities not in the vicinity of Jerusalem.

One name I had heard before was Ahitophel, who lived in Giloh to the south. Another notable adviser was Hushai, whose family lived to the north in the area of Tyre and Sidon. Hushai was primarily a military strategist. He wasn't born to the Twelve Tribes and wasn't familiar with our history. However, he had a home in Jerusalem as well as another home among his own people. He was respectful of our customs and was accepted. Ahitophel was a spiritualist and a seer. Some perceived him to be a bit like Samuel with a direct link to Elohim. The two didn't particularly like each other. Their priorities were entirely different.

David consulted Ahitophel before he approached the ark again. Ahitophel wasn't very approachable, even by a king. He asked David what he had done with the ark to cause a man's death, implying that it was David's fault. When David mentioned the ox cart, Ahitophel responded with, "Of course a man died!" He continued rather vehemently, "The ark is not to be transported on a cart! There are heavy metal rings attached to the four corners of the ark. The rings accommodate poles, and the poles are carried on the shoulders of men. Do not look into the ark and do not touch it! It is sacred."

David didn't speak to me about whether or not he appreciated Ahitophel's demeanor. David had been a general/king long enough by then not to be too open to being patronized. What he did appreciate and what he appreciated for the rest of his life was correct information. David may well have missed his mentor, Samuel. Ahitophel was a bit like Samuel, albeit without the modesty. Ahitophel had a lot of knowledge, but he had a reputation for arrogance.

David had the Mighty Men who were willing to tell him the truth or the truth as they saw it, and he also had Ahitophel and Hushai. Of the two, Hushai was more tactful and more likable. But either of them could be called upon to offer advice that wasn't rooted in self-advancement.

David tried again, and this time, the ark was lifted up on poles and carried by priests. The priests found the rings right where Ahitophel said they would be, and there was a huge effort to insert the poles without touching the ark. This time, the ark came to Jerusalem without incident. Its procession through the streets of Jerusalem became a huge festival. Many, many people lined the streets, and there was singing and dancing and musical instruments in celebration.

David's own enthusiasm knew no bounds. He leaped and danced before the ark with every ounce of energy, and it became apparent that he wasn't wearing anything under his linen loin covering. I will concede to being a bit judgmental. Kings need more dignity and more decorum. The ark was slipped into the tent that had been erected for it, and David offered burnt offerings and fellowship offerings for the occasion.

I might have been appalled at David's lack of modesty, but I was entirely taken aback by the sacrifices. Wasn't this what my father had done and incurred the wrath of Samuel in the name of Elohim? David was no priest! Zadok and Abiathar were the high priests of the Twelve Tribes. Abiathar had actually been present when my father destroyed the community of priests at Nob, and he had fled to David's camp. I'm puzzled as to why they stood by while David usurped their authority, but they did. Samuel hadn't been so tolerant of my father. When David strolled toward the palace, I was in a mood. I met him outside.

"What in the world do you think you're doing? There are any number of slave girls who are giggling at your expense. Kings cover themselves!"

David was about to enter the palace to bless the household. My strong words were completely unexpected. He had been dancing uninhibited and almost certainly didn't know what he looked like.

David retorted, "I danced in honor of Elohim, the same Elohim who selected me to replace your father. I can be less dignified than this before Elohim, and even though you don't approve, those slave girls will respect me for it."

David stalked away. Our household didn't get its blessing. I saw David on his deathbed when he asked for me. But I never saw him again otherwise. I tried and tried and tried to apologize, but he wouldn't see me. He was very well guarded. There was no option to catch him alone. He was never alone. When he decided he wouldn't see someone, his retainers made it happen.

My name is in the chronicles, too, albeit not for bearing children. I have to assume that David relayed my remarks to a scribe, and the scribe interpreted them. The chronicles say I despised my husband.[41] That's quite a strong statement. It was all about disapproving of his behavior at a specific moment and saying so. Many people know how it feels to say what shouldn't be said. Saying the wrong thing certainly isn't rare. It wasn't the only time I made questionable comments, but it was these comments that were recorded for posterity. One of my regrets.

Throughout his reign, David offered plenty of sacrifices to Elohim without the benefit of priests. Now late in life, I am still pondering why Elohim rejected my father when he did it, but it was perfectly fine for David to do it. David didn't lose his throne for it, and he was succeeded by his son.

David's life seemed spectacularly blessed, at least in his early days as king. He did not have a holy man reprimanding him for offering sacrifices.

At one time, Samuel was confident that Elohim had selected my father. I can only conclude that my father was specifically disobedient when he usurped Samuel's authority. And, again, maybe the sacrifice my father offered when Samuel failed to appear, while annoying to Samuel, wasn't really the problem. Maybe the larger problem with my father's behavior was his unwillingness to annihilate the Amalekites, his willingness to massacre the priests of Nob, and his aggression against Gibeon.

---

[41] 2 Samuel 6:16.

CHAPTER 35

Year 445

David was a warrior. I'd suggest that his life was plagued with battles against the Philistines, the Ammonites, the Aramaeans, the Amalekites, the Moabites, and any other neighbors who were not part of the Twelve Tribes. But I'm not sure David would appreciate the word *plagued*. He thrived on battle, and so did his Mighty Men and his armies in general. Battles made everybody rich. Well, battles that were won did, and the armies of Israel were quite successful. David was almost always at the head of the troops with one notable exception.

It was the second month. Winter was over, but it had left David with a hacking cough that hung on and on. I had prepared what amounted to soup that had a large amount of thyme in it. I sent it to the palace, and I do hope David took some of it, though I told the messenger to be vague as to where it had come from. I was, after all, in disgrace. I specified that it was best served hot. I also gave the servant a quantity of crushed up mustard seeds and told him that his lord would benefit from soaking his feet in hot water with the mustard seeds in it. I had no way of knowing whether David received any of my remedies and whether he found them to be useful, though after a while, it was clear that the king was feeling better.

In the meantime, Joab and the army had left Jerusalem and were making life difficult for the citizens of Rabbah, which was the capital of the Ammonites. David wasn't with his armies, fighting the enemy, and time weighed heavily on his hands. He was strolling along the roof of his palace one day and could see a lot of the city from his vantage point. Jerusalem had become an elegant new city that David had in large part designed.

The first time I heard Bathsheba's name was from Joab. Joab was commanding the army, as usual. The siege was going well, and Joab knew that his pregnant wife was near her time. He left his brother Abishai in charge and returned home with just a few men.

When Joab got home, I was attending to his wife, Damaris, and Damaris had just delivered her second child. Childbirth is always a worry. Many things can go wrong. Praise Elohim, this was a very ordinary labor. The child was a son and Damaris was healthy. Joab looked in on us and inquired after Damaris. Damaris, exhausted, was dozing with the new baby on her chest. I told Joab that all was well, and he had a son to add to his family. Joab already had an older daughter.

The two of us left the house as quietly as we could. Joab and I strolled into the garden at the back of the house. I should have asked who was the gardener in the family. At the time, I'd never seen a garden like this. It was completely different from either my mother's garden or the garden I cared for in Jezreel. This area was more of a cultivated park. I was assuming that Damaris was the gardener, mainly because Joab was away from home a lot. The garden was very well-kept, and after the obvious planning that went into it, it required maintenance. There were myrrh shrubs and frankincense shrubs, and if they weren't exactly thriving, they were at least alive. These were not common, and they weren't easy to grow. I made a note to speak to Damaris at a more convenient time just because the sap of both of those plants could be used for healing.

There were several large rocks around the perimeter of the garden, and between those were rock roses in various shades of color. They were in bloom and the scent was heavenly. There was also the scent of rain. The garden was wet and the odor of moisture hung heavily in the air.

I have a habit of worrying about what my behavior might look like to others instead of focusing on friends and their pain. Maybe I have reason. It did feel like any number of my acquaintances were more than willing to watch me, gossip about me, and report me to anyone who would listen. I had reservations about strolling in a garden in the evening with a man who wasn't my husband, and it didn't help that David had specifically warned Joab to stay away from me.

Be that as it may, I managed to look outside myself long enough to notice that Joab wasn't rejoicing over his new healthy son like most fathers would be. I certainly didn't expect what happened next, when Joab sat down on a wet rock and started sobbing. I was at a loss. What was my role? Could I be there for Joab while his wife was recovering from childbirth? Should I be? I remembered Deborah in that moment, and I remembered slipping away unnoticed and pretending not to witness her grief. No. This time would be different. I would not abandon Joab to his nightmare. I took a seat on the adjoining wet rock and pleaded that he speak to me.

Joab started with, "Uriah is dead." Uriah was one of David's Mighty Men. Asahel had been a Mighty Man, too, and he was dead. "Uriah is dead, and I killed him."

I was speechless. What? Joab was clearly in distress. I reached out my hand. My impulse was to touch Joab, and I almost did. It wouldn't have been proper. Proper! I'd spent my life not being proper, and I'd made plenty of trouble for myself. If Joab had been a woman, I most certainly would have joined him on his rock and wrapped my arms around him. No, it wasn't allowed. I reminded myself that Joab's wife was just inside the house, and even if David had long ago given up on my behavior, it might come as a surprise to Damaris.

Joab continued, "It all started when David recalled Uriah to Jerusalem rather suddenly. It wasn't a good time in the course of the battle to let him go, but the king sent for him. So Uriah went to Jerusalem. Insofar as I can tell, David needed Uriah to sleep with his wife, Bathsheba."

Now I remembered. Uriah was the young man who had made a trip to Gibeah to claim a bride, and I'd met him.

Joab went on, "Since Uriah knew that his fellow soldiers and Mighty Men were on the battlefield, he refused to go home. He went to Jerusalem, as summoned, but not to his house. He slept in the barracks. So David sent him back to the siege with a note for me to put Uriah in the thick of the fighting and then draw the soldiers back from around him so he'd be killed." It took all of Joab's determination to spit out that sentence, and his body was wracked again with emotion. "He was my friend, he was my friend, and I did it!"

I had to ask, "Wasn't he David's friend too? What happened?"

Joab had been out of the city. Rumors were flying, of course. "As near as I can figure, David saw Bathsheba and took her. She got pregnant, which wasn't part of the plan. There was no way she would have been able to pass off the child as Uriah's. So David took care of the problem. It will be clear soon. Bathsheba will mourn for her husband for a suitable period, and then we'll all see what happens. Right now, I hate David and I hate myself more!

"Michal, Uriah's father-in-law, was there too. When the men drew back and left Uriah to his fate, Eliam refused. Eliam isn't dead, but he's gravely wounded."

We both heard a small new baby cry and went back into the house to check on Damaris. I picked up the baby and swaddled him. Damaris opened her eyes and saw her husband. Joab kissed her on the head and then kissed the baby on the head.

He asked, "How are you feeling?" Damaris was a little weak but ecstatic.

She simply responded with, "Isn't he perfect?"

"He's perfect," Joab agreed. "I won't be here long. The army is besieging Rabbah of Ammon, and we are winning."

Joab passed quite close by me as we were entering the house again, and I caught the scent of something unpleasant and threatening. There are lots of battlefield scents. Active soldiers are sweaty and unable to bathe when they'd like to. I knew those odors, and this wasn't one. That was when I noticed a large filthy bandage on Joab's right upper arm.

"Joab, I've got to look under that bandage." In his usual impatient way, Joab advised me that it was nothing. "It is something," I said. "I can smell it. And it's got to be very painful."

Joab reluctantly let me strip off the bandage, and I saw an angry deep slash in a variety of colors. The odor was very noticeable when the bandage came off. Damaris wrinkled her nose. Right then, Joab's four-year-old daughter entered the room. She should have been sleeping, of course, but can a child really sleep through her mother's labor? She was so cute I wanted to drop what I was doing and cuddle her. Instead, we helped her up on the bed with her mother and introduced her to the new brother.

I got back to Joab's wound. There was clean hot water left from the birth preparations, and there were also clean bandages or maybe, more specifically, rags. Clean rags make good bandages, and in Damaris' case, I hadn't used them all. I put the water back on the fire for just a few minutes and grabbed a rag.

"Joab, this is going to hurt." I cleaned up the jagged edges of the infected wound. I saw Joab cringe, but he made no sounds. I used the rag to separate the edges just a bit to make sure there were no foreign objects deep in the wound. The field physician had done a good job in that respect. "This is your sword arm, isn't it? Joab, would I make a good torturer?"

Joab answered, "Yes!" through gritted teeth.

The wound was as clean as I could make it. I asked Joab if he had any spirits. There was a small bottle, and I dumped the contents into the wound. Joab yelped! The baby, who had dutifully latched onto one of Damaris' breasts, jumped but didn't let go.

I then turned to Damaris and asked if I could use her honey. I'd seen some. She agreed, but they were both mystified. I took the largest clean rag to use as a bandage and smeared some honey on it. Then I applied the honeyed part to the wound and wrapped up the arm. I told them that honey has healing properties. Joab was afraid he'd attract insects.

"Just leave the bandage on for a day or two. Well, maybe leave it on until there's some opportunity to wash the area." We got back to the subject at hand, which was the new baby boy.

Damaris asked Joab what he wanted to name his son, and Joab replied, "Asahel."

Joab went back to that battle for Rabbah. Shortly after he arrived, he was able to send word to Jerusalem that the tribes of Israel had taken Rabbah's water supply. David left Jerusalem with the rest of the army and was present when the city fell. It's inhabitants were set to hard labor. Once Rabbah had been neutralized, David, Joab, and the armies of Israel also captured other Ammonite cities and enslaved their populations.

The armies of the Twelve Tribes returned to Jerusalem and to their various tribal land allotments after a number of successful battles and with large amounts of booty. There was a huge welcoming festival. David made a triumphal entry into Jerusalem at the head of the portion of his army that lived in Jerusalem. The men had been gone for a long time, and the vast majority had survived. Families joined together in joyous reunions.

I saw Damaris standing with her children alongside the street beside Abishai's wife. I saw Joab and Abishai being heartily welcomed home. I was surrounded by a great crowd of people and felt lonely. Even if I wasn't in exile, so to speak, I would have been tripping over other women in an effort to get to our mutual husband. I didn't stay. I walked back into the palace and the women's quarters.

I pondered these events on lackluster days and sleepless nights. I pondered how David, all self-righteous, took murder and made it look like a battle casualty. It probably fit his personal model of what constitutes a heroic death. After all, Uriah had died in battle. Appearances counted. David was a politician.

All eyes were on Bathsheba. She mourned for Uriah for the appropriate number of days and was then taken into David's palace. She was obviously pregnant by now. Bathsheba actually lived in David's quarters for a while and made her way to us in the women's quarters later on. Bathsheba delivered a son. I was not present.

During this period, the Holy Man, Nathan, visited Jerusalem. He had words with David, and they were not words of encouragement. To hear Joab tell it, Nathan pointed out in no uncertain terms what David had done to Uriah—and to Bathsheba, for that matter. Nathan predicted the death of the child, which occurred.

Please don't think I would accuse Joab of rejoicing in a child's death. Children are valued by our society, all children, and by Joab as much as anyone. I had been something of a confidant to Joab over the years, and I believe that he said things to me that he wouldn't say to anyone else. There is nobody to admonish a king. Joab actually tried to do so himself on some occasions, but this incident left him speechless. I know for a fact that he was gratified that Elohim had noticed and that David's behavior didn't stay hidden.

I had feared a bit for Bathsheba just because I thought David took her in a moment of lust, intending all along to put her back into Uriah's bed. Maybe David meant to do that but didn't count on Bathsheba getting pregnant. I have never thought that David was solicitous of women. He surprised me when he did right by Bathsheba. Bathsheba became David's wife and bore him other children. She was his chief wife during his lifetime. Bathsheba's second son is our present king.

News travels quickly. Because Nathan publicly confronted David, a lot of the country became aware of David's actions. What does it take to denounce a king's behavior? It takes a brave man. Nathan may have been convinced that Elohim would protect him. David was aware enough, at least when it was pointed out, that he'd done something terrible. He never tried to punish the messenger.

Ahitophel was appalled. His son was near death and his granddaughter had been dishonored. He and his wife came to Jerusalem to be at the bedside of their son. Eliam never regained consciousness, which can be a mercy when the body has been ravaged. They waited and watched with their daughter-in-law, but their son didn't recover. After Eliam died, Ahitophel sold his house in Jerusalem and retreated with his wife from public life to their home in Giloh. Bathsheba remained in Jerusalem, but her mother went to Giloh with her in-laws.

CHAPTER 36

When Michal spoke, the room was quiet. When soft footsteps came through the door, everyone heard them. Asher slowly approached the sheepskins on which Michal and Abishag sat. "I have news," he said. "Bathsheba has passed."

Michal asked if she should assist with the preparation of the body for burial, but Asher replied that the process was already underway.

"Ladies, do not ever take life for granted. David and Bathsheba made a love story for the ages, and now they're both dead. I cannot wish Bathsheba any more days of mortal life just because her body was in such awful condition, but with her goes one of the last links to my youth. David and Bathsheba's love story was tainted when David used his power to take a married woman.

"The law tells us not to covet what doesn't belong to us.[42] We all have at least some control over what we wish for. We can turn our attention to something else before what we wish for becomes an obsession and we can also practice gratitude for the things we have. Covetousness is destructive. It destroys our own peace, and it can impact other people. You all know what happened to Zeta. It isn't common knowledge what happened to the woman who attacked her, but she's gone. I doubt it was anything good.

"Ladies, I need to rest. Bathsheba was a friend of mine, and even if her passing was inevitable, it's still painful. It's difficult to know what sort of final ceremony will be granted to the mother of

---

[42] Exodus 20:17.

the king. Whatever it is, we all need to support it. I will return to this room on the day after tomorrow."

Michal stood up with some difficulty and with assistance from both Abishag and Asher.

All the ladies gathered early the next morning outside their dwelling. The body of Bathsheba was lying on a litter, properly wrapped and scented. Solomon appeared, as did his wife, Amneris. Solomon directed the bearers to pick up his mother's litter, and he and his wife followed it outside the city walls.

The ladies of the harem, including Michal, helped make up a procession. Asher walked with the ladies, specifically Michal. Michal hadn't walked that far in a very long time, and she was wheezing. Bathsheba was to be buried in a cave outside the walls of Jerusalem. The area was quite beautiful, including some flowering bushes and trees. The cave was behind some of the bushes, and it was clear that somebody in the gathering had to know where it was. The opening wasn't obvious.

Michal, as always, was scouting for plants that might have healing properties. It wouldn't have been appropriate to gather plants during a funeral procession, but she could make a note. What she really needed was a place to sit down. Michal was breathing hard. Solomon and the daughter of Pharaoh followed the litter into the cave, but everyone else waited outside.

Asher tried to guide Michal to a little hill that would have made it easier for her to settle down and to get up. But Michal had spied a cluster of poppies and instead pulled Asher in that direction. She flopped down to one side of the poppies, and Abishag sat herself down, somewhat more gracefully on the other side. Both women very discreetly pulled off a few seed pods and secreted them within their clothing.

Michal commented, "I know I said we shouldn't use this occasion to gather plants. But Bathsheba benefited mightily from the poppies, and hopefully, she would approve."

There wasn't any dramatic ceremony. Bathsheba's remains were interred in a carved-out slot inside the cave, and Solomon and his wife reemerged. The procession returned to Jerusalem in silence or insofar as a large group can be silent. Michal continued her narrative the following day as planned.

"Good morning, ladies! I'd like to formally thank the number of you who turned out to pay their last respects to Bathsheba. We had a well-attended procession to her burial place. Can I assume that most of you didn't even know Bathsheba? I almost never walk that far, and the journey was difficult for me. I also had barely slept the night before. *I miss Bathsheba!*"

Michal sniffled and a tear rolled down her cheek. She continued. "Bathsheba was one of my last contemporaries. Some of you understand how rivalries emerge in a harem, multiple females vying for the attention of a male. It wasn't like that between Bathsheba and me, especially after David rather publicly rejected me and wrote about it. I wasn't competing with anyone. Bathsheba and I supported each other over the years. We had shared experiences. I cuddled her children. Now I weep for her, but as you must realize, it makes me feel guilty. At the end, Bathsheba's life was awful. I don't begrudge her peace, but it's always hard to lose a friend.

"How many of you have never seen Solomon before? I know some of you are even married to him. There are things about Solomon that remind me of my brother, Esh-Baal. Neither of them were soldiers. Both of them reveled in education and read everything they could find. Solomon also reminds me of his very handsome brother, Absalom, who wasn't so different from his father, David, in his youth. But Solomon's mannerisms aren't his father's. If I could be so bold, Solomon also reminds me of my father's concubine, Rizpah. There is a sensuality about him. I haven't sat down and had a conversation with him, so I don't know how he thinks. It's his demeanor, the way he moves, especially his long, thin fingers, and the way he dresses."

CHAPTER 37

Year 450

David's children grew up as children do more quickly than anyone expects. David's oldest children, the ones who were born in Hebron, found their way to adulthood. Bathsheba was only the first scandal of David's reign. Some of his sons didn't behave like princes. Or did they? Do princes have a reputation for reaching out and taking whatever they want? David had an unfortunate tendency to ignore what went on within his family, but if he'd been paying attention, he would have noticed history repeating itself.

Just like his father, David's oldest son, Amnon allowed himself to lust and to become obsessed. The object of Amnon's lust was his half-sister, Tamar. I think back to my first meeting with Amnon as a child, and I wouldn't have predicted this sort of behavior. Amnon had grown up to be sly and impulsive. He tricked his father into thinking he was sick, and he tricked Tamar into entering his house. Tamar resisted her brother's advances as it was forbidden for brothers and sisters to be intimate.[43] Amnon overpowered Tamar and raped her. Then he rejected her and very literally threw her out.

Tamar was devastated. She tore the elegant robe that the virgin daughters of the king wore, put ashes on her head, and wandered around the neighborhood like she was lost. It hadn't escaped notice that Amnon pined for his sister. When Tamar's full-brother, Absalom, found her wandering listlessly, he specifically mentioned Amnon's name. Tamar told him the story with many sobbing interruptions. Absalom guided his sister to his house instead of the women's quar-

---

[43] Leviticus 20:17.

ters of the palace, and she lived there in seclusion. It was reported that King David was angry when he heard about it. However, he wasn't angry enough to confront Amnon.

Absalom was livid, but he bided his time. Absalom waited two years. He decided to host a celebration up in Baal Hazor where his many sheep were being sheared. Sheep-shearing is hard work, but it's also a social gathering. There is eating and drinking and the promise of an infusion of wealth when the fleeces are sold. He invited his father and his father's advisers, but they declined. Then he invited all of his father's sons. Amnon was among the participants. Once Absalom had gotten Amnon away from the palace, Amnon was in Absalom's power. Absalom's retainers killed him.

The people around Absalom were caught off guard. We all believed Amnon's behavior had been forgotten. There is also some vague understanding that women aren't all that important. Too bad for Tamar! I will concede to being somewhat gratified that Absalom thought she was important. He believed strongly enough in justice for her that he accepted banishment.

Absalom ran for his life and fled to Geshur where his mother's relatives lived. His half-brothers returned from Baal Hazor to Jerusalem with the news. Tamar left Absalom's house and returned to the women's quarters of the palace. She is still here.

I said earlier that I was surprised at the man Amnon had become. I was less surprised at who Absalom became. Absalom was used to doing any questionable thing that occurred to him and then begging forgiveness. He always got it. It was just a matter of time before his actions became outrageous.

David was horrified. He had real trouble understanding what had taken place and why. Why did David not understand that Amnon had committed a criminal act and that he had ignored it? Because the act was perpetrated against a woman? A woman who happened to be his daughter as a matter of fact? Absalom was gone, and David behaved like he was in mourning. He wasn't decisive, he wasn't assertive, he wasn't king-like. It became very clear during this time that Absalom was the favorite son, and even if David was trying to do the right thing, he was desperately unhappy. He missed

Absalom a lot more than Absalom deserved. I don't know whether David felt guilt, but that, too, might have been part of his problem. With the death of Amnon, Absalom's status had risen to oldest son, but the title wasn't doing him any good in Geshur.

My information, as always, came from Joab who complained at length about David's lethargy. This wasn't the exuberant boy with whom he'd grown up, and this wasn't the leader of men that David had become. This wasn't the creative, optimistic person I had married years ago.

Joab, ever the man of action, got very impatient with the king's moping. He eventually devised a scheme to trick David into recalling his favorite son to Jerusalem. This process was tedious, but in the end, Joab's chicanery was successful. David relented and allowed Absalom to return, but then he wouldn't see him. I know all about that, personally! David could be extremely stubborn, in addition to being surrounded by men who did his bidding.

In those days, David's nephews were the most powerful men in the kingdom. They had access and David listened to them. Maybe it was because of their power that David at times felt threatened by them. But still, they were absolutely loyal to David in his lifetime. I told you that I tried very hard to see David after my mouth said some unfortunate things, but I never got past the guards.

What I didn't do was to set Joab's barley field afire. No, that never occurred to me! But it occurred to Absalom. Resourceful! Joab had clout, and Absalom essentially demanded that Joab intercede for him. Joab had already gotten Absalom recalled from Geshur, but that wasn't enough. I found out after the fact that Joab could also be pretty elusive. When David wouldn't see Absalom, Absalom tried to see Joab. Joab said later that he felt he'd done what he could, and the rest was up to Absalom and David. He didn't want to discuss the matter, and he avoided Absalom until Absalom did something he couldn't ignore.

I never took a lesson from Absalom, but his tactics worked with Joab. Joab finally met with him and then tried harder to have Absalom received at court. David received him at long last. It made a huge difference in David's demeanor. David overcame his apathy and acted like a king again.

Life went along placidly and without incident for about four years. Absalom desperately wanted to return to his former life and he did, but what David didn't realize is that Absalom never forgave him. Actually, David probably never understood his own role in the situation, especially after Absalom had taken matters into his own hands and meted out his version of justice. David had forgiven Absalom and what else could be required?

If David was a master politician, so was Absalom. Absalom got himself some horses and a chariot, and he employed fifty retainers. Then he made himself available to the population at large to people who were coming into Jerusalem and sympathized deeply with their complaints. Did he actually sympathize? Whoever knows how any politician feels? But he was an excellent actor. By the end of the four years, he had a loyal following of people from all over the Twelve Tribes. Absalom made the citizens feel like he understood them and their situations.

CHAPTER 38

Year 456

Never let it be said that Absalom was all talk and no action. Never let it be said that Absalom wasn't a careful planner. He had proven when he killed his brother that he could bide his time and wait for the right moment. He was deliberate and had a goal. He had made his impression on the population and moved his following to Hebron where he had himself crowned king.

David's former counselor, Ahitophel, joined him in Hebron. People came from everywhere at the sound of the trumpets, and Absalom found himself in command of an army. People are way too easily led. It can be as simple as telling them what they want to hear or making promises that can't realistically be kept. People routinely do not ask how an objective can be reached, though they should. Absalom didn't hesitate. The new army marched on Jerusalem.

We who lived in the palace were petrified. My mother's words came back to me with force. "Boring is good!" David made the decision to flee. David must have gotten dire information about the sort of army his son had been able to raise. Abandoning the city with all his loyal followers was extreme. The residents of the palace, including myself, were running back and forth, here and there, attempting to throw together tents, blankets, and food. David and his entire household, including the harem, left the city.

Let me rephrase—the entire household, with the exception of ten concubines, left the capital. David told Joab that these ten concubines were left to take care of the palace. What? They were a sacrifice to Absalom, and I have every confidence they knew it. I can't imagine what it was like to be left behind on that basis. Those women must

228

have been more frightened than those of us who were faced with getting out of town in a hurry. We were a large group. Could any of them have simply joined us and become lost in the crowd? I don't know, but I do know that all ten did as they were told.

In the meantime, an old friend of David's arrived from Gath. Ittai had come into Jerusalem the previous day with 600 retainers. His men were by no means rested. It must have been quite a surprise to find the entire city in chaos and the king preparing to leave. I heard the conversation.

David and Ittai greeted each other with kisses. Ittai exclaimed, "What's going on here? I was greatly looking forward to seeing your capital city, and now you and your household are heading where?"

David explained, "My son has raised an army and is marching on his father. Where are we going? Right now, we are trying to get out of Jerusalem, and we'll worry about the destination later. Ittai, just go home. Or better yet, just remain in Jerusalem and await King Absalom. Your men are exhausted. You have my blessing."

Ittai said, "My men and I have nothing to go back to. You know Achish is dead. His successor and I do not get along, and my men and I have very good reasons for leaving. Our land in Gath has been confiscated. None of us feel safe in the land where we've lived since our youth. We had to find a safe haven, and we had very few options."

David laughed a bitter laugh. "A safe haven? Ittai, my friend, my friend, accompanying David is not a safe haven."

"My men remember you as a formidable warrior and a fair leader. Again, David, who else would have us? You'll forgive me if I have no faith in your son. My men and I have no history with him. Perhaps he, too, is a formidable warrior, but he is untried. We are your men, David. Life or death comes for all of us, and come what may, ours will be beside you. I'm sorry my men are tired, but they are also the toughest soldiers in the world. They will not slow you down. And you'll see—we will all return to this place and will return together in triumph."

"Ittai, what did you see? You and your men came from Gath to Jerusalem. My son's forces were somewhere in between."

"We did see a very large force which apparently didn't see us. It was moving north. My small force had no desire to encounter it. We were hoping it wasn't heading for Jerusalem, but we admitted that it could have been. David, it has a *lot* of soldiers. Still, my men combined with your men are also formidable. We are not afraid. You have an army. I have some very, very good soldiers. What if we made a stand together here? Is Jerusalem defensible?"

"Ittai, thank you so much for your vote of confidence. This city has its strengths and its weaknesses. I have made a decision to let Absalom have it and see what happens after that. If I were totally honest, and I'm trying to be, I am absolutely determined that my son not be killed. Please don't call me foolish. I realize my son is behaving like an enemy, but I still have hope for the future. I'm not certain I can go on living without him, and maybe much later, the two of us can reconcile if we're both alive. Maybe I will have to face him in battle, but I will do what I can to delay the moment. "Your soldiers and you are most welcome, but it is a poor welcome."

"We stand with King David."

David gave it up and simply sent Ittai and his men out of the city and alongside the women and children. This migration, which included wives, children, soldiers, and the Mighty Men, was a tremendous undertaking. We marched or walked or carried children in a large procession.

Marching to an unknown destination is taxing on both body and mind. As we continued, while still exhausting, the effort became routine and monotonous. My mind started pondering the conversation between David and Ittai. I remembered in David's youth, he had offered services and soldiers to Achish of Gath. Now in middle age, Ittai of Gath was offering services and soldiers to David. The circle is round! Our present king is something of a philosopher. He has started to write down his thoughts, and I've read a few of them. Solomon says there is nothing new under the sun.[44] History is one big circle, eternally rotating the old back to the new.

---

[44] Ecclesiastes 1:9.

One bright spot, we were met fairly early on by a caravan of donkeys carrying supplies. This helped morale. The person who organized the donkeys was the steward of my brother Jonathan's son. He told David a tale of how my nephew remained in Jerusalem in the expectation that Absalom would make him king of the northern tribes in my brother's place. We all appreciated the supplies, but it was a failure on David's part to simply believe the most recent voice in his ear. He was more than willing to take Ziba's word for it. My nephew, who was badly crippled, would have had a terrible time evacuating. He had the opportunity to speak for himself, but this was months later.

As we fled in haste from Jerusalem, at first, the people lining the road and watching our progress were crying and mourning as we passed. Later on, in the area of Bahurim, a man of my father's clan came out and started throwing rocks at us. The population was divided, some in favor of David, others in favor of Absalom. The man throwing the rocks supported my father's family, which may have constituted a third faction? A lost cause!

Our procession stopped on the banks of the River Jordan. We learned that en route, David's adviser, Hushai, had met him on the Mount of Olives. David was distraught, as were the rest of us who'd trudged up the hill with him. Part of David's distress was a direct result of learning that Ahitophel had actively joined Absalom's rebellion. I know why Absalom welcomed him. He thought Ahitophel was key to at least some of his father's successes, and he thought with Ahitophel's help, those successes would fall to him. And by definition, not to his father. David greatly feared Ahitophel's influence. I also knew why Ahitophel joined Absalom. He hated David.

Hushai was prepared to join our caravan to somewhere far from Jerusalem, but David persuaded him to go to Jerusalem instead. He wanted Hushai to join Absalom and thwart any advice coming from Ahitophel. Hushai agreed to do so, and he took his leave. He was admitted into Absalom's inner circle but not without some discussion. Ahitophel was actively opposed and told Absalom not to trust him. When Absalom asked on what basis Hushai was proposing to abandon David, he simply pointed out that he wasn't born to the

Twelve Tribes. He would support whoever the ruler was, and David's time was over. Change had come.

Absalom certainly believed Hushai's words and agreed that accepting himself as king was the practical thing to do. Hushai took his place among Absalom's advisers and, as David had hoped, had the opportunity to disagree with Ahitophel's proposed tactics. Absalom pondered for a while and ended up taking the advice that was counter to Ahitophel's. We learned long afterward that Ahitophel encouraged Absalom to sleep with his father's concubines who had been left in the palace. The symbolic appropriation by the new leader of the old leader's women.

There were two priests in Jerusalem who were loyal to David, and they each had a son. The sons acted as messengers. Zadok's son was named Ahimaaz and Abiathar's son was named Jonathan. The young men showed up with news of the meeting between Absalom, Ahitophel, and Hushai just before sunset. The camp was eating the evening meal, and one of the slaves made sure Ahimaaz and Jonathan were given food and drink. They joined David and David's advisors around the campfire.

David held his tongue long enough for the messengers to catch their breath and to refresh themselves. He finally asked, "Well?"

Ahimaaz swallowed quickly and said, "We were concerned about being seen in Jerusalem. We weren't actually there. We camped at En-Rogel and waited for word."

Jonathan added, "We knew one of the slaves who served wine at the meeting, and she agreed to listen closely to the conversation. After she was dismissed from her duties, she met us at our camp. She is smart and trustworthy. We believe her account, and so can you."

Ahimaaz continued, "In short, Ahitophel counseled that Absalom pursue you, my Lord, immediately, and Hushai counseled that Absalom consolidate his army first. Absalom had to choose one tactic, and he chose to delay. Still, my Lord, the delay will be short. Please take the opportunity to cross the Jordan now."

David answered, "It's almost full dark. I've crossed the Jordan before, but never at night."

"You must. It can be done. The Jordan, happily, is low in this season. The sky is clear, and there's some light from the moon. Hushai had bought you some time. Please don't squander it."

David gave the order. "Everyone is tired and I'm sorry. But we cross the river tonight. Pack up!"

He added to Ahimaaz and Jonathan, "Where will you go?"

"We'll join your party. Absalom knows we left, and we assume he knows why. He sent soldiers after us, but we eluded them. Our fathers will understand."

Jonathan said, "Our fathers will be relieved!"

David asked, "Will your fathers be safe? It wouldn't be the first time priests have suffered for my sake."

Ahimaaz said, "We don't know and we can't know. What we do know is that Absalom knows our loyalty lies with you. Perhaps he will be too occupied with other things to take notice of the fathers of a couple of rebels. But in any case, Jonathan and I can't go back until your army returns victorious to Jerusalem."

We crossed the River Jordan by moonlight. It's true that the river was low and sluggish, and if it hadn't been, I would have despaired of keeping the children safe. As it was, the older children thought the crossing was a big adventure. There was a tendency to squeal when they were sprayed by stray drops of water. Silence would have been desirable, but nobody believed it was remotely possible. The children had their fun, and the whole procession crossed the river before morning.

This particular day of our march or rather day and night was strenuous. We didn't simply camp on the other side of the river once we reached it. The soldiers among us knew of a water source well away from the river, and we spent more than half a day getting to it. On that day, we didn't spend the whole day traveling, which was what we'd become accustomed to doing. The children, if they were lucky enough to have a mule, were asleep in their saddles. All of us were exhausted. David called a halt at the pool in the afternoon, and we set up camp. We stayed through the night and woke up feeling a lot better.

As we walked, day after day, we found ourselves traveling together in groups. For instance, David's wives were a group. We journeyed in the same part of the caravan, and there were at least thirty of us. I didn't try to count. I knew I didn't get along with all of my sister-wives, but it wasn't that difficult to avoid them. I tried, and they probably also tried. Amongst our group were the smaller children. We spent our energy on them and on walking, and none of us had the strength to carry on a feud.

The king's older children walked in a group, although the oldest of David's sons were now part of the army. Adonijah, Shephatiah, and Ithream were officers by this time, serving under Joab. These three sons had been born in Hebron and had been children when I arrived there. There was a group of children who weren't old enough to be soldiers but who were too old to be seen in company with their mothers. This was a mixture of royal children, soldier's children, and servants' children.

The army was all around us. David was leading soldiers at the front, and Ittai was leading soldiers toward the rear. Joab and Abishai each had a contingent, and their men flanked either side of the women and children. We all believed we were fleeing for our lives, and there was a lot of tension associated with the undertaking. Still, to some degree, we felt protected by the omnipresent soldiers.

Absalom followed us, but days later. Our journey took us all the way to Mahanaim, Esh-Baal's former capitol. It was a dry, hot, dirty, exhausting march. The weather wasn't a constant hazard, but it was bad enough. The rains came, the tents were inadequate, and the roads, such as they were, were slippery with mud. David doesn't always get kind words from me, but I do give him credit—he shared his soldiers' hardships, despite being king and being older than the average soldier. We tried very hard to protect the children from both the elements and from dehydration. It was a long monotonous journey, and the children survived.

At night, I shared a tent with Ahinoam and Abigail, whom I counted as friends. There was another woman, Bathsheba, whom I didn't know well, and she had a two-year-old son. I knew *of* Bathsheba, of course. Everyone did. But she'd been ensconced in the king's quarters, and none of the other wives had gotten to know her. She was thrown together with the rest of us rather suddenly. I hope we were welcoming. It was wives like her with small children of whom the rest of us tried to be especially mindful.

Abigail posed a neutral question, "What's your baby's name?"

The child wasn't really a baby. He was very mobile and very curious.

Bathsheba answered, "Solomon."

Ahinoam actually got down on her knees, to Solomon's level, and started to play with him. He had never encountered any of us before, but he wasn't particularly shy. If Ahinoam wanted to play, Solomon would accommodate her.

I'll never forget one of the first things Bathsheba said to me. It wasn't just to me. We were all there in the tent, Ahinoam, Abigail, and I. Bathsheba was the youngster of the group. We were away from Jerusalem in a rather uncomfortable shelter, and she said, "I'm so glad to be out of the king's quarters."

The king's quarters were the most comfortable and luxurious quarters in the country, so I had to ask, "Why?"

Bathsheba replied, "They're stifling. And it's lonely there. And if any of David's advisers happen to come in, I can feel their disapproval. Oh, they stare at me the way men stare at women, but it's when they think I'm not looking. It's unnerving. Some of the slaves speak kindly to me, but I don't have anyone there I could call a friend. I suppose the women's quarters are crowded, but I am tired of spending so much time alone or in the company of my son.

"You must know I was married before David, and my situation wasn't so different then, albeit without any children, left alone for weeks at a time while my husband was out fighting battles. I am hoping—well, I hope a lot of things. Maybe I should hope first for our husband's success. But I hope to return to Jerusalem and hope to live in the women's quarters with other wives."

Abigail said, "I hope you won't be disappointed. There are certainly things about the women's quarters that are stifling."

I continued, "You would be most welcome. You'll find female company there. There are many personalities within a small space, and you'll undoubtedly find that you are more compatible with some wives than others. If we propose to venture outside, our movements are quite restricted. We *can* leave as long as we're escorted. Maybe that's better than your present situation."

"I believe it will be. I'm looking forward to it. I feel a freedom out here in a tent that I haven't felt since I was a girl. I fear for the safety of my son, but when I'm not fearing for him, I feel a sort of exhilaration in these circumstances, a sort of loosening of the usual rules. Maybe danger is exhilarating."

The four of us and Bathsheba's son spent all of our nights together in the tent. We got to know Bathsheba a bit. I was the exception, as usual. I'd never borne a child. The other three were all mothers who'd lost sons. Bathsheba was the newcomer to the group, but there were times when I felt like the outsider.

Bathsheba had been blessed with another healthy son, though she was far from gloating about it. The first years of any child's life were the most dangerous ones. She was right to fear for Solomon on this rigorous journey.

CHAPTER 39

Year 456

During the course of the journey, I tried one more time. It may be that I found some inspiration in Absalom's boldness. No, I don't mean his insurrection. But he used a very unlikely method of getting Joab's attention, and it worked for his purposes at the time. I also felt that Bathsheba was probably right when she mentioned the relaxing of the usual rules.

Most of my attempts to see David consisted of getting from the women's quarters of the palace to the king's quarters. I never got past his security. The situation in which we found ourselves now was entirely different. There were plenty of soldiers at hand but no palaces! There were none of the usual protocols. I took advantage of the moment.

I was in the tent with the usual group and we were trying to sleep. The camp was noisy. First of all, the wind was a distraction. It wasn't gale-force, but it was strong enough and there were drops of rain in it. I would hear a *ping* against the tent sides every so often. There were dogs barking, and there were children crying. The soldiers were making the noises soldiers make, cursing under their breaths and jangling their weapons and armor.

As far as I could tell, my tent-mates did fall asleep. I gave up trying, got dressed, and found my heavy cloak. I put the cloak over my hair and body and wrapped it as tightly as I could. I knew where David's tent would be and set off in that direction. I watched for guards. I thought I could avoid them, but it's not easy to avoid anything with one's cloak wrapped around one's head. I knew the ground was uneven, and I was trying to be aware of that too. I couldn't see very well.

Not too much later, I was grasped from behind. I screamed, more out of surprise than fear. A female scream can be jarring. I didn't know how much attention it would garner above the noise of the camp, but there was some. Joab came out from a small tent that was behind the king's. He asked the soldier what was going on, and the soldier pulled off my cloak. Joab sighed audibly. He took my cloak and wrapped me back up in it. He dismissed the soldier and said he would handle the intruder, specifically me.

"Joab, I just need to talk to him for five minutes. I'm not a threat, I promise!"

Joab laughed. I had to laugh too. The journey had been so stressful that there hadn't been any laughter for a long time, and it felt good. In those days, not many people called me by my given name. I was either the daughter of Saul or the wife of David and was entitled to certain honorifics. But Joab had known me too long. I was his best friend's wife, and that was all. He guided me to one of several wooden benches around a fire and sat down beside me. There were a few soldiers seated there, and some were sipping beer.

"Michal, I know you're not a threat. And Michal, I sympathize with your position. I sympathize, but not enough to disobey a direct order. I have mentioned your name a time or two to David, and it hasn't helped at all. He believes your disrespect is unforgivable. It's not, but that's what he believes. Right now, tonight, the greater problem is that David isn't alone."

"You? Unwilling to disobey a direct order? That's hard to believe!"

Joab smiled. He'd been known to disobey an order or two, and unbeknownst to me, he'd even tried to advocate for me. But David was stubborn. Joab guided me to one of the benches facing the fire and sat down beside me. The two of us absorbed the warmth in silence.

Then Joab said, "I am having an unexpected opportunity to get to know Adonijah a bit. I hadn't thought much about him before. He seemed like a peacock. But I'm impressed. We are far away from the easy life at the palace, and Adonijah has adapted better than I thought he would. He also seems to be able to command men."

I answered, "So what does Adonijah think about his brother, Absalom? I had always thought the two were quite close. If they were as close as I thought they were, surely Adonijah had to make a decision which king, if you will, to support."

"I asked him that, and believe it or not, Absalom didn't invite him. He didn't go to Hebron and he had no idea of Absalom's plans until those plans became public knowledge. It may be that Adonijah is a little bit insulted, but he says he was prevented from having to make a decision that would have been a hard one. I asked him directly. He said he doesn't know whether he'd have sided with his brother or not, and now he can't know. He will bring whatever leadership skills he possesses in support of his father. In the meantime, he's learning for the first time about a soldier's life. He's making the best of it."

Joab asked if I wanted a bowl of beer, and I said no. Joab was a general, but he still took ribbing from his men occasionally.

One of the soldiers near the fire spoke up. "Hey, Joab! Pretty little bit you've got there!" I assume at least some soldiers could have identified Joab's wife. My cloak was still on, but it had slipped off my head. My face and hair were fully exposed.

Joab almost stood up. I performed the forbidden gesture of putting my hand on his leg. I surprised him and myself. I jerked back my hand as soon as I became aware of what it was doing, but it was too late. Joab sat back down. As many times as I'd almost reached out to Joab like a brother, the eventual act was inevitable.

The three soldiers across the fire watched us with interest. The soldier who'd spoken up, who had probably drunk one bowl of beer too many, caught both of us off guard. I had a casual, comfortable relationship with Joab and wasn't nearly concerned enough about what it looked like from the outside. Now I had touched him, and in public no less. I'd given the soldiers reason to believe we were behaving improperly.

After Joab recovered from my touch, he defended himself. "This is one of King David's wives."

I mumbled, "I need to leave." I'd done enough damage. I knew my face was flaming red, but the warmth of the fire would have disguised it. I stood up, pulling my cloak over my hair, and went back to my tent. The raindrops in the wind were becoming more noticeable. I never tried again.

That endeavor certainly didn't help me sleep. I tossed and turned some more and must have at least dozed. When dawn broke, it was a relief. The camp was awake and preparing to continue the journey.

Our caravan went as far east as Mahanaim, a location with which I was somewhat familiar. David may have left Jerusalem with no real destination in mind, but when we got to Mahanaim, we stopped. It turned out that David had an ardent supporter there named Barzillai who was elderly and wealthy. Barzillai used his own resources to meet the daily needs of a large group of refugees. We were relatively comfortable in the quarters that were found for us.

We wives and children were housed in the dwelling that Esh-Baal had built for himself and that had served as his headquarters and palace. It hadn't been lived in since my brother's death. It had been built well and hadn't been devastated by weather or scavenging humans. It could have been cleaner. There were signs that small animals had taken up residence. We had brought enough slaves with us that they made the place habitable quickly.

Once we had adequate shelter, we all collapsed for a day or so, even the slaves. Our sojourn in Esh-Baal's palace was a terribly uncertain, frightening time. Those of us who had followed David to Mahanaim had a real stake in the eventual outcome and a lot to lose if all didn't go well for David. I thought that the children would have no choice but to reflect the anxiety of the adults, but that wasn't true. Maybe our acting skills were better than we thought. The children did what children everywhere do—went outside and found local children to play with.

Mahanaim—we women with our children got the luxury of resting there. Clearly the soldiers didn't. They did rest, but not for long. Joab had everyone up and practicing drills after a couple of days. It didn't take long for Esh-Baal's palace to feel small. It was harder than it had been to avoid Maacah and Haggith.

I doubt there was a private conversation to be had. Everyone heard everything. So I wasn't surprised to hear a conversation between Maacah and Haggith, even if I wasn't actively eavesdropping. There was something about Maacah's voice that was harsh, maybe high and nasal. I knew immediately who was speaking, whether I saw her or not. I can't have been the only one within earshot, and the words weren't entirely discreet. Maacah wasn't known for her discretion. She might have been even less likely to think before she spoke than I was!

"This entire palace, or should I say house, is on the edge of hysteria. I still don't understand the urgency. We're talking about my son here. This place can't honestly be called a palace. It's tiny! My son is a perfectly reasonable man. He sees a need for a change in leadership, and since his following is huge, he's not the only one. It's our mutual husband who's being unreasonable."

Haggith's voice was less distinctive and less grating. I simply assume Maacah was talking to Haggith because I can't imagine her saying what she said to anyone else.

"So you are caught between your husband and your son? You have nothing to fear from whatever results from this miserable journey? You win whatever the outcome? Yes, the rest of us are married to David and aren't Absalom's mother. How should we feel about what could happen to us? To me, it's much more likely that if your son wins, David's wives lose."

"Haggith, you will not lose. I will protect you."

"Will you protect my son?"

I didn't hear anything else. If Maacah answered the question, she whispered it. I can't pretend I've been privy to all the conversations between Maacah and Haggith, but this one caught my attention. I actually hadn't known that Haggith was smart enough to be afraid and afraid for her son. On the other hand, we lived in an atmosphere of fear and everyone felt it. I was also surprised to see that Haggith had enough backbone to at least nominally stand up to Maacah.

In general, the Twelve Tribes didn't exhibit an obvious preference of the old king over the new young blood. Whatever the outcome, their lives wouldn't change. We, David's wives, learned to pray. The residents of Mahanaim, possibly due to the influence of Barzillai, had taken a stand with the old king. They had given the old king shelter; they were now complicit. They, too, had a lot to lose if it turned out that they'd supported the wrong army. The vast majority of the Twelve Tribes, of course, was sitting back and watching and waiting.

Some of us thought Elohim was on our side. Was that arrogant? All these years later, looking back on my life and times, I have to ask whether Elohim approves of war in general. War is ugly! War is ugly, but tradition has it that Moses and Joshua were tasked with taking the land around the River Jordan by force, which requires war and which was at least theoretically sanctioned by Elohim.

We heard that Absalom had been crowned king in Hebron. We didn't hear that he'd been anointed. David had been anointed a total of three times, always with consensus of the tribal elders. We hoped it was he who was the Lord's Anointed and not Absalom.

I am no martial strategist, but occasionally, I have wondered why David decided to evacuate Jerusalem. It was an ordeal in and of itself and it was hazardous. Yes, I remembered the conversation with Ittai and, yes, I remembered that David thought the evacuation would help his son's chances of survival. What about his own? Did David have no concerns about his own life? The rest of us did!

David went to war against his son. It appeared to David's following that it couldn't be avoided, though maybe David thought it could. Is it possible that David thought Absalom would be happy with the southern tribes and with Jerusalem while David ruled the northern tribes? History repeating itself! When Absalom's army pursued David all the way to Mahanaim, the answer became clear. Absalom was prepared to kill his father. Absalom's army was advancing. By the time it arrived in our environs, David's men had the advantage of being somewhat rested.

David organized the men who had accompanied us in exile and explained a strategy that involved meeting the pursuing army in the forests of Ephraim. David used Joab, Abishai, and the Philistine, Ittai, to lead three different divisions. The forest was a treacherous place. David chose it for the battlefield once he finally conceded that there would be a battle. The army that chooses the battlefield has an automatic advantage. The fighting within the forest was very difficult and close.

There was a huge amount of tension within the walls of Esh-Baal's house and too many people crowded within it. I do believe that once the battle began, some of the tension eased. The anticipation was driving us all crazy. We'd reached the point of no return. There would be an end and soon.

Absalom was extremely handsome. In fact, he was more beautiful than any man should be allowed to be, and he knew it. He was very vain about his hair. It was very long and very thick, and occasionally, he would have a public haircut. The cut hair would be weighed at such time as Absalom got tired of carrying it around, and it often weighed about five pounds. Absalom must have gone longer than usual without cutting his hair because it literally caused his death.

Absalom's soldiers were being defeated by David's soldiers, and Absalom was retreating on a mule. The forest was David's friend. How does a man not notice a low-lying tree branch? Maybe Absalom looked behind him one too many times. His mule hurried efficiently under the branch without a lot of regard for his rider. Absalom was jerked off the mule when his head got stuck in a forked branch of an oak tree. The mule went on its way while Absalom was left dangling. Absalom's beautiful hair got tangled in the smaller branches, which made his predicament worse.

Absalom was unmistakable. His predicament was noticed by one of Joab's men, who told Joab. The soldier who came upon the helpless Absalom had no intention of touching him. David had made it known to Joab, Abishai, Ittai, and everyone else that he didn't want his son killed. Joab and ten armor-bearers killed him anyway. The rebellion effectively ended with the death of its leader, leaving David the victor. Cause for celebration!

Instead of encouraging his soldiers who had given their all for their king, probably saved his life, definitely saved his throne, and had won a difficult battle, David retreated to a room to mourn. Joab was incensed. He demanded that David quit moping and commend his soldiers. David did. But David's relationship with his sister's sons was strained. It had suffered when David ordered a comrade's death, and now Joab had killed his extremely disloyal son.

David wasn't the only one moping. I never thought I'd see a subdued Maacah, but she was severely impacted by the death of her golden son. Was it only that now she would never be queen mother? If what Maacah ultimately craved was power, there would have been a sort of power in that forever unattainable position. She made the journey back to Jerusalem with the rest of us, but she wasn't the same person. Thank goodness for Tamar! Maacah got support from both Tamar and Haggith, but her downward spiral almost certainly began with Absalom's death. She was no longer my sworn enemy, which should have been a relief. I can be spiteful, but I never rejoiced in any woman's loss of a child—even an adult child.

CHAPTER 40

Year 456

David's family was large. It wasn't surprising that some of his relatives had supported Absalom. Joab and Abishai were sons of one of David's sisters, and Absalom's main general was the son of another sister. Absalom, Joab, Abishai, and Amasa were cousins. David was furious with Joab and decided to take this opportunity to replace him. He named Amasa as his new general.

Their conversation reverberated across Mahanaim.

David shouted, "You killed my son! What did you expect me to do? Reward you?"

Joab answered, "David, I killed the man who almost certainly would have killed you, given the chance, and the man who plunged the Twelve Tribes into civil war. What did *you* expect *me* to do?"

"What did I expect? I expected you to follow my orders!" David's anger gave way to grief, and he started weeping. "Absalom, my son, my son! Why couldn't it have been me who died? Joab, how can you know that Elohim wouldn't have blessed my son? He may well have been a better king than I. I want you out of my sight and want Amasa in your place."

Joab pointed out, "I have been loyal to you over the years and against many enemies. One would hope that after all this time, you could at least recognize your enemies. Amasa is not your friend."

David ended the conversation by walking away. I noticed how Joab had called the king by his given name, even in front of all of us who'd journeyed to Mahanaim. Typical Joab! I wondered whether David would now shun Joab in the way he shunned me? Should Joab be grateful that David didn't have him struck down? How dangerous is it to display anger toward a king? Still, if David were to take this approach, we would almost certainly have had another civil war. Some soldiers would have been loyal to David, but others would have been loyal to Joab. David chose not to resort to violence. A demotion was enough, at least for the moment.

It was time to go home. The caravan began the preparations to return to Jerusalem, and Joab bided his time.

So began the dry, hot, dirty, exhausting march back to Jerusalem. Yes, the return journey was all of those things, but I sound like a whiner. At this stage of my life, I had done a certain amount of traveling and had lived in more than one location. I hope I was observant enough to find beauty. We were spending most of our waking moments outside, and the natural beauty of the terrain was harder to miss. We didn't have to trudge through the mountains, and I had conversations with soldiers who had. It's arduous, and at least our path was moderately level. But mountains are beautiful if you're not trying to cross them. Rivers are beautiful and so is the area around them, lush and green. I had occasionally seen the River Jordan high and fast with speeding white water.

During those times, I wasn't trying to cross it, and it was certainly more beautiful than the low, meandering brown version of it. I thought about the mighty Jordan and wondered what our upcoming crossing would look like. Olive trees, heavy with fruit, are beautiful. Rainbows are beautiful. We all experienced many sunrises and sunsets, some ablaze with color. Beauty is there if a person is willing to look up!

David and his army were almost spent. We had the same number of children going back, and now we had wounded soldiers. I had brought a few of my healing potions with me when we all left Jerusalem but by no means enough. I used the ointments I'd brought. There were some besides me who had some basic knowledge of cleaning wounds. We assisted the wounded to the best of our ability. We learned that several slaves had some healing knowledge. We were all fully occupied in addition to putting one foot in front of the other.

We used those same tents on our return journey and shared space with the same women with whom we'd shared before. Everyone was weary, but we women had the advantage of not having spent our energy fighting in an overgrown forest. We huddled in our tents at night and tried to sleep. I was up late one night, having to urinate. I've made note of the fact that military encampments aren't really quiet, but there can be something very peaceful about a starry night. During the journey, we were never alone. The lack of solitude sometimes made me anxious. I took advantage of the moment. I walked back close to the tents and just sat on a rock for a few minutes, gazing up. More beauty—a clear night!

I became mindful of weeping from one of the tents. It was Maacah's voice between sobs. Haggith's voice was present too. I didn't make out any words. But I did recall the conversation the two of them had earlier when Haggith asked Maacah if she expected to win no matter which army took the day. That was a nice sentiment, but it wasn't true. Maacah was still alive and was still the wife of the king, but she wasn't feeling victorious as the dust settled. She had lost her shooting star son. He'd made a huge, brilliant display and crashed to the ground.

I surprised myself by feeling some sympathy, though I never would have intruded on Maacah and Haggith in the dead of night. They wouldn't have appreciated it! I didn't sit on the rock long. I got cold quickly. I reentered my tent as carefully as I could and wrapped myself up in the bedding I'd brought. I made another effort to relax and sleep.

The journey back felt longer than the journey away. It wasn't longer, but it was slower. I remember the weather wasn't too bad, but it was windy enough to be unpleasant. The constant breeze seemed to encourage the small biting insects. There is also something about wounds that attracts insects, though the other women and I wrapped any wounds as best we could. We did battle with insects the entire way back along with the usual difficulties, like uneven ground, rocks, rain, and mud.

When we finally reached the River Jordan, close enough for us to see the Benjaminite city of Gilgal on the other side, we were met by some of David's supporters who had remained in Jerusalem. They helped us cross the river and also escorted us back to Jerusalem. It was another uneventful river crossing which none of us would ever take for granted. We all witnessed the joyous reunion of Zadok and Abiathar with their sons. We hadn't expected Absalom to take out his anger on priests, and he hadn't.

My nephew was among the crowd who met us at the river, his crippled condition notwithstanding. He rode a mule, which helped. This was the man whose steward told David that he was waiting to share the kingdom with a triumphant Absalom. That was not the story my nephew told, and in the end, David didn't try to punish anyone.

My crippled nephew, Mephibosheth, told us all the rest of the story of Ahitophel. I have to assume that Ahitophel, not that he was any great friend of mine, had some difficulty dealing with the death of his son. And he would certainly and justifiably have blamed David. When Absalom took Hushai's advice instead of his, he was devastated. He simply gave up. It was reported that he went to Giloh, put his affairs in order, and hanged himself.

I thought about being proven right. Ahitophel was proven right, though being dead, he never knew. If Absalom had taken his advice, would Absalom be king now? King of all twelve of the tribes? Ahitophel could have been rewarded with a powerful government position. But since all of that didn't happen, Ahitophel's position would have been untenable had he survived.

The River Jordan was kind to us again. If it was higher than it had been when we crossed to the east, it still wasn't dangerous. We had all seen dangerous. All of us got across, those of us who were physically healthy assisting those of us who weren't. We got daylight this time, which was a relief. David was the last to cross. He was saying farewell to Barzillai who had come with the caravan as far as the river. David wanted Barzillai to come to Jerusalem. Barzillai was old. He didn't want to radically change his life at his age, and he preferred to be buried in his father's tomb. He declined and returned to Mahanaim.

David had barely gotten out of the river. Our group was approaching Gilgal when we all became aware of a loud squabble. The Twelve Tribes had a tendency to divide naturally into Judah to the south and Israel to the north. The men of Israel complained that the men of Judah had spirited David and his family away from Jerusalem with no input from them. There were harsh words exchanged.

These were followed by more than words, an overt act of division. It didn't take much. The northern tribes were feeling slighted. They, too, were being ruled by David, and yet the men of Judah felt justified in ignoring their interest. His name was Sheba, and he was of the tribe of Benjamin. He blew a trumpet and shouted to all who would listen, "We have no share in David, no part in Jesse's son. Every man to his tent, O Israel!"[45]

The men of the northern tribes, feeling offended, saw an opportunity to support somebody else, and they left their brothers of Judah and followed Sheba. Why? Who was Sheba? A great warrior? Not yet! David had been intent on restoring unity. He hadn't attempted to stop the supporters of Absalom from fading unmolested into the villages and forests, but there were limits to his tolerance. He wasn't prepared to allow Sheba and his followers to defy him, especially right as he was reclaiming his throne. If Sheba got anything out of this enterprise, beyond notoriety, I have no idea what. He managed a few seditious statements, caught the attention of some defeated and resentful soldiers, and ran for his life with his newly created following. The would-be army got as far as the fortified city of Abel Beth Maacah.

The civil war that both David and Joab tried to avoid happened anyway, albeit a very small one. David wanted to try out his new general, Amasa, and gave him three days to send word through Judah and mobilize some soldiers. Amasa wasn't back in three days, and David lost patience. But he didn't approach Joab. He approached Abishai and sent him off in pursuit of Sheba. Joab stayed at his brother's side. Amasa caught up with the army near the great rock of Gibeon. Joab did almost the exact same thing to Amasa that he'd done to Abner—stabbed him in the stomach. This was Joab's stock response to the

---

[45] 2 Samuel 20:1.

losing general. One of Joab's men proclaimed, "Whoever favors Joab and whoever is for David, let him follow Joab."[46]

If David had intended Abishai to supplant Joab, it didn't work. Joab led David's forces to Abel Beth Maacah and laid siege to the city. The city wasn't interested in supporting a rebel to the death and threw Sheba's head down to Joab's forces. Joab's forces put the head in a basket, dispersed, and returned to Jerusalem with it. The city fathers of Abel Beth Maacah politely and strongly invited the followers of Sheba to leave their city.

While the healthy soldiers of David's army pursued Sheba, the rest of us proceeded to Jerusalem. I was concerned about the concubines who had been left behind. I would have gone to them to make sure they were well, but David had already had them taken from the women's quarters. He put them in a house a little ways away and he set a guard at the door. I was allowed to visit them. Absalom had indeed taken all of them to his bed, and one of them was pregnant. David rejected them all after that. He made sure they had the daily needs, but he didn't visit them nor invite them to his bed. He just locked them in a house and forgot them. I did assist the one pregnant concubine when her time came. She bore David a grandchild whom he never deigned to acknowledge.

I truly sympathized with the ten concubines, though there wasn't much I could do for them. I was allowed to visit them, which I did occasionally. It wasn't that they really lacked anything I could have brought. I was never clear on whether they appreciated my company or not. I'd bring news of the outside world to the best of my ability. Most of it came from Joab.

I have met many women in my day, some of whom enjoyed a certain amount of autonomy—Bathsheba, the daughter of Pharaoh, the Queen of Sheba. But other women, and I numbered myself among them, were very little more than the possessions of some man. Men mostly definitely hold almost all the power, and for the most part, don't view women as competent. Symbols! I understood the concept but really hated it insofar as it applied to human beings. I

250

tried not to dwell on the shortcomings of our society, but sometimes I grieved over people whose choices were so much limited by other people. Some people don't mind being cared for all their lives. Some people feel imprisoned.

The ravished concubines aside, we were elated to be home. We all hoped for a lot less excitement in the future.

CHAPTER 41

Year 457

I always believed that Israel's god, Elohim, didn't demand human sacrifice. He certainly didn't require babies to be laid on white-hot altars, but I did witness human sacrifice, and it was in the name of Elohim. No, it wasn't called that! I don't care what it was called. That's what it was! I am now in danger of being struck down for blasphemy before I can finish my story.

The crops need sun at the appropriate times and rain at the appropriate times. There is great hardship when the seasons don't bring the conditions on which our farmers rely. Our country suffered many years ago from a famine that lasted three years. Joab told me that David consulted Elohim and that Elohim pointed him toward the city of Gibeon. I do not begin to understand Elohim's timing, if indeed David got his information from the Lord's mouth. Joab thought he had. This famine occurred *long* after my father's death.

David commanded that the elders of Gibeon send a delegation to Jerusalem, and he questioned them about the famine. The Gibeonites had a long-standing grudge against my father for leveling their city despite the treaty signed by Joshua.[47] The Gibeonites saw an opportunity for vengeance against my father, and they took it. It is written that the sons bear the consequences for the sins of the fathers.[48] My sister and I watched those events play out. The Gibeonites demanded seven male descendants of my father to be

---

[47] Joshua 9:15.
[48] Exodus 20:5; Numbers 14:18.

killed and exposed on a hill to the foxes and the birds. They assured David that the famine would end after this act.

David knew about my father's sons and grandsons. My father had five grandsons in Meholah, the sons of my sister, Merab. The youngest was five years old. My father and Rizpah had two surviving sons in Mahanaim. David sent out two companies of soldiers, one to Meholah and another to Mahanaim. I wasn't there. I can only imagine the shock of the families when David's troops took away their sons.

My sister and her husband followed her sons to Gibeon. So did Rizpah. When I heard about it, I demanded an escort to Gibeon. I met my sister and her husband in Gibeon. My sister has always taken pride in her appearance, but when I first saw her, she didn't look good. The journey itself was long and hard, and she was following her sons who were under arrest for nothing. She was beside herself. Her face was swollen and red. Her clothing hung on her body. Her husband tried hard to be strong, and he succeeded better in some moments than others.

"Adriel, what is going on? Do you understand any of this? Rizpah, what's going on?"

Rizpah said nothing. She collapsed into tears, and my sister joined her.

Adriel had a little more success with speaking. "We have all felt the effects of the famine. It's devastating our food supply, not to mention our water supply. The elders of Gibeon have told King David that Elohim sent a famine to punish King Saul for breaking the treaty. Since King Saul has been dead for many years, and since King Saul rests in the hands of Elohim, I do not see how this can be. What more can Elohim want of him? But King David believes it. The Gibeonites have demanded the lives of seven of King Saul's male descendants, and King David is accommodating. My sons, my beautiful sons!" Adriel could no longer hold back the tears.

David handpicked the seven males. I knew specifically of another grandson of my father whom David protected. He was Jonathan's son, Mephibosheth, and he lived in the palace. We had approached the city of Gibeon as part of a military procession. There were a lot of soldiers, there were the condemned individuals, there were family members, and the usual curious onlookers. Were the elders of Gibeon "curious onlookers?" We saw them standing on the other side of the field. They were clearly there to make sure David kept the agreement. I stared at them and tried not to hate.

It might be easy to hate your parents for thrusting you into a king's harem. It might be just as easy to hate Solomon for not taking notice of you. I looked at my own response to the executions of my nephews and my half-brothers and realized how easy it is to hate. Hate is destructive, and the individuals I was proposing to hate would never know it. The only person affected by my hate would be me. It's a futile and negative emotion. It's all very well and good to analyze hate as an emotion to be avoided, but sometimes...did I hate David? I can't answer that.

Those of us who were there to bear witness were held back by soldiers when Merab's and Rizpah's sons were marched up a low hill adjacent to a field. They were positioned in a row with a soldier behind each of them. I watched the soldier behind Merab's five-year-old son, Obed. Obed was crying. He was scared. The soldier behind him towered over him and seemed detached. It all happened very quickly after that. The soldiers slit the throats of the descendant of my father whom they were guarding, and they acted almost in unison. The bodies dropped to the ground, and the soldiers withdrew. The bodies were left where they fell.

I stood with my sister, her husband, and Rizpah and watched the executions. Merab sobbed and shook. I cried and held her. Rizpah collapsed. I was focused on Merab, but there were women near Rizpah who did their best to minister to her. Adriel cried. This was in the eighth month. I do not regret making my feeble attempt to support my sister in her grief. But it was the most horrible sight I have ever seen.

I mentioned Solomon's spies and his insistence on keeping the peace. Is this what soldiers do, day-to-day? Is this how peace is kept? I wondered if slitting throats was a commonplace activity for soldiers who were between battles. The whole process seemed nonchalant. How often did soldiers kill children? There were no altars and there was no fire, but there was a lot of blood. The seven deaths were just as real.

It has been difficult for me to come to terms with the concept that sons should be held responsible for their fathers' shortcomings. I knew the famine existed. I was a rather sheltered wife of the king, but the famine affected us all. We in the women's quarters got food, but it hadn't been good quality for some time. We got water, but it was limited. We didn't bathe when we wanted to. The water was meant for drinking and for cooking. I didn't believe that executing seven innocent males would solve the problem. But after it was done, the rains came almost immediately. How was this possible? If Elohim doesn't control the weather and the way the land produces, then who? Since it was harvest time, those rains weren't entirely welcome. This was the only execution I ever saw. Most executions are public. A person who wishes to observe one can do so. I choose not to.

I've expounded at length about symbols, women as symbols of a man's power, blood as a symbol of atonement. Is rain a symbol of cleansing? For whatever reason, I found some comfort in the gentle rain that washed my face and hands and washed away the blood of my relatives. We all got wet, of course.

We had all taken shelter with various families in Gibeon, and as it rained, we all retreated to those homes. I was the notorious daughter of the man who had inflicted devastation on Gibeon, and so was Merab. I have to assume the townspeople knew who we were, but they didn't make us feel unwelcome. Any mother of Gibeon had great sympathy for Merab.

Adriel, Merab, and I were all housed in the same dwelling, one of the larger ones in Gibeon. The three of us had a whole room in which to sleep. We arrived back cold and wet. There wasn't an option for a warm bath at that time, though bathing would become commonplace again in the future. We were treated to hot tea and warm coverings for our feet. There was a blazing fire in the hearth of the main room, and our clothing dried fairly quickly. We were all planning to partake of supper, and we sat together with the owners of the dwelling as we waited and warmed up.

The owner of the home was an older man named Hiram. I was trying to guess his age, and I didn't quite deem him to be a contemporary of my father. But he was heading into infirmity, and he walked slowly, using a stick. His voice was still strong and his hearing seemed good. I'm not sure about his eyesight. His mind was intact. And so were his memories, for better or for worse.

Hiram told us his story, the story that featured our father. He wasn't trying to make us feel bad, but like so many people, he thought his story should be told before he died. And he believed that the perfect audience would be the daughters of the king in question.

CHAPTER 42

Year 416

"I was a boy. Gibeon had been at peace for all of my short lifetime, just because our city was under the protection of the Twelve Tribes. Or so we thought. We had the basic training in weapons that men and boys get, but we weren't battle-hardened. We also had very few weapons, though we all had knives and scythes.

"King Saul and his army swooped down upon us one early morning like a swarm of locusts. We were shocked. We understood that the Twelve Tribes' government had evolved to include a king, but it never occurred to us that our daily lives would be affected by it. I didn't follow politics then, but my parents, at least, were aware that the old treaty had been updated and presumably with the blessing of the king. Our city was still upholding our end of the treaty, specifically gathering wood and carrying water for the cities surrounding us, the cities occupied by the descendants of Israel.

"It was a massacre. My father faced down a mounted soldier who held a sword. My father armed himself with the knife he used to skin rabbits. I watched because I couldn't help myself as my father's head flew off his body. The men of Gibeon were very brave, and the mounted soldier found himself distracted by the feeble resistance that was offered. My mother, my two sisters, and I faded into the woods on the other side of a flat field. We were very visible on the field, but we were also lucky. It didn't take too long to cross to the trees, where we were effectively hidden. That was where we encountered other residents of our town.

"We slogged through the woods with a goodly number of people, a lot of whom were children. It was difficult. The woods were thick with low-lying branches, thickets, thorny bushes, and lots of dead leaves covering the ground, hiding any hazards like holes or tree roots. There was some concern about wild animals, and we did hear some, though we didn't see any. We got all the way through the woods to a clearing where we found a different section of the stream that feeds Gibeon. We all collapsed there in exhaustion with no food and no shelter, though we managed to be grateful for water. We didn't dare light a fire. We spent that first night in the open, trying to sleep, but assigning watches. It seemed clear by morning that there wouldn't be any pursuit. So we busied ourselves with details like finding shelter and food.

"The stream watered trees and grasses, but it also cut through a stretch of low, rocky hills. We found a cave system, which certainly isn't a comfortable shelter, but it's a shelter, which is more than we had on our first night. We explored enough to find two entrances, and we lit fires near both of them. After that came the effort to obtain food, and if I may, I'll use the word *luck* again. We were farmers. We planted and we harvested. We weren't hunters, though some of us were able to snare some rabbits. I hope you're not offended by rabbits. Yes, I know that rabbits are forbidden to members of the Twelve Tribes,[49] but as you know, we citizens of Gibeon weren't part of your community, and we weren't bound by your dietary laws. At the time, when rabbits were food and were available, we were grateful for the fact. We were also well aware that our present predicament had everything to do with essentially being outsiders. We caught a few fish. Some women gathered edible plants. We pieced together very limited meals. We subsisted. Maybe we could have grown adept at this way of life with a little practice, but we weren't actually refugees for long—for which we were most grateful.

"We spent about a week in the cave, and after that, we sent out two scouts. Two of the older boys who were fit and who could move with grace volunteered to go back to our town to see if there were still soldiers there. Before they left, we made sure to give them an additional share of food. They came back and reported that the soldiers

---

[49] Leviticus 11:6.

were gone but that there wasn't much left. We left the cave and made our way back to what used to be our town.

"Some dwellings were burnt to the ground. A few were intact. The first priority was to bury our dead. My mother took on the task of finding my father's head and his body. I couldn't—"

Hiram broke down and wept. One of his daughters held out his bowl of beer, and he sipped.

"It was a long time ago. But there are some things a person never forgets. We all applied ourselves, house by house, to rebuilding. And field by field to replanting. Our town isn't without scars, but then I have to assume that all towns have scars. It has been many years since this atrocity against us, and we have only now been granted retribution. I was there. I witnessed the deaths of the sons of Gibeon's great enemy. Am I satisfied? It is written: a life for a life. The survivors of Gibeon didn't demand of David the destruction of a city.

"But now that the family of Saul has paid, it all feels hollow. Our town has been rebuilt, there are new crops, there are new children. We, the survivors, the foundation for the next phase of the life of Gibeon, witnessed a great irony. This king who tried to destroy our town moved his people's tabernacle to our high place. The high place of Gibeon wasn't touched. The circle is round."

CHAPTER 43

Year 457

I watched Merab, who had just lost five children. She seemed almost detached. Her expression never changed. She sat still as a statue. I'm not sure she heard a word Hiram said.

We, the family members of Saul, left the following day. When my sister and her husband returned to Meholath, I returned to Jerusalem.

I found out later that Rizpah had stayed and had lived rough, outside, keeping the scavengers away from the bodies of her sons and my nephews. She never touched the bodies, but she guarded them through the nights. She did this for several months. David eventually found out, and when he did, he arranged for the decent burial of those bodies, plus the bodies of my father and my brother, which had been resting in Jabesh Gilead.

David sent a contingent of soldiers back to Gibeon to collect the remains. I got permission to accompany the soldiers, and I spoke to Rizpah there on the slope. Even a few months later, Rizpah was much changed. Living outdoors isn't good for the human body. Rizpah looked wild. Also, childbearing takes its toll as a mother ages. Rizpah looked more dumpy in her elder years and less curvy. I offered her sanctuary, if you will, in the women's quarters of the palace, but she refused. I didn't hear of her after that. I'm not sure what her options might have been with her sons dead and her lover dead. I hope some of her daughters were well and in happy marriages. She might have found support there. It made me start thinking about Sarah. I can't believe I failed to ask Rizpah about Sarah when I had the chance.

The soldiers completed their grisly task of gathering up the remains of my nephews and Rizpah's sons at Gibeon. Joab and Abishai led that battalion that was sent to Gibeon and later to Jabesh Gilead to collect human remains. Neither one of them was impressed by drawing grave duty. I didn't speak to Abishai on that occasion, but as always, I met up with Joab.

Joab was complaining, "I can't believe David needs a general to gather up remains for burial. He specifically sent Abishai and me to supervise this task. Maybe I shouldn't be so surprised. I did kill his son, after all, and it's been difficult for him to stand the sight of me. Abishai had nothing to do with that, but of course, he's guilty of being my brother."

For the most part, the task was completed, though Joab and I were walking across the slope just to make sure. It had been a busy day and the sun was going down. We didn't see any bones the soldiers had missed. I didn't find a lot to say. I wasn't feeling charitable toward David either.

The evening was mild. We could feel the grass of the low hill under our sandals. It was green now, not that bristly brown of the bad days of the famine. We saw no other people. Anyone who'd participated in the search for remains was tired and probably settling down to supper. We passed by the ruins of the stone foundation of some abandoned structure. We couldn't tell what had stood there, but it hadn't been large.

Then lightning struck. Some of you are very literal-minded and won't comprehend how lightning struck on a perfect evening as the moon was rising. I search for words at times. Language seems inadequate, and lightning is the best I can do. Doesn't lightning usually strike the tallest object in the vicinity? Tall, old, strong trees can be destroyed in an instant, and sometimes they take the surrounding forest with them. The tallest thing standing between Joab and me was David, and in an instant, his presence disappeared in a firestorm of sparks. Joab and I were engulfed.

Joab was standing quite close to me, and suddenly, I felt his hands on my shoulders and his lips on mine. It was a hard kiss. It was a needy kiss. I kissed back with all the urgency of years of physical deprivation. He held my body against his, and I felt his muscles ripple through my thin linen shift. I felt a stirring in his groin and mine. I wasn't even aware of my clothing hitting the ground, but it did. So did his. He eased me down to the ground behind the stone wall.

For a big man, Joab had a surprisingly gentle touch. His fingertips caressed my skin and made their way to my secret place. I gasped! My thoughts were completely overtaken by the sensations of my body. I couldn't even consider my responsibilities as somebody else's wife. I know all of us control our own actions, and in some very vague way, I was even aware that I'd probably regret this action. But I didn't care. My body was aflame, and the responsibilities in question were very distant.

My fingers were occupied with returning Joab's caresses. They wandered down to his secret place, and I squeezed. It was Joab's turn to gasp. I opened my legs for him, and we joined our bodies in the way that male and female bodies have been joined down through the centuries. We mated there in the grass. It was rather primitive. I was breathing hard, and my heart was beating fast. I did my very best to stay silent. It wasn't easy.

I am not trying to tell you that Joab raped me. We were both utterly filled with pent-up resentment, and it exploded into something that was almost violent. It wasn't lust either. We both desperately needed release, and we got it.

Joab and I came together and spent our frustrations. We spent our energy too. I lay in his arms on the grass. With my physical needs sated, the realities of my life and Joab's life were creeping in. It was full dark now. It was full dark except for the half moon and the brilliant stars. It was a clear night.

Joab started to speak, "Michal, I—"

I reached across his chest and put my forefinger against his lips. It was another intimate gesture, but the two of us had officially achieved intimacy. One more intimate gesture didn't matter now.

"Joab, if you are about to say you're sorry, don't. I'm not, and I don't want you to be. And don't tell me you love me either."

Joab was silent. Then he said, "I wanted to tell you that you're beautiful, Michal."

My head was on his shoulder, and we were both focused on the sky with its tiny lights. I lifted myself up on one elbow and actually looked at Joab. His hair was turning gray. When had that happened? And was it happening to me? His face was very weathered and lined. Was he old? Was I old? I leaned over his body and traced an angry scar on his right arm.

"I remember this wound, Joab. The Ammonites did this to you." I traced another long scar on his chest. "Who gave you this one, Joab?"

Joab said, "My body is a maze of scars. I don't even necessarily remember the circumstances of all of them anymore, but that particular wound was inflicted by the Philistines. Since we fought so many battles against the Philistines, it may be safe to say that most of my scars came from them. I've got a jagged scar on one leg from the Amalekites. Is it time to find our clothing?"

We groped around for our clothing, put them on, and stood up. That was when we realized that we'd been seen. Rizpah was prowling the grounds in the darkness, and there she was. She stared at me, and I stared at her. She said nothing. We said nothing. We all went our separate ways toward the homes where we were staying. Rizpah, too, had been taken in by one of the residents of Gibeah. It was no longer necessary for her to spend her nights outdoors. Joab and his brother were sharing a tent in the same area as the soldiers under their command.

*****

The next morning, we all left for Jabesh Gilead to pick up the remains of my father and my brother. My father and brother had been buried before their bodies decomposed, so it was a less onerous task. David clearly knew that my father's and Jonathan's remains were at Jabesh Gilead, but this was news to me. I could have asked what happened to their bodies, but I wasn't sure I wanted to know. I knew that the victors in any battle would have been likely to abuse and mutilate the bodies of the leaders of the vanquished. I learned that the citizens of Jabesh Gilead had rescued these bodies and buried them. After all, the very first act of my father as king was to rescue Jabesh Gilead.

I never saw my sister again. I heard that she'd died in childbirth. I don't know whether her last child was a boy or a girl, and I don't know if the baby survived. I have no information from Meholah, though I think about the family and hope Adriel and his children are well.

CHAPTER 44

Year 480

I have contemplated David and Joab over the years. David was my husband, and I loved him dearly, but life and other people came between us. Joab was a true friend to me in a culture where male/female friendships didn't exist and over many, many years. Both men were valiant warriors. David was also a poet, a musician, and a politician. Joab was much more practical and much more direct.

Looking back at the two of them, both dead, I have some sympathy for Joab. I have said that in my father's lifetime, David was loyal to him, even to a point where he refused to kill my father when he could have. Joab was that same loyal servant to David, and David used him. In David's defense, David at least didn't try to kill him!

Joab allowed David to stand aside as if he had clean hands, all the while holding onto his kingdom. We all knew that David had specifically ordered his generals not to kill Absalom. Joab just as specifically disobeyed. What would have been the result if Joab had protected Absalom? Another insurrection in five years' time? Perhaps a king lying dead in his bed before his time? Joab took the side of the tribes of Israel against its king. David never forgave him. David clearly had an emotional investment in his son, but what about Abner and Amasa? They had both participated in efforts to kill David, and neither one qualified as "the Lord's anointed."

Solomon does not excuse rebels. He may not be a warrior, but he has spies everywhere. And we live in peace.

On the subject of rebels, King Solomon is dealing with one I could name who achieved a certain notoriety. Presumably, other rebels exist as well. I heard these things when I went to the other palace, both from Solomon's more prominent wives and from the soldiers stationed there.

Jeroboam was a young man of the tribe of Ephraim, and he came to Solomon's attention. He was effective and hardworking, and he was put in charge of one of Solomon's labor forces, one that included his native tribe. The labor forces of the Twelve Tribes under Solomon are generally overworked and discontent. They work long hours and often spend days or weeks apart from their families. Solomon's projects are very grand and require heavy taxes. Jeroboam had begun to sympathize with the laborers whom he was supposed to be supervising. The work forces, Jeroboam's and others, were almost openly critical of the king.

Then came the oracle, and it was completely unexpected. There was a holy man of Shiloh who met with Jeroboam one day as Jeroboam was leaving Jerusalem. He prophesied that the Twelve Tribes would once again be split and that Jeroboam would become king of the ten northern tribes.[50] Solomon heard about it and tried to have Jeroboam killed. This all sounds so familiar to me since my father tried to do the exact same thing. Jeroboam slipped through the lines of the search party and sought refuge in Egypt. The pharaoh Shishak is protecting him.

The search party's commander was embarrassed, and Solomon was disgusted. Did Solomon believe the prophecy? He didn't discount it. Solomon hasn't tried to assassinate Ahijah, but that wouldn't be wise. He is a holy man to the people of Shiloh and to those in the surrounding area. Samuel prophesied some very negative things about my father, and my father didn't try to kill him. He tried to kill the object of the prophecies, David.

As David's reign became mostly peaceful and somewhat monotonous, David saw Joab as a traitor, but it had nothing to do with the taking of the king's wife. I am confident that David never found out about our little indiscretion. He certainly wouldn't have heard it from Rizpah! David's relationship with the sons of his sister suffered. The sons of his sister? I meant Joab and Abishai, though there were

---

[50] 1 Kings 11:29–40.

other sons of other sisters. Did Joab tell Abishai about the starry night in Gibeon? Probably. There was no turning back for Joab and me. We were not "friends" anymore. It was inevitable, but I grieved a little bit.

David had a *lot* of sons. In fact, some of them were involved in governing. Adonijah, Solomon, and a number of younger sons were being introduced to the intricacies of running a country. Solomon was the scholar and the conscientious one. Adonijah was smart enough but unmotivated. He liked his luxuries and his privileges. I had heard Joab's opinion of him, but in the routine setting of the palace, I didn't see Adonijah as being particularly hardworking. He had a tendency not to be where his half-brothers thought he should be.

Joab outlived his two younger brothers. Abishai wasn't a lot younger. He died in battle against the Philistines. For a soldier, dying in battle is the most desirable death. Joab and his two brothers operated almost as a unit. They were as close as brothers could be. Surely, Joab grieved for both of them. Did he feel incomplete without them? It must have felt strange to him. Unlike David, Joab didn't have the burden of outliving any of his children. As a general and soldier, perhaps Joab would have wished to die in battle. It wasn't the death he got.

CHAPTER 45

Year 480

Michal got out of bed stiffly. Abishag was usually there to help her, but not this morning. She found a mirror and tried to inspect her long, gray braid that hung down her back. It had not suffered too much from being slept-on. Michal reached for a head covering and put it on. She dressed and started toward the dining area, thinking to meet up with Abishag there. After dressing, Michal sat back down rather heavily on the bed. She was dizzy. She stood up and tried again.

The dining area was empty. She approached the public room where she'd been telling her story to a large number of women. It was empty too. She became aware of music coming from outside, and she followed the sound to one of the windows. The windows were crammed with women, and so was the doorway. Michal wormed her way through the door and stood outside in front of the palace. Then she fought the crowds and made her way to Solomon's new palace as close to the entryway as she could get. Along with many others, she stood outside and watched.

There was a huge parade. There were many camels, many mules, there were tumblers, there were jugglers, there was music, there was the beat of a drum. Everywhere. there was color. There were many, many people marching in procession, and all were darker-skinned than the people of the region of the tribes of Israel. It felt like an exotic festival. Michal asked the woman nearest her what was going on, and she didn't know. Nor did anyone else.

Michal liked music, but this music was not like what the troubadours of the Twelve Tribes played. The instruments were different and the drum was unusual. Michal liked it, but it was unfamiliar.

As the procession approached Solomon's palace, the spectators took note of a woman being helped down from a palanquin. Clearly, she had servants and retainers, but she didn't seem to be specifically escorted by a man. There were men in the entourage in general, and some carried the weapons of an escort.

The women from the women's quarters of both palaces watched in fascination. There was a lot of excited whispering, specifically about the woman in the palanquin. Michael and the rest of the women of the harem were used to assessing other women. This was the most beautiful woman Michael had ever seen. Her clothing was a blaze of color and swept downward to her feet. Her skin was perfect and as black as obsidian—and just as shiny. She moved with a grace that was accentuated by her flowing clothing. Michal couldn't see her hair under her ornate turban, but of course, this was the custom among the Twelve Tribes too. Women generally covered their hair. The mysterious queen disappeared into Solomon's palace.

We learned she was a queen and that she came from a country far to the south. The name of the country was Sheba, but none of us had ever heard of it. Sheba! I thought back to a traitor named Sheba.

The tumblers, jugglers, and musicians continued to perform. Camel after camel approached the entrance to Solomon's palace and knelt down. The servants unloaded one, and then its handler would take it away for food and rest, and the next camel would come to replace it. After the camels, the mules were unloaded, and the goods were taken into Solomon's palace. After the last animal made its way toward the stables, the tumblers, jugglers, and musicians were also allowed to rest. The effort had taken several hours. It wouldn't have been true that the environs of the palace became silent, but the joyful noises of the caravan were replaced by the common noises that people and animals make doing everyday tasks. Eventually, the last spectator made her way back to her quarters. It had been an exciting morning, and nobody wanted to leave.

Michal didn't go inside right away. She'd met up with Abishag in the crowd, and the two ladies took the opportunity to stroll through the garden. The garden was less crowded than it sometimes was. Many of the ladies were inside, breaking their fast or simply resting. Michal and Abishag went to the fish pond and sat down on two of the surrounding rocks.

"What *was* that?" asked Abishag.

Michal answered, "I don't really know, but it was certainly entertaining. If we can trust the gossip, Solomon has a very high-level guest from a far country. I wonder how long those people have been traveling? And did you notice the jugglers and tumblers? They performed those acts for hours. They're entitled to a long rest, and I hope they get it."

Neither Michal nor Abishag had eaten that day. They were both hungry, but they were resigned to waiting until supper. It was easier than fighting the crowds. The pond area was blissfully deserted, and the two of them were enjoying it. Michal wanted to continue her story, but at this point, it would be the next day.

The next day was much more routine. Abishag appeared at Michal's bedside to help her get up. Then she combed and braided Michal's hair. The two of them broke their fast together, and then strolled in a leisurely fashion into the public room. There were a number of ladies already there, seated against the walls on the usual rugs.

"Ladies, welcome back to the continuation of my story. But let us start by making mention of yesterday's excitement. It is extremely unlikely that I'll be invited to meet the Queen of Sheba. Possibly some of you will be. She will certainly be presented to Solomon's wife, the daughter of Pharaoh. I wish you all could have seen Bathsheba in her youth. Bathsheba was very beautiful, but this woman is spectacular insofar as I got to see her. She didn't linger long in the courtyard!

"Ladies, you have been most tolerant of my musings about life and status. Can I muse publicly about princesses and queens? A few of you are princesses, and you're married to a king. I was a princess, but sometimes I view myself as a fake princess. I was not born into a royal line, but that said, my father became a king in title and in fact.

He didn't establish a dynasty. I was married to a king but was never a queen. Maacah was born to a royal line, and she was never a queen. If David had a queen, it was Bathsheba, but even so, Bathsheba was not of royal birth, nor did she make decisions of state. She had access and influence, and she produced the heir. I see the same in Pharaoh's daughter, who is Solomon's wife. Is she a queen? Her royal line goes back centuries. But she's very like Bathsheba—access and influence.

"Now we have all seen a queen—a female ruler who packed up camels, packed up retainers, and made a journey to a distant place at her convenience and because she wanted to. Hers is a status that seems unique. The heads of state with whom we are all familiar are men.

"I suppose you're all very curious about my 'friendship' with Joab. I was rebellious enough to believe that men and women could be friends, and it did seem to be true of Joab and me for a long time. Have I proven our culture to be right in its belief that friendship isn't to be found between opposite genders? Perhaps. I am guilty of adultery, certainly, and this time I can't blame my father. Joab and David are both dead, and that's why I dare talk about it at all. Nobody alive today cares what an old woman did years ago. Joab and I had a one-night sexual relationship. It never happened again. And our friendship? It didn't survive. It couldn't. We'd both betrayed a person we cared about, and there was no going back. The guilt came between us. I told Joab that I wasn't sorry, and I still say that. I did regret the loss of our easy conversations, though."

CHAPTER 46

Year 469

David was very proud of his army. He was a king, a general, and a soldier, and his fighting men were second to none. There must have been a few defeats here and there, but I don't recall anything specific about that. David's armies consistently returned home victorious and wealthy. David decided to count his soldiers.

I won't try to tell you that I participated in any way, but the topic was on every soldier's lips. The concept wasn't unprecedented. In the time of Moses, there were two censuses,[51] both of them sanctioned by Elohim—according to Moses, that is. Moses was the one who recorded my people's history as he saw it, and he also recorded the numbers of the censuses. My uncle long ago suggested that the historian may bring his own bias to the subject matter. I do believe that. I'm not suggesting that Moses was dishonest. But some information is subjective, and also, there are 400 years of oral history between Moses' and David's censuses.

David's census was not ordered by Elohim, and Joab tried to talk him out of it. Joab was afraid the effort would be seen as a point of pride on David's part, and it was. Joab eventually followed David's orders. The effort took Joab and his assistants nine months, and even at that, Joab purposely overlooked the tribes of Levi and Benjamin.

Joab finally returned with his report, which was a series of numbers. Very shortly after David got the numbers, he was confronted by a holy man named Gad who assured him that Elohim wasn't pleased. There would be consequences. Gad presented David

---

[51] Numbers 1, 26.

with three options of punishment for his arrogance, none of which directly affected the king. But David was the one who was required to choose. His pride, his decision.

The options were all painful. David chose the option that took the shortest span of time, which was three days of plague. The tribes suffered the loss of 70,000 men.[52] So David's ill-advised census became inaccurate overnight.

I didn't see this and didn't hear it from David. But various members of David's court say that David insisted he saw the angel of the Lord striking down his subjects with plague.[53] The angel had gotten as far as the threshing floor of Araunah, one of the elders of the former city of Jebus, and had paused. Gad told David to build an altar there. David purchased the threshing floor, built the altar, and sacrificed oxen to Elohim. This act marked the end of the plague.

David did great things for the Twelve Tribes, not the least of which was to give the tribes as much unity as they had ever had. He built a city and built a palace. He, much more than my father, defined the word *king* for the tribes of Israel.

But after this misbegotten census, David started to age quickly. I tried to find out if any of my bits of medical knowledge might be useful. Joab was no longer the person to whom I went for information, but for something as general as the king's health, there were others who knew. David was listless, he was distant, and he had no energy. David had exhibited these symptoms before when his favorite son was in exile. Now his hair was white and his face was wrinkled. He was also very thin. The attendants in his circle didn't believe he suffered from anything but old age, which is incurable.

After a while, David took to his bed. David took to his bed without publicly naming a successor, which wasn't wise. His advisers should have insisted on it. David's most notable symptom was that he couldn't get warm. There are times when I wonder what his advisers were thinking. There are times when I wonder whether

---

[52]   1 Chronicles 21:14.
[53]   2 Samuel 24:17.

Abishag's arrival was intended to be a distraction from something else. Adonijah's behavior, perhaps?

Abishag as a very young girl was brought to David's bed to serve him and to keep him warm. Abishag, I've often wondered how that worked out? Oh, I'm sure you served him well. But did anything, even you, keep him warm?

It was after Abishag's arrival that David relented and called me to his quarters. I'd have said his bed, which was accurate, but it wouldn't be the sort of male-female bed activities that the phrase implies. The bed was there, and David was in it. He no longer got out of it very often.

It hadn't felt important to me for many years to concern myself too much with my appearance. I have always covered myself modestly, but I don't believe for a minute that you ladies of the harem are interested in what I wear. When I was summoned by David, I tried a little harder. I found a brilliant yellow linen sheath and a matching head cover. Both garments were new. Abishag was there for our conversation.

Abishag, were you shocked when I crawled into bed with David and initiated my own feeble attempt to help him get warm? I didn't succeed. But we had a very close and almost private, conversation for the first time in decades. David hugged me and said, "Michal, I'm so sorry I didn't give you children."

That was a surprise. It led me to believe that David had thought about me over the years, which I never would have guessed. It's so hard not to be bitter. But do I direct my bitterness at David or at life? There were opportunities for me to conceive, and I didn't. I would have liked to blame David, but I couldn't. I started crying.

"David, I'm so sorry about what I said when you and others were celebrating the procession of the ark of God. Maybe if I had been celebrating, too, I wouldn't have been watching you with critical eyes. I loved you, David, when we were both young. It's hard to be permanently rejected, and it's also hard to be one of multiple wives. But I need you to know I did love you."

David snorted. "Multiple wives! What a concept! I have been prideful, and Elohim has dealt with me. What man needs fifty wives?

At some point, when my name became known, the kings of the region all wanted to give me their daughters. It was flattering. But it has occurred to me how unfulfilling it must be for the wives, and truth be told, it wasn't all that fulfilling for me. It became a huge responsibility. An obligation. I will rest with my father very soon, and it's hard to look back now and understand exactly why I thought it was important to have fifty wives.

"You were my first princess, Michal. I told you once that you were precious to me, and I meant it. I was in shock when I found out that your father had given you away to another man. I respected your father. I respected your father a lot, but he did me wrong in a number of ways."

I was silent. I thought, *When I was sent to Jezreel, you were in Ziklag with two new wives. You were building up an army and consorting with the Philistines. Why do I not believe you thought one time about me?* Do the chroniclers write down what wasn't said? Of course not! It doesn't exist anywhere but in someone's mind. And over the course of years, I have concluded that's not a bad place for it. If life has taught me anything, it's not to say whatever pops into my head. David and I were having an intimate, cordial conversation for the first time in decades and, yes, I could have ruined the mood. This time, I didn't. This time, I feared it would be David's and my last conversation. The words that passed my lips were, "It's good to be back."

"Michal, I know it's no consolation now, but please realize that children aren't always a blessing. I would know. I had too many children. I was a valiant warrior and hopefully a decent king, but I was a terrible father. My son raped his sister, and I did nothing. My other son meted out his own justice. My son rebelled against me and quite possibly would have killed me, had the battle gone his way. He incited a civil war, and even if I survived, a number of good soldiers didn't. We all pray to have children. But what children? Any children?"

David began to weep. I wrapped my arms around him and held him. David went on, "I haven't forgotten Tamar. I grieve for you and I grieve for her now that it's entirely too late."

David's violated daughter never married. After some mutual grief, we both harked back to those much younger days when our lives were before us and anything was possible. We shared magic all those years ago. We shared joy.

I said, "Yes, David, you will rest with your fathers, as will we all in due course. You're looking back now on your mistakes, and again, we've all made some. Do you find any satisfaction in your successes? After my father died, there was a need to bring the Twelve Tribes back together, and you did it."

I never got an answer. David had drifted off to sleep. I got up and left. I was enormously grateful that I was given the opportunity to say goodbye.

CHAPTER 47

Year 470

If David was growing old, so were we who lived in the women's quarters. Many days were exactly the same as the one before, and sometimes the days dragged on and on. I tried to add something productive to each interminable day. I won't say interesting. Finding something interesting to do was asking too much.

When the weather was nice, I took the opportunity to visit my garden, which was much closer to the palace then than it is now. I would go through the gate, pull some weeds, and see whether the plants should be watered. I wasn't opposed to pulling weeds, if there weren't too many of them, but when it came to carrying water, I enlisted some slaves. I could only stand being down on my knees or in a crouching position for just a short period, and when I got up, I'd need a moment to catch my breath.

On one otherwise unremarkable day, I was sitting in the large public room, in this same room, in fact, with Bathsheba when Asher entered the room. We were both doing needlework that bored women do—I was embroidering a sleeve, and she was tacking up a hem. Asher came to advise Bathsheba that there was a holy man to see her. Bathsheba looked surprised. "Gad?" she asked.

"No, Nathan."

Bathsheba responded in a way that I didn't expect. She and I had shared confidences over the years, and we'd talked about everybody and anybody. But until now, Nathan's name hadn't come up. Her immediate response was, "What does he want with me? I'm sorry, Asher, I don't suppose you asked."

Asher shook his head, indicating that, no, he hadn't.

"Nathan can't have anything to say that I want to hear."

"Lady, should I send him away?"

Bathsheba thought for a moment and then said, "No, bring him in. I'm not very interested in making conversation with him, but then again, I'm not very interested in finishing this garment either. Perhaps a visitor, any visitor, will alleviate the tedium."

Asher showed Nathan into the women's quarters public room. I tried to be sensitive, all the while being very curious. I did ask both Bathsheba and Nathan if they preferred some privacy. Nathan said it wasn't that sort of conversation. There was nothing secret about it, or at least, there soon wouldn't be. Besides, the room wasn't empty. There were various groups of women here and there, either doing their own needlework or simply conversing. When a male entered the room, they looked up and took notice. My eyes were on Bathsheba. She was sitting quite stiffly and had folded her arms in front of her body.

Nathan started the conversation with the usual pleasantries. "Greetings, Your Highness and Bathsheba! I trust you are both in good health?"

We agreed that we were. I knew that Bathsheba was feeling a little bit of pain in the upper part of her torso and that she had a lump in her breast, but she wasn't about to mention it to Nathan. She and I had talked about it privately. I did know about alleviating pain, but I couldn't begin to guess how the pain came to be there. I don't always voice my fears to people who consult me, but I hadn't forgotten my mother and her pain. I worried a bit.

He went on, "Did the king tell you that your oldest son would succeed him as king?"

Bathsheba answered, "Yes, Solomon will be our next king."

I hadn't heard this before. Solomon may have been Bathsheba's oldest son, but he wasn't David's oldest surviving son. It wasn't traditional.

Traditional—what does that mean? My father's oldest son hadn't succeeded him, though Esh-Baal got a taste of being king of a divided kingdom. I was under the impression that David hadn't named a successor, and here was Nathan, suggesting that he had.

David had apparently named Solomon, and Nathan and Bathsheba knew it. Did others know it?

Nathan told us a little of the history of Adonijah, the son of Haggith. The women generally didn't make a habit of watching any of the king's sons who weren't theirs. Adonijah had been calling attention to himself for some time, assembling chariots, charioteers, and horses, and he employed fifty retainers to clear the way ahead of him. Maybe clear the way isn't entirely accurate. It was more a matter of announcing his arrival to anyone already in the vicinity. If it all sounds familiar, it was because Absalom had done the exact same thing when he was amassing followers.

Nathan went on, "David knew about it. David watched Absalom do it, David watched Adonijah do it, and David said nothing.

"As the king is dying, Adonijah has made his move. No one would disagree that the king is dying. Adonijah went to the spring of En-Rogel with a significant number of supporters and had himself declared king. He presided over a huge sacrifice of animals.

"Perhaps I shouldn't be shocked, but I wasn't invited. Many of Adonijah's brothers were invited, but Solomon was not. Joab is there, but the Mighty Men are not. Abiathar, the priest, is there, but Zadok, the priest, is not. Bathsheba, David is all too willing to let his sons do whatever occurs to them, but in this case, I am confident he doesn't know. He needs to know. I greatly fear for both you and Solomon if David dies and Adonijah takes power."

Bathsheba uncrossed her arms and leaned forward a bit. "Nathan, why don't you tell him?"

"I can't get near him. I have tried. That's why I'm here. David will see you. If you agree to request an audience, I'll accompany you."

I had just seen David a few months ago. On some level, I knew it would be the last time, and he himself even referred to sleeping with his fathers. He knew. What I hadn't been considering, and what I should have been considering was the inevitable transfer of power. The death of a king and the elevation of his replacement is a dangerous time in all cultures. It's hard on a king to die without an heir, but what about too many heirs?

I never realized that if the wrong son came to power, Bathsheba would be in danger. Maybe I should have. I'd heard the story of Abimelech after all. All I knew about Adonijah was that he was the son of Haggith, that he was David's oldest surviving son, and that he was almost as handsome as Absalom. Obviously, I knew something about Haggith who, by the way, had died several years ago, but I wouldn't have concluded that her son would have inherited his mother's venom. If Adonijah believed that he'd have to kill David's sons to consolidate power, why did he invite most of them to his celebration at En-Rogel? I worried that Solomon had been set apart when he wasn't included, and perhaps he was the only son Adonijah viewed as a threat.

I was concerned about Bathsheba. I was concerned about Solomon. But most of all, I was concerned about Joab. To separate himself from the Mighty Men—this was unlike Joab, and it didn't feel wise. I also wondered at the separation of the two priests. They had led worship together for all of David's reign, and they apparently weren't in agreement anymore.

I had to ask, "Nathan, was Adonijah anointed? You said one of the priests was there. Was he crowned?"

Nathan answered, "I heard a shout go up from the crowd, 'Long live King Adonijah,' but as to your two questions, I don't know."

Bathsheba immediately requested an audience with her dying husband, and she was, of course, granted one. I knew she, too, would have a care for how she dressed, and I offered to help her. Bathsheba had a maid servant for that. She found a vivid blue garment and cream-colored head covering. I walked with her through the palace to David's chamber, though I didn't approach David myself. I stood in the back of the room. Nathan followed behind but close enough that he would have been perceived as part of Bathsheba's entourage.

I will assume at least some of the people surrounding David were aware of this turn of events. However, David learned of the situation from Bathsheba. Poor David! His life was utterly plagued by rebellious children, and Adonijah was just one more. I never got to have a conversation with Adonijah. I just wonder whether he perceived himself as a rebel? He was the oldest son, after all, and his father was dying. Some of the things he was doing were right out in the open, and his father hadn't said a word. But when I consider the fact that he didn't invite Solomon to witness his big moment, and he did invite his other half-brothers, it makes me think he wasn't quite sure of his position. Or of Solomon's.

David mustered the strength to give orders, and these orders were given to Benaiah, the commander of the Mighty Men and to Zadok, the priest. David commanded that Solomon be brought to Gihon, the spring that feeds Jerusalem, and there be publicly anointed king.

Bathsheba and I were part of the procession, as were some of the ladies of the women's quarters, a company of priests, the Mighty Men, and lots of private citizens. The music was majestic. There were voices and flutes and trumpets that shook the ground. Zadok anointed Solomon at Gihon, and the cry, "Long live King Solomon!" echoed loudly enough to be heard at En-Rogel. Adonijah and his supporters were in the middle of a big celebration when they realized that there was a serious dispute about the succession. Adonijah watched his erstwhile supporters discreetly disappear.

In turn, he panicked. He raced to Gibeon, where the tabernacle stood, and took hold of the horns that were attached to the holy altar in the hope of keeping his life. The tabernacle and altar were places of sanctuary.

The tabernacle, the ark of God, and the altar were all built around the same time in the Sinai Desert 400 years ago in the time of Moses. All were designed to be portable. The altar was made of acacia wood overlaid with bronze.[54] The altar was square. The bottom corners had bronze rings attached. The altar, like the ark of God and the tabernacle itself, was carried on poles on the shoulders of men. The top corners of the altar were decorated with horns, which were symbols of power.

I saw the ark of God once from a distance, when it was being brought into Jerusalem. It is the most sacred of the three items, and it is not available to be viewed in public anymore. It rested in a little

---

[54] Exodus 38:1, 2.

tent in the king's palace for a while, and since Solomon completed his temple, it rests there. Only the priests see it now. The altar and the tabernacle itself have always been available to the public. When my father moved the tabernacle to the high place of Gibeon, the altar went with it.

Solomon was mounted on his father's mule with his father's royal trappings and escorted to the palace and to the throne. I was most honored to be able to participate in history, though I will admit to being winded. It was a glorious day, but it required more physical exertion than my usual embroidery. Solomon viewed the day with solemnity and gratitude. It was not a day for executing his brother. He was told where Adonijah was, and he sent men to bring Adonijah back to Jerusalem. Adonijah swore allegiance to Solomon along with David's other sons, and Solomon considered the matter closed.

Solomon, too, was anointed twice, both times by Zadok. The second time occurred before the death of his father. There hadn't been any sacrifices at the spring of Gihon, and sacrifices were important. Adonijah knew that! Zadok honored Elohim with a thousand bulls, a thousand rams, and a thousand male lambs to commemorate the beginning of a new reign. This event took place at the altar David had built on Araunah's threshing floor in Jerusalem. It was a grand festival to which anyone of the Twelve Tribes was invited. Everyone ate and drank their fill. Bathsheba and I were there, along with most of the ladies of the women's quarters.

Some days later, Solomon and his father had a heart-to-heart discussion in David's chamber. Abishag was there in the background, but she heard very little. All she knows for sure is that the name Joab came up more than once, loudly and angrily. Very shortly after Solomon's coronation, David died. Abishag and I did not attend the funeral. David's body was taken to his home town of Bethlehem and buried in his father's tomb.

At the time of David's death, the women's quarters consisted of his wives only and some of the younger children. I can't claim that our lives changed. But there was an odd feeling of disconnect. We were wives without a husband. We were all heavily protected from that situation that can arise in which a strong man attempts to claim the former ruler's women. If we were sequestered before the death of our mutual husband, we were more sequestered after. As per the laws of nature, we started to die. And as the new king amassed huge numbers of wives, some of them found a home among us in the old palace.

CHAPTER 48

Year 480

Michal paused and tried to stretch. Her legs were cramping. She tried to get up, and Abishag moved toward her to help. The audience had been sitting in one place too long, and other ladies were obviously repositioning themselves. It was time for the evening meal.

Michal said, "Ladies, did my story end with David's death? I'm still alive. But somehow there is so little left to tell. I survive, along with all of you, in the women's quarters of the old palace, and I haven't been anywhere at all since my last trip to Gibeon. Ten years ago, I helped celebrate the crowning of a new king, a momentous event, but even then, strenuous. I feel my lack of strength at times and fear that if I had to travel anywhere, I wouldn't make it. Abishag has been a huge blessing to me in my elder years. She does have some things to say, and for those of you who are interested, you can listen to her tomorrow morning."

Abishag and Michal went to eat supper, as did the ladies who'd been listening to their stories. They had bread and vegetable soup accompanied by bowls of beer. Michal tried to do more than pretend to eat. Food had no flavor these days. Abishag noticed, of course, and Michal made the effort to finish her soup. After supper, Abishag assisted Michal to her cubicle and then proceeded to her own sleeping mat. Michal laid down dutifully and pretended to be comfortable. She didn't want to keep Abishag from her own sleep. But Michal didn't sleep well and could tell when the effort was going to be futile.

After a while, Michal simply got up and wandered around the building. There was some moonlight coming through the windows, and she was careful not to step on any sleeping women. She found her way outside and leaned up against an outer wall of David's palace. The night air was mild, and the sky was clear. There was a fragrance on the breeze. Something was in bloom. Michal took a deep breath. She smelled roses and something else, something spicier. The night sky was brilliant. Michal enjoyed the unaccustomed solitude and the silence. She remembered her tryst with Joab on this same sort of night. She thought about regrets and decided that her regret was the loss of the friendship and not her adulterous behavior. Her husband had denied her intimacy after all.

Joab and David…and Paltiel. David had pointed out how children aren't necessarily a positive factor, but her lack of children would always be one of Michal's regrets. A missed experience. She was feeling sentimental, especially after having put the story of her life into words and sentences. One of her husband's poems popped into her mind in the cool of the night. "Be still, and know that I am God. I will be exalted among the nations. I will be exalted in the earth."[55]

Jerusalem was a city with a large population and was, in fact, a seat of government. The silence couldn't last. Michal became aware of a group of women giggling loudly and passing by the old king's palace, heading for the new king's palace. Well, Solomon's palace wasn't exactly new anymore. But still, there were people alive who remembered the old king David, and still, there was clearly an older palace and a newer palace. *Drunk*, Michal thought.

Michal found herself walking less and less. There wasn't any need to. Most days, a walk consisted of moving between her cubicle, the public room, the latrine, and the eating area. She found herself considering a walk in the garden despite the fact that it was night. It was a clear night, though there would be less light under the trees. Michal decided to venture out and hope to smell if not see the flowers. She knew where the paths were. She knew it would be important to pick up her feet. The stone paths were very welcome, but they weren't perfectly level, and under the circumstances, she wouldn't be able to see them.

---

[55] Psalm 46:10.

She entered the garden and walked to the place where she'd once maintained her medicinal herbs. There were several thriving rosebushes in that spot now. The problem for Michal's short plants had been lack of sun after Solomon designed a formal garden with a stone wall. Michal still tended a garden and her garden still had a fence around it, but now it was at the edge of a field. Michal wasn't prepared to leave the palace environs at night to see to her own plants, but then it wouldn't be practical in the darkness anyway. She could enjoy Solomon's garden without venturing too far afield. She couldn't see too much, but she felt the solitude that she sometimes craved.

Michal could definitely smell the roses. When the roses were in bloom, their odor overpowered the more subtle flowers. Michal was astonished to meet another human being in the garden at night, and she was startled enough to jump. She heard a soft, if heavily accented voice, saying, "Shhhh, it is I—Bilqis."

Michal found herself face-to-face with the queen of Sheba. Like Michal, she was arrayed in her sleeping garments, though her sleeping garments were more eye-catching than Michal's. It was hard to gauge the color in the dark, but the garments were filmy, floaty, and multicolored. Her hair, black and kinky, was uncovered.

Michal had been most curious about the mysterious queen and hadn't expected to meet her. Now that she had met her, she didn't know how to act. Was she supposed to bow? Still, the queen had introduced herself by her given name, and Michal took that as a cue that she didn't intend to stand on ceremony. Bilqis continued in her accented Hebrew, "I know who you are. You are the daughter of Saul."

Michal countered, "I know who you are too. You are the queen of Sheba. But I am very puzzled. You are the most unique individual in this city right now, but how would you know who I am and who my father was?" Michal found a low bench and added, "Please sit with me, Bilqis. I want to hear about your country. I want to understand what it's like to rule a kingdom. I want to hear your impressions of our country and our king. I have never traveled, even within the kingdom of the Twelve Tribes. I have lived in Gibeah, in Jezreel, in Hebron, and finally in Jerusalem. I will never see your part of the world."

Bilqis gave a very soft, tinkling laugh. "You have many questions! We will talk, but we have only this night. My stay in Solomon's palace has been enlightening and a true adventure, but it's time to leave. If the packing goes well, my entourage and I will begin our return journey in a week. Perhaps I have already been away too long, but I like to think that my travels are part of my education and that educated rulers are a benefit to their populations.

"Believe it or not, I knew Saul had a daughter here, and I was hoping to meet her. You have come to Solomon's palace since I have been in residence there, but when you did, I was meeting with the king. You were gone before the meeting was over. This setting, a deserted garden at night, is much better. It feels private, though if it's not, we'll never know. I asked one of Solomon's wives to describe you to me, and you may be more striking than you think. Both of us have uncovered hair tonight. Your thick silver hair makes you stand out, though without that gleam of moonlight, I might have missed it.

"As for your father, we in Sheba didn't know him, but we knew of him. He was a thorn in my mother's hand, though he was dead before I became queen. Sheba is a wealthy realm, but only because of trade. Our ships are our living. We have a major hub in Gaza, in Philistine territory. From Gaza, Sheba's trade goods go all over the world. If your father made himself unpopular in our eyes, it was the effect his battles had on Gaza."

Michal interjected, "Gaza is very far south. Did my father raid the city?"

"No, it was more indirect than that. When he raided other Philistine cities or tried to, Gaza would send reinforcements. If one of our ships docked during this time, there was no one to unload it. It was annoying and time-consuming, and per my mother, it happened a lot. It wasn't really damaging to our economy, but it upset our schedules.

"My country is very different from what I've seen of the Twelve Tribes' territory, though clearly, I haven't seen all of the territory. I prefer to call my country a realm as opposed to a kingdom. 'Kingdom' is a misnomer in a land that has never been ruled by a king. My realm is in the desert. Water is precious. But the desert blooms and is indescribable. This garden of Solomon's is spectacular, but so is our desert in spring. Our climate supports frankincense and myrrh trees. I made sure to bring some to your king, though I can only hope they will thrive here. I was surprised to see that this garden already supports a few. The desert doesn't support roses, and I'll miss these when I'm gone.

"As for your king, he is an enigma. He has great knowledge and has great wisdom and is full of surprises. I haven't found a topic yet that he can't discuss intelligently. I consider myself to be well-educated, but I am not his equal. He's also obviously handsome. Solomon is very famous. I made this journey because I was tired of hearing about him, things that didn't seem believable. A great many people talk about him. And yet my impression now is that everything that's said about him is true."

Michal made the comment that Solomon wasn't a warrior, and she asked if Bilqis had ever led an army. Bilqis said no. Her realm indeed had an army but like the Twelve Tribes; it had enjoyed peace in her lifetime. "Your husband was a warrior of renown, yes?"

Michal remembered. "I like to think that David laid a foundation for Solomon's peace, but David seemed to fight constant wars. My husband fought the Philistines too. Did he also impact your country's trade?"

"Not as much. David had an accommodation with Gath, which made a difference for the affairs of Sheba and the port of Gaza."

The conversation turned to frankincense and myrrh and to the art of healing. Michal became animated as she talked about the properties of poppies, and then suddenly, she blushed. It was dark, and she assumed Bilqis wouldn't be aware of the blush. It also led her to wonder whether a blush would even be noticeable on Bilqis' smooth, dark cheeks.

Michal stuttered. "I know Arabian doctors are famous the world over for their knowledge and their expertise. You undoubtedly have the world's best physicians within your reach."

Bilqis laughed her musical laugh. "I love your enthusiasm. I know very little about healing, but as you say, I have access to very good doctors."

The ladies were surprised to see the first hint of dawn brightening the tops of the trees and the top of the wall. Michal hadn't seen a sunrise in many, many years, and she was enjoying it.

Bilqis broke the mood. "I must go. I will be missed if I haven't already been missed. I have very much enjoyed our conversation, Michal." As Bilqis headed in the direction of the new palace, Michal became aware that she'd been sitting in one position for too long. She got up slowly and stiffly and wandered back toward her familiar cubicle.

Abishag came in at the usual time the next day to help Michal out of bed. She was instantly concerned that Michal wasn't in the bed. It was difficult enough for her to get up that she usually waited for Abishag. Michal appeared in the doorway just as the ladies sleeping on the floor were starting to stir. Michal explained that she'd been out for an early morning solitary walk in the garden. Abishag picked up the rumpled blanket and folded it. The two of them continued to the dining area to break their fast.

CHAPTER 49

Year 470

My name is Abishag. I come from the town of Shunem to the north of Jerusalem in the Jezreel Valley. I was fifteen years old when I was taken to Jerusalem. I did not come here to the women's quarters then. I went to the private quarters of a man who was old enough to be my grandfather, and I was married to him. Married! Michal is trying not to be bitter, and so am I. Neither one of us has children, and now it's too late. I was a caregiver and a maid. I was King David's last wife, if I can call myself that. Legally, I was a wife.

I have a story. My story overlaps with Michal's, but I will try not to repeat what she has already told. I met Michal for the first time the day she climbed into bed with my husband! I was in the room, as I always was in those days, and I was surprised. I'm not sure I had even heard Michal's name, though I knew, of course, that my husband had many wives. Michal, we both have regrets, but I do not regret meeting you. Michal is teaching me many things. I help with the plant remedies and I help with the babies. I am learning to read a little. I don't have any babies. I want to be useful, and I hope I can find some meaning in this life that is mine.

Before I left Shunem, I had learned a little bit from my mother about plants. My mother didn't read or write. She did not grind up herbs in the manner that Michal does to use later. My mother dried whole plants so she knew what they were and ground them as she needed them. She never kept a lot of plants at the same time. My childhood in Shunem wasn't so different from Michal's in Gibeah. I gathered wood and carried water, like all the other girls. We children played some games when the daily tasks were done. I did not get schooling before I left. Michal has taught me enough letters to read the labels on the bowls.

When I came to Jerusalem, I spent a year in David's quarters, where I mainly met slaves. David's advisers came in sometimes, and I almost said they took no notice of me, but they did. If they thought I wasn't looking, some of them stared at me. They didn't speak to me. Since I was the king's wife, they thought they were being discreet.

I had something to do in the odd moments when David wasn't asleep. I was there to keep the king warm. That wasn't possible. I did try. I tried with my body and I tried with hot bricks that were wrapped in a blanket. It's very discouraging to be given an impossible task and to be expected to spend the rest of my day staring at the wall. My job was to be available.

One of the slaves took pity on me and brought me something to sew. I sewed a little bit in Shunem, and my skills improved in the king's quarters. Was I grateful not to be carrying water and picking up firewood? No! In those days, I wanted to go outside so badly that I would have done any menial task.

I was in the room with David when Bathsheba came. I'm not sure what I expected. I'd heard Bathsheba's name and heard that she was very beautiful. She was old when I first saw her. I could tell that she was very nicely dressed, but she didn't move easily and couldn't sit for any amount of time. It seemed like the journey from the women's quarters to David's quarters took some effort. She came right up to David's bed and sat down on a stool. David greeted her and asked about her health. She said she was fine and asked about his. He said he was fine. Neither one of them was fine!

I remember they tried to talk about the weather, but neither one of them had been outside. They only spoke about what they could see through the window, and yes, it was a pleasant day. I viewed the world through a window too. David eventually asked why Bathsheba wanted to see him. Bathsheba stood up. She could see David's face better, and besides, those stools aren't very comfortable.

She said, "Your highness, did you not promise me that my son, Solomon, would succeed you as king?"

David answered in just a word, "Yes."

Bathsheba went on, "Who else knows your wishes? I know and the holy man, Nathan, knows, but do your advisers know? Does the army know? Your son, Adonijah, has followers now, and they have declared him king. Some of your most trusted supporters are now supporting him."

Bathsheba was interrupted by Nathan, and when David agreed to see him, Bathsheba withdrew, but she didn't leave the king's quarters. She came over to speak to me. I offered her a stool but then offered her my bed. She seemed grateful to lie down. She didn't want to sleep. She wanted to talk.

"He isn't fine, is he?"

"Of course not. He's dying," I answered. "And you, Lady? Are you really well?"

I could tell that Bathsheba hadn't spent her life complaining, and she wasn't going to complain to me. "Oh, I have my good days and my bad days. You will undoubtedly find some day that growing old can be difficult. Still, I can move from here to there. I eat with the ladies in the dining area. Does David ever leave his bed? And does he eat at all? I have never seen him so thin. I haven't seen him in some time, and he has changed."

She went on, "Nathan came to me and told me that some followers of David had proclaimed his oldest son, Adonijah, king. I had no idea, and as far as I can tell, neither did David. I believe nobody before me has approached him with that bit of news. Are David's advisers afraid to tell him what's going on? Is it all about being cautious of David's coming death and needing to support the right successor?

"When Nathan told me that Adonijah had invited the sons of David, with the exception of my son, to his celebration, I became very much afraid. If the other sons aren't a threat, and if my son is, things will not go well for us once David passes. I firmly do not believe my son would kill his brothers in an effort to consolidate power, but Adonijah might.

"Nathan came to me with news. I don't like Nathan. I am capable of being polite, but only with great effort. Do you know any of my history with the king?"

I know I said something vague. "I've heard rumors, but I haven't paid a lot of attention."

"I had a husband before I was married to David. I am old and can say anything I want now. I committed adultery with David before my husband died. Did I have a choice? I don't know whether it's wise to say no to a king or not, but I didn't. I barely knew my husband. He was a soldier and was constantly away with the army. My first husband didn't spend enough time with me to give me a child. One time with David—I committed adultery once with David and became pregnant.

"My husband was away fighting Ammonites. If it wasn't Ammonites, it was Philistines, and if not Philistines, then Amalekites. Do I blame Uriah? I'm not being fair, but I was heartily sick of it. There was always some nation to fight. Let me add that we were wealthy. Uriah was always bringing home the spoils that he'd taken, and we had a comfortable life. David's armies didn't lose many battles. When I realized I was pregnant, I sent word to David. There was no possible way my child would be perceived as my husband's. But the problem corrected itself. My husband got killed. No big surprise!

"I sent word to David because I had no intention of being a martyr. But neither did I know what I could expect of him. I'd met him once, and the two of us did indeed enjoy each other's bodies. Women get pregnant all the time, and in very many cases, the problem, if you will, is theirs. It's much easier for a man to deny a pregnancy than a woman. David actually married me. I was fortunate. But it's also true that there was love between us. There still is.

"Nathan believed that David caused my husband's death. Well, kings send men into battle all the time and some of them die. Nathan prophesied against me and against David's and my child who died soon after he was born."

Bathsheba burst into tears. How long ago was this? She still grieved over her lost baby? I brought her a little bowl of beer, and she sat up and sipped.

"I do not like Nathan and he doesn't like me. I corrupted his king. Now Nathan seems to be of a mind to support my son, Solomon, but I wonder why. My first child, the one who died, was a son. Solomon is also my son. Yes, David told me many years ago that Solomon would be king, but who else did he tell? Michal didn't know. If Nathan knew, he must have heard it from David."

I said, "I saw Michal once, but I didn't speak to her. She slid into bed beside David. I'm trying not to be surprised by anything, especially since I have so little knowledge of David's life before I came. But she surprised me."

Bathsheba added, "Michal has been a friend to me. The women's quarters is so alive with jealousy and rivalries it's exhausting. Michal has her own history with David, and I don't know all of it, but she's always been cordial to me. Did you know she's the daughter of King Saul? I appreciate your willingness to allow me to ramble. What was your name?"

I told her, "Abishag.

"Abishag, you're very beautiful. I do not envy your position in this place. I am reminiscing a bit, and I remember being beautiful."

I assured her that she was still beautiful, but she was impatient.

"Yes, maybe I still display the remnants of beauty, but age and beauty are quite different from youth and beauty. I was young, beautiful, and proud. I had a secret place up on a rooftop. It was a bathing pool. I had an impression that it was something left over from the Jebusites as I never saw anyone else there. And I didn't tell anyone. It was my secret. Have you ever taken off your clothes and felt the breeze on your skin? I doubt it. It's a luxury, and not many women would be brave enough to do such a thing outdoors. Again, I thought my spot was private, and at the time, I was proud of my young body. My pool was high up but not high enough.

"I went to the pool regularly on sunny days. I enjoyed feeling a breeze on my skin, but the sun also felt heavenly. And while I knew that the king's palace overlooked my pool, I never noticed anybody up on the heights of it. The inevitable happened. I got noticed and by no less of a personage than the king himself.

"What does a person do when the king calls the person to his presence and sends along two soldiers as an escort? I went with them, of course. You know what happened after that. I found out later from palace guards that David knew exactly who I was before he called for me because he made inquiries.[56] So who corrupted whom? Is it always the woman's fault for being where she shouldn't be and for wearing what she shouldn't wear? There are definitely people who believe that, and if I may say so, they're all men! David saw me from afar, and he certainly saw more of me than I should have allowed, but still, the decision to send messengers and initiate a relationship with me was entirely on him."

It turned out that Nathan said to David the exact same thing Bathsheba had said about Adonijah, and David asked her to come back to the bed where he lay. I went with her, at least close enough to hear what was said. I felt Bathsheba lean on me just a little. David swore an oath that Solomon would be king, and Bathsheba knelt and said, "May my Lord, King David, live forever."[57]

I know, I know. It was the correct thing to say, but it was so ironic, right after Bathsheba, and I had discussed the state of the king's health.

Michal has already told what happened next. She and Bathsheba got to walk in Solomon's procession. I did not. I knew now that two of David's sons, leading two different groups of followers, had been pronounced king. I had some vague idea who Absalom was and what had happened when two men wanted to be king of the same kingdom. David had moved the whole family out of Jerusalem.

For David, this was not an option now. He would lie in his bed and be killed by the victor if civil war erupted. Well, by Adonijah, anyway, if Adonijah was the victor. David threw his influence publicly in favor of Solomon who would have no reason to view his father as a threat. Would I simply become the property of the next king?

There was no civil war. Adonijah's followers abandoned him, which left him very vulnerable. Solomon took the throne with his father's blessing and happily with the blessing of the Twelve Tribes.

David died. I can't have served him for more than a year. I was still very young when I became what society called a widow. I took my

[56] 2 Samuel 11:3.
[57] 1 Kings 1:31.

place in the women's quarters. None of the wives went to Bethlehem for the burial. But I did see some of the people who went, and one of them was David's son, Adonijah. I'd heard Adonijah's name, but I didn't know who he was. He was beautiful! Michal said that David was beautiful when he was young. Michal knew Absalom who died before I came. He was beautiful too. Adonijah also saw me, and at the time, people said I was beautiful.

The group who went to Bethlehem to bury David returned after a week or so. Adonijah was with them. He hadn't forgotten me. I was a wife to David in name only. But there are old laws against taking your father's wife[58] that some people remembered. Adonijah wanted me, and I so much wanted what everyone wants—a real husband and some children. I was no different. Did I want the man whom Bathsheba was afraid of? All I knew at the time was that Adonijah was handsome and that he might be a pathway for me to leave the harem. Is that enough? I thought so then. Sometimes Elohim saves us from ourselves.

I almost had my desires. We were so close! Adonijah knew that Solomon would not want to grant him favors. He actually approached Bathsheba to speak for him, for us. Adonijah's power evaporated when his following dispersed, and Bathsheba wasn't afraid of him anymore. I knew she had some sympathy for me. Bathsheba asked her son for permission for Adonijah to marry me. I will admit that I felt a little sorry for Bathsheba. She can't have expected her son to fly into a rage, but he did. He was very frustrated that his mother did not understand the position I was in and the position he was in.

If I was sorry for Bathsheba, I was sorrier for Adonijah. He lost his life. Solomon already knew his brother wasn't trustworthy, and now he thought to take the former king's wife. I understand the whole thing now, but I didn't then. Solomon, a very new king, could not allow it. The taking of the former king's wife was symbolic of the taking the former king's power. And my wishes? My wishes, if I had any, were as unimportant as could be. Nobody asked how I felt and nobody cared how I felt. We in the women's quarters have very few

---

[58] Leviticus 20:11.

options. Our lives are controlled by powerful men. It's easy to lock us away and pretend we don't exist.

Back when Adonijah organized his almost-rebellion, Joab took his side. When Adonijah died, Joab had no side. He ran to the same altar where Adonijah had taken hold on the day Solomon was crowned. Is there really protection in an altar? Both Adonijah and Joab thought so. So much of my thoughts are about me and my wants. But I have to deeply sympathize with Benaiah, one of David's Mighty Men. Benaiah fought at Joab's side for decades. And now the new king demanded that he kill his former commander. Benaiah did, even while Joab gripped the altar by the horns. It must have been very painful.

But that was the end of the old. Solomon swept it all away and put in place soldiers and officials who were loyal to him. The wives of the old king were secured out of sight in the women's quarters of the old palace.

When I started living in the women's quarters, I saw Michal coming and going, especially to help with childbirth. I was interested, and Michal thought I might be capable. I wanted something to do after Adonijah died. I tried not to dwell on becoming a mother and found another path.

I have come to terms with being a widow. I completely understand why no man would ever dare ask for me. I spend my days in much the same way you all do, but Michal and I do a few other things too. I help with her garden. I help with the grinding of the herbs, and sometimes the two of us go out beyond the palace grounds to look for plants we don't have. We don't do this very often anymore. Michal simply can't walk far. I hope Michal would agree that I have become a competent midwife.

CHAPTER 50

Year 480

Michal and Abishag sat together in the garden. It wasn't raining anymore, and the sunlight had begun to creep through the tree-tops. Michal and Abishag had ventured out in a light drizzle, which sometimes prevented the garden from being crowded. They noticed more women strolling now, enjoying the garden and enjoying the fresh scent of rain and wet grass. Michal and Abishag were seated on adjoining stones that bordered the fish pond. The stones were wet, and Michal felt the damp through her shift. She didn't care. This was a place of beauty. It took some effort to walk this far these days, and she was going to make the most of it. It had been some days now since either one of them had addressed the women in the public room. Their stories, like their lives, had overlapped, and there was no more to be said.

Abishag broke the silence. "Michal, you have no idea how much I appreciated your story. I thought I knew you well, but now I feel like I knew nothing *about* you. You saw so much before you were isolated in the harem of a king."

"Abishag, I enjoyed your story, too, and if it's taught me any-thing, it's that hardships are part of life, but everyone has different hardships. I was not locked in a room with an old man at the age of fifteen, and it never occurred to me to be grateful for it. I didn't enjoy as much freedom as I wanted, but it was more than you got. Do you think that the women who spend their whole lives gathering wood, carrying water, and bearing children envy us? As I get older and less mobile, I might concede that I appreciate the safety and the luxury of the harem more than I used to."

Abishag said, "I know. I know we have ease and luxury and even safety. I see these young wives of Solomon, some hauntingly beautiful, and realize in my elder years how quickly beauty fades. Solomon almost never makes his way to the old palace, and these wives may never be noticed. I am just like them. Michal, can I ask a deeply personal question?"

"I have no secrets now, Abishag!"

"You had two husbands, real husbands, and even a lover. I am a virgin. A virgin wife. How ironic! I see these young women who have no contact with their husband, and I see myself. What is sex like? Does it hurt?"

"Yes, well, like I said, everyone has different hardships. To lose your virginity is somewhat painful, but no, otherwise, sex doesn't hurt. In fact, with a considerate lover, sex is exhilarating. It's very hard to describe to somebody who's never experienced it. As for pregnancy, well, you and I both missed out on that experience."

"Michal, why did you take Joab as a lover? I never met him. By the time I got away from the king's quarters, he was dead."

Michal didn't say anything for so long that Abishag was afraid she'd overstepped. Finally, she said, "At the time, I might have told you I loved Joab. Love is a tricky word. There are many different kinds of love. When I was very young, my mother tried to explain it. When David and I were young, we had a passion for each other. This wasn't that kind of love. It was a familiarity, like a favorite pair of old sandals. He and I had been thrown together so often over the years that we didn't have too many secrets. Sort of like you and me.

"David had rejected me long ago. I still lived in the women's quarters, and I was still his problem, but if you don't mind my saying so, he was my problem too. Sex can be a burning desire, though not so much when you're old. David deprived me of my rights as a wife. Now we both know plenty of women who have that hardship.

"Joab was dealing with his own rejection by the king. Maybe Joab shouldn't have expected forgiveness when he killed Absalom, but all I did was say something stupid. David could be extreme. He could be stubborn. He could be self-righteous. Joab and I were thrown together one more time on a glorious night, in a strange city without our spouses, and both frustrated with David. As you know, David not only allowed my sister's children to be killed, he selected them. Joab initiated a brand-new relationship with me, and I willingly participated. By the way, Joab was a pretty good lover!

"I have had a lot of time to consider whether the two of us succumbed to lust. I don't like the word at all, and I'd rather not apply it to myself. But I have to. The stars were aligned, and the conditions were perfect. People like to say sometimes that their adultery just happened. No. Joab and I had free will, and we changed our relationship in an instant. We both spent our frustrations like a couple of goats."

"Did you ever see him again?"

"No. It made me sad, but I knew we couldn't ever go back. It's just how it was."

Michal and Abishag became aware of hurried footsteps along the path. This was unusual. The ladies who frequented the garden never hurried. There was much beauty to take in and nothing in the garden was urgent. When the owner of the footsteps came in sight, Michal saw that it was Asher. And Asher was moving more quickly than usual.

"Good morning, Asher," Michal greeted him. "Have we ever seen you in the garden before? Welcome!"

Asher shook his head. He seemed greatly agitated and was having trouble speaking. He was also breathing hard. Michal stood up and approached him. "What's wrong, Asher?"

Asher answered, "Highness, do you remember Solomon's Moabite wife, Ahsia? You assisted in the birth of her child a couple of months ago."

Michal said, "Yes, I remember her, even if Solomon doesn't. Does Solomon sleep with so many women he can't remember their names? I remember feeling sorry for her. As I recall, Ahsia had a son. Do you know whether the child has a name yet?"

Asher looked surprised. "Did Solomon not acknowledge Ahsia's son?"

"I hope he did. After Rehoboam was born, I mentioned Ahsia and her son to Solomon, who at least was present for Naamah. Anyway, Asher, what did you come to tell us?"

All Asher could do was shake his head. Michal motioned for him to sit down on one of the rocks, which were now dry. Michal stood beside him. "Asher, what?"

Asher managed to organize his thoughts and put them into words. His voice trembled a little. Eventually, he continued, "Last night, Ahsia and her ladies got drunk and went to the high place of Chemosh. I don't know whether the baby had a name or not. He's dead. They sacrificed him."

Michal and Abishag were speechless. Was there silence in the garden? Were Solomon's expensive, imported birds hanging on Asher's every word? No, there was a loud chirp followed by another. Michal looked at Abishag. Abishag looked at Michal. They both turned to Asher. Michal finally whispered, "Solomon's son was sacrificed to Chemosh?"

Asher nodded. Michal very quietly collapsed and died. Both Asher and Abishag reached for her as she toppled over and both missed.

Abishag gasped. Asher dropped to his knees and put two fingers against Michal's neck. He shook his head. Silent tears rolled down Abishag's face. She had started to stand up but fell back somewhat heavily on the rock where she'd been seated. Ouch! Asher, ever practical, directed some slaves to take Michal's body back to the vicinity of the palace and prepare it for burial.

Abishag couldn't think. She deliberately put one foot in front of the other and managed to walk with Asher back to the old palace. She entered, but she couldn't settle. She walked across the public room. She walked back. There were a few ladies in the public room but nobody she knew. She walked into the dining area and walked out again. She stepped outside the door. Michal's body was being scented and wrapped. Abishag walked to where it was being done but burst into tears and left. She tried finding solace in the garden, but the garden was getting crowded.

Abishag went to the area where the ladies slept and to Michal's cubicle. The blanket was still folded. There was Michal's favorite red and white bowl sitting in the cubicle where Michal's head would have been. She saw the various bowls of dried herbs along one side of the cubicle. She was now able to read the labels, but she really didn't read well otherwise. Abishag couldn't stand it. She sat down and sobbed, eventually curling into a ball on the folded blanket. She fell asleep.

Abishag went into the public room the next morning. There were some ladies there. Abishag wondered if they hoped there was more to her story than what she'd already told. *I have no story*, she thought. *I've been moldering in this place for over ten years*. Still, if she could phrase it that way, she was Michal's successor, her protege. She addressed the women in the room.

"Good morning, ladies. Please forgive me. It isn't a good morning for me. You must know that Michal is dead. She had a long life and she had a good story and she even got to tell it all. I will do what I can to continue her work. I don't know enough. I had a few years with her to learn a few things. Michal's body has been prepared for burial. It is time for us all to escort Michal to the cave where we buried Bathsheba."

There was the usual procession of ladies, very similar to Bathsheba's burial ritual albeit without the presence of the king. The wives of Solomon's father were dying with some regularity. Solomon knew Michal by sight, but the women of the harem didn't know whether anyone had even informed Solomon. Processions were well-attended, even if the participants didn't know Michal. It was an opportunity to get some exercise, to enjoy a lovely day, and just to do something outside the usual routine.

Abishag accompanied the group, which was back before sunset. Life without Michal would be a lot different, and she needed to find a way to come to terms with it. Her feet took her to the dining area, but she wasn't hungry and didn't know why she was there. She walked out into the garden but couldn't find a solitary spot. She headed back into her quarters and decided to take a closer look at the bowls of herbs in Michal's cubicle. *I need to know what's there*, she thought.

Michal's cubicle was a prime spot in the sleeping quarters, and Abishag felt that she could inherit it. The ladies who might have competed with her for the privilege would be put off by the dried plants, some of which were dangerous. Abishag wanted the space because it had been Michal's and in order to keep an eye on the remedies.

Asher found her there. "There is a soldier at the door, and it seemed appropriate to ask you to speak to him."

Abishag was on her knees, trying to memorize the contents of the bowls. She stood up and went to the door. A soldier at the door of the women's quarters was always something of a novelty. Some of the curious ladies followed. Abishag had seen most of them before, but she didn't necessarily know any of their names. Oh, yes, Zeta was there—Zeta with the stab wound and the flaming hair. Abishag asked, "Zeta, are you well?"

Zeta said, "I am fine and am staying out of knife fights!" Abishag noticed that Zeta stubbornly wore the gold ring that had brought her to a malevolent person's attention in the first place.

The soldier addressed Abishag and said, "Lady, we need a midwife at the other palace."

Abishag glanced at the women who were within earshot. "Are any of you interested in assisting with childbirth?"

Zeta said, "I am."

"Then, Zeta, come with me. The circle is round."

ABOUT THE AUTHOR

Barbara was born long ago and far away in a sleepy little town called St. Paul, Minnesota. She lived in various places after that, though she considers her home town to be Long Prairie, Minnesota. She moved to New York City in her twenties to work at LaGuardia Airport. She met her husband there.

Barbara and Steve raised twins in Indianapolis. Barbara was an airline ticket agent, and Steve was a chef. They spent most of their working years in Indianapolis but, after retirement, left the snow belt for sunny South Carolina.

The pandemic of 2020 struck after Barbara, and Steve relocated. *The Circle* was born as a pandemic project.

Lightning Source UK Ltd.
Milton Keynes UK
UKHW042128041222
413345UK00001B/125

9 798886 441055